About Us

About Us

SINÉAD MORIARTY

SANDYCOVE

an imprint of

PENGUIN BOOKS

SANDYCOVE

UK | USA | Canada | Ireland | Australia
India | New Zealand | South Africa

Sandycove is part of the Penguin Random House group of companies
whose addresses can be found at global.penguinrandomhouse.com.

First published 2021
001

Copyright © Sinéad Moriarty, 2021

The moral right of the author has been asserted

Set in 13.5/16 pt Garamond MT Std
Typeset by Integra Software Services Pvt. Ltd, Pondicherry

Printed and Bound in the United States of America by BVG

The authorized representative in the EEA is Penguin Random House Ireland,
Morrison Chambers, 32 Nassau Street, Dublin D02 YH68

A CIP catalogue record for this book is available from the British Library

ISBN: 978–1–844–88535–0

This book is dedicated to all those who lost loved ones to Covid, and to Lily Capot

A true relationship is two imperfect people refusing to give up on each other.

– Unknown

I

Ann wiped down the grey marble island and rinsed out the cloth. She hung it on the spout of the tap to dry. The door to the lounge was open and she could hear Ken muttering and cursing as he watched the news.

She ran her hand over the clean counter. She'd been so proud of the fancy marble top when she'd had the kitchen done up ten years ago. It had been her dream to have an island with four stools lined up against it. She used to love handing the kids their dinner and watching them eat as she leant against it, chatting to them about their day. She missed it. She missed the chatter and the noise. She missed being needed. The kitchen was so quiet and clean. She yearned for Zoë and John's muddy trainers and boots to clatter through the door. Why had she been so irritated by the mud splatters? If only she'd known then how much she'd pine for them one day.

She glanced at her watch: seven o'clock. The evening stretched before her, like a heavy weight. Watch TV, rinse her wine glass, take off her make-up, moisturize, brush her teeth, fold her clothes on the chair in the bedroom, put on one of her three pairs of silk pyjamas and go to bed. Read for half an hour and turn out the light.

The same routine over and over again. It changed only when her kids called in, or if she and Ken were meeting friends for dinner. How often did that happen? Ann frowned as she tried to remember the last time she and Ken had gone out for a meal. Of course, Marie's sixty-fifth, about six weeks ago. The four friends had gone to that posh new restaurant in town – Larry had booked it for Marie's birthday night. It was gorgeous, all low lighting and red velvet booths. The food was delicious and they'd had pink champagne as a treat. At dessert, the staff had sung 'Happy Birthday' to Marie and the manager had offered them a drink on the house.

But then the bill had arrived. Ken had presumed Larry was going to pay as it was his wife's birthday and he had booked the expensive restaurant and invited them, but instead he had pulled up the calculator on his phone, and announced, 'Two hundred and ten euros per couple, including tip.'

Ann had thought Ken was going to have a heart attack. She could see him struggling not to say something. He'd rummaged around in his jacket pocket for ages, eventually pulling out his wallet and thumping his card on the table. Ann had told some silly story about the kids to try to distract them all from Ken's irritation at having to pay so much for a meal. Ann liked Larry and Marie. They were one of the few couples that Ken agreed to go out with and she was terrified he might make a comment that would ruin the night. He was so short-tempered, these days. She wasn't going to let the bill cause a problem between them, so she had talked and talked until they'd said goodnight to each other and climbed into separate taxis.

In the taxi, Ken had been apoplectic. 'Bloody cheapskate. His wife's birthday and he books one of the most expensive restaurants around and then expects me to pay for it! He orders champagne, not prosecco, oh, no, actual champagne for his wife, and *I* have to fork out for it. I don't drink champagne. I didn't even have one sip of it. Does he think I'm made of money?'

Ann was going to point out that she had enjoyed the champagne and had drunk three glasses, it had been a truly lovely treat, but she'd kept her mouth shut. There was no point in talking to Ken when he was on one of his rants. She'd looked out of the window and tried not to let him ruin the night. She'd enjoyed being out in town. They did it so rarely. On the few occasions they went out together or met up with friends, it was always local restaurants, casual dining. That was fine, but it had been really nice to get dressed up and go somewhere fancy. Ann had even had her hair blow-dried and had worn her favourite red dress. She'd felt excited and had really looked forward to the evening. But Ken had burst her bubble of happiness with his moaning and groaning.

He had huffed as the taxi fare ticked upwards with each mile. Once home, he'd stomped upstairs and gone into his bedroom with a perfunctory 'Goodnight.' Ann had sat up and watched an old movie, too awake from the bubbles to go to bed. She had poured herself a glass of wine and tried to block out Ken's negativity.

That had been six long weeks ago and there were no plans to go out again. Ann stood in her tidy, quiet kitchen and reached for her phone. No messages. She had three new emails offering her a holiday to Borneo, a deal on shoes, and an anti-ageing cream. She missed the days when her phone was constantly hopping with texts and messages from the kids, or other school mums, or sports coaches, or the school. Her phone used to ping non-stop. Now it was silent most of the time.

Maybe she'd bake some brownies. That would kill an hour. But she'd end up eating them all. Ken would have one, Zoë was in Spain with a girlfriend, and John probably wouldn't call in to see her until the weekend. So, Ann would scoff the lot, then feel guilty about the calories.

She drummed her fingers on the counter. She could go

for a walk, but it was drizzling outside and it would make her hair frizz. She pulled the book she was reading from her bag but couldn't concentrate on it.

She would be turning sixty-five in May. Sixty-five years of age. The age when you officially became old in the eyes of society. Panic seized her. Was this it? Was her life reduced to clock-watching and killing time? She pushed down the fear. She had to get control of her emotions. It was normal to feel anxious as big birthdays approached. Sixty-five was another milestone, the official age of retirement. The official age of you 'no longer having any real purpose in the world'. The dread she was experiencing was not unusual. She breathed in for ten, and out for ten, trying to calm her pounding heart. These moments of panic were getting worse. Maybe she needed to see her GP. She'd never been an anxious person before, but lately she'd been very jumpy and on edge, and she wasn't sleeping well at all.

Ken called, 'Ann, any chance of a cup of tea?'

'Sure.'

She turned to fill the kettle. As she set about making tea for her husband of thirty-eight years, she imagined pouring it over his balding head. Would he react? Would he look up from grumbling about the news and actually acknowledge her? Would he look her in the eye and have a conversation with her?

When was the last time they'd properly chatted? Not about the kids, or putting out the bins, or paying car tax, but a real conversation about life, their hopes and dreams and fears.

Not for a long time, Ann thought. Not for a very long time.

Ann made the tea, just the way Ken liked it, strong with a drop of milk. She went into the lounge where he was sitting in his big brown leather chair. Ann reckoned it was his favourite possession. If there was a fire, she was fairly certain he'd push her aside and try to heave the chair out of the front door. He'd bought it three years ago, on his sixty-fifth birthday, a present to himself, and had rarely been out of it since. It had a bit at the bottom that flipped out so you could rest your legs on it and a big cup-holder on the side. It was possibly the ugliest thing Ann had ever seen, but Ken had insisted on buying it, claiming it would help with his bad back, aching hips and whatever other ailment he chose to moan about.

Ann knew all about aches and pains. She'd had her hip replaced three years ago and it had made a big difference to her life. The constant ache in her side was gone and she was able to get back to her daily walks. She'd told Ken to get his hips checked out, but he was one of those men who liked to complain about pain but never do anything about it.

Ann had raised two kids. She didn't need a third. After months of nagging Ken to get his hips seen to and making two appointments to which he hadn't shown up, she figured that he could just bloody well sort it out himself if they hurt that badly.

She handed her husband the tea.

'Thanks,' he said, giving her a half-glance. 'Would you look at this fool? What an idiot. This is the man running our health system. What has this country come to?'

On and on he ranted, as Ann stood leaning against the top of the oversized chair. His words rolled over her, down her back, along the carpet and out of the door.

She'd found herself doing this a lot lately – switching off. When Ken went off on one of his monologues, she'd drift into her own thoughts. He never said anything new. He'd thought the previous health minister was a fool, and the one before that, and the one before that. Same old, same old.

Ann slipped out of the room while Ken was still talking. He didn't notice. She sat at the kitchen table and pulled out her iPad, opened Solitaire and began to play. A solitary game for a solitary woman.

The next morning Ann cooked Ken his two rashers, one fried egg and a slice of brown toast and handed it to him on the plate with the blue flowers. He thanked her and ate heartily. They discussed the weather and what a busy day he had ahead of him. Ann wondered if he really was that busy any more. She knew that Jason Ackler was taking over from him and that Ken was handing over most of his work as he wound down to his retirement in June. Ann said nothing. She smiled, nodded, and made a kissing sound when Ken pecked her cheek.

After he left, Ann got herself ready, grabbed her bag and keys and headed out to the car. As she drove to work, she fretted about Ken retiring. What on earth was he going to do all day? He had no hobbies. Was he going to sit in his big chair watching sport? Would she have to come up with things for him to do? They had barely anything to say to each other as it was. What would they do with all this extra time together? Maybe Ann could work extra days in the shop. It made sense, given that it was the only thing that made her feel good.

Second Chance charity shop had been her unexpected lifeline for the past two years. She'd started working there when John had left home. She'd found the empty nest very difficult to accept so she'd decided to do something about it. There was an ad in the window of Second Chance, looking for part-time staff. The cancer charity that ran the shop could only pay their staff the bare minimum wage, but Ann didn't care. She wasn't doing it for the money. She did it to keep herself from going crazy. The two and a half days she worked were the highlight of her week.

She pulled into the small car park at the front and parked in the space reserved for staff. She sat there, staring through the windscreen, and realized she couldn't remember the journey. She had absolutely no recollection of driving through streets, traffic lights or junctions. She sat in the car, paralysed. Was this what it felt like to have a breakdown? Did it start when you were living inside your own head so much that you disassociated from real life?

She was trying to remember something about her journey, desperately trying to jolt herself back into the world, when there was a knock on the window. Ann almost jumped out of her skin.

'Hey, stop daydreaming and open up,' Milly said, taking off her bicycle helmet.

Ann opened the door.

'You look like you've seen a ghost. Sorry, did I give you a fright?'

'Yes, actually, you did,' Ann said. Mind you, these days every loud noise made her jump. It was as if her senses were heightened and she felt raw, as if a layer of skin had been removed.

'Whaddaya think?' Milly pointed to the thick silver ring in her eyebrow.

'Oh, my goodness.'

Milly grinned. 'Do you like it?'

'It's . . .' Ann searched for the right word. Milly acted like this super-confident feminist, but she was a bundle of insecurity and mush underneath. 'It's very striking,' Ann said, pleased with her choice of word. 'Did it hurt?'

'Like hell, but *so* worth it.' Milly wriggled her eyebrow. 'I'm still not used to it. It feels weird, but I love it. I got it done to mark moving on from that dickhead Harvey.'

7

'Good for you.' Ann hoped that this statement meant she wouldn't have to listen to Milly crying over Harvey any more. The boy had treated her like dirt and cheated on her all the time. For someone claiming to be a hard-nosed feminist, Milly had chosen a really awful boyfriend with no respect for her. It was about time she moved on. 'Now, you're not to take him back again, no matter what he says. A leopard never changes its spots. You deserve someone who treats you like a queen.'

Milly chewed her already bitten thumbnail. 'I know, but he's so fit and the sex is unreal.'

'Sex won't keep you together, though. Love and respect will,' Ann told her.

'I guess.' Milly didn't sound too sure. She was mad about Ann, but she was old and probably hadn't had sex in decades. She reckoned that Ann had probably forgotten what sex was like, and Harvey really was good in bed. Still, she didn't deserve to be cheated on. Ann was right about that. It was definitely time to move on.

Mind you, Ann's husband was no picnic. The one time Milly had met Ken she'd thought he was a grumpy old fart. He'd called into the shop and gone mental with Ann because she'd taken his car keys by mistake and he was late for a meeting. Milly thought he was going to have a stroke, his face was so red. Ann had been all flustered and apologetic. Milly's blood had been boiling and she'd wanted to tell Ken to sod off and stop shouting at his wife over a stupid mistake. Ann was cool for an oldie and she deserved a nice husband who didn't shout at her.

Ann patted Milly's arm. 'Take your time before you go out with someone else. Don't rush into anything – you're only twenty, you have your whole life ahead of you. I met Ken when I was twenty-two. I settled down too young. I should

8

have travelled more first. Seen the world.' She unlocked the shop door and switched off the alarm.

Milly turned on the lights. 'I'm never getting married,' she announced. 'I don't want to be stuck with the same man for ages. It must be so boring, looking at the same face every single day, over and over again.'

Ann smiled. 'I suppose it can be sometimes, but it's also nice to have someone in your life you've been through so much with.'

Milly threw her bag behind the counter. 'Why don't you go travelling now? You're fit for an old person – you could head off with a backpack. It's never too late. Look at that really old guy, David Attenborough, the one Greta Thunberg talks about. He's, like, a hundred and he still goes and makes documentaries about animals and the climate and stuff.'

Ann tried not to take offence at the 'old person' remark. At twenty, anyone over thirty seemed ancient. 'Ken doesn't like to fly. He gets anxious on planes.'

Milly shrugged. 'So go without him. I travel on my own all the time. To be honest, it's easier. You don't have to do the boring stuff your boyfriend or friend wants to do. There are loads of cool places you can go, and you can meet up with other single travellers and have great fun.'

Ann laughed as she pictured herself backpacking around South America, hanging out with young people on gap years, trying to find themselves. 'I'm not sure I'd blend in.'

Milly stuck a nicotine patch on her arm and pressed down. 'Age is only a number. That's what my granddad says.'

Although Ann didn't admit it to Milly, she had thought about travelling alone, but she was too nervous to do it. What if she got sick, stung, bitten, mugged, assaulted, lost or murdered? A single older woman was easy prey. She loved the idea of heading off into the sunset, not knowing what the

9

future would bring, not having the same old routine day in, day out, but her sensible side always made her think of the dangers.

They spent the morning sorting out the bags people had donated. Well, Ann sorted them out while Milly tried on anything she thought she might like. Her style was eclectic and she was good at customizing and altering clothes, so she got most of her wardrobe from the charity shop. As she liked to say to Ann, 'The pay is crap, but the clothes are a pretty cool bonus.'

In the two years Ann had been working there, she had found only two donated things that she'd liked enough to buy. A navy wrap dress and a deep purple scarf with bright blue butterflies on it. Milly had persuaded her to buy the scarf because 'You need to funk yourself up!' and whenever she wore it, she felt cheerful.

The shop was kept busy with people donating, browsing and occasionally buying. The older browsers tended to ask Ann for advice while the younger ones were drawn to Milly. They worked well as a team and Ann enjoyed Milly's chatter. She was so full of life, hope, ideas and freedom. Ann envied her. Oh, to be young again with no responsibilities and the world at your feet. She'd definitely do things differently if she had her time over. For a start, she wouldn't have taken that boring, dead-end job in the bank that her father had got for her. She would have gone travelling and lived abroad for a while. Maybe Rome or Barcelona or some other cool European city where you sat in cafés sipping espressos and smoking while you watched the world go by. She would have drunk more wine, worn shorter skirts, danced more and had passionate love affairs. She'd done none of that . . . not one single thing.

Milly watched the clock, and at exactly five, she rushed over and locked the door.

'I've got an hour to transform myself into a goddess,' she said. 'I'm going clubbing with the girls. Maybe I'll meet Mr Right tonight, or Mr Wrong but smoking hot.' She winked at Ann. 'Any plans yourself?'

Ann shook her head. 'Not really. Probably just a quiet night in.'

'You need to get out more,' Milly said, stuffing her phone into her bag and rummaging for her helmet. 'Get your lazy-arse husband off the couch and go dancing. It's so much fun and it always makes you feel better.'

Dancing, thought Ann, sadly. When was the last time we went dancing? Suddenly the thought of going home, cooking dinner and watching TV again made her feel physically ill. She wanted more. She wanted change. Her life was drifting by and she didn't know how to stop it.

2

Niall sat back on the couch, drinking a glass of red wine with Kanye West playing on Spotify. He didn't particularly like the music, but he was trying to get into it. He didn't want to be one of those dads who had no clue what music young people were listening to. The door burst open and Alice stood in front of him.

'So, how do I look?' She twirled.

Niall thought, Like a mother of four in a dress that's kind of frumpy. But he said, 'Yeah, nice.'

Alice frowned. 'What's wrong with it?'

'Nothing. I just said it's nice.'

'Nice is what you say to your granny when she turns up in her good coat. Nice is not what you say to your wife when she's just spent an hour getting ready. And it's a miracle that I look in any way normal because I had to get ready with Poppy and Ted crawling all over me and trying on my make-up.'

'Alice, you look great. Let's go or we'll be late.'

Niall knew that if she went upstairs to change, they'd be an hour late. The old Alice would throw on a tight black mini-dress, high heels and some red lipstick and they'd head out. These days she wore clothes that covered her up. Niall missed seeing her legs in short dresses. She'd always had great legs. It was the first thing he'd noticed about her. He stood up and put his wallet into the back pocket of his jeans.

'Right, let's grab our coats.'

Alice looked at her husband. He was wearing very tight

dark jeans and a shirt she'd never seen before. 'Where did you get that shirt?'

'In a shop across the road from work. Cool, isn't it?'

It was a navy shirt with a swirly pattern on it. Alice thought he looked ridiculous, like a middle-aged man who was trying too hard to look younger. Niall's stomach was straining the bottom button, which looked dangerously close to bursting.

Ted and Poppy came running in, followed by the babysitter. Poppy's face was covered with red lipstick and she was holding the stub in her hand.

'Poppy! I told you not to play with that one. That's my best lipstick.' Alice groaned.

'Stay away from the bloody couch! You'll ruin it!' It was a cream colour and Niall had spent a fortune on it. He grasped his six-year-old by the waist and pulled her back.

Alice had told him it was completely impractical and not to buy it, but Niall had wanted one room in the house where they could get away from the kids. A room where he and Alice could sit on a couch not covered with marker pen, chocolate or biscuit crumbs. A room where he could pretend his life hadn't been completely taken over by his four children. But Alice rarely went into the room. She was always busy with the kids or in bed at nine o'clock. Niall spent a lot of time in there on his own. Not that he was complaining: it was a relief to have somewhere in the house he could go without having Lego impaled in the sole of his foot or one of the kids pulling out of him.

Poppy glared at him. 'Daddy said a bad word.'

'Yes, and he's sorry, aren't you?' Alice said.

'Yes, sorry. Slap me.' Niall proffered his hand to his daughter. She walloped it. For a six-year-old, she had a lot of strength.

Ted wrapped his arms around his mother's legs. 'Mummy, I want you to read me a story.'

'But I told you, sweetie, Daddy and I are going for dinner now, so Danika is going to read to you tonight.'

'I don't want stinky Danika to read. Her voice is weird and I don't understand her.'

Alice was mortified for poor Danika. She'd only babysat twice, but she was so kind: she tidied up after the kids went to bed, which to Alice was a slice of heaven.

'Ted, don't be rude. Danika has a beautiful accent and she speaks excellent English. Now, she is going to read and I am going out with Daddy.'

'But I don't want you to go out. *Pleeeeeeeease*, Mummy, read me a story.'

'Just one, Mummy,' Poppy chimed in.

Alice wavered. 'Well, I suppose I could read one.'

'For the love of God, Alice, the taxi will be here in two minutes. I'm paying Danika ten quid an hour so she can read them the bloody book.'

Poppy smacked his hand again. 'Naughty Daddy.'

'Mumm-*yyyyyyy*,' Ted whined.

'I'll run up and read a quick one. I'll be down in two minutes.' Alice led the twins out of the room and headed upstairs.

Niall refilled his wine glass and tried not to throw it at the wall. She always, always put the kids first. Now they'd be late – again.

When they arrived at the restaurant, Max was sitting at a high table with bar stools. Alice hated those tables: she could never get comfortable on the stools. The footrest was always too low, so she had to either perch at the edge of the stool or sit back with her legs swinging in the air.

Music was blaring and the place was full of slinky, scantily clad twenty-somethings. Alice felt like a complete granny. Her dress was all wrong. It was far too conservative for a place like this. They'd only just walked in and she already had a headache from the blaring music.

Max waved at them. His T-shirt, which was too tight for him, said, 'MY BODY WILL NOT BE A TOMB FOR OTHER ANIMALS'. Alice tried not to roll her eyes. Beside him, holding his hand, Lizzie, his ridiculously young new girlfriend, was wearing a very short, very tight silver dress and killer heels. She had legs like a giraffe's and was having no trouble reaching the footrest on the stool.

Alice had to fight the urge to turn around and go home. She hadn't wanted to meet stupid bloody Max and Lizzie. She felt disloyal to his ex-wife, Sally, but Niall had insisted.

She and Sally weren't best friends, they'd met through their husbands, but Alice liked her and thought she was a great wife and mother. Her kids were so well behaved, unlike Alice's four wild offspring. Sally had done everything for Max – she'd literally devoted her life to him – and he'd still dumped her. He'd just announced to her that he wasn't happy with her any more and had walked out without a backward glance. Alice was furious with him: he had tossed aside an amazing wife for this Lizzie, who looked barely twenty. While Sally was at home devastated, Max was out and about wearing stupid T-shirts and looking annoyingly smug.

Niall bounded over and gave Lizzie a very warm hug and kiss. 'Hello, Lizzie, so nice to meet you. Wow, what a great dress. You look fantastic.'

Alice tried not to mind her husband's enthusiasm over Lizzie's dress, which was obviously more than *nice*. She gave Max a peck on the cheek and shook Lizzie's hand. She was even more stunning close up. All glossy hair and glowy skin. Alice wished she'd worn her Spanx, but they were so tight that they made her feel sick. She pulled her stomach in and tried not to stare at Lizzie's toned, flat one. Lizzie's dress had probably used a quarter the amount of material in Alice's. She had never felt so frumpy and unsexy in her life. Lizzie's youth and sexiness highlighted her own total and utter lack of both.

'Interesting T-shirt,' Niall said to Max.

Max grinned. 'Thanks. Lizzie got it for me.'

'Isn't it a little ironic for a man who loves steak?' Alice asked, as she tried to hoist herself onto the high stool.

'Not any more. Lizzie's persuaded me to become vegan and I feel fantastic.'

'You? Vegan?' Niall was shocked.

'Seriously, guys, you should do it.'

'Ha, I'd like to see Niall give up steak.'

'OMG, you really should. It's not just about diet and nutrition, it's all about saving the environment too,' Lizzie gushed.

'How long have you been vegan?' Alice asked Max.

'Two weeks, but the difference is amazing. I've lost three kilos already and my energy levels are so much higher. I need it to keep up with this one.' Max kissed Lizzie on the lips. It wasn't a peck. Alice looked down at her menu.

'He's so selfless.' Lizzie wiped lip-gloss from Max's lips. She even made that look sexy. 'He just said, "Lizzie, if it means that much to you, I'll do it."'

Oh God, give me a puke bucket, Alice thought. She looked at Niall to wink or roll her eyes discreetly, but he was gazing at Lizzie in rapt attention, as if she was explaining the meaning of life.

A gorgeous young waiter came over to offer them a drink. 'It's on the house,' he drawled. 'Ben wants to buy you a round.'

'Aww, that's so nice,' Lizzie said. 'Ben, the manager, is one of my clients at the gym,' she explained.

'Large gin and tonic for me,' Alice said.

'I'll have the same,' Niall said.

'We'll just have sparkling water with a slice of lemon, thanks,' Lizzie told the waiter.

Niall stared at his best friend. 'What? You're not drinking?'

'Not tonight. Lizzie's taking me on a ten-mile hike up the Wicklow hills tomorrow morning.'

'Are you winding me up?'

Max grinned. 'I know. It's a whole new me. This woman has changed my life in the three months we've been together. I feel ten years younger.'

Lizzie rubbed Max's arm. 'You were just stuck in a rut, babe.'

A rut of married life and raising children. The same rut my husband is in, Alice thought darkly. Thankfully, the gin and tonics arrived and Alice almost downed hers in one gulp.

The waiter took their food order. Max and Lizzie ordered lentil stew. The menu was completely vegan. Alice watched, amused, as Niall looked up and down the pages.

'I'll have the, uhm . . . the vegan pizza.'

Alice ordered the sweet potato curry and a second gin and tonic. She needed to numb herself to get through the evening.

'So, Lizzie, how is your personal-training business going?' Niall asked.

'Really well, thanks. I've actually just been asked to do some work with Gavin Jackson.'

'Wow!' Niall's eyes widened.

'Who's that? Why are you wowing?' Alice asked.

'Gavin Jackson is the captain of the Irish football team,' Niall explained. 'Alice doesn't watch sport,' he said to Lizzie, in an apologetic voice. He made her sound like some kind of ignorant fool he was saddled with. Alice really wanted to spike her husband's head with her fork.

'I do watch sport, actually,' she said.

Niall smirked. 'When?'

'I watched the rugby last weekend.'

Niall laughed. 'Coming into the room and asking me to turn the TV down does not constitute watching sport.'

Alice wondered if throwing a knife at your husband's smug face was considered a sport. She reckoned she'd win a gold medal.

'Gavin has a recurring back problem they want me to help him with,' Lizzie explained. 'I had him doing Pilates yesterday and he found it really helped.'

Niall leant forward. 'I hear Pilates is excellent for bad backs. I might take it up myself. Do you do classes for beginners like me?'

Alice glared at him. Why the sudden interest in Pilates? He played tag rugby on a Tuesday and the odd game of golf at the weekend, which had been enough for him until now.

'Oh, I'd love to help but I'm afraid all my slots are booked up. My friend Molly could do a one-on-one with you. She's a bit younger than me but she's brilliant.'

Alice almost choked on her drink. Younger? How old was this friend? Seventeen? 'Don't be ridiculous, Niall. You don't have time for Pilates, and there's nothing wrong with your back.'

'Actually, Alice, it's been at me lately. I just haven't moaned about it.' Niall smiled at Lizzie. 'Alice isn't exactly Florence Nightingale.'

Alice felt rage boiling inside her. 'I have four young children swinging out of me morning, noon and night, so I'm sorry if I don't have a whole lot of time to pat your brow.'

Before Niall could reply, their food arrived. Alice looked at her sweet potato curry and wanted to cry. She wanted to go home, put on her pyjamas, open a box of chocolates and watch Netflix in bed. She did not want to sit here holding her stomach in, feeling old and chubby, eating a dinner she didn't want and knew she wouldn't like, watching her husband make a fool of himself, drooling over a twenty-three-year-old fitness instructor.

'This is actually quite nice,' Niall said, chewing his pizza.

'See?' Lizzie beamed. 'You just need to try good vegan food to realize how great it is. Max loves it now.'

'Maybe we should go vegan, Alice,' Niall said.

'Sounds like a brilliant plan. If you're willing to shop and cook and persuade your four children to eat it, I'm in,' Alice snapped. Her husband hadn't cooked in ten years.

'I could hook you up with some really good vegan apps that have amazing recipes,' Lizzie offered.

Alice smiled. 'Thanks, but trying to persuade my kids to eat three peas with a meal is a feat worthy of a UN peace negotiator. I don't see them appreciating veganism.'

'It's all about getting to kids when they're young,' Lizzie ploughed on. 'I bet if you cooked your kids vegan lasagne, they'd love it.'

Alice snorted. 'Yeah, right. Sorry, but you clearly have no clue what kids are like.'

'You should try it,' Niall said. 'It'd be good for the kids.'

'Like I said, if you want them to eat vegan, you cook it,' Alice hissed at him.

Niall rolled his eyes. 'Alice is a bit stuck in her ways, I'm afraid.'

Alice thought of all the things she'd like to stick into Niall's head. She took a big gulp of gin and willed herself to stay calm. She was dangerously close to crying. *Stuck in her ways?* It was so dismissive. He might as well have stood up on his bloody high stool and announced that he was sick of being married to such a boring woman. She felt completely humiliated.

Lizzie put a hand on Max's head and ran her fingers up and down the back of his neck. Max was stroking her thigh.

'I'm going to pop to the loo,' Lizzie said, winking at Max.

As she walked away, her pert bum and toned legs turning heads, Max groaned. 'She is so hot. I swear, the sex is unreal.'

'I can imagine.' Niall grinned.

'She's mad for it. Any time, anywhere. I need to be fit to keep up.'

'She's a cracker,' Niall said.

Alice wondered if she should offer him her napkin to wipe up his drool.

'I'll be back in a bit. I'm just going to check on her.' Max winked at them and scurried after Lizzie.

'Jesus, do you think they're having sex in the loo?' Niall asked.

'I think that's pretty much what Max was spelling out there, yeah.' Alice pushed away her half-eaten curry.

'Wow.' Niall looked impressed, jealous and shocked all at the same time.

'It's pathetic,' Alice said. 'Max is a sad man going through a ridiculous mid-life crisis. I pity him.'

Niall sipped his gin and tonic. 'What's so pathetic about being with a hot woman who hangs on his every word and wants to have sex with him all the time?'

'He's not eighteen, he's forty-two.'

'So what?' Niall sounded exasperated. 'Why can't you have great sex at forty-two? Jesus, we're still young, Alice, but we live like old people.'

Alice flinched. 'What do you mean?'

'Our life has become so boring. When was the last time we did anything spontaneous or fun?'

'We have four young kids! We don't have time to be spontaneous. When they're older it'll be easier.'

'Stop using the kids as an excuse. We can get a babysitter and go clubbing. I'm sick of staying in and watching kids' movies. It's so dull.'

What? Alice didn't want to go clubbing. The thought of staying out past midnight made her weepy. She was up every single night with one or other of the kids and she hadn't had more than four hours' continuous sleep in ten years. Besides, she liked snuggling up and watching Disney movies with them, getting an early night. She loved family time. Why was Niall belittling their lovely life?

Before she could ask him what was so difficult about being part of their family, Max and Lizzie came back, holding hands and giggling like naughty teenagers. Max had a spot of white powder on the side of his nose. So, the teetotal vegan was snorting cocaine. While his ex-wife and kids were at home, heartbroken, he was out snorting drugs and pretending he was a footloose, fancy-free, twenty-year-old.

'Sorry, guys, this one is *craaaazy*,' Max said, kissing Lizzie's neck.

'I just can't keep my hands off him, he's so hot.' Lizzie nibbled his earlobe.

Jesus, get a room, Alice thought. This was like watching bad porn. They continued to paw each other for the rest of the meal.

When they finally got up to leave, Max announced that he and Lizzie were going to meet some of her friends in Club Monaco. 'Come, it'll be great. Lizzie's friends are really cool.'

'I thought you needed an early night for your big hike,' Alice said.

Max laughed. 'It's only half eleven, Alice. We're not ninety.'

'The club sounds great.' Niall's eyes shone with excitement.

'No, thanks,' Alice said firmly. There was no way she was going to a nightclub with a bunch of twenty-somethings, all hot bodies, pert bums and boobs that hadn't been sucked into shapeless, droopy calamities. She felt frumpy enough as it was. She didn't need to feel any worse about herself.

'Come on, Alice, let's go,' Niall pleaded.

'You can if you want to. I'm going home. I told Danika we'd be back before midnight and Sarah has hockey at eight thirty tomorrow morning.'

'For Christ's sake,' Niall grumbled. 'It's always about the kids.'

'I said go if you want, I'm not stopping you.' Alice had had enough of Niall and Max and Lizzie and their let's-pretend-we're-teenagers-again crap.

Niall sighed. 'No, I'll come with you. Sorry, guys, it sounds great. Next time.'

Max and Lizzie walked off, his arm around her, her hand tucked into the back pocket of his jeans, groping his bum. Alice and Niall climbed into a taxi. They didn't speak on the way home, but after she had walked Danika to the front door and waved her off, Niall grabbed Alice around the waist.

'What are you doing?'

'Come on, Alice.' He began to kiss her neck and tug at her dress.

The last thing Alice wanted was sex. She wanted to run upstairs, hide her flabby stomach under her baggy pyjamas, hop into bed, watch an episode of *Poldark* and sleep.

She pulled away. 'I'm tired and I'm up at seven.'

'Come on, it's been ages! I'm horny as hell.' Niall reached his hand up her dress.

Alice pushed him back. 'Not tonight. I'm not in the mood.'

Niall threw his hands into the air. 'You're never in the mood, Alice. You're always tired, feeling sick, have your period, a headache, or one of the kids is sleeping with us. It's been ten weeks since we had sex. That's nearly three months. My dick's going to fall off from lack of use.'

'Jesus, Niall, there's no need to be so aggressive.'

'I'm sick of it, Alice! I'm sick of all this. We're living like pensioners. This is bullshit.'

Niall stormed into the lounge and slammed the door.

Alice left him to calm down. She climbed the stairs, got undressed and cuddled up in bed. She set her alarm for seven a.m., then pulled out her iPad and put on *Poldark*. She needed to block out the voice in her head telling her she was fat, unattractive, unsexy and frumpy.

3

Lulu reached over, raised the cup of watery black paint and splashed it all over Nathan's drawing.

'Miss Orla!' he howled. 'Lulu wreckted my painting.'

He held up his painting. Orla could see the outline of a crooked house covered with wet black splodges.

'Lulu is a pig. I hate her,' he bawled.

Orla went over and put her arm around Nathan. Getting to him before he wound himself into full-blown histrionics was the key. She rubbed circles on his back and said she'd help him paint a new house and then she handed him a 'special' light blue sheet to draw on.

When Nathan had calmed down, Orla took Lulu to the cosy corner of the classroom, where beanbags were spread about and the children went for circle or reading time.

Lulu plopped down on a red beanbag while Orla sat on the rug and crossed her legs, so she was at Lulu's eye level. 'Lulu, you're such a lovely girl and usually you're so helpful and kind. Why did you splash black paint all over Nathan's house?'

Lulu's dark pigtails swung as she shook her head. 'I didn't do it.'

'Lulu, I saw you. Now, you know it's really important to tell the truth, don't you?'

Lulu's eyes flashed. 'Well, mummies don't tell the truth.'

Orla knew she must tread carefully. Lulu had been acting up for a few days now. Something was obviously upsetting her at home.

'Why would you say that, Lulu?'

'Cos Mummy lied to me.' Lulu's lip wobbled. 'She saided that I was her only princess, but now she has another girl baby in her tummy.'

So that was it. Orla knew that Lulu's parents were separated, but now the poor little girl was all confused because she had to deal with a new sibling.

'But, Lulu, you will always be your mummy's first girl, the first princess. She loves you very much and that won't change when the new baby arrives.'

Lulu jumped up from the beanbag and screamed, 'Yes, it will. That stinky baby will be all new and shiny and I'll be the old princess that nobody wants.'

Before Orla could stop her, Lulu had rushed over to Nathan, ripped his new blue page in half and punched him on the nose.

Mayhem ensued. Nathan howled like a banshee, and when the other kids in the class saw blood coming out of his nose, they all began to scream, too. Orla asked Harriet, the trainee teacher who helped her two days a week, to keep an eye on the kids, while she rushed Nathan to the boys' cloakroom and tried to stem the flow. The poor child was traumatized and it took a while to calm him down.

When she got back to the class ten minutes later, Lulu was sitting in the corner on her own, while all the other kids glared at her. When they saw Nathan, they surrounded him and love-bombed him with hugs and offers of treats from their lunchboxes.

Orla crouched beside Lulu. Her little face was streaked with tears. 'Sweetie, I know you didn't mean to hurt Nathan, but you did hit him and you know that's absolutely not okay. I need you to come and apologize to him now.'

Reluctantly Lulu walked over to Nathan, clinging to her teacher's hand. 'Sorry, Nathan,' she muttered.

'You should be super-duper sorry, Lulu. You broked his nose,' Ruby said.

'She didn't break his nose.' Orla was firm.

'My mum is going to be *so* angry with you, Lulu, when she sees all the blood,' Nathan said, holding a tissue to his no longer bleeding nose.

'I said I was sorry!'

'I'm not your friend any more.' Nathan walked away from her.

'Me too. You're mean.' Ruby followed Nathan.

Lulu's head drooped and she wiped her eyes with the back of her hand.

'I'll still be your friend,' Poppy said to Lulu. 'I'll make Ted be your friend, too. He does what I tell him. Anyway, he thinks Nathan is silly cos he doesn't like football.'

'I wish I had a twin,' Lulu said.

'You can borrow Ted but he can be a pain sometimes,' Poppy said.

'Okay, Poppy, back to your desk now.' Orla ushered her to it and clapped her hands. 'Now, class, what Lulu did was wrong. Hitting someone is not acceptable. But she has apologized, and we are her friends so we're going to accept her apology and move on. Nathan is going to be fine. Let's remember how important it is to be nice to all our class-mates. Kindness costs nothing, but it's the best gift of all. Now we'll open our Irish books and find out what happened to Spot's ball.'

That afternoon, Orla spoke to Nathan's mum in the school-yard. She explained what had happened, playing it down a little, but Pam Lyons was having none of it.

'That brat could have broken his nose. I want to speak to her parents. This can never happen again.'

'I will be speaking to Lulu's parents and she is aware that what she did is unacceptable. She's normally a very sweet girl, but she's not herself at the moment. She's upset about something. She's very sorry and she apologized to Nathan.'

Pam Lyons huffed. 'If a child is this violent at six, what hope have they in the future? She'll end up a delinquent. Such behaviour should be nipped in the bud. I want a full apology from her parents ASAP. And in the meantime, I don't want her anywhere near Nathan, either inside the class-room or out in the yard.'

'I understand. I'll be in touch.'

As she walked away, Orla sighed. Poor Lulu, she was in for a roasting. Orla knew exactly what it felt like to be young and confused.

She remembered, long ago, her father being called to school when she'd slapped a boy, who'd said, 'You killed your mammy.'

Orla had foolishly thought her father would defend her, but instead he'd told her that she was a 'silly girl' for losing her temper and that what the boy had said was true. 'You can't go around hitting everyone who says things like that, Orla. People here in town know the story of your mother's tragic death and you have to learn to ignore the comments.'

Orla felt tears prick her eyes at the memory. She had been only seven. Had he had no heart, no compassion?

Zoë stood in front of Orla in her Wonderbra and thong. Holding up two dresses, one red, one black, she asked, 'Well?'

'The black,' Orla said.

'I'm thinking the red.'

Orla wondered why Zoë bothered to ask her for fash-ion advice when she always chose what she wanted to wear anyway.

27

'What are you wearing?' Zoë wanted to know.

Orla didn't want to go out, but she knew that if she told Zoë, her flatmate would hound her relentlessly until she gave in. After three months of living together, Orla knew that it was easier to agree to go. She would try to slip home early when Zoë was distracted with whatever guy she picked up tonight.

But it was exhausting. Just the thought of having to get dressed up and go to a bar, then a nightclub, chat to men and pretend . . . The pretending was draining. Orla just wanted to curl up on the couch with a book. She didn't want pressure, she didn't want to perform, she just wanted to be left alone.

But Orla was a good actress: she'd had to be. She'd been acting all her life.

'I'm going for skinny black jeans and the silver top,' she told Zoë.

'Ooh, sexy. We're going to get lucky tonight, I can feel it!' Zoë whooped. 'Right, get dressed, and we'll have a few glasses of wine before we head out.'

'Great.' Orla feigned enthusiasm.

Two hours later, she was still feigning enthusiasm when the taxi pulled up outside Club Monaco. Zoë strode ahead into the nightclub. She was swaying slightly. She had drunk most of the bottle of wine. Orla had had one glass – she liked to pace herself. She never got drunk any more because she knew that if she did things could go wrong. She'd tried that tactic and it hadn't worked out. Alcohol didn't help. When they bought each other drinks and it was Orla's turn to order, she always had Diet Coke, no vodka. It meant she got tipsy but never drunk.

The nightclub was full and the dance-floor was packed with people throwing their bodies around.

'Oh, my God, look at that old guy! What a total idiot.'

Zoë pointed to the edge of the dance-floor where a much older man was doing dad dancing, wearing a T-shirt that said, 'EAT PUSSY NOT ANIMALS'. He was with a much younger woman in a slinky silver dress – she looked even younger than Orla.

Zoë tapped him on the shoulder. 'I find your T-shirt offensive.'

'Lighten up, it's a joke. No need to burn your bra over it. I'm Max, what's your name?'

'My name is – Take the T-shirt off, you tosser.'

Orla giggled into her drink. The old guy stood open-mouthed at Zoë's back as she pushed past him into the middle of the dance-floor. She began to dance with a group of guys. Within minutes, she was grinding up against one of them. Orla had to hand it to her: Zoë knew how to get what she wanted, and what Zoë wanted was sex. Lots of it. Loud, shouty sex. The apartment walls were paper thin, and after the first month, Orla had ended up investing in noise-cancelling headphones. They were not easy to sleep in, but anything was better than listening to Zoë's multiple orgasms – fake or real.

Zoë came off the dance-floor holding hands with the guy she'd been dancing with. One of the others followed them.

'Hey, this is my flatmate, Orla.' Zoë introduced her. 'Orla, this is Gary and this is a guy we just met dancing. I told him my flatmate was here and that you're single.'

Orla blushed. Zoë was so forward – she didn't do small-talk: she thought it was a waste of time. Her take on it was: 'Why waste oxygen and energy chatting to a guy who isn't available? My first question to every guy I meet is "Are you single?"'

'Hi, I'm Will,' the dance-floor stranger said.

Will was Orla's type. He was tall, for starters. At five feet nine, Orla liked tall men. He was in good physical shape and had green eyes. She was a sucker for green eyes.

Will moved closer to her as Zoë and Gary began to kiss passionately. 'Your flatmate's a live wire.'

Orla laughed. 'Try living with her. She's great fun, though,' she added, not wanting to appear disloyal.

'Sure. So, what do you do when you're not in nightclubs?' Will asked.

'I'm a teacher.'

'Cool.'

'You?'

'Electrician.'

'Busy?'

'Out the door.'

Orla sipped her drink while she tried to think of something to say. While Zoë didn't see the point of small-talk, Orla did – she was just rubbish at it. She knew it was a form of dance: you started slow with chit-chat and built up to more meaningful conversations, but she'd never really acquired the knack for chit-chat.

'You look really fit. Do you work out?' Will asked.

'I run,' Orla shouted, over the music. She ran most days. She'd started when she was about ten and never stopped. It helped to push away the pain and anxiety. She needed it in her life. When she ran, she thought of nothing but putting one foot in front of the other.

'It shows.' Will leant in. 'Blue eyes, too. I love blue eyes.'

'I like green ones,' Orla replied.

Will moved in and kissed her. It was slow and nice. Orla responded to him. She put her hand up to his face. They kissed for a long time.

'Has anyone ever told you that you're a great kisser?' Will whispered in her ear.

Yes, Orla wanted to say. I'm a good kisser, and I'm good at lots of other things too, except one. One vital thing.

The lights went on and the crowd groaned. Zoë came bounding over with Gary in tow. 'Gary's coming back to ours. Are you guys coming?'

Will put his arm around Orla. 'Sounds good to me.'

Orla needed to take control of the situation. 'Actually, how about I come back to yours instead?' she asked.

Will nuzzled her neck. 'Fine with me.'

Thankfully, Will lived in the opposite direction, so Zoë and Gary got into one taxi and they got into another.

In the back of the taxi, Will leant over and kissed Orla. She felt his hand go up her top. It crept higher and higher and then slipped into her bra, cupping her breast. It felt so good, she wanted to close her eyes and go with it. Maybe this time it would be okay. Maybe Will would be the one. But she knew it wouldn't, and he wasn't. She pulled his hand down and leant forward to ask the taxi man to pull over.

'Hey, what's wrong?' Will was alarmed.

'Nothing. I just need to get out.'

'I'm sorry, did I go too far? I thought you . . . I mean, I thought we were going back to mine. What's going on, Orla?'

The driver pulled the car over to the side of the road.

'You didn't do anything. I just need to go now. I'm sorry.' Orla opened the door and hopped out.

'I can drop you home,' Will called after her.

'I'm fine. Please just go away.' Orla needed him to leave before she started to cry.

'Fine. You're a bit of a prick-tease, you know,' Will muttered, as he rolled up the window.

Orla pulled her leather jacket around her. She looked at

her watch. Three a.m. She had three hours to kill. If she went home before six, Zoë would ask too many questions.

Orla pulled her bag up on her shoulder and made her way to the usual spot. Thank God for all-night Starbucks. She'd treat herself to a hot chocolate and a blueberry muffin. There was some comfort in that. She had her book. Her English teacher used to say, 'You can never be lonely if you have a book.' But that wasn't true. Orla had felt lonely her whole life. Books helped, but loneliness was Orla's norm. She'd always been different. She'd always felt like a bit of a freak. People had always talked about her.

All she'd ever wanted to be was normal. Just a normal person, with a normal history and a normal body.

4

Ann arranged the flowers in two pretty bunches and placed the vases on the table. She straightened the white linen cloth and smiled. It looked lovely, warm and welcoming.

'I don't know why you're fussing. It's just the kids coming for dinner,' Ken said, as he carried the good glasses to the table.

'I want it to be nice. I want them to want to come back for dinner,' Ann said. 'Besides, Zoë is bringing her flatmate, Orla. She's from somewhere near Limerick and I don't think she knows many people here.'

Ken plonked the glasses down roughly. Ann tried not to wince. They were delicate and needed to be handled with care.

'They'll come anyway,' he said. 'All kids want to come home for a good meal.'

No, they don't, Ann thought. Kids leave and never look back. Sure, they'd call in the odd time, but she wanted them to call in a lot. She missed them desperately. Zoë and John were the glue. They were what had held this family together. They were what she had fought so long to get. They were the reason she had put her body through years of IVF. They were her miracles, her late babies, Zoë born when she was thirty-nine, John when she was forty-two. Both all the more precious for having taken so long to arrive, after years of disappointment and heartbreak.

But now they were grown-up and had moved out. Ann felt lost. She had no purpose really. Gone was her reason for getting up in the morning. Gone was her reason for doing big supermarket shops. Gone was her reason for feeling excited when she heard the front door opening. Apart from her shifts in the charity shop, life was just one big, endless, dreary drudge. She felt her stomach twist. She couldn't live like this: it was destroying her. She needed more – she wanted more. Sixty-four was too young for a lifetime of endless nights in front of the TV and no excitement. She had to do something before it was too late.

'Hello! We're here,' Zoë called, from the hall.

Ann took a deep breath, pushed aside her thoughts and rushed out to greet her daughter.

Zoë clapped her hands when she saw the table. 'Oh, Mum, this looks so lovely.'

'Thanks so much for inviting me.' Orla handed Ann a bunch of flowers.

'Delighted to meet you, Orla. How do you find living with this firecracker?' Ann asked.

Orla smiled. 'Zoë's great fun.'

'Wild is what she is,' Ken muttered, as he held out a hand to shake Orla's.

Zoë rolled her eyes. 'Dad thinks having more than three beers is wild. You need to live a little, Dad.' She poked him in the stomach and he pulled her in for a hug.

'Your mother's been cooking all day,' Ken grumbled. 'She's worn out making this dinner. I told her to keep it casual, but she insisted on all this fuss.'

'Well, I like it! Thank you, Mum.' Zoë leant over and kissed her cheek.

'It looks wonderful,' Orla agreed. She handed Ann a tinfoil-wrapped parcel. 'I made this for you. I hope you like chocolate fudge cake.'

'It's Ken's favourite.' Ann beamed at her.

'You can come again, Orla,' Ken said, patting her shoulder.

'Well, I have to confess I had insider information. Zoë told me you liked it.'

'Thank you, Orla. And feel free to teach Zoë how to make it.' Ken winked at his daughter.

'Dad, you know I hate cooking. It's a complete waste of time,' Zoë announced. 'But I do appreciate Mum's amazing dinners.' She squeezed her mother's hand.

Ann wanted to put her arms around her daughter and hold her. She missed their physical closeness. She missed the days when Zoë would climb in beside her in bed and tell her all of her boyfriend woes, or which friend she was arguing with, or gossip about who was dating whom. They'd drink mugs of tea, eat chocolate biscuits and chat for hours, Zoë often laying her head on her mother's shoulder and falling asleep.

John had also been very physically affectionate towards her, often picking her up and swinging her around to make her laugh. He was always the one who brought lots of friends back to the house, and Ann would make fresh scones, then offer pots of chicken curry or beef stroganoff. She loved feeding them and listening to their banter as they relentlessly poked fun at each other.

She missed them. Her kids were her life.

'Can I help with anything?' Orla asked, as Zoë and Ken chatted to each other.

Ann could see the young woman felt a bit awkward, so she decided to give her a job. 'Actually, pet, you could. Would you mind putting the dressing on the salad for me?'

'Of course.'

Orla followed Ann into the kitchen and mixed the dressing into the salad. Zoë's home was just how Orla wished her home had been. A mother cooking dinner, welcoming you with open arms, and a father whose face lit up when he saw you.

Ann stirred the beef stew. 'So, Orla, where are you from?'

'I'm from a small town called Ballystone. It's about eighty miles from Limerick.'

'How long have you lived in Dublin?'

'I moved here straight after school to do teacher training. So it's been six years now.'

'What age do you teach?'

'I've got senior infants this year, the five- and six-year-olds.'

Ann put a hand up to her chest. 'Oh, that's a magical age. I remember my two, adorable they were.'

'Yes, it's fun.'

'Have you brothers and sisters?' Ann asked.

'No, I'm an only child.'

'How did you find that? Some people love it and others find it a bit lonely.'

'I'm more of the lonely variety, I think.' Orla smiled.

Orla didn't like being asked too many questions, but Ann was lovely and warm, so she tried to be polite without saying too much.

'It's not easy having all that attention and focus on you.'

Ha! Attention and focus? If only Ann knew. Orla might as well have been invisible her whole life.

'Do you go home much?'

Orla shrugged. 'Probably not as often as I should.'

'Ah, sure, when you're young you should be out having fun and not worrying about your parents. Although I'm sure they appreciate it when they see you. I know I love it when Zoë and John call in. I miss them.'

'It's just my dad and he's busy with the farm, so . . .'

'Oh, I'm sorry, pet. When did you lose your mother?'

'A good while ago.' Orla fudged the question.

'That's very hard on you. My mother died when I was nine. It's lonely, isn't it?'

Orla nodded. 'Yes.'

'I think that's why I was so desperate to have children. I wanted to be a mother more than anything. Children who lose their mothers young have a hole in their lives that they need to fill. Thankfully, Zoë and John filled mine. I'm sure teaching helps you fill yours.'

Orla looked at Ann. She got it. She didn't totally get it – no one could, Orla's life was so complicated – but Ann understood about the gaping hole that not having a mother had left. 'You're right, it does help.'

Ann patted her arm. 'Good for you. Those children are lucky to have you.'

Orla tried not to get emotional. 'Thank you.' She wanted to hug Ann and tell her how much those words meant to her.

'Right, we'd better get this food out.' Ann led the way as Orla followed.

They sat down to dinner and Zoë told her parents about her car acting up and how smoke had been coming out of the bonnet by the time she'd arrived home that afternoon.

'I'll sort that out for you. I'll come over tomorrow after work,' Ken said. 'You must keep your car properly serviced, Zoë. You can't go letting it fall apart. I'll drop over at about seven.'

'Thanks, Dad. You're the best.'

Ann laughed. 'You've always had your father running around after you.'

'He likes to help and I like to accept help.' Zoë grinned.

The door opened and John walked in. Ann jumped up and rushed over to hug him.

'The prince has arrived,' Zoë said, making a face. 'John is the apple of Mum's eye,' she explained to Orla.

Lucky him, Orla thought.

John greeted them and sat down. 'You look a bit rough,' he said to Zoë. 'Late night?'

'Very,' Zoë said, smirking at him.

'How do you live with her?' John asked Orla. 'She's so messy and loud.'

'I'm not that bad, am I?'

Orla smiled. Yes, you are, she wanted to say. You are messy and you make the walls shake when you have sex. But Zoë was also nice and didn't ask too many questions, which suited Orla. 'Zoë's a lot of fun to live with.'

John laughed. 'You're very polite, Orla.'

Ann fussed about, making sure everyone had enough on their plates and giving out second helpings. They chatted easily about this and that. Ken was quiet, but he chipped in every now and then. A normal family, Orla thought. A lovely, normal family.

'Zoë, have you met any nice boys recently?' Ann asked.

John snorted. 'A nice boy would be scared of her.'

Ann swatted him with her napkin. 'Any boy would be lucky to have her, just like any girl would be lucky to have you. Gems, you are.'

'This cake is delicious. Have you a boyfriend, Orla? I bet he loves your baking,' Ken said.

'Dad!' Zoë cut across him. 'Don't ask Orla that. It's rude.'

'Why is it rude?'

'Because that's her private life. Anyway, neither of us has a boyfriend and we don't want one either. Being single is way more fun.'

'You could do with settling down,' Ken said.

Zoë rolled her eyes. 'You're so old-fashioned, Dad. I'm

twenty-six, not sixty-six. Besides, I'm never going to get married, so you need to park that dream.'

Ken shook his head. 'I don't understand young women now. You're all so strident. You can't even give a woman a compliment or hold a door open for her or you'll be accused of harassment. What happened to old-fashioned values – and when did getting married and having a family become so undesirable?'

'Women nowadays do not want to get married, give up work and be stuck at home with screaming kids. They don't want to rely on their husbands for money and support,' Zoë replied.

'Your mum did, and she was happy to do it.'

Was I? Ann thought. Yes, when she finally had the kids, she wanted to be at home to savour every second. But she hadn't liked having to rely on Ken for money. That had been hard after working for so many years and having her own income. But she had been grateful that she'd had the choice to stay at home with the kids. Ken had provided that choice and given her that security.

'Are your family like this?' John asked Orla. 'Always arguing about everything?'

Orla shook her head. 'No, but I'm an only child, so I guess it's quieter.'

'Sometimes I wish I was an only child,' John said.

Zoë thumped her brother's shoulder. 'Thanks a lot.'

John put his arm around her. 'You know I love you, even though you are kind of nuts.'

Ann smiled at them. Her two greatest creations. She loved that they were close even though they were so different. Zoë had always been a bit wild and loud. John was quieter and more reserved. Together they complemented each other's personalities perfectly.

John reached over and helped himself to more cake. 'Actually, I have some news,' he announced.

'You've finally decided to study medicine?' Ken asked.

Ann saw John's jaw set. Ken was always so hard on him. He hadn't hidden his disapproval when John had said he wanted to do nursing. 'Nursing is a woman's job,' Ken had said. John had been hurt, but he had ignored his father and gone on to become a very competent nurse and he loved his job.

John turned away from his father and directed his conversation to his mother.

'I applied for a job in Australia and I've been accepted. I start at the Royal Alfred Hospital in Sydney in two weeks. The salary is almost twice what I'm earning here and I'm going to move in with Larry and Suzie. They've been there almost a year already and love it. They're the ones who encouraged me to apply. They have a spare room, so it's all sorted.'

Ann felt the room spin. She was afraid to open her mouth. She wanted to scream, *Nooooooo, please don't go. Don't leave me.*

Ken slammed his knife down on the crisp white tablecloth, staining it with chocolate. 'Why the hell are you going to Australia? That's what kids do when they're eighteen, not twenty-three. Running off to Australia? It's nonsense! You need to stay here, get on the property ladder with a mortgage before it's too late.'

'Gee, thanks, Dad. I knew you wouldn't be over the moon, but I didn't expect that outburst.' John's voice was icy. 'I was going to add that I've been given a position as one of their senior nurses and they've offered to put me on their training course to qualify as a theatre nurse while I'm there.'

'Wow, John, that's amazing. I'm so proud of you, bro.' Zoë got up and threw her arms around him, cutting through the awkwardness.

Orla hurriedly excused herself to go to the toilet. Ann realized the poor girl had left to escape the tension in the room. She needed to smooth things over. She cleared her throat. 'That's wonderful, John. I'm really happy for you.' She went over to him and put her arms around him. 'I'm going to miss you so much, though.'

John smiled at her. 'Come and visit. Golden beaches, blue skies, great food . . . Come, Mum. You've always said you wanted to go to Australia. Now you have a great excuse.'

Ann nodded, afraid to speak for fear she'd start bawling. Her beautiful boy was going to be living on another continent.

'We won't be travelling halfway around the world at huge expense, I can tell you that. I'm nearly seventy and I'm not spending twenty-four hours cooped up in a plane.'

John turned to his father. 'I never expected you to visit, Dad. I know you hate travelling. I'm talking about Mum coming.'

'Don't be ridiculous! She's not going all that way alone.' Ken snorted. 'Your mother gets lost going to the shops.'

Ann briefly considered upending the remainder of the chocolate cake on her husband's head.

'Mum can do anything she wants.' John winked at his mother.

Ann kissed her son's smooth cheek. People always talked about the special mother–son bond. They were right. John was her only son and her ray of sunshine. The thought of him moving across the world made her heart shatter. But she had to pretend to be happy for his sake. This was what he wanted, and it would be good for him and his career. But she knew she'd spend every day praying that he didn't fall in love with Australia – or an Australian – and never come home.

'When do you leave?' Zoë asked.

John held his mother's hand and squeezed it. 'Next Tuesday.'

Ann gasped. 'So soon?'

'I know, Mum. I didn't want to give you too much time to be upset. I thought it was best to tell you as close to the leaving date as possible.'

He knew her so well. Ann wiped away the tears that had fallen down her cheeks and forced a smile to her face.

'I'll get that bottle of champagne your dad got from a client. We kept it for a special occasion.'

'I was keeping that for your birthday,' Ken objected.

Ann spun around and glared at him. 'Turning sixty-five is nothing to celebrate. John getting a brilliant job and forging ahead in his career is.'

Ann fetched the bottle and asked John to do the honours. They were all trying their best to look jolly, but there was an unmistakable tension in the air.

Orla returned to the room and slid nervously into her seat. You could have cut the atmosphere with a knife. It was time for her to go. She picked up her bag and stood up. 'I've to head off now. Thank you so much for a really gorgeous dinner.' She made for the hall before anyone could try to stop her.

Zoë caught up with her at the front door. 'I'm so sorry. Our family dinners are normally a lot calmer.'

'Please don't worry, it was really lovely.'

'Poor Mum, this is going to break her heart. She adores John. I'll really miss him too.' Zoë looked upset.

Orla squeezed her arm. 'You can go and visit him as well. It'd be amazing to go to Oz.'

Zoë smiled. 'Yeah, you're right. Maybe I'll bring Mum

with me.' She gave Orla a hug. 'Thanks, and sorry again. I'll be home in a while.'

'See you later,' Orla said.

When Zoë came back, they drank the champagne, with Ann downing most of it. She needed the alcohol to numb the pain of John's departure. The atmosphere was still tense and it was obvious that Zoë and John were anxious to be out of there. As soon as the champagne was finished, they gathered their things and headed towards the front door.

As Zoë hugged Ann goodbye, she whispered, 'Don't worry, Mum, I'm still here.'

Despite her intention to be stoic, Ann sobbed into her daughter's shoulder and then cried into John's.

'I'll Skype you every day, Mum. It'll be okay. And I promise to come home for Christmas,' John said, to his distraught mother.

Ann stood in the doorway and waved her children off until they were specks in the distance.

'Come inside – you're letting all the heat out,' Ken grumbled.

Ann closed the door. She picked up a half-bottle of leftover white wine and a glass, then went into the lounge. She sank into the couch and proceeded to drink and cry while Ken tidied up.

When Ken had finished clearing the dishes, he went to see how his wife was doing. He stood in the doorway, watching her. She had mascara streaks down her cheeks and her eyes were half closed as she finished the last drop of wine.

Damn John! This was going to kill Ann. He was furious with his son for upsetting her. John was probably right to go and get ahead in his career, but Ken was protective of

Ann and knew how heartbroken she would be. He knew how much the kids meant to her. He had held her up through all the miscarriages and the failed first two IVF attempts. He had begged her to stop. He hated what it was doing to her emotionally and physically and, truth be told, to their marriage. Having children had consumed them for twelve long years. They had sat through endless christenings and kids' birthday parties while inside they ached.

Ken would have given up on kids years before Ann. His wife was enough for him. He loved Ann more than anything in the world. Sure, he wanted kids, he was heartbroken too, but he wanted his wife more. The primal urge to have children took up all of her attention. She was consumed by her need to be a mother and she was never going to stop until she had a baby. She had been strong enough to keep going. And then she had given him the two most beautiful children. Ken thought his heart would burst when he held Zoë in his arms and then, a few years later, John. All the pain and years of struggle disappeared when he looked into Zoë's eyes for the first time.

It was Ann's determination that had led to their two miracles. Ken was awed at his wife's ability to push through the pain of fertility treatments with her eye always on the end game. And it had been worth it – it had been worth all of it to see her so happy, holding her babies and radiating pure joy.

'Okay, Ann, let's get you to bed.'

'My heart is broken, Ken,' she slurred, as he lifted her up from the couch.

'Come on now. John'll be back. It's just a couple of years, and you can Skype him every day.'

'But I want him here, near me, not way over there.' Ann flung out her arm, smacking Ken in the face.

'Ouch. Okay, let's keep the hand movements down. Come on, up the stairs we go.'

He half dragged, half carried Ann up to the bedroom. Ken hadn't seen her so drunk in a long time.

Ann flopped onto the bed. Ken knelt and took off her shoes. Then he sat her up and pulled down the zip of her dress. Ann leant forward and kissed him.

He drew back.

'Come on, Ken, kiss me like you used to.' She pushed her tongue into his mouth.

'You're drunk, Ann. You need sleep.'

'No, I don't.' She began to sob again. 'I need affection. We never have sex, we never even touch. You sleep in a different room from me. I'm so lonely,' she bawled.

Ken stood up. 'You're just feeling down because of John. A good night's sleep will do you the world of good.'

She clung to his shirt. 'No, Ken, I don't want to be alone.'

He moved away from her. 'You'll feel better in the morning. You'll see. Goodnight, Ann.'

He hurried out of the room and closed the door behind him.

5

Poppy was standing with her hands on her hips, screeching into Alice's face. 'I have told you a zillion, trillion times that I *hate* ham sandwiches. I had nothing to eat for lunch today and I'm *starving*.'

Alice wanted to tell her that she was lucky to have any sandwiches at all. That there were children all over the world who had nothing to eat, but she knew that would only lead to Poppy's usual reply: 'Send them my sandwiches, then. I bet you *they* wouldn't even eat them.'

As Poppy banged on about her human rights being violated by having a sandwich filling she didn't like, Alice tried to tune her out. Her head was pounding. She'd been up again with Jamie: he was still wetting the bed at eight and didn't look like stopping any time soon. At first she'd worried that he was being bullied, or was unhappy, but he was by far her happiest and most content child, she'd taken him to the doctor, had an ultrasound done, and the diagnosis was that he had a small bladder, slept deeply and would grow out of it. When Alice asked when that would happen, the doctor had shrugged and said, 'They usually grow out of it by their teens.' Alice had tried to block that out of her mind.

Alice wondered if she should just buy plastic sheets. Jamie refused to wear pull-ups, despite wetting the bed at least three times a week. Alice was worn out with changing sheets at two a.m., never mind the washing it added to her already huge pile. But she didn't want him to be self-conscious about it, so she told him not to worry and changed his pyjamas, sheets and duvet covers in her half-sleep each time it happened.

The problem was, once Alice had been woken up, she found it really difficult to fall back asleep. Last night she'd lain awake for almost two hours, doing lists in her head of all the things she needed to do, while Niall snored beside her, oblivious. Jamie had clearly inherited his deep sleeping habits from his father.

Niall thought she had an easy life as a stay-at-home mum, able to give up work and spend lots of time with her kids. But some days Alice secretly yearned to go back to work, even though the thought made her feel horribly guilty. She wanted to be at home with the kids. It had always been her dream. But the reality wasn't quite what she'd imagined. It wasn't all home-baked scones and singsongs in the car. Her days were crammed full of busyness, but it was busyness that was mind-blowingly boring. Grocery shopping, cooking, driving, laundry, homework, cleaning and general admin – and often she was doing those things not just for her own family but for Niall's dad, who lived on his own: she cooked and delivered batches of meals to him every week. She also helped her uncle Theo because of his bad arthritis, doing a weekly grocery shop for him as well as his ironing.

The most trying part of her day, though, was homework-time because it came when she was tired and trying to cook a meal that all four children would actually eat. Jamie had a particularly bad memory, so doing spellings with him was a form of torture. She had once, and she wasn't proud of this, flung his copybook across the kitchen in a moment of pure frustration. By that stage, he had spelt 'chicken' incorrectly fifteen times.

Alice was ashamed of her reaction and Jamie had ended

up not having to learn any more spellings and getting a Kit-Kat in return for 'not telling your teacher about this'.

Niall seemed to think that Alice swanned around all day doing yoga and drinking chai lattes with other school mums. In fact, Alice didn't do either. She never felt cool enough to be with the in-mums, and the not-so-cool mums never asked her, so she fell between the groups. She had two best mates from her own schooldays, but they both worked full-time. Alice often found the days very lonely. She liked picking the kids up, because there was chat and activity, but after ten minutes they'd start fighting and she'd wish she could drop them back at school again.

She had thought about going back to work when the twins turned five and went to big school last year, but she didn't know what to do. She'd been out of work for almost eleven years and hadn't loved her job anyway. She had been a sales manager for a range of healthy vegetable juices and soups. It had been exciting at the beginning but the guy running the company, Garret, was evangelical. Early on in her career with him, Garret had found her glugging a full-fat Coca-Cola one morning and gone nuts. Alice had been out with Niall and some friends the night before and had ended up drinking far too much and going to a nightclub until three a.m. She was hung-over and tired, and she needed the sugar rush from the Coke to get through the morning. A kale, cucumber and lime juice just wasn't going to do it. Garret had given her a thirty-minute lecture on the evils of fizzy drinks.

Alice had tried to get into the juices and soups, but they all tasted like grass. She never drank Coke in front of Garret again and she sold his products into supermarket chains as if they were the second coming of Christ. She ate and drank her non-healthy snacks when she was on the road, hidden in the back of car parks, tucked away from prying eyes.

She knew Garret suspected her of being a non-believer, but she was very good at persuading people to stock his products so he mostly left her alone.

When Sarah came along, she'd packed it in. The long hours and travel around the country were too hard to juggle with a baby. Niall had been happy for her to give it up. His mum hadn't worked and he thought it was 'better for the kids' to have a parent at home.

Alice had grown up with a mother who was always at work. She had been a latch-key kid, she and her sister, Lisa, coming home from school every day to an empty house and cooking their own meals. When she had kids of her own, she wanted their lives to be different from hers. She wanted to be the at-home-baking-buns kind of mother because she'd craved that as a young girl. She'd been so jealous of her friends whose mums were always at the school gate to pick them up, made them fabulous costumes for the school plays, cooked them hot school lunches that they packed in Thermos flasks, volunteered to help out at school functions and always seemed to have time for their kids.

Alice didn't blame her mother for not being around: she knew she'd had no choice. After her father had died, when Alice was eleven and Lisa was thirteen, her mother had gone from working part-time in the family pharmacy to running it, which was a full-time job with very long hours. Alice didn't see her much. Her mother was an incredibly strong person. She'd got up the day after the funeral and gone to the pharmacy to open up and begin running it full-time. She never complained, never moaned about being tired, sad, overwhelmed, lonely . . . She just got on with it and provided a good life for Alice and Lisa.

Alice appreciated all that her mother had done for them, but she wanted to be a different type of mum. She wanted

49

to be the mum who was at all the school plays and cake sales. The mum who was always at the school gate at pick-up time. The mum who volunteered to go on school outings and spent as much time with her kids as possible.

But what Alice was realizing now was that it was also better for Niall to have her at home because it gave him complete freedom. No need to rush home from work to let the nanny go, no drop-offs or pick-ups from crèches or schools, no lunch-making, no long division, no laundry, no cleaning, no organizing their kids' busy sports schedules . . . Niall just swanned off to work every day and Alice did the rest.

But, then, Alice knew she was lucky to be able to stay at home and not have to work and juggle kids. Perhaps her own mother would have preferred that if she'd had the choice. Alice also knew that Niall worked hard for his family, but she felt lonely and kind of worthless a lot of the time. The stay-at-home-mum life she'd imagined was nothing like the reality.

Alice left her screaming daughter, still roaring about her hatred of ham, and went into the small laundry room. She reached up behind the spare bulbs and batteries in the corner shelving unit and pulled out her secret box. Inside was her emergency stash – cigarettes and two packets of chocolate digestives. She put the box back into its hiding place, sat on the washing-machine and ate three biscuits, welcoming the sugar rush.

'*Muuuuuummy! Muuuuuuuummy!* Where are you?' Poppy bellowed. 'Ted just spilted his Ribena all over the couch.'

Alice swallowed the last bite and went to deal with it.

'Look!' Poppy squealed. 'Ted knows we're not allowed to drink juice in here, but he did anyway and now it's all ruined.'

Alice examined the large purple stain on the blue couch in the TV room.

'You're a tell-tale.' Ted shoved his twin roughly. 'I'm sorry, Mummy.' His bottom lip quivered.

'No ice-cream for you tonight, Ted, and no TV for the whole weekend.' Poppy took charge of her twin's punishment.

Ted's eyes watered. 'But it was an accident.'

Alice put her arm around her now howling son. 'It's okay. Ignore your sister. Just stay out of the room while I try to get rid of the stain.'

Poppy was furious. 'Not fair. If I didded it, you'd have been *waaaay* stricter to me.'

Poppy had been born with a persecution complex.

'No, I wouldn't. Now go and get me the kitchen roll, please,' Alice said. 'I need to soak this up.'

Ted and Poppy raced off to get the kitchen roll and a fight broke out over who got to bring it in.

'*Muuuuuuuum!*' Jamie roared. 'There's smoke coming out of the pot.'

Damnit, the pasta. Alice ran to snatch it off the hob. Ted and Poppy had managed to unroll the entire kitchen roll and were ripping it from each other's hands. The kitchen was covered with torn squares of tissue.

Alice cursed under her breath. The pasta was burnt, but she hadn't got to the shops earlier because she'd had to take Niall's dad to the doctor. She had sod-all else to feed them.

Sarah looked up from the kitchen table where she was doing her homework despite the chaos around her. Alice marvelled at her daughter's powers of concentration.

'Mrs Jenkins says that people who curse are ignorant and lazy,' Sarah told her mother.

'Mrs Jenkins doesn't live in a zoo,' Alice hissed.

'You created the animals who live in it, so you should control them, like a zookeeper would.' She was only ten but Sarah could argue like a razor-sharp barrister.

'Thank you, Sarah, for your helpful advice.'

'I'm starving.' Jamie groaned.

Alice peered into the saucepan. The bottom half of the pasta was burnt but maybe she could salvage the top. She scraped it into a bowl and removed the bottom half.

'Yuck. That looks like vomit.' Jamie gagged.

'I'm not eating vomit,' Poppy shouted.

'Me neither. No vomit.' Ted threw the tube from the kitchen roll into the air and tried to catch it.

'Gross,' Sarah said. 'And it stinks of burnt food in here now.'

Alice counted from ten backwards. 'I don't have anything else. I didn't make it to the shops.'

'What did you do all day?' Sarah asked, sounding uncannily like her father.

'A million things,' Alice answered. She *had* done lots but, truth be told, after she'd dropped her father-in-law home, she had sat down and watched an episode from series one of *The Crown*. She'd seen it almost as many times as she had *Poldark*, but she loved it. She felt guilty. She was failing at her one job. She was not the supermum she had planned to be. She was falling short in all aspects of motherhood.

'So what *exactly* are we supposed to eat?' her obstinate ten-year-old asked. 'I've already missed a meal because of those disgusting sandwiches you gave us all. Mrs Jenkins says a good diet is vital for a healthy brain.'

Mrs Jenkins had better watch out, Alice thought. She might just find herself getting mown down in the school car park some morning by a mother who had heard enough of her 'wise' sayings.

'I need food now.' Jamie clutched his stomach.

Alice opened the fridge. Four eggs, a packet of out-of-date bacon, a large hunk of Cheddar, two litres of milk, six yoghurts. She had a box of Cornflakes in the cupboard and some crackers.

'We can have a small omelette and some cheese and crackers and, I guess, cereal too.'

'How is that a good diet?' Sarah asked. 'The food pyramid clearly shows that kids need carbohydrates, and fruit and veg most of all.'

'Yes, well, just for today you'll have more protein and dairy.' Alice turned her back on her daughter and began to gather the leftovers for dinner.

At nine o'clock, when she had finally got everyone into bed, Alice poured herself a large glass of wine and had one of her emergency cigarettes. She sat on the back-door step and took a breath for the first time in hours. She had toothpaste all down her top from trying to break up one of Ted and Poppy's gazillion arguments. She had found Jamie drinking a glass of milk just before bedtime, which meant he'd definitely wet the bed tonight, and Sarah had told her very firmly that she had 'not been a good mother today'. Her daughter had explained to her that she had been undernourished, and that if she failed to get into a top university in the future, it would be entirely Alice's fault.

Alice exhaled and watched the smoke blow away in the light breeze. She'd given up smoking years ago but every now and then, after a particularly trying day, she'd have one with a glass of wine. It was currently happening more frequently. Instead of getting easier as they grew older, as she'd expected, the kids were harder to manage. She'd have to nip the cigarettes thing in the bud before the habit got worse. She pinched her stomach. She'd have to give up the chocolate biscuits, too. She'd put on nine pounds in the last two months instead of losing them. Alice sighed. She was a chubby, useless mother, who secretly smoked and lusted after Aidan Turner in *Poldark*.

While her mother ran a successful pharmacy, always looked immaculate, exercised regularly and had her life perfectly under control, Alice was a big fat failure. She had only one job – parenting – and she was failing to get that right. She was a pathetic excuse of a mother.

She was grinding her cigarette butt into the ground, about to pick it up and hide the evidence, when she heard a taxi pull up outside the house. Niall was home. He'd gone for a few Friday drinks after work so he'd be tipsy and horny.

Alice closed the back door and bolted up the stairs before her husband had put his key into the lock. She turned off the bedroom light and jumped under the covers.

She heard Niall looking for her downstairs, then coming up. He walked into the bedroom smelling of beer. 'Alice,' he whispered loudly. 'Are you awake?'

Alice didn't move.

'Alice.' He leant down and kissed her cheek. 'Are you really asleep?'

Alice kept her eyes shut. She wanted him to go away. She did not want to have sex. She felt fat and unsexy. She just wanted to be left alone to sleep. She needed to drop off quickly because Jamie was going to be up with pee-stained sheets again.

Niall's phone pinged. He looked at the message and sighed. 'Lucky bastard.' He threw his phone onto the bed and went into the adjoining bathroom. Alice picked up his phone. It was a message from Max: *Just got a blowjob in the disabled toilets in the Intercontinental. She's insatiable!*

Bloody Max and his hot young sexy girlfriend. Alice would have to have sex with Niall soon. Just not now, not tonight: she was too tired, and she felt bloated after all the biscuits. Maybe she'd feel up to it next week.

6

Herby, it won't hurt again...and the
day, so he then ...as I'd so...and the men, so when the
and...for...glad...with less...and gift...an explaining
Much the 11w ing wanting...mes

Orla looked down at her ringing phone. She didn't want to
answer it, but she knew she had to. 'Hi, Dad.'

'Hello, Orla. Happy birthday.'

'Thanks, Dad.'

'Twenty-four years ago today.'

Orla flinched. 'Yes.'

'I miss her every day.'

'I know, Dad.'

'The love of my life.'

Orla said nothing. What was there to say? She knew her
mother was the love of her father's life. He'd told her a million times and it always stung. Time, and the fact that she
was now an adult, made it a little easier to bear. It had been
much more hurtful when she was younger, but it could still
make her feel queasy.

The thing that hurt most was that he never, ever thought
about how Orla felt. He never seemed to take into account
that she had lost her mother. That she had never known her
mother. That she had a huge, aching gap in her life where her
mother should have been.

No: Dad was all about his pain, his loss and his heartbreak.
Sometimes Orla suspected he almost enjoyed wallowing in
it. He was the tragic man who had lost his wife in childbirth.
Joseph Kane, the man whose love for his wife never faded.
The man who placed flowers on her grave every Sunday,
rain, hail or shine. The man who had never looked at another
woman. The man who was a martyr to his one true love.

When she was a teenager, Orla used to pray that he'd meet someone, fall in love and stop being the town martyr, or that he'd have a sordid affair with Mrs Hegarty and her huge boobs so that his saintly halo would fall off and smash to the ground. But he never did. Oh, no: Joseph Kane was a one hundred per cent bona-fide victim.

The complication in his story was that his own daughter, the child he was supposed to love and cherish, had 'killed' his beloved Sheila.

Orla the murderer. Orla the innocent child, born with the burden of having taken her own mother's life.

'It's like every time he looks at you he thinks of her,' Shannon, Orla's best friend, used to say. 'I mean, technically your birth did kill her, but obviously not on purpose. It's a pity she didn't die of cancer or in a car crash. It'd be much easier on you if your dad couldn't blame you for it.'

But Sheila Kane had died during childbirth and Orla was the culprit. Instead of entering the world to be embraced by loving parents, Orla was handed to the nurses and left to one side while all around her people mourned.

Sheila's parents, who lived in Canada, had flown over to be with their granddaughter and had offered to take Orla back to Canada and look after her until Joseph had recovered. But Joseph had refused. His child was not leaving his sight. So, Orla had got stuck with her cold, distant father, who had never forgiven her for killing his wife.

He wasn't purposely cruel or unkind. He just couldn't help himself. He had become the king of grieving husbands and he wore the crown proudly.

'I've sent you a few bob in the post for your birthday,' he said.

'Thanks, Dad, but I've a good job now. You don't need to.'

'Sure, you might as well enjoy yourself while you can. Lord knows what awful tragedy is waiting around the corner.'

Orla decided to move onto safer ground. 'How's the farm?'

'Ah, sure, it's breaking me. All this mumbo-jumbo about people not eating red meat. What am I going to do with all my cattle if people turn away from meat? I'll starve, and so will the cows. I never heard such rubbish in all my life. God made animals so humans could survive.'

'I don't think the masses are going to stop eating red meat any time soon, Dad. You'll be okay.'

'The world's gone mad, so it has.'

Orla tried to think of something to say. Conversations with her father were always a struggle.

'Paddy sends his best,' Joseph said.

Orla cringed. 'That's nice.'

'You should come home soon. He'd like to see you.'

Over my dead body, Orla thought. Her father had somehow got it into his head that she'd end up marrying Paddy, his right-hand man on the farm. They'd get married, run the farm and her dad would live with them until he died.

The minute Orla had finished school, she was on the train to Dublin. There was no way she was getting trapped in that town, with those memories, all those people who looked at her with either pity (the poor baby who lost her mother) or blame (the baby who killed her poor mother).

'I'm really busy, Dad. I won't be down for a while. In fact, I'd better go now or I'll be late for school. Thanks for calling.'

'Sure, how could I ever forget this day? I'm off up to the grave now.'

Of course you are, Orla thought. She had to hang up before she got upset. 'I won't keep you, so. Bye, Dad.'

'Right well, happy birthday, bye, Orla.'

Happy birthday! What a joke. She'd never had a remotely happy birthday and it didn't look as if she ever would.

Orla pressed end call and looked down at her right hand.

Her nails had dug four little half-moons into her palm. One had even broken through the skin and drawn blood.

The door opened and Lulu's dad walked in. Orla recognized him from pick-up time, although it was usually Lulu's granny who collected her.

'Hi, I'm Paul, Lulu's dad.'

She shook his hand. His shirt was wrinkled and his hair needed a cut, but he had a kind face, and when he smiled, his eyes crinkled, which Orla always thought was a good sign. It meant the person was genuine. Orla had spent most of her life not smiling with her eyes, faking happiness. She knew all about it.

'Please take a seat,' she said, and Paul sat on one of the little kids' chairs.

'I feel like an elephant on a toadstool.' He grinned.

Orla smiled back, with her eyes.

The door opened and a waft of expensive perfume preceded Lulu's mother into the classroom. She was proudly showing off her pregnancy bump, wearing a tightly fitted dark green dress and impressively high heels.

'Right. I have a conference call in fifteen minutes, so let's get this sorted ASAP.'

'Nice to meet you, Mrs –'

'Ms O'Hare, but call me Sonja.' She gave Orla a bone-crushing handshake.

'Please have a seat.'

Orla tried not to smile as Sonja attempted to fold herself into the small chair.

'Oh, for goodness' sake, I need a proper chair – I'm pregnant. I'll take yours if you don't mind.'

Sonja plonked herself behind Orla's desk before Orla had the chance to answer.

Orla leant over, picked up her notes and sat down beside Paul. Sonja tapped her nails on the desk.

'I called you here today to talk about Lulu's behaviour.'

'Yes, I know she punched some soppy kid called Nathan and his stupid mother is causing a fuss. What do we need to do to make this go away?' Sonja asked.

God, she was rude. Orla took a breath. 'This is not just about Lulu punching Nathan, this is also about Lulu's general behaviour and demeanour. She has been very anxious and angry lately. I think she may be feeling a little put out about having a new sibling.'

Sonja flipped her hand in the air. 'All kids act up when a new baby is on the way. It's normal. She'll be fine.'

Paul stared at her. 'It's not normal for Lulu to punch a kid. It's not normal for her to be crying herself to sleep when she's with me because she's worried her mother will love the baby more than her. Maybe you could work a bit harder at reassuring her,' he said.

Orla noticed an edge to his voice. The crinkly eyes weren't smiling now.

'Maybe if you didn't mollycoddle her all the time, pandering to her every whim, she'd be able to take things in her stride. I've told her a million times that the baby won't change the way I feel about her. She's just looking for attention, like all kids do. If you stopped running to her every time she whimpers, she might actually sleep through the night.'

'If you stopped trying to toughen her up she might actually have a childhood and not turn out to have a heart of stone.'

'Like me, you mean?' Sonja said. 'I take that as a compliment. I'd rather Lulu grows up to be tough and resilient than weak, Paul. Weak girls get walked over.'

'And tough ones walk over other people. I don't want that for Lulu, thanks.'

Yikes, these two had serious issues. Orla wondered how they had ever got together. Sonja was very good-looking, dark hair, hazel eyes, great figure. Paul had probably been dazzled by her. But what had drawn her to him? He was a little pudgy around the stomach, looked like he hadn't ironed his shirt properly and didn't care much about his appearance . . . and he seemed like a big softy. Orla didn't get it. Sonja was so polished and perfect and hard. It must have been a case of polar opposites attracting.

Orla cleared her throat to interrupt them. 'Okay. Let's talk about what Lulu needs to do going forward. Nathan's mother has requested a written apology from Lulu to Nathan and an assurance that she will never lay a hand on him again.'

'God, she's an awful woman,' Sonja said impatiently. 'I had her on the phone practically having a nervous break-down over a stupid little incident. Really and truly, you'd think Lulu had ripped his eye out. I cut her off in the middle of her rant, told her I had a meeting.'

'To be fair, if Lulu came home with a bloody nose, I'd want an apology,' Paul said.

Orla kept going, trying to keep control of the conversation. 'If you could sit down with Lulu and help her write a note to Nathan, I think that would really help. And to help Lulu adjust to having a sibling, I think she would benefit from both of you reassuring her that the baby won't take her place. I've seen this with lots of children. It's a fear of being replaced. They just need lots of support.'

'Of course, we'll do that,' Paul said.

'Fine, I'll talk to her again,' Sonja said. 'But I think her bad mood also has to do with the fact that her father insists on having her every second week. If she lived with me and he saw her on weekends, she'd have much more structure to her life. Besides, he keeps her up too late. When she's with me she's in bed by seven thirty.'

Paul's face reddened. 'That's never going to happen. Lulu will continue to stay with me every second week as we agreed in court. And I do not keep her up late. Nine o'clock is perfectly reasonable. She gets eleven hours' sleep. I like hanging out with her. I don't clock-watch until I can put her to bed so I can have more time with my boyfriend.'

Sonja slow-clapped. 'The perfect father. Superdad.'

Paul's jaw clenched. 'No, Sonja, just a dad who prioritizes his kid, unlike you, who put your boyfriend and work first.'

'Shoot me for having ambition and investing time in my relationship.'

'Lulu's life has already been turned upside-down by our break-up. Now you're pregnant with another man's kid. Could you just spend some of your precious time reassuring her and making sure she feels valued?'

'Don't tell me how to raise my daughter,' Sonja snapped.

'Well, do it properly,' Paul snapped back.

Poor Lulu. Orla hoped that her parents didn't go at each other like this in front of her. Kids just needed love and reassurance, hugs and kisses. Orla knew this only too well. She felt Lulu's worry acutely and wanted to help the little girl. She knew what it was like to feel alone, confused, unloved and unwanted. She didn't want any child to feel like that. It was one of the reasons she had become a teacher.

'I think what Lulu needs,' Orla said firmly, 'is consistency, support and perhaps, for now, some extra love and cuddles. In the meantime, I need that note for tomorrow morning. Is she staying with you, Sonja?'

Sonja shook her head. 'No, she's with her dad.'

'I'll make sure she writes a grovelling apology and hopefully that will keep Nathan's mother happy,' Paul said.

'Excellent, thank you. I'll let you know if Lulu behaves out of character again, but hopefully this was just a blip. You have a beautiful little girl. You should be very proud of her.'

'We are,' Paul said.

'I am,' Sonja said, at the same time.

Orla stood up and shook their hands. Sonja barely said goodbye as she rushed out the door for her 'very important conference call'.

Paul thanked Orla and apologized for his ex-wife. 'She can be kind of rude sometimes. She doesn't actually mean it – she just gets very caught up in Sonja world.'

Curiosity got the better of Orla. 'Have you been separated long?'

Paul nodded. 'Almost two years. We limped along for a few years after Lulu was born, but we both knew it was a lost cause. Sonja met Oliver at a work conference and that was that.'

'Sorry to hear that.'

Paul grinned, his brown eyes twinkled. 'I'm not. She was a nightmare to live with. Oliver's welcome to her.'

Orla knew it was unprofessional, but she laughed.

'Anyway, I'd better go. I left Lulu with my mum. I'll make sure she writes the most amazing note and I'll tell her a million times how much we love her. Thanks for being so nice about all of this. Lulu adores you. She talks about Miss Orla all the time. She's lucky to have you as her teacher.'

Orla blushed. 'She's a great kid. Honestly, she's a joy to teach.'

'Thanks. I know it's not the done thing to boast, but I think Lulu's incredible.'

'You're perfectly entitled to boast.' Orla smiled.

Paul shook her hand between both of his warm ones. 'I can see why Lulu likes you so much. Thanks again.' He walked off to pick up his little girl.

Orla looked down at her hand. It was tingling.

7

Ann hadn't stopped crying since John had left for Australia. She'd taken to her bed the day he'd left and not got up for two days. She hadn't done that since the second IVF failed.

Ken didn't know what to do. He hovered beside her bed, asking her if she wanted anything, bringing her up trays of toast and tea. Eventually, on the second evening of non-stop tears, he told her to stop being silly, that John was only in a different country, not gone for ever. 'Come on now, Ann, don't you think you're overreacting a bit? He's not dead, for God's sake.'

Ann cried harder and he left the room.

At a loss as to what to do, he ended up calling Zoë to come over and talk to her mother. She arrived half an hour later, walked straight into the bedroom, climbed into the bed and hugged her mother tight. She hadn't said a word, just held her mother in her arms and comforted her.

Ken realized he should have done that, but it felt awkward. They weren't a huggy couple. They weren't one of those pairs who held hands on the street or kissed across dinner tables in restaurants. Ken didn't understand people who did that. It was like 'Look at us, we're so in love.' If you were in love and happy, you didn't have to show it off. He loved Ann and Ann loved him. They didn't need to shout about it.

Ken left Zoë and Ann and went downstairs to put on the kettle. He had finished two cups of tea by the time Zoë came down.

'How is she?' Ken asked.

'Heartbroken, Dad.'

'I know it's hard on her. I've tried to talk to her but, I mean, he's not dead.'

Zoë sighed. 'Jesus, Dad, try to be more sympathetic. She's devastated. Australia is a long way away, and he may never come home.'

Ken shrugged. 'Kids leave home and live their own lives. It's what they're supposed to do. He'll be back to visit at Christmas. When I left home my mother didn't shed a tear.'

Zoë shook her head. 'Granny was a cold, hard cow. Mum's the opposite. Just be nice to her, okay? Buy her flowers, treat her to a pedicure at her favourite beautician or something.'

'I don't know what beauty place she goes to.'

'Well, you should. Now go up and just hold her. Don't say anything because you'll say the wrong thing. Just be there for her. She'll be fine in a day or two. She just needs to get it out of her system. You know how she adores John. We all do. Don't you miss him?'

'He's been gone two days!'

'But aren't you sad he's gone?'

Ken shrugged. 'Not really. It seems like a good career move and he was excited to go.'

'That's a bit cold.'

'I dunno, Zoë, maybe I'm old-fashioned, but I don't see how my son getting on with his life is a tragedy.'

Zoë sighed. 'Australia is on the other side of the world. Mum wouldn't be this upset if he was in London because he could pop home any time. But Sydney is so far away.'

'I know that, but she can Skype him and chat to him any time she wants.'

'It's not the same. Look, you have your work to keep you

occupied every day, Mum doesn't have that daily focus. I think she feels a bit lost.'

Not for long, Ken thought glumly. He'd soon be retired and then what? What would his days look like? How would he fill them? He'd have to take up golf or something. Maybe he could do the accounts for Ann's charity shop, or read all the books he hadn't read, or paint the outside of the house . . . He'd have to find something. Ann would probably come up with ideas – she was good like that. She always had a plan. She was the one who organized everything. She probably had a list of things for him to do already. It was hard, though: work was all he knew. In a few months, it'd be over. Forty-eight years of working life. Kicked to the kerb, while a younger, pushy, ambitious guy moved into his office and took over his life. Ken knew he had been lucky to stay until sixty-eight. Most employees left the firm at sixty-five. But now his time was nearly up and he had to go.

'Just be nice to her, Dad. Show her some affection. Maybe actually hug her for once in your life.'

'We're not that kind of couple,' Ken said.

Zoë threw her arms in the air. 'No, Dad, *you* aren't affectionate, but Mum is. She's always hugging me and John. Maybe you need to start hugging her.'

'I show my affection by looking after you all. I know my wife. Ann will be fine. She just needs to get out of that bed and get on with life. Wallowing never did anyone any good. A busy mind is a happy mind.'

Zoë shook her head. 'Seriously, Dad, don't say things like that to her, just be nice to her or I'll start hugging *you* all the time.' She grinned, throwing her arms around him.

Ken kissed her head. 'Thanks for coming. I'll try to say the right thing.'

Zoë left and Ken went upstairs. He stood outside the

bedroom door, listening. He had never been good with tears. He didn't know what to say. When Ann had cried about her failed pregnancies, he'd just held her hand and told her it'd be fine. She'd cried harder and shouted, 'It won't be fine until I have a baby in my arms.'

Later on, after the failed IVF, he'd told her they needed to stop and just be happy with each other, which was the wrong thing to say too. Ann had told him, through gritted teeth and tears, she would never, ever give up on having a baby.

It was hard to get it right. Ann had always been the one to comfort the kids when they were upset. She was good at it, really good at it. Ken never seemed to say the right thing. He'd been brought up in a house where showing emotion was considered weak. He had a tough father and a cold mother. If you were upset about something, you just got on with it. No crying, no moaning, just 'get on with it'. They never discussed feelings or cried at home – ever. When Ken had left home and started dating girls and they cried, he hadn't had a clue what to do or say. He thought he'd got a bit better over the years, but apparently not much.

One of the things he loved about Ann was how much she adored the kids. She was a fantastic mother, so loving. But maybe she'd been too close to them. She'd made them her life. Now they were gone she was falling apart. But that was life. Kids moved out and moved on. Ann needed to 'get on with it' now, but Ken wasn't going to tell her that.

He took a deep breath and opened the door. Ann was lying on her side, wiping her eyes with a tissue. Ken moved over to the bed. He sat on the edge. 'Are you feeling better now?' he asked.

Ann shrugged.

Ken reached out to take her hand, but it felt really awkward, so he just patted her arm. 'There, there,' he said, as if to a small child who had hurt their knee.

Ann said nothing.

'You should get up now, Ann. Have a shower and get dressed. You'll feel better. Lying around crying is no good for anyone. Come on now. Kids leave and move on with their lives. It's the way it is.'

'Don't you feel upset, Ken?' she asked, looking at him with eyes bloodshot from crying. 'Don't you feel anything about our son moving thousands of miles away to a different continent? Is there a beating heart in there, Ken?'

'I . . .' Ken started, but he didn't know what to say. Why was she angry with him?

Ann sighed deeply. 'Maybe you're better off. Maybe I think too much, feel too much. I'm here crying my eyes out and you . . . well, you seem to be fine.'

Ken stood up and tried to smile. 'I'll turn the shower on. A long, hot shower will do you the world of good. Then get dressed and come downstairs. I'll rustle up something for you. Might not be much, but you need to eat.'

'I feel lost, Ken,' Ann said quietly.

Ken turned. 'What?'

'I don't know who I am. I used to be a mum, but now what am I?'

'Well, you're you, Ann.'

'But who is that?'

Ken frowned. 'I don't know what you're talking about. You're you, you're my Annie.'

'I feel so lonely, Ken.'

'Lonely? I'm right here in front of you. Zoë was here a minute ago. Look, all this lying about, crying and festering, isn't good for anyone. Have a shower and shake it off. You'll feel better.'

'What if he never comes home?' Ann said. 'How many sons have left the country and said, "It's only for a year or two," and never come back? Sydney is so far away and so sunny and beautiful. He'll probably swim after work or surf, get used to the weather and the lifestyle and never want to come home. He'll meet a beautiful Australian girl and settle down and have babies. We'll never see them – only on Skype. As if that could ever make up for human contact and touch. I'll never hold my grandchildren, Ken.' Her voice caught and she sobbed.

Ken looked at her in shock. This was crazy talk: the boy had barely left the country and she was talking about grandchildren. For goodness' sake! 'Ann, he's been gone two days and he'll come back for Christmas. You need to calm down and stop catastrophizing all the time. Come on, up you get.'

He tried to take her arm and help her out of bed, but she swatted him off. 'Go away, Ken. You don't understand anything.'

'John getting on with his life is not a tragedy, Ann.'

Damnit, he hadn't meant to say that, but she was wallowing and it was bad for her.

Ann glared at him. 'How can you be so cold? He's our only son. Don't you feel anything?'

Ken sighed. 'He's a young man making his way in the world. I guess I feel glad that he's growing up and being independent.'

Ann turned her face away from him. 'Without the kids, I don't know who I am or who we are.'

'Please, Ann, please get up now and stop all this nonsense.'

Ann threw her soggy tissue at him. 'Go away,' she shouted.

Ken gave up and left her to it.

*

When Ken woke up that Sunday morning, he was surprised to hear noises from downstairs and smell bacon. He lay back and smiled. Ann must be feeling better. Thank goodness for that. Four days in bed was far too much wallowing. She needed to get out and start living again.

He put on his dressing-gown and went downstairs. Ann was dressed and seemed her usual self as she handed him a plate of toast and bacon.

'Thank you. I didn't expect you to be up so early. Did you sleep okay? Do you feel better now?' he asked.

Ann sat down opposite him, holding a cup of coffee. She spoke slowly and clearly. 'Ken, I want you to listen to me very, very carefully. I've had a lot of time to think over the last few days. John leaving has made me realize that I can't live like this any more. I'm dying inside. I feel more lonely than I ever thought possible. For that reason, I'm going to book us in to see a woman I heard on the radio. She's a couples' therapist.'

Ken put down his toast. 'Hang on. What are you talking about? Ann, you're all emotional because of John. You just need to calm down and get used to him being gone.'

'No. I'm sad because John has left, but the loneliness has been going on for years now. The kids leaving home has just made it more obvious. You and I have grown apart and I'm very worried about our marriage. I was going to book this woman a few months ago, but then I thought I'd wait and see if things improved. But they haven't, and John leaving has made me see that I need to act.'

Ken felt anger build inside him. 'Hold on a minute here. Don't start picking holes in our perfectly good marriage because you've too much time on your hands. All that crying and navel-gazing isn't good for anyone. You're just finding problems where there are none. You need a hobby, Ann, something to keep your mind occupied.'

Ann placed her two hands flat on the table. 'A hobby is not going to save our marriage, Ken. We live like strangers in the same house. We need help before it's too late.'

Ken opened his mouth to reply but Ann held up a hand. 'This is not open for discussion. I'm booking us an appointment with this woman. Her name is Maggie Purcell. I cannot live like this, and if you're honest with yourself, Ken, you know we need help.'

With that, she picked up her car keys and headed to the front door.

8

Alice was in a deep, blissful sleep when she heard a noise. As her brain tried to push its way into consciousness, she felt a sharp pain in her leg.

'Jesus Christ,' Niall roared beside her.

'Daddy said a bad word!' Poppy squealed.

'What the hell?' Niall sat up in bed rubbing his ankle as Poppy rolled on top of him and Alice.

'We're dive-bombing Mummy for her birthday,' Ted said, as he stood at the top of the small stepladder they had dragged to the end of their parents' bed. He launched himself onto his mother.

Alice braced herself for the not insignificant weight of her six-year-old landing on her.

'I want to do it.' Jamie came into the bedroom to see what all the commotion was about.

'NO!' Niall roared at him. 'No more dive-bombing. Give Mummy a hug instead.'

'You're all so immature.' Sarah walked over to her mother, kissed her and handed her a card.

'Thank you, sweetie.' Alice opened the card. Inside was a message: *Dear Mummy, 42 is old but you are still qwite pretty and not too rinkly. I love you (most of the time), you are a good Mummy. Love Sarah.*

Alice tried to ignore the passive-aggressive tone and hugged her spiky daughter. 'Thank you, darling.'

'We done a card, too,' Ted shouted.

'Did,' Niall corrected him.

Ted handed his mother a piece of paper with a drawing of a woman with straw-coloured hair and brown eyes. It wasn't far off, except the woman had a stick body and Alice's was definitely round. The twins had written: *Happy Birtday Mummy, we love you SOOOOOOOOO much. You are the bestest Mummy in the hole wurld!*

Alice pulled them in for a big hug. 'It's the best card ever,' she said, as they beamed with pride.

'I didn't make you a card cos they're soppy, but I got you this.' Jamie handed her a gift wrapped in a page ripped from his copybook and covered with Sellotape.

It took Alice a while to break through the tape and open it. A bar of Cadbury's Mint Crisp fell out. 'Oh, Jamie, my favourite. You're so sweet.'

Jamie's chest puffed out. 'I got it yesterday when we were in the shop and the twins went missing. I used my money that Granddad gave me.'

Alice hugged her son tightly. 'You're the kindest boy in the world.'

He really was. Jamie was born kind. The other three would never offer Alice a lick of their ice-cream cone or a square of their chocolate bar, but Jamie always did. Alice had worried he'd be walked over by the boys in school, but he'd managed to find a little group of boys as sweet as he was.

'What about me?' Ted wasn't happy.

'You're the joint kindest.' Alice smiled at him, lying to avoid a meltdown.

Niall reached under the bed and pulled out a box.

Alice had dropped many unsubtle hints to her husband about a day in the Escape spa in town. A full day of pampering away from the kids was her dream gift. The box Niall was holding was quite big, but she hoped it was a ruse to put her off and that inside was a spa voucher.

'Okay, kids, go downstairs and watch TV. Daddy wants to give Mummy her present now.' Niall shooed them away.

'We want to see it,' Poppy said.

'No, Poppy, this is private Mummy-and-Daddy time. Now scoot. You can have pancakes if you go now.'

'With Nutella?' Poppy saw an opening.

'Fine.'

'Really?' Ted clapped his hands.

'Yes. Now go – and close the door.'

They all scurried out, thrilled to be getting Nutella pancakes on a regular Saturday morning.

Niall handed Alice the box. He was grinning at her. She had a bad feeling about this. She unwrapped the paper. It was a box with 'Love Honey' written on it.

Alice's stomach sank. She pulled off the lid. Inside she saw red lingerie. She stared at it, trying not to cry.

'See?' Niall pulled out the knickers. 'They're crotchless, how hot is that? And the bra is open at the nipple. Max told me about the shop. Lizzie shops in Love Honey all the time. It's an online shop. I ordered it two weeks ago to make sure it arrived on time.'

Niall was looking at her, his face full of lust. Alice wanted to scream, 'You complete dickhead! I wanted a day away, not hooker underwear.'

'Put them on. I want to see them on you. The kids are downstairs – come on, Alice, let's have some fun.'

Niall pressed his erect penis against her hip. Alice felt the urge to rip it out of its socket. She didn't want to put on the stupid underwear. She would look ridiculous and completely unsexy in it, and Niall had bought size ten: Alice was now a size twelve, if she was lying to herself, fourteen if she was being honest. 'Uhm, I think they're too small.'

Niall rubbed up against her. 'It doesn't matter, put them on.'

'They won't fit,' she said.

'Fine, forget about them, just take off these granny pyjamas.' Niall tugged at the bottoms. 'I'm horny as hell.'

Alice just couldn't. She couldn't have sex with him because she was so disappointed in the gift and in him. He didn't get her. He had no clue what she wanted. He didn't listen to her hints. He had bought her a present that he wanted, not her. Alice needed a day away from her daily grind. She craved a little pampering and rest, not crotchless bloody knickers. Tears flowed down her cheeks and she began to sob.

'What the hell?' Niall was confused. 'Why are you crying?'

'Because I wanted a spa day, with massages and peace and quiet, and you got me prostitute underwear.'

'Fine! I'll buy you a spa day – I'll do it today. Calm down, Alice. Come here.' He pulled her in and hugged her, but within seconds he was putting his hand up her pyjama top and rubbing her nipples.

Alice shoved him back. 'Jesus Christ, Niall, I do not want to have sex with you. I'm upset. Really upset.'

'Why? Because I bought you sexy underwear to try to revive our dead sex life? Because I want to have sex with my wife? Are you crying because I want you? Come on, Alice, I give up. You never want sex any more. I'm a man, I have needs. We used to have great sex. You used to want to be with me. Now you never come near me and push me away all the time. I'm sick of being rejected. Couples are supposed to have sex. But not us apparently. It's been months. What's wrong with you?'

Alice glared at him. 'What's wrong with me? I'm utterly exhausted! I spend all day every day looking after our four kids and they are hard bloody work. I love them, but it's relentless.'

'I'm tired too, Alice. I work my balls off. But I still want

76

to have sex with my wife. Jesus, you used to want it too. We had fun in bed. It was a place for us to get away from the kids and have some us time. Now all you do is turn your back to me and sleep. If I even try to initiate sex, you push me away. Being rejected all the time gets old, Alice, really, really old. We have a problem here, a serious one, and we need a solution.'

Alice went cold. What did he mean, 'a solution'? Was he going to leave her? Oh, my God. Her heart was pounding. 'What are you saying?' she asked, her voice shaking.

'We need help. I've found someone. I booked us in for next week.'

'What are you talking about?'

'We're going to see a relationship and sex therapist. I can't live like this. I heard her on the radio, talking about couples who stop having sex and how dangerous it is. So I called and made an appointment.'

Alice was shocked. 'What? You booked us in to talk to someone about our sex life? There's no way I'm going.'

Niall looked at her, his face sad. 'No, Alice, I booked us in to talk about our relationship and our lack of a sex life. We have to do something before it's too late.'

'Are you threatening me?'

'No, I'm just telling you how I feel. Our marriage is in trouble, Alice. You know it too.'

Ice-cold fear ran through Alice's body. 'No, it isn't. This is just a bad phase. All couples go through times when they drift apart and have less sex. It happens when the kids are young. We'll get back on track. Just give it time.'

'I have, I've tried, but we need help. Our appointment is at nine thirty on Tuesday. She's American, a straight talker, sounded very nice and professional. Now I'm going to have a cold shower – again.'

Niall locked the bathroom door, leaving Alice crying in bed. Sex therapy? How the hell was she going to get through that? She was mortified. She didn't want to talk about her sex life. It was private. She'd wait until Niall had calmed down. She'd have sex with him when he came out of the shower and then maybe he'd change his mind. She had rejected him a lot lately. But she just never felt sexy any more. Was that wrong? Was she a freak? Was sex part of your marriage vows? Did you have to have sex with your husband even when you didn't want to? Wasn't that messed up? What did men do for their wives that they didn't want to do? Men didn't fake orgasms but women did, all the time. Why were women supposed to do things they didn't want to and pretend to climax to make the man feel better? Why was sex so important? Alice loved Niall – well, most of the time she did. She was happy to be with him; she didn't need regular sex.

Then again . . . She thought back to the times when they'd been all over each other, ripping their clothes off, having sex in the kitchen, the TV room, the bath. It had been fun, and she'd always felt closer to him after sex. But that was then. Now she was a mum of four with no energy after nine p.m. That was just life.

Alice whipped off her cosy pyjamas and waited for Niall to come out of the shower. She decided not to put on the underwear because her flabby stomach would just hang over the pants and make her feel worse about herself.

As she heard the shower click off, Alice tried to get into a sexy mood. Just as the bathroom door opened, Poppy burst in.

'MUM! Ted fell and there's blood everywhere.'

As Niall came out of the bathroom, he saw his naked wife charging out of the bedroom door.

9

Orla was hanging the children's paintings from the day before when she heard a knock on the classroom door.

Ted, Poppy and their mum walked in. 'Hi, Orla.'

'Morning, Alice.'

Alice was one of the parents Orla saw regularly. Some she never saw: nannies picked the kids up or they just grabbed and ran, and a good few got the school bus home with older siblings. But Alice was always at the gate at home time. Orla thought she seemed like a lovely mum. The twins always raced out to her and she'd hug them tight, asking them about their day. She looked exhausted now, though.

Orla turned her attention to the twins. 'Uh-oh, someone's been in the wars.'

Ted had a big bandage on the right side of his forehead.

'Yes, that's why we're here. Sorry to barge in on top of you before class begins, but I just wanted to explain about Ted's head.'

'Jamie pushed him off the high stool cos he ated the last pancake,' Poppy piped up.

'No, he didn't. Stop blaming Jamie.' Alice frowned at Poppy. 'They were arguing over the last pancake and Ted's stool toppled backwards. Poor old Ted had to have four stitches, but he's rested all weekend and the doctor said he's fine to be in school today but no sports. I wasn't going to send him, but he said he wanted to come. If at any point he needs to come home, please call and I'll be straight over for him.'

'How do you know what happened to him, Mummy, when you weren't even there? You were in the bedroom with Daddy having private time,' Poppy noted.

Alice blushed, and Orla stepped in. 'Is it still sore, Ted?'

'No. I got loads of treats and I slepted in Mummy's big bed with Mummy so she could mind me, and Daddy had to sleep in my bed. And Daddy even let me lie on his white couch and watch football.'

'Dad never lets anyone sit on his special couch,' Poppy explained.

Alice's face was even redder. 'Okay, kids, that's enough talking.'

'And it happened on Mummy's birthday, which was a bit bad because she spented the whole day in hospital,' Poppy added.

'Oh dear. Well, I hope you'll be especially good for her this week to make up for it,' Orla said.

The door swung open and Sonja came in, a pale Lulu trailing behind her. She was perfectly made up, beautifully dressed and wearing sky-high heels.

'Hi, it's Orla, right? Sonja – you'll remember me from our chat the other week. Anyway, Lulu has a very slight temperature, but she's fine really. If she gets worse, though, call her dad. I have back-to-back meetings all day so he'll have to pick her up. I've given her Calpol and she said she feels all right. Bye, sweetie.' She blew a kiss at her daughter and swished out of the door, leaving a waft of perfume behind her.

Alice caught Orla's eye. 'Wow,' Alice said. 'I bet she's good at delegating in work.'

Orla smiled but said nothing: it wasn't appropriate to discuss parents with other parents – but, my God, Sonja was cold. She'd even give Orla's father a run for his money in the icy-parenting stakes. Thank God Lulu had her dad for cuddles and compassion.

'Your mum is so pretty,' Poppy said to Lulu, clearly awed by Sonja's brief, but memorable, appearance. 'And she smells so nice and her hair is so shiny. My mummy didn't even brush her hair today.'

Orla felt Lulu's forehead. 'You do seem a bit hot. Are you sure you're feeling okay?'

Lulu nodded. 'I'm hot and a bit tired, but not sick-sick.'

'Well, we'll keep a close eye on you.'

'Looks like you have your hands full. Maybe I should take Ted home,' Alice said.

'Not at all,' Orla replied. 'He seems absolutely fine. Sure, there's always some little drama with a class of twenty-four.'

Alice smiled. 'God bless your energy. I find my four exhausting.'

Orla laughed. 'I get to hand them back in the afternoon.'

'I suppose that's true. Good luck, and don't hesitate to call me if you need me to pick Ted up.'

Alice bent down to hug the twins, then left Orla to it. No wonder the twins liked school so much this year: Orla was lovely and clearly very capable.

That Sonja, though – bloody hell, she was terrifying. Poor little Lulu. Alice felt sorry for the kid. She'd seen the dad a good few times at pick-up but never the mum. Perfectly groomed women like Sonja made Alice feel completely inferior physically, but on the other hand they made her realize she wasn't such a bad mother. As much as she often felt she could do so much better, at least her kids were actually kissed and kept home from school when they were ill.

*

As the morning wore on, Lulu became quieter and paler. At breaktime, Orla brought her to Reception to check her temperature. Poppy insisted on coming with them.

Thirty-seven point nine: quite high.

'Lulu, pet, do you feel sicker now?'

Lulu nodded.

'Would you like to lie on the beanbags in class until home time?'

Lulu shook her head. 'I want my daddy.'

'My daddy never, ever collects me. He's always too busy in work,' Poppy said.

'My mummy's always busy in work too,' Lulu said.

Orla asked the school secretary for Paul's number and called him.

He answered after one ring. 'Hello? Is Lulu okay?' he asked, clearly panicking at seeing the school number flash up on his phone.

'It's Orla, Lulu's teacher, sorry to alarm you. Lulu is fine, but she does have quite a high temperature that seems to be getting worse.'

'Where's her mother?'

Orla hesitated. 'Uhm, she dropped her in this morning with a slight temperature, but thought she'd be okay. She said if Lulu got worse to call you as she was in meetings all day.'

Paul cursed. 'It's her week. Never mind, I'm on my way. Can you put me on loudspeaker so Lulu can hear me?'

Orla pressed the button. 'Go ahead.'

'Hi, sweetie, are you feeling poorly?'

'Yes, Daddy.' Lulu began to cry.

'I'm on my way, pet. We'll go home and get you some medicine. Then we'll snuggle up and watch movies.'

'Thank you, Daddy.'

He hung up.

'Wow, your daddy's super-nice,' Poppy said. 'My daddy never wants to watch movies with me. He pretends he does, but he just looks at his phone all the time. Mummy gets cross with him. She says, "It's family time and you have to turn your phone off."'

'My daddy loves kids' movies. He says they're better than grown-up ones.'

'My mummy says that too.'

'My mummy says kids' movies are silly and you're never too young to learn, so we watch stuff about the planet and animals.'

'*Boooooriiiiing.*' Poppy rolled her eyes.

'Yeah, but my daddy lets me watch whatever movies I want. He's the best,' Lulu said.

Yes, he is, Orla thought. The notion that her father would ever have sat down and watched a film with her was laughable. He'd barely sat in the same room as her in the eighteen years she'd lived with him. Mrs Long had cleaned the house and cooked for them. Orla would eat when she got home from school and her father would eat when he got in from the farm. Never at the same time. The only meal they had together was lunch on Sunday when their parish priest, Father Pierce, would join them. Orla would sit and listen to the two men talk about the state of the world, politics, farming, gossip about the locals, the loose morals of young women 'these days' and on and on.

Orla had taught herself to switch off. She would sit still while her mind took her away to Hogwarts with Hermione and Harry or to Panem with Katniss Everdeen or to Narnia with Lucy and Edmund. Orla read to escape her lonely life, and those books were where she retreated to in her mind during those long, arduous Sunday lunches.

She smiled at Lulu and walked her back to the classroom.

She settled her on the beanbags, Poppy insisting on lying down beside her. They were becoming fast friends.

Within ten minutes Paul had knocked and rushed into the room. He scooped Lulu into his arms and rested his lips against her forehead. 'Oh, yes, you are hot. Right, let's get you home.'

'I'm sorry to call you out of work,' Orla said.

'Not at all, I'm glad you did. Clearly her mother is too busy to look after her sick child, even though it's her week,' he muttered. Then, turning to Lulu, he said, 'It's great, though, because I get to hang out with you for the afternoon.'

'I hope you feel better soon,' Orla said to Lulu.

'I will. My daddy is better than any doctor.'

'Come on, pet.' Paul held Lulu in his arms and left without a backward glance.

Orla knew it was ridiculous, but since the tingle in her hand after their last meeting, she'd been thinking about Paul a lot. But just now he hadn't even looked at her. She might as well have been invisible. Then again, Orla was good at being invisible – she'd been a ghost most of her life.

She felt a tug on her arm.

'You look sad, Miss Orla. Are you feeling sick too?' Poppy asked.

'No, Poppy! I'm fine – see?' She fake-smiled.

'Oh, good, cos I don't want you to be sick. I don't want any other teacher. You're the bestest in the whole world.'

Poppy put her sticky little hand into Orla's and the teacher felt herself melt. Her students would fill the gaping holes in her life. They'd have to, because nothing else would.

Ann studiously ignored her husband as he stomped around the house getting his car keys and coat, slamming cupboard doors and generally making his feelings known.

She didn't give a damn. They were going and that was that. She stood calmly at the front door, coat on, handbag over her shoulder, waiting for him to stop faffing about, wasting time. She wasn't sure what you should wear to a counselling session, so she'd opted for a burgundy midi-length dress, the bright scarf that Milly had insisted she buy from the charity shop, and her best navy coat with the brass buttons.

Ken walked towards her. 'Let's get this over with.'

As Ann stepped outside, he slammed the front door and locked it.

They drove in silence. Ann looked out of the window. She was nervous but strangely excited, too. They were finally doing something. They were going to be shaken out of their godawful limbo. They would communicate properly and really talk about how they felt. She was hopeful that Maggie Purcell would save them.

She'd heard her talking about relationships on the radio and she'd sounded very capable. That she was American was an added bonus. She was an outsider, while an Irish therapist would no doubt end up being someone's cousin or sister-in-law. Ann felt safe going to see Maggie. Besides, on the radio she'd said that she'd started out as a relationship therapist but ended up specializing in sex therapy as it was the cause of so much angst in Ireland, where she believed people were still so repressed about sex.

Ann liked the sound of that. She wanted someone who would persuade Ken to talk about why he didn't want to make love to her any more. Someone who was a straight-shooter: their marriage needed this.

They arrived at the address and Ken parked the car. It was a pretty mews house with a little studio attached to the side. The main front door was painted a bright cherry red, but the studio door was a muted grey. It looked like a warm, welcoming place.

When he turned off the ignition, he turned to Ann. 'I'm doing this for you, but if this woman turns out to be one of those hippy-dippy weirdos and asks personal questions, I'm leaving.'

'Fine,' Ann said. She wasn't going to start a row now, outside the therapist's rooms. Besides, was Ken stupid? Of course she was going to ask personal questions. That was the whole point.

Ann pulled her coat tightly around her and walked towards the studio door, with a plaque that said 'Dr Maggie Purcell'.

She rang the bell. The door was opened by an attractive woman who looked to be in her early forties. She was tall and lean with shoulder-length auburn hair and was wearing thick, black-rimmed glasses. Ann was glad to see that she was dressed in smart black trousers and a pale grey cashmere jumper. Ken would approve of her business-like attire. It might make him a tiny bit less uptight. He'd probably been expecting a woman in a flowing kaftan wielding scented herbs. Hopefully, this neat professional would be easier for him to talk to.

Maggie smiled. 'You must be Ann and Ken. You're right on time. Please, come in, you're very welcome.'

There was a small reception room, with four comfy chairs,

all muted grey, and a glass table covered with magazines. It had everything from *Psychology* to *Vogue* to *Car.* It felt very classy and clean. Ann wasn't sure what she'd been expecting, but she was in a professional place and she felt they would be in good hands.

They followed Maggie through to her consultation room. She had three big armchairs. The two facing her were charcoal grey and hers was a deep green. To the left, a desk was surrounded by floor-to-ceiling bookshelves. The thick carpet was pale lilac and the walls were painted dove grey. Everything was very soothing, calm and uncluttered.

Maggie took their coats and hung them on the coat-rack beside the door. She motioned them to the grey chairs and sat opposite. Between them a small coffee-table held a large box of tissues, a jug of water and three glasses.

'Welcome to both of you. My name is Maggie Purcell. I'm a therapist who specializes in relationships and also in sex therapy. Now, you both look a little shy, so I'm guessing this is your first time doing a counselling session.'

They nodded.

'And I'm guessing you've been married for some time.'

'Thirty-eight years,' Ken said defensively, 'and we've never needed any outside help in all that time.'

'That's an achievement,' Maggie said. 'But asking for help is not a sign of weakness. In fact, it's a sign of strength. Couples come here to explore the issues they're having and to be honest with each other in a safe and respectful environment. Honesty is the key to moving forward in a relationship. There will be things you will both hear today that may upset you, but it's important that you are completely open and speak your truth.'

Ken looked a bit put out by this, but Ann instantly warmed to Maggie.

Maggie turned to her. 'So, Ann, we spoke briefly on the phone and you said you wanted to come here with Ken to discuss your relationship. I'm interested to hear from both of you as to why you're here, and what you hope to get from counselling.'

Before Ann could answer, Ken sat forward. 'This was Ann's idea and I'm here because she forced me to come. I think the whole thing is ridiculous. We don't need an outsider to fix our marriage, whatever you might say.'

'Okay. I'm aware that this isn't easy for you, Ken, that you're dubious about its potential to effect change. All I ask is that you keep an open mind. There is a reason you're both here and it's important that we try to confront and discuss that reason honestly. How about you, Ann? How are you feeling about this?'

'I booked this appointment because I'm at the end of my tether.'

Ann felt Ken tense beside her, his hands bunched into tight fists. Suddenly she felt nervous and emotional. But she had come here to save her marriage, and her sanity, so she took a deep breath and began to speak.

'I feel that Ken and I have fallen into a rut. We seem to do the same thing every day. We talk, but we don't communicate. We're like two strangers living in the same house.' She didn't add that she sometimes wanted to run far away and never come back. She didn't add that she thought she might be falling out of love with Ken. She didn't add that she was worried it was too late for them, that their marriage might be unsalvageable. She didn't add that she fantasized about having sex with other men. Steamy, passionate, raunchy sex, the kind she'd never really had.

'Ken, do you feel that's true, that you and Ann have grown apart and are like strangers to each other?' Maggie asked.

'Strangers? That's daft. We've been married for thirty-eight years, we have two grown kids. We know each other inside and out. We have a normal, solid marriage.'

'I'm wondering how well you think you and Ann communicate?' Maggie asked.

'We talk all the time. That's why this is ridiculous.'

Ann wrapped her handbag strap around her index finger. 'No, it isn't, Ken. We talk about who put the bins out or what we're having for dinner, but we never talk about our feelings and the fact that . . . the . . . well . . .'

'It's okay, Ann,' Maggie said gently, 'you're here to express how you feel.'

'The fact that we sleep in separate rooms. We're more like housemates than husband and wife.'

'Why do you sleep in separate rooms?'

Ann looked at Ken. 'I'll let you answer that,' she said.

'Well, it's simple,' Ken said. 'Because Ann had her hip replaced and I moved out so she could sleep in peace without me rolling into her by accident or bumping her or whatever. I gave her the master bedroom with the en-suite bathroom and I moved into Zoë's old room. I wanted her to be comfortable and peaceful.'

'That was very considerate,' Maggie said, nodding. 'And how long ago was this?'

'Three years,' Ann said.

'No, less than that,' Ken said.

'Three years and two months,' Ann said firmly.

'So you're long recovered from that operation,' Maggie said. 'When you were recovered, did you want Ken to move back into your bedroom?'

'Yes, I did. I asked him to.'

'Is there a particular reason you didn't move back in, Ken?' Maggie asked.

Ken shifted in his chair. 'I suppose, maybe, I'd just got used to sleeping alone. I'm an awkward bugger to sleep next to, to be fair. I often wake up at night, and being in a room on my own means I can put the light on and read or watch TV. If I was sleeping with Ann, I'd just disturb her. It wouldn't be fair on her.'

'Would you agree with that, Ann, or would you like Ken to move back in with you now?'

'Yes, I would,' Ann said.

'Ken, would you like to move back in with Ann and share a bed again?'

'Well, yes . . . I mean . . . you know . . . I think I'd drive her nuts. Like I said, I'm up a lot at night so . . .' He fell silent.

'I understand that you're now used to sleeping alone, Ken, and habits can be hard to break, but would you consider moving back in, even just one night a week? Would that be possible?'

Ken shrugged. 'Sure, maybe.'

'It obviously means a lot to Ann, so taking that first step would show her how much you care. Do you visit each other's rooms, or have the separate sleeping arrangements caused a lack of intimacy?'

Ann nodded.

'When was the last time you had sex or were intimate physically?'

'What?' Ken spluttered.

'Before I had my hip replaced,' Ann answered.

'So, that would be over three years ago?'

'Yes.'

'It's not been that long,' Ken snapped.

'Yes, it has, Ken.'

'No, there was that time when . . .' He trailed off. 'Look, Ann, this is all wrong. I don't want to discuss our private life with a total stranger. We can talk about this at home, just the two of us.'

'But we never do. That's the problem. And whenever I raise the subject, you cut me off,' Ann pointed out.

'Why do we have to talk about everything? Why can't we just be married? We've been happy for decades. Why are we suddenly not okay? I don't get it. We have the same marriage, we're the same people. Why is everything that was absolutely fine now suddenly wrong?'

Ann looked at her husband. 'Because it isn't fine. Our marriage has changed, Ken, and it upsets me that you can't see it. We haven't been close for years. We aren't like a couple any more. I came here because I want to see if we can fix it and find each other again.'

'Well, I don't agree. I think we're just fine. I came here because I'm a good husband. I came here because you asked me to. Well, if the truth be told, you threatened me. None of my friends would do this. None of my friends would put themselves through this humiliation.'

'I understand that this is a big step for you to come here today, Ken,' Maggie said. 'It sounds to me that Ann is trying to tell you she doesn't feel heard when she speaks to you.'

'I listen to her all the time. Only last week she said she liked those scones in the bakery near my office and I brought her home two.'

'I said I liked the brownies, Ken. You don't listen. You think you do, but you don't.'

'And what about you, Ken? Do you feel that Ann listens to you?' Maggie asked.

'Yes, I suppose so. She's the talker, though. I guess I'm kind of quieter.'

'I want to revisit the question of intimacy. It's a key part of any marriage, I think you'll both agree. I'd like to know if you both miss having intimacy in your relationship?'

'I do miss being physically close in terms of sex, but most of all I miss affection,' Ann said.

'Ken, how do you feel about it?'

Ken was staring at his wife. 'What are you talking about, Ann? We are close. We have a good life together. I've always worked hard to provide it for you and the kids. I've never had an affair or anything like that. What is your problem? I'm a good husband. Look at Fintan! He went off and shagged his secretary. Look at your brother, for God's sake! He abandoned his family for some young one he met on the bloody internet. I've never cheated on you. So why the hell are you trying to make me feel like I'm not a good husband? It's not all about sex. Other things are just as important, if not more so.'

'But we never have fun any more, Ken. We never do anything spontaneous. We've become old before our time. We never kiss or hold hands, never mind have actual sex.'

Maggie went to speak, but Ken slapped his hand on his knee, making Ann jump. 'Damnit, Ann, what do you want? You want to leap out of a plane, go ahead. You want to learn to tango, go ahead. I'm not stopping you. To be honest, I think this is all just a big waste of time. Since the kids left, you've had all this time and you're just festering. You need a hobby. Take up golf or bridge or something to occupy your mind and stop looking for trouble where there is none.'

Ann held up her hands. 'I'm not saying this to hurt you, Ken. I'm saying it to make you open your eyes. It's the truth. We're like strangers and our marriage is falling apart.'

'I don't understand where all this is coming from. I'm nearly seventy and now suddenly everything between us is wrong? I don't get it.'

Maggie handed Ann a tissue. She hadn't realized she was crying. She dabbed her eyes. How could she get through to her husband? He was right, he didn't get it. Not screwing around did not make you a great partner. Where was the old Ken? The funny Ken, the Ken who had energy and wanted to get off the couch. Who was this grumpy old man who was so closed off and defensive? Was her Ken still in there?

'I'd like both of you to take a deep breath. Feeling angry is natural and it's good to air those feelings, but I'd like us to return to a calmer frame of mind now. Let's go back to the beginning, when you first met. Tell me about that, Ken. What is your first memory of Ann?'

'Ann knows when we first met. She was there too.'

'I'd like to hear the story,' Maggie said. 'What attracted you to each other?'

Ken sighed, leant back in the chair and closed his eyes. 'We were at a party. I was with my friend Harry. He passed away two years ago. Heart attack. Anyway, we were chatting to each other when this girl walked in. Red hair, green eyes, in a short, tight black dress. She was a knockout. I'd just come out of a two-year relationship and I was really not looking to meet a girl, but then I saw Ann. She looked around the room, saw me staring at her and smiled. That was it, I was smitten. I've always loved her smile – it lights up her whole face.'

Ann wiped the tears that were sliding down her cheeks. She remembered that night so well. She'd thought Ken had forgotten, but he hadn't. Her Ken *was* still in there. Ann felt relieved. Maybe they could find their way back.

'Ann, is that how you remember it?'

Ann smiled. 'Yes, I was taken with him, too. He was so strong and handsome and confident. He was ambitious and hard-working, and I knew he was someone I could trust. Someone who would never let me down.'

'And I haven't, have I?'

She shook her head. 'No, you haven't.'

'Then why are we here, Ann?'

'Because I feel as if I've lost you, Ken. That Ken, the man who smiled at me across the room and wanted to kiss me.'

'But you haven't. I'm right here, beside you.'

'No, you're not. You live your life and I live mine. I miss you. I miss us.' Ann sobbed into her tissue.

'Is that hard for you to hear, Ken?' Maggie asked.

'It's not true. We are together. We are a couple. She's just missing the kids and all that. It's a phase, empty nest. She'll be fine.'

'The kids left home ages ago,' Ann said. 'This is not a phase.'

'You've been in a slump since John went to Australia. Our younger child, John, moved to Australia recently and Ann has got herself into a state about it,' he explained to Maggie.

'This is not about John leaving. Yes, I'm upset he's gone, but I was sad and lonely already, Ken. I have been for years.'

'Ann has said she feels the relationship has changed, and that's why there's a new distance now, one that wasn't there before. Can you see that point of view? Do you also feel that your relationship has changed, Ken?' Maggie asked.

'No, I do not.'

'So for you the relationship is the same as it always was and you're satisfied with your level of intimacy and general closeness.'

'Yes,' Ken said, crossing his arms over his chest.

'Come on, Ken, be honest for once,' Ann said. 'You can't say what we have is satisfying. I miss the physical and emotional closeness, the cuddles and the holding hands. I miss waking up to you beside me. I miss our night-time chats and the way we used to laugh in bed. We don't seem to laugh any more. I just can't believe you don't see all this. You have to. I mean, if we haven't had sex for three years, something's wrong. That's just logical.'

'Ann, have you tried to initiate sex with Ken?'

'Yes, but he always comes up with an excuse.'

'There could be many reasons for that,' Maggie said. 'You're both over sixty now, so it can be the case that the body isn't as cooperative as it once was, and that can prove a major obstacle if it's not discussed. Is there any problem for you physically, Ken, that prevents you responding to Ann's advances? Have you, for example, experienced erectile dysfunction that has led you to avoid sex out of a sense of embarrassment?'

Ken jumped out of his chair, his face bright red. 'There is no problem with my body at all, thank you very much. That's enough. I'm not discussing these intimate things with you, Maggie. Ann, come on now, this is our private life.'

'This is a place where we can talk honestly, Ken. I've worked with every type of couple you can imagine, so I'm well used to discussing things like erectile dysfunction. I'm not being disrespectful by asking you that question. It can be a difficult thing for men to talk about, so I just want us to rule it in or rule it out. Please, sit down.'

Sweat formed on Ken's brow. 'I do not . . . I will not . . . I'm not . . . This is . . .'

Ann and Maggie stared at him.

'I do not have erectile dysfunction,' Ken said, through gritted teeth. 'I'll be seventy in two years, for God's sake. I just feel tired after work and my back acts up and . . . Well, frankly, it's none of your business. Ann, please, can we go? I can't stay here another minute.'

Ann sighed and stood up.

Maggie glanced at the clock. 'Okay, the session is almost over, and I think we've actually made progress today, even though it may have felt like pulling teeth,' she said, smiling at Ken. 'I want to thank you both for coming here and talking to me. I think communication is a key issue here. You've made great strides on that today, and we can continue to work on it. With that in mind, I'd like to give you some homework to do before next week's session. Would that be okay?'

'Christ,' Ken muttered.

'I'll go easy on you with the first lot, I promise,' Maggie said. 'All I'm going to suggest is that every night when you're watching TV, sit close together on the couch and hold hands. That's all. Just hold hands. I'd like you to feel comfortable physically with each other again, but we'll take baby steps with that, okay?'

Ken put on his coat and helped Ann into hers.

'Thank you, Maggie. Sorry for the waterworks. See you next week.' Ann shook her hand.

'Never apologize for crying in here,' Maggie said. 'This is a safe space to express whatever you want. It was lovely to meet you both and I'll see you next week. And don't forget your homework.'

Ken rushed out of the door like a hare running away from a pack of hungry dogs. Outside, he breathed in the fresh air and tried to get his heart rate down. 'A hundred and twenty euros for that claptrap. Bloody daylight robbery.'

Ann climbed into the car, saying nothing.

'She'll be waiting until Hell freezes over before I ever set foot in there again.' Ken started the engine. 'Well, I went, so you can't say I didn't try.'

Ann remained silent.

'Ann? I went, I tried, and it's a load of rubbish. We're fine. I'll try to talk to you more. Okay?'

Ann continued to look straight ahead. 'Ken,' her voice was calm but there was a hint of ice in there too, 'we haven't had sex in over three years. We haven't actually touched each other for three years, except the occasional peck on the cheek or pat on the arm. We never laugh or have fun together. This is not living. This is existing. We can't go on like this. You're going to be retiring soon, and then what? Are we going to spend our days watching TV and talking about the weather? We're healthy, we're lucky, we should be embracing life.'

'When did you become so unhappy with everything?' Ken said, gripping the steering wheel. 'What is it you want? Hugs and kisses and flowers and chocolate all the time? Is that it? Do you want to be appreciated more? Fine, I'll buy you flowers on my way home from work today. There, happy?'

'No,' Ann said quietly. 'I'm not happy. I don't want flowers or chocolates. I just want you to see me, Ken. I want us to be a couple again.'

'For the love of Jesus, I see you as plain as the nose on my face. You're wearing a dress and a weird scarf.'

'I see a man who won't look at me, touch me or talk to me.'

'I've had enough,' Ken said wearily. 'I'm going to drop you home and then I'm going to work. I hope to God that by the time I get home this evening you'll be back to normal.'

Ann closed her eyes to stop any more tears falling. Her husband had just crushed her fragile hopes of solving their problems.

11

Alice threw a handful of nuts into her mouth and watched the front door of the restaurant. She was starving and needed food to give her energy. She'd been up for hours the night before. Ted had woken with a bad nightmare, and after she'd soothed him back to sleep she'd been awake for hours, worrying about Niall and their therapist appointment. Her head ached and her eyes prickled from lack of sleep.

Why was he making her do it? She didn't want someone asking her personal questions. They were just in a little slump – all couples went through them. She was dreading the appointment in two days' time. But Niall was firm: she had to go. She'd decided she would go to one appointment to shut him up, then have sex with him more regularly so he'd calm down.

She'd wanted to cancel tonight, too, but she knew her mother and sister were keen to take her out for a belated birthday dinner, so she'd slapped on lots of concealer and tried to make herself presentable.

Her mother and Lisa arrived together, looking like clones of each other. Slim, elegantly dressed, blow-dried hair and subtle, but perfectly applied, make-up.

Alice was glad she'd worn her Spanx under her dress. At least it hid her muffin top. She waved them over.

'Hello, sorry we're late. We had a crazy day. That nasty flu seems to be doing the rounds – the pharmacy was packed,' her mother said.

'No problem.' Alice smiled. They were always late. The

pharmacy was always busy. Initially, Alice had been jealous that her mum and older sister worked together – the Johnson Pharmacists, mother and daughter, side by side. The smart, focused daughter and the smart, focused mother building their pharmacy, expanding, being successful, while the not-so-smart daughter drowned in nappies. But then Alice had realized she had no business being jealous because it had been her choice to be a stay-at-home mum.

They ordered a bottle of wine and some olives. Then they turned their attention to Alice.

'So, how are you? You look tired,' her mother said.

Great. They'd barely sat down and already Alice felt worse about herself.

'Yeah, you do,' Lisa agreed. 'Here, we got this new concealer in – it's supposed to be amazing.' She fished in her designer bag and handed Alice a tube.

'Thanks.' She shoved it into her bag. She didn't need concealer, she needed uninterrupted sleep.

'Why are you so tired?' her mother asked.

'Ted was up with a nightmare,' Alice said, leaving out the marriage-therapy anxiety.

'Alice, you mollycoddle those kids. You have to stop rushing to their sides all the time. Children need to build up resilience,' her mother said.

Alice tried not to let the comment sting. Her mother was the most capable woman she had ever met. But the steeliness that had allowed her to raise two girls on her own after her husband's death, while running his pharmacy, had also translated to how she was with her daughters. When Alice had had nightmares, which she often did after her dad died, her mother would march her back to her own bed, tell her to think nice thoughts and remind Alice that she had to be up at six to go to work and needed her sleep. Yes, they were well cared for, but Alice and Lisa were definitely not mollycoddled.

'He was upset, Mum.'

'You are a bit overprotective,' Lisa added.

You don't have kids so keep your opinions and judgements to yourself, Alice wanted to shout. Her sister lived with her barrister boyfriend – marriage was too conservative for Lisa – in a penthouse filled with sharp-edged furniture and cream rugs. She had chosen not to have kids and that was fine, but it didn't give her the right to criticize Alice's parenting.

'You should have stopped at two,' her mother said, for the zillionth time. 'The twins are too much. Four children is a zoo.'

Alice took a large sip of her wine. 'Thanks, Mum, but I happen to love my twins and thank God every day that I have them.'

'I know you do, but four is a handful. You need to go back to work and get yourself up and running again. You've been at home with them long enough.'

Alice bit her tongue so that she didn't say what she was thinking – she found herself biting her tongue more and more often, these days. *I don't want them to grow up like I did. I'm sorry, but I hated coming home to an empty house and having a mother who was always working. I wanted a mum like my friend Juliette had. An Aga-mum, who baked scones and buns and collected her from school every day and made amazing costumes for the school plays and sat in the front row at the concerts.*

Alice accepted that her mother had had to work to support them. She admired her hugely for it, but it was not the life she wanted for herself. Why couldn't her mother accept Alice's choice?

'I just worry that if anything happened to Niall, you

wouldn't be able to support the children. You never know what's going to happen in life, Alice.'

'I know that, Mum, but I'm not going to rush back to work on the tiny chance that Niall dies. The kids need me.'

'You could get a nanny,' Lisa said.

'A nanny would probably cost more than I'd be paid for in any job I could get.'

'You should have studied pharmacy,' her mother said.

'I wasn't smart enough to get into pharmacy, Mum. I'm not bursting with brains like you and Lisa.' This also stung. Alice had always been the dumb one in the family; the 'funny cute one' or the 'not-so-smart one'.

'You didn't exactly kill yourself studying in school either,' Lisa reminded her.

True, she hadn't. She'd been too busy having fun. But even if she'd studied day and night, she knew she wouldn't have got the grades to go into pharmacy.

'Anyway, how are you both?' Alice shifted the focus.

'Good. Carl and I are going to Paris next weekend,' Lisa said.

'And I'm going to Barcelona with Derek,' her mum said, referring to her partner of five years, Derek the divorcee.

Alice quite liked him. He adored her mother, and it was nice to see her being spoilt and treated. She deserved it after so many years on her own. 'Lovely,' she said. 'I hope you both have a great time.'

'How's Niall?' her mother asked.

'Busy, never home until after nine, which is a pain. It means I have to do the kids' bedtime alone every night.'

'Well, someone has to work,' Lisa pointed out.

'I know that, but it's after nine every single night of the week.'

'All the lawyers I know work late,' Lisa said. 'The ones who want to make senior partner do anyway.'

'It's good that Niall's driven,' her mother added. 'You need to support him in that.'

'But he's also a father who never sees his kids,' Alice snapped.

Her mother put down her glass. 'You married an ambitious man, Alice, much better than a lazy one. Don't criticize him for working hard to provide you all with a good life.'

Alice felt her cheeks flush. 'I'm not criticizing him. I'm just saying he needs to spend more time with his kids.'

'Doesn't he see them at the weekends?' Lisa asked.

'He often goes into the office for a few hours, and when he's home, he's always on his phone or watching sport on TV. He sees them a bit, but it's not enough. They need their dad.'

'They'll be fine. I barely saw my father when I was growing up,' her mother said. 'People expect too much, these days. Working full-time doesn't allow for all this "down-time" and "family time". You work hard to look after your family, and if you don't get to play hours of Monopoly with them, so what? They'll survive. Honestly, I'm so sick of hearing our young employees complaining because they don't have enough me-time or time with their kids. Niall is a good man, who's climbing up the ladder in his profession. His job allows you to be at home with the kids. You wanted that, so you should be grateful.'

Alice had missed having a dad in her teenage years and beyond. She had felt his loss acutely. He had been stolen from her by cancer. He had been a great dad and had adored her and Lisa. Alice wanted her kids to have a close relationship with Niall. She knew how important a dad was in a child's life. Hers had missed her secondary-school years, her wedding and the birth of her children. She wanted Niall to be there for all of the important events, and for the children to want him to be there. But he needed to be present, to engage with them, to get to know them before they grew up and were gone.

'I know all of that, Mum.' Alice tried to keep her voice even. 'I'm just saying that it's not easy being on your own with four kids all the time, and on the weekends Niall could make more of an effort.'

Her mother nodded, then saw someone she knew waving at her. 'Oh, it's Brendan and Hazel – I'd better go over and say hi.' She got up and walked across to her friends.

Lisa turned to her sister. 'How are you and Niall getting on?' she asked. 'Are you just angry about the work thing or is it something else?'

Alice felt a lump form in her throat. 'Well, we're arguing a fair bit.'

'Be careful, Alice, nobody wants a nagging wife,' her sister warned her. 'Carl's friend just left his wife because she nagged him all the time and he couldn't take it. Every time he came in from work, she was complaining about the kids or the house or something. Eventually he snapped and left.'

'Thanks a lot, Lisa. Very understanding. Look, I don't nag him. I just think he needs to see his children more, for their sake as much as his.'

'Men don't want to come home to conflict. Maybe he's working late because he doesn't want to come home. You need to be careful, Alice.'

Red-hot anger rose in Alice. 'Why?' she demanded. 'Why do *I* need to be careful, Lisa? He needs to be careful that he's being a good husband and dad, as he promised. Why am I a big, horrible nag because I want him to see his own children and engage with them more? How is that such a terrible thing to ask of him?'

'Calm down, Alice. I'm not attacking you. I'm just giving you an objective view on it. It's not the fact that you want him to see his children, it's the way you say it and how you react. You seem really angry about it and I'm sure that comes across to him,' Lisa said.

'I *am* angry. I'm sick of parenting alone,' Alice said. 'It's no fun, doing it all by yourself. It's exhausting and thankless.'

'But, Alice, you wanted lots of children and you wanted to stay at home with them. You wanted this exact life and Niall has to work to provide it for you,' Lisa reminded her.

'But how come my friends' husbands manage to work hard and still spend time with their kids?'

'Oh, God, whatever you do, don't compare him to other men. They all hate that,' Lisa said, 'and it'll drive him away, seriously, Alice. The best way to keep a man happy is sex. I always find that sex helps release tension and reset the connection. Give him plenty of sex and he'll come home earlier.' She laughed.

Alice emptied her glass in one gulp. 'Why is it always about sex and what men want? What about what women want? How about if Niall thinks about me for a millisecond and decides to come home and help put the kids to bed, or get up with the kids in the middle of the night once in a blue moon so I can get a full night's sleep? Or maybe he could consider the possibility that I don't want to have sex until I lose weight and feel sexy again.'

Lisa raised her hands. 'Okay, okay, I've obviously hit a nerve. I'm sorry. I'm just saying that sex can help ease tension between a couple.'

Alice rubbed her eyes, then reached over and took Lisa's hand in hers. 'Sorry, I shouldn't be giving out to you. I'm just freaking because Niall is making me go to couples' therapy. Don't tell Mum.'

'Are things that bad?' Lisa asked quietly.

'I didn't think so, but apparently because we haven't had

sex for a while, he thinks we need help.' Alice began to get emotional.

'Define "a while".'

'Four months.' Alice winced. It sounded bad when she said it out loud.

Lisa's eyebrows shot up.

Alice sighed. 'I know, I know, it's a long time. I'm just always up at night with one of the kids and then I can't get back to sleep and I'm constantly wrecked and I don't feel sexy.'

'It's a very long time, Alice, and if you don't use it, you lose it. So much about sex is habit, and if you get out of the habit of having sex, it's harder to get back into it. Just pick a night and do it. When you've done it once, it'll be easier to do it the next time.'

Alice nodded. Her sister was right: she needed to try harder.

'I'll drop this new vitamin booster in to you as well. It'll take a week or two to kick in, but it should help give you an energy lift.'

'Thanks, Lisa.' Alice paused. 'How often do you have sex with Carl?'

'Twice a week.'

Alice groaned.

'I schedule it in. Saturdays and Wednesdays.'

'Seriously?'

Lisa shrugged. 'If I don't, I know it could slip. It keeps both of us happy. Even on nights when I don't feel up to it, once we get going I always get into it and feel good afterwards. It's kind of like working out. You need to get into a routine and stick to it.'

'Do you ever have spontaneous sex?' Alice asked, remembering all the spontaneous sex she used to have with Niall.

'Yeah, but usually when we go away for a weekend or something. On a normal week, it's Saturdays and Wednesdays.'

'Do you think once a week is enough?'

Lisa laughed. 'Of course. Even once a fortnight, but once every four months, Alice? No.'

'I'm scared of therapy, Lisa. I'm scared he's going to say he wants to leave me for a younger woman who wants sex all the time. Like his stupid friend, Max, who's dumped his family for a twenty-something.'

'Niall's mad about you, Alice. Don't freak out about therapy – I think it'll help, actually. He wants to sort things out – he's showing you he cares. Go with it. It might help you sort out what you want in life, too. I mean, do you want to stay at home long-term now that the twins are in school?'

Alice sipped her wine. 'I don't know any more. But I'm starting to feel like maybe I need to do something to shake my life up. I think I'd like to work, but only part-time. I'd want something that fits into my life so I could still pick the kids up from school and go to their concerts and plays, not work in the holidays, and be able to stay at home if they're sick. But who is going to hire a woman who hasn't worked in eleven years and wants more time off than she spends in the office? I'm not exactly a prime candidate.'

Lisa grinned. 'You certainly have a lot of demands, but maybe you could help in the pharmacy. I'd have to think about what you could do, but leave it with me.'

'I don't need a pity job but, thanks, I appreciate the offer.'

Before Lisa could reply, their mother came back. 'What did I miss?'

Lisa and Alice looked at each other and laughed. 'Not much. Just me giving out about Niall,' Alice said.

'You need to mind Niall. Plenty of women in his office

would run off with him. He's handsome and charming,' her mother said.

Alice sighed. 'Thanks, Mum. Thanks for that, I feel so much better now. Why is it always "mind your man"? Why don't people say "mind your wife"?'

'I'm being honest, Alice. I've lived a lot longer than you have and I've seen many marriages break up. You do need to be careful, pet. You mustn't be grumpy and resentful. And you need to look after yourself, too, keep fit and dress nicely. When you look good, you feel better in yourself and it does wonders for your self-esteem. You need that, darling.'

'This leads nicely to your birthday present,' Lisa said, grinning at her. 'I have a fantastic new personal trainer, Dione, and I've booked you ten sessions with her as your gift. I think if you lost a few pounds and were fitter, it would help your energy levels too. Just call her to schedule it in. It's all about schedules, Alice.' Lisa winked at her.

Alice rolled her eyes. Great. As well as never saying a cross word to Niall about never being at home, she had to lose weight, get fit, dress up every day, be smiley and happy and have sex with him all the time.

And now she'd been given another birthday gift she didn't want. She had to suffer the humiliation of some gym bunny who was going to shout at her and make her run and jump up and down and tell her what to eat and make her lift heavy weights and . . . oh, God. Just the sound of it was exhausting.

Alice poured herself another large glass of wine and glugged it down.

12

Orla listened to Zoë's dramatic moans and groans through the paper-thin walls. The guy she'd brought home last night was obviously fit. They'd done it three times since they'd stumbled in at three a.m. She should never have lent Zoë her noise-cancelling headphones when she was working from home. Now they were on the desk in Zoë's bedroom and Orla was subject to all of Zoë's sound effects.

Orla closed her eyes and imagined having sex with Paul. She'd been thinking about him a lot since their meeting about Lulu. She imagined his smiling eyes gazing into hers, his strong, warm hands all over her body. Orla moved her hands over herself. She moved them over her breasts, then down and into her pants.

Stop it, she told herself. It'll never happen, you stupid fool. He had barely looked at her when he'd picked up Lulu the day she had the temperature. Orla pulled her hand back and snapped her eyes open. There was no point. No point in fantasizing about something she knew could never happen. She was a freak. A freak no man would ever want to be with. A freak, who would never have a relationship. A freak, who would never have children. A woman, who wasn't a real woman, and never would be.

While her flatmate climaxed loudly in the next room, Orla turned her face into her pillow and wept.

Orla was back from a run, having a late breakfast, when Zoë appeared from her bedroom looking dishevelled.

'Oh, my God, have you been for a run already?'

'Yeah, I couldn't sleep so I decided to get some exercise in.'

'You don't need to go running to get exercise.' Zoë grinned. 'I got plenty of it.'

You don't say? Orla wanted to snap. I was forced to listen to every bloody minute of it.

'So who's the guy?' she asked her flatmate.

'I met him in a bar last night when we went for Friday-night drinks. He's so fit! Wait until you see him.'

Orla really didn't want to meet another of Zoë's one-night stands. She'd met enough to last her a lifetime. Zoë had a phenomenal sex drive. Orla knew she'd have to move out soon. All the sex going on beside her was making her feel even worse about herself. But it had only been four months and finding a nice place close to the school had been really difficult.

She'd have liked to live alone, but the rents in Dublin were crazy. Still, sharing with Zoë was doing her head in. She'd have to go out and find a nice quiet flatmate who didn't shag every man she met.

'How was your night? Any luck?' Zoë slathered a slice of bread with butter.

'I just went to the movies.'

'With workmates?'

'Yeah,' Orla lied. She'd gone to the cinema alone, like she always did. The other teachers were either married or coupled up. It was a small primary school, and of the ten staff, she was the only teacher who was single.

Everyone always seemed to have plans. Lots of plans. Busy-busy all the time. Everyone except her. Orla hated weekends. She'd either be bullied into going out with Zoë, which led to her pretending to go home with a guy, ditching him as soon as Zoë was out of sight and spending another night in Starbucks. Or else she'd avoid Zoë by making up fake plans and wandering about the city on her own, going to the cinema, sometimes seeing two films in one day.

Sundays were the worst. Zoë would go home to her family and Orla would pretend she was meeting colleagues for brunch, so she didn't have to witness any more family meltdowns with Zoë's parents. There was tension in that house and she felt uncomfortable around it.

'I know the last time probably put you off, but you're welcome to come to Sunday dinner at my parents' house tomorrow if you have no plans.'

'Thanks, but I'm meeting a friend,' Orla lied, for the third week in a row.

'God, I wish you were free. Since John left those dinners are a bit gloomy. My parents barely speak to each other. Honestly, I'm never getting married. They don't even sleep in the same room. It's so grim.'

'Were they always like that?' Orla wondered.

'No, they used to go out and have fun together, but not for ages now. I dunno, Dad's always been old-fashioned but he's got really set in his ways, and Mum's a bit of an enabler. She's always looked after Dad and us. I think she devoted herself too much to all of us. Now we're gone and it's just her and Dad, and he never wants to get out of his big TV chair to do anything.'

'I suppose when you've been married that long, you just get into a habit and accept things about each other that you can't change.'

Zoë chewed her toast. 'Yeah, I guess so, but it's depressing. They barely ever go out. It's the same thing every day. I don't know how Mum will cope when Dad retires in June. He'll drive her nuts, sitting around the house all day. I'd go mad. Marriage is a prison. Being single rocks – you make your own decisions and do what you want when you want.'

Zoë finished her breakfast and went back in to check on her latest conquest.

Orla sipped her coffee. Choosing not to get married was freedom. But when you had no choice about being single, because no one would ever marry you or even date you, well, that was a real prison, and a very lonely one.

Orla found the loneliness hard to bear. The weekends were always difficult. The one person who knew Orla, who knew her past, who understood her, was Shannon, but she was in America now. She'd got the hell out of Ballystone as soon as they'd finished their Leaving Cert exams. She'd got on a plane to New York and never come home. They WhatsApped and occasionally caught up on FaceTime, but less so recently. Shannon had a big job in sales, a Canadian boyfriend and an eight-month-old baby. Her life was filled with happy things, and Orla was delighted for her. Shannon deserved happiness. While Orla was pitied in town for having killed her mother, Shannon was pitied for having an alcoholic father.

The two town losers, Shannon had labelled them.

'We might be losers,' she'd say to Orla, 'but we're going to get away from this dump and live brilliant lives, full of adventure and happiness.' Shannon had been true to her word.

Orla had got out of Ballystone, too, but her life was not full of adventure. In fact, her life had become smaller. Once she had realized she was a freak, she had retreated into herself and kept people at a distance. She didn't want a new best friend because best friends asked too many questions. She needed distance to protect herself. She didn't want drunken conversations about the meaning of life. She didn't want to 'share'. She needed to hide her weirdness. If it got out, she'd be a freak all over again. Not the freak who killed her mother, but the freak who couldn't . . . Well, that girl.

Later that day, when Zoë and her new sex-buddy had gone out for food, Orla was sitting on the couch flicking through the TV channels when the doorbell rang. She went out to answer it.

'Hello, pet, how are you?'

It was Ann, Zoë's mother. 'Oh, hi, come on in.' Orla held the door as Ann walked into the small living and kitchen area. Ann had dark circles under her eyes. Her shoulders drooped. She seemed to have aged since the last time Orla had seen her.

'Is Zoë here?'

'Uhm, no, you've just missed her. She went out for some food.'

'Ah, pity. I was just passing by and I thought I'd pop in on the off-chance. Sure, I'll see her tomorrow for dinner. You're very welcome to join us, Orla.'

'Thanks so much, but I'm afraid I can't.' Orla felt like an almost professional liar.

Ann nodded. 'Right, well, I won't keep you.'

Keep me from what? Another long day of boredom, waiting for Monday to come so I feel I have some purpose in the world? 'Would you like a cup of coffee, Ann? I was just about to make one.'

'I don't want to take up your time.'

'I'd be glad of the company, honestly. Sit down.' Orla could sense Ann's loneliness. She knew the signs all too well.

'That'd be lovely, thank you.'

Ann sat on the couch and Orla busied herself with the coffee and cutting two slices of the banana bread she had made the day before, when she was trying to fill her afternoon.

'So, how are you doing? It must be hard, now that John's gone to Australia?' Orla handed Ann a mug and a plate.

Ann nodded. 'It's harder than I thought. I miss him so much. We Skype all the time, but it's not the same. Ken thinks I'm being ridiculous, but I'm terrified he'll never come home.'

'I'm sorry you're struggling. Zoë misses him, too. Would you go to visit?'

Ann sipped her coffee. 'I would, but Ken would never come with me. It's funny . . . As I get older, I yearn to travel. Maybe it's because I know I haven't got all that much time left and there is so much of the world I haven't seen.'

'You're not old,' Orla said.

'I'll be sixty-five soon. Life goes by so fast. Do all the things you want, Orla. Live life to the full.'

I want to, Orla thought, but it's not that easy.

Ann bit into the bread. 'Oh, my goodness, this is delicious. You're an amazing baker.'

Orla blushed. 'Thanks, but it's a really easy recipe. So if you could go anywhere, where would you go?' she asked Ann.

Ann smiled. 'Buenos Aires. I've always dreamt of going there and learning the tango. What about you?'

'Peru. I've always wanted to walk the Inca Trail.'

Ann laughed. 'Isn't it funny that we both want to go to South America?'

'Peru just seems so far removed from here, so exotic, full of history and natural beauty.'

'You should go. Book it and go this summer. The great thing about you teachers is the long holidays. Have you a pal to go with or would you go alone?'

'I'm not sure,' Orla lied. Of course she would go alone.

She did everything alone. 'I don't think it'll happen this year or next.'

Ann leant forward and patted her knee. 'Do it, Orla. Do it while you can. Don't put things off.'

They ate their banana bread in silence until Ann asked, 'Did your father ever meet anyone after your mother passed?'

'No. He says she was his one true love.'

'That's very romantic,' Ann said.

Not when it's shoved down your throat every day and you're blamed for ruining that true love.

'How long have you been married?' Orla asked.

'Thirty-eight years. We've been together for over forty.'

'Wow, that's amazing. It must be so lovely to have met your soulmate.'

Ann put her coffee cup down. 'To be honest with you, Orla, marriage is hard. It has its ups and its downs. But we've managed to muddle through.' She picked at the crumbs on her plate. 'Have you your eye on anyone?'

Could Orla admit that she had a crush on a school dad who barely knew she existed?

'Kind of, but I'm not sure he's even noticed me.'

Ann patted her hand. 'Orla, you're a gorgeous young woman. Of course he's noticed you, and if he doesn't give you all the attention and affection you deserve, move on. You're a gem.'

Orla's throat tightened. She wished Ann was her mother. She wished she could lay her head on her shoulder and tell her everything. All the worries and burdens she carried.

She swallowed and croaked, 'Thank you.'

'I'm serious now. You deserve a wonderful man and don't settle for anything less. Life can be difficult and you need to be with someone very special to get through it all.'

Life couldn't get more difficult, Orla thought sadly.

'Let him taste this banana bread and he'll be yours for life.' Ann smiled.

Orla laughed. 'If only it were that easy!'

'I've taken up enough of your time now. I'm sure you've pals to meet. I'd better go. Ken will be looking for his dinner. I've spoilt him – he can barely boil an egg. Thank you for the lovely coffee and cake.' Ann stood and picked up her bag. 'Now remember, pet, you're welcome for dinner any time – and take my advice. Book that holiday to Peru.'

'And you should go and dance the tango.' Orla smiled.

Ann laughed and opened her arms to hug Orla goodbye.

Orla tried not to cling to her. She didn't want Ann to know how needy she was for love and affection. It was all she'd ever really wanted – just to be loved.

She saw Ann out, then tidied up and resumed her position on the couch with a bowl of muesli and yoghurt. She wondered if Zoë knew how lucky she was to have such a gorgeous caring mother. To be fair, Zoë always spoke fondly of Ann, and Orla knew she loved her mum, but she wondered if kids in general knew how magic it was to have someone who loved you unconditionally and wholeheartedly. It was a gift that Orla would never receive, and some days that really hurt.

She snuggled under a soft blanket and switched on the TV. She flicked around and came across a rerun of a weekday afternoon talk show. An American woman, Maggie Purcell, was taking calls from people with relationship problems. One call was about a cheating partner, another about erectile dysfunction, but then a woman rang in and said she found it difficult and painful to have sex.

'In what way?' the therapist asked.

'Uhm . . . well . . . it's hard to explain. It's embarrassing. I'm sorry, I can't . . .'

'Oh dear,' the glossy presenter said. 'We seem to have lost that call.'

The therapist lady held up her hand. 'I think that woman hung up because she felt ashamed. This may not have been her exact problem but a lot of women, far more than you would think, suffer from a condition called vaginismus.'

'What's that?' the presenter asked.

'It's a condition in which the muscles in a woman's vagina literally close up and prevent her having or enjoying penetrative sex. It affects everything from using tampons to having smear tests. A lot of women out there are suffering in silence and I urge them to seek help. Therapy can help. It doesn't cure everyone, but seeking help will, at the very least, allow you to come to terms with having vaginismus and give you tools to work around it so that you can live a full life with it.'

Orla sat bolt upright on the couch. With trembling hands, she typed the name Dr Maggie Purcell into her phone. It was a sign. It had to be. What were the chances of her switching on the TV at that exact moment and hearing those words?

Maggie Purcell's website came up on her screen. There was a contact number. Orla saved it in her contacts list. Maybe, just maybe, this woman could help her. Maybe she could fix her. Maybe she could make her normal.

13

Ann handed the bag to the lady and thanked her.

'Scabby old witch,' Milly said, as the shop door closed behind the customer, 'haggling over three euros. It's a charity shop, for feck sake.'

'Language, Milly.'

'Seriously, though. Did you see the diamond ring on her finger? It was huge. It's not like she couldn't afford the three euros.'

'You never know what's going on in someone's life. Maybe she's having a tough time.'

Milly tried on one of the hats on the shelf and looked at herself in the mirror. 'You're too bloody nice, Ann.'

Ann laughed. 'I'm not. I've just been around a lot longer than you and I know appearances can be deceiving. You never know what's really going on behind closed doors.'

'I suppose.' Milly put down the hat and came over to the counter. 'So, what are you going to wear to this party tonight? You have to dress up, wear something sexy, give all those old men a heart attack.'

'Seventy is not that old, Milly. I'll be seventy in five and a bit years!'

'You don't seem old, but my nan seems ancient and she's sixty-six. Anyway, you should go sexy. You've got great legs. You should show them off – and get a push-up bra, show some cleavage. I bet your Ken would like it.' Milly winked. 'Short skirts and push-up bras always work for me.' She giggled.

They used to work for me, too, Ann thought sadly. Ken was a big fan of short skirts. He always said he was a legs man. He used to whistle when she came down the stairs in a short skirt, and caress her legs under the table in restaurants. He'd liked it when she wrapped her legs tightly around him during sex. She had always known that if she wore a short skirt, it would turn him on. It used to be so easy. When had it got so difficult?

'How about this?' Milly held up a short black satin mini-dress.

Ann burst out laughing. 'Milly, if I wore that, people would think I'd lost my mind. I need something that goes to the knee.'

Milly wagged a finger at her. 'Ann, you need to shake it up. You have a young vibe, so stop hiding it. Right, how about this one, then?' Milly held up a yellow dress with spaghetti straps.

'No, thanks. Yellow was never my colour. I have a nice black cocktail dress that I'll wear. I always feel good in it.'

'But do you feel sexy in it?' Milly pressed.

'Actually, yes, I do,' Ann admitted.

'Because, Ann, you're hot. Like, I know you're older and all, but if you wore better clothes, you'd be smoking.'

'What's wrong with my clothes?' Ann looked down at her black trousers and beige polo-neck.

'I mean, they're fine. Smart, I guess. But a bit, I dunno, boring. You have a good body – you should be wearing skinny jeans and cool shirts with lots of gold necklaces and stuff. Look at Elle Macpherson. You should dress like her. She has a very cool vibe. I think it would suit you cos you're tall and skinny too.' Milly searched for photos of Elle Macpherson on her phone and showed them to Ann. To be fair, her clothes were lovely. Casual but very stylish.

'She's fabulous, but she's also a supermodel,' Ann pointed out.

Milly grabbed Ann by the shoulders and gave her a little shake. 'Ann, you may not be a supermodel, but you are gorgeous in your own way. You just need to shake it up.'

Ann hugged her. 'Milly, you are a dote. A ray of sunshine and a tonic.'

Milly beamed. 'Thanks.'

'Right, let's lock up and get out of here so I can get ready for my party and you can go to yours.'

They collected their belongings and locked up the shop.

'Have a great night, Milly,' Ann said. 'See you next week.'

'See ya,' Milly called, as she hopped onto her bike.

As she walked towards her car, Ann felt a spring in her step. Milly was right. She should shake it up and maybe that would help with Ken, too. They had tried to hold hands on the couch, as Maggie had prescribed, but it had been so awkward. They'd sat stiffly, holding hands, until Ken had pretended he needed to go to the bathroom and pulled away.

Ann wanted to put some spice back into their relationship, to remind Ken of why he'd fallen for her. She'd put on her black cocktail dress and maybe some red lipstick to sass it up a bit. She'd wear her really high black shoes. They killed her feet, but she'd drink wine to numb the pain. She'd be the Ann of old, figure-hugging dress and heels, and maybe that would encourage Ken to find his younger self and have a bit of fun.

Ken stood at the bottom of the stairs swinging his keys. 'For the love of God, Ann, hurry up! We're going to be late. You know I like to get out early and home early.'

Ann reapplied her red lipstick and slowly walked down the stairs, careful not to topple on her sky-high heels.

Ken glanced up. 'You're very dressed up,' he said.

'Is that a compliment?' Ann smiled and struck a pose.

'I just think you're a bit dickied up for Peter's seventieth birthday. It's just twenty people invited to the house.'

Ann tried not to mind, tried not to be hurt. 'I thought I looked good,' she said.

'You do, just a bit overdone is all. You always say those shoes hurt your feet, so why are you wearing them?'

'Because I was making an effort, Ken.' Ann felt deflated. Was it too much to ask for a compliment? Was it too much to hope that her husband would tell her she looked nice? 'Let's just go,' she said, as she put on her coat.

'What? What did I say?' Ken looked confused.

'Forget it.' Ann walked to the car, trying not to break her ankle on the driveway.

When they got there, lots of people complimented Ann on how well she looked and she began to feel better. She drank two glasses of wine in quick succession to numb the pain in her feet. Ken stood to one side of the room, discussing business with Dan and Tom, while Ann chatted to the other guests.

She was with Keith, hearing about his recent walking trip in Portugal, when Peter tapped his glass and asked for silence. 'Thank you all for coming to celebrate my birthday. I can't believe I'm seventy. I feel thirty, and when I catch a glimpse of myself in the mirror, I wonder who the old guy staring back at me is. But I feel very lucky. I have three great kids and I'm still married to the love of my life. Cathy is the best thing that ever happened to me. I still can't believe she agreed to marry me. I look at her every day and think, Wow, I won the wife lotto. I love her more now than I did the day we got married. We have so much fun together and I still fancy the pants off her.'

Lots of whoops and cheers from the audience. Cathy roared with laughter.

'Thanks for coming to celebrate with us. Now, have some food, drink lots more and be merry. Life is short. Fill it with love, laughter and adventure.'

Keith handed Ann the cocktail napkin from under his glass.

'Oh, gosh, thanks.' Ann dabbed her wet cheeks. 'I'm such a sap.'

'It was a great speech.'

'I'm a sucker for a romantic speech,' Ann said.

'I get it. Peter's words were moving. They almost made me miss Marcie.' Keith grinned. 'But then I remembered what a psycho my ex-wife is.'

They both laughed.

'Peter's right, though, we do need to laugh more and be more adventurous,' Ann said. 'Well, you don't, Keith, you're always doing exciting things.'

Keith shrugged. 'I keep busy, but a lot of the time I'm running away from being alone. When Marcie and I split up, I was relieved. It had been toxic for so long. Life felt full of opportunity and possibility again. I dated a bit, had some short-lived relationships, but never found someone I wanted to share my life with. To be honest, Ann, I found retirement difficult. Suddenly I had all this time and no sense of purpose. It pushed me into being more adventurous. That was when I joined the group hiking holiday in Spain, which started me on these trips. They're great fun. You meet interesting characters, a few nutters too, but mostly lovely people.'

'And do you ever have holiday romances?' Ann asked.

Keith winked. 'One or two. In fact, I met a very nice Swedish lady on my last holiday. I'm going to Stockholm next week to see her.'

Another man – Ann didn't recognize him – came over to chat to Keith.

Ann studied Keith as he chatted. She wondered if she could have sex with him. She tried to imagine dragging him into Peter and Cathy's guest bedroom and having steamy sex. No, he was too small and she didn't like beards. She looked at Ken. He was her type. Tall, strong and clean-shaven. She still found him attractive after all these years. But clearly he didn't feel the same. Ann couldn't have looked any better than she did tonight. Everyone at the party had told her she looked fantastic. So why didn't her own husband fancy her? Maybe she just needed to go out to a bar or nightclub and have random sex with another man. Maybe that would satisfy her.

But it was Ken she wanted. She missed him. She missed the way they used to laugh together. They'd always found the same things funny. She could look at him across a room and he'd know exactly what she was thinking. Now she had no idea what he was thinking. Was he thinking at all? He seemed so shut off.

Zoë had noticed it too. 'Why is Dad so grumpy?' she asked constantly. 'He's so impatient and short-tempered. What's wrong with him?'

The sad thing was, Ann didn't know – and she wasn't sure Ken did either. It wasn't about his retirement, although that was definitely making him worse. But, he'd been getting grumpier and less active for years.

Ken looked up and saw her watching him. He walked towards her. She smiled at him, but in return he tapped his watch. 'We'll go soon.'

'It's only a quarter to eleven, Ken.'

'I know. Eleven is a good time to leave.'

'But it's fun. I want to stay.'

'Well, I'm talked out and I'm tired.'

'It's Saturday night, we have nothing to get up for. We can sleep in.'

'Ann, I want to go.'

'Well, I don't,' Ann said, putting her foot down. She was sick of leaving parties early with Ken. When had he got so dull and old? He used to be the one she'd have to drag home. He'd be drinking beers and telling funny stories until the wee hours.

They glared at each other. Peter came up and put his arms around them.

'My favourite couple.' He was slurring slightly now. 'You know, Ken, we're two lucky sods, marrying Cathy and Ann. Two incredible women.'

Ann kissed Peter's cheek. 'It was a beautiful speech, Peter. You made me cry. What you said about Cathy was really touching.'

'I meant every word. Ken and I know how lucky we are, don't we, Ken?'

Ken nodded curtly but said nothing. Ann could see that he was still seething about being dragged to therapy and her saying she didn't want to leave the party. He couldn't even manage to say, 'Yes, we are.' Ann hated him for it.

Peter wandered off to hug some more of his guests. He was full of love and joy and wanted to share it with his friends.

Ann walked away from Ken and went to talk to Cathy, whom she could see through the window. She was outside having a cigarette.

Ann joined her, and sat beside her friend at the garden table. 'Hey there, can I have one?'

Cathy was surprised. 'You don't smoke.'

'Well, I do tonight.'

Cathy handed her a packet. Ann pulled out a cigarette

and lit it. She inhaled deeply. It felt good. She'd only ever been an occasional smoker but ten years ago she'd stopped completely.

'It's a gorgeous party, Cathy. Well done on organizing it.'

'I wanted it to be special for Peter.'

'He certainly appreciates it, and you.' Ann tapped her ash into the ashtray on the garden table.

'Ah, he's a teddy bear. We drive each other nuts, but we're still mad about each other. Like you and Ken.'

The wine had loosened Ann's tongue. 'I don't know, Cathy. Ken and I are . . . we're . . . we're drifting.'

Cathy patted her friend's arms. 'Hey, we all drift at times. All men go a bit funny when they get close to retirement. Peter was very tricky around the time he retired. He's used to it now and is enjoying it. Don't worry, Ken will settle down.'

'It's not just that, it's . . . In the last few years he never seems to want to do anything. He's cold and distant. I can't reach him.'

Cathy put out her cigarette. 'I guarantee it's because he's panicking about ageing and retiring, how to fill his days. Maybe you should encourage him to do one of those how-to-retire courses. They're supposed to be really good. Men are useless at filling their time. It took Peter a good six months to find a routine. And to give you a heads-up, when they have all this spare time, they're looking for more sex. Thankfully, that's settled down too. Peter was mad for it, morning, noon and night. Jesus, I was worn out.'

Ann tried to laugh with her friend. 'Thanks for the warning,' she said. She knew for sure that Ken was not going to be pestering her for sex when he retired. All it would do was make their lack of closeness more acute. While Peter was looking for more sex, Ken was looking for none.

But it was too personal and painful to discuss. Ann wanted

to ask Cathy how often she had sex with Peter now, but she was afraid of the answer. She was deeply ashamed to admit that she and her husband never even touched.

Ann avoided Ken until he stood in front of her at midnight and said enough was enough, they were leaving. He'd ordered a taxi and would pick up the car in the morning.

Ann had stopped drinking and had the beginnings of a hangover. She rubbed her temples as they sat in the back of the taxi, in silence.

'Headache?'

'Yes.'

'You drank too much wine.'

'Yes, I did. I enjoyed every drop.'

'How are your feet?'

'Sore as hell.'

'Told you not to wear those shoes.'

'Yes, Ken, I know you did, but I wanted to look good and, believe it or not, I got lots of compliments from everyone . . . except you.'

'I told you that you looked nice.'

'No, you didn't.'

'Well, you do.'

'It would be nice if you were to tell me occasionally.'

'I always think you look nice, Ann, dressed up or not.'

'Forget it.'

They pulled up outside the house and Ken paid the driver. Ann took off her shoes and carried them up to the front door. She opened it and headed for the kitchen.

'Would you like me to make you a cup of tea? Or do you want to take some paracetamol for your headache?' Ken asked.

'No, Ken, I would not.'

'Hey, why are you so cross? What did I do?'

Ann threw her shoes at him. 'You never do anything, Ken. That's the whole point. You never say nice things, you never hold my hand, you never tell me you love me, you never hug me or hold me or even look at me. Did you hear Peter tonight? He was so loving about Cathy. It's like I'm just part of the furniture to you. I'm here, in front of you. I'm your wife. Why can't you see me any more?' She began to cry.

Ken looked at her helplessly. 'I don't understand, Ann. We're going in circles with this. Why are you so unhappy? We have a good life.'

'No, we don't. It's an empty sham of a life.'

Ken shook his head. 'I really am sick of you knocking our life. We're lucky, Ann, very lucky. We have everything we need. Why the hell are you so dissatisfied? It's driving me crazy. What do you want? What exactly are you looking for?'

'My husband. I'm looking for my husband. I feel invisible and lonely, so lonely, and the fact that you can't see it means we have no hope.'

Before Ken could say another word, Ann ran up the stairs and locked herself into her bedroom. She threw herself onto the bed and cried herself to sleep. Ken sat downstairs in the kitchen, wondering where his calm, contented wife had gone and if she was ever coming back.

14

Alice hugged Poppy and Ted extra tight.

'Ouch, Mummy,' Ted complained.

'Sorry, darling, I just love you guys so much.'

'Why are you crying, Mummy?' Poppy asked, as Alice wiped the tears from her eyes.

'I'm just being silly and thinking I'll miss you today.'

'So take us home. We can eat sweets and watch movies, like Lulu's daddy does with her,' Poppy, never one to miss an opportunity, suggested.

Alice wished with all her heart that she could say yes. But Niall was waiting in the car. Waiting for her to get back in, so they could get to their stupid appointment.

Alice let the twins go and walked slowly back to the car.

She tried one more time to persuade Niall that this was unnecessary. 'Can we not just sort this out ourselves? Please, Niall.'

Niall shook his head. 'Alice, I've tried talking to you about our sex life. I've tried having sex with you. I've tried not to mind when you keep pushing me away – but I can't go on like this. I love you and I want to fix this. We are going to see this woman, Maggie Purcell, today and hopefully she can help us.'

Alice gritted her teeth. One session. That was all she was doing. One session and that was it. She'd just grin and bear it for Niall.

*

Maggie looked about Alice's age, but Alice reckoned she was probably older. She looked like she'd had really good work done. Botox and fillers, Alice thought. Lisa would know straight off. She should probably get some done herself. All her friends were doing it. And, of course, Lisa kept telling her that she should do it before it was 'too late'. Alice was afraid to, though, because knowing her luck she'd have a reaction to it, or something would go wrong and she'd end up with a droopy face. Also, as she was carrying an extra ten kilos, Alice's face was round and less wrinkled than her skinny friends' and sister's. It was the only good thing about carrying extra weight.

Alice kept crossing and uncrossing her legs. She could not have been more out of her comfort zone. This confident, well-groomed American woman was probably sex-mad and thought women should shag their husbands twice a day. Oh, my God, what if she made them do stuff, like touch each other or try tantric sex or something? Alice tried not to hyperventilate.

Maggie handed her a glass of water. 'Here, Alice, you look like you need this.' She smiled at her. 'Don't worry. No one is going to ask you to do anything you don't want to. This is a safe space for you and Niall to talk about how you're feeling and what's going on in your relationship.'

Alice took a gulp and tried to calm down.

'So, why don't we talk about what brought you here today and what you're hoping to address during the session?'

Niall clasped his hands together and jumped straight in. 'Alice and I haven't had sex in almost five months now. It's constant, relentless rejection. When I try to initiate sex, she always has an excuse – tired, headache, period pains, feeling bloated, kids . . . The list is endless.'

'Not endless.' Alice bristled. 'And it hasn't been nearly five months.'

'Yes, it has. Before this particular dry spell,' Niall continued, 'we were only having sex about once every five or six weeks anyway.'

'We have four kids,' Alice said. 'It's full-on, all the time.'

'I'm not demanding hours of your time, Alice. A quick shag takes five minutes,' Niall replied.

'Okay, let's take a moment to talk this through,' Maggie gently interrupted them. 'Are we agreed that it has been five months since you were last intimate with each other?'

'Yes,' Niall said firmly.

Alice nodded miserably.

'So your intimate life has slipped off the agenda, which, as Alice pointed out, is a very busy and demanding agenda. Alice, what's it like for you when you hear Niall saying that the two of you are not having enough sex?'

Alice's face reddened. This was mortifying. She never liked talking about sex. She wasn't one of those women who told everyone about their favourite positions or whether they liked giving or receiving oral sex. She was suspicious of women who talked about their sex lives all the time, women who banged on about how much they loved sex. She thought a lot of it was bluster and exaggeration. Sex was private: it was between you and your partner. Maggie was looking at her, waiting for an answer.

'I don't know, really. I guess I just have a lower sex drive now because I'm tired. But it's not like I've shut down or anything. I'm not frigid.'

'A lot of women find their sex drive declines after having children and becoming sleep-deprived. Energy levels can really fall drastically and it has an effect across all aspects of their lives.'

'Exactly,' Alice said. Maggie understood her. Alice felt better.

'However, I'm hearing from Niall that he's struggling with this because he feels rejected by you.'

'Exactly,' Niall said. 'And everyone knows that the longer you go without having sex, the harder it can be to get back to it.'

Alice crossed her arms defensively. 'It's not like it's been years. It's just a couple of months.'

'But even before this, it was always me reaching for you,' Niall said. 'You never initiate sex any more, and even when I hug you in bed, you push me away. You never want to be with me.'

'That's because you never just want to hug me, Niall. If I thought it was just a hug, I'd hug you. I'd love a big hug, but it's always you wanting sex. People talk about spooning. We've never spooned. You spoon me and then you want sex.'

'What's wrong with wanting sex with my wife? It's normal, Alice. Couples have sex. A lot more than we do.'

Alice turned on him. 'This is all about Max, isn't it? You were fine before Max dumped his wife and rocked up with sex-mad Lizzie. Now he's having sex everywhere, all the time, and you're jealous.'

Maggie held up her hands. 'Can you tell me who Max is and why Niall might be jealous of him?'

Niall sighed. 'Max is my best mate. He left his wife six months ago and is now dating Lizzie, who is twenty-three, and yes, he's having a very active sex life and lots of fun.'

'Well, that can be a difficult situation. When people close to you have a complete change of lifestyle, it can make you re-examine your own in a new light. Is that how you feel, Niall?' Maggie asked.

'Not really, but would I like to be having great sex with my wife? Damn right I would.'

'How do you feel about Max leaving his wife?' Maggie

asked Alice. 'Does Max leaving her and taking up with a much younger woman make you feel uneasy, off-balance?'

Alice paused. She felt more angry than uneasy. But maybe the anger was hiding the fear. Underneath it all, she was scared. What if Niall did fall for one of Lizzie's gorgeous Pilates-instructor friends and leave her?

'It just makes me furious more than anything. Sally, Max's ex-wife, is lovely. The four of us were good friends. We used to go out together and we got on really well. But then Max had his pathetic mid-life crisis and left her and is now going to nightclubs, snorting cocaine and getting blowjobs in public toilets. He thinks he's God's gift. I think it's pathetic. I think *he's* pathetic, and I hate what it's done to Niall. Niall thinks Max is great and he's jealous of his new life. I can see it. He practically drools every time he mentions Lizzie's name.'

'How does Niall's jealousy make you feel?'

'Well, I suppose it scares me a bit. I can't believe how easily Max dumped Sally and moved on. He barely skipped a beat. If they didn't have two kids together, he'd never have seen Sally again. Fifteen years of marriage just flicked away. He's acting like a horny teenage boy. Niall doesn't see how pathetic it is. He has Max on a pedestal.'

'No, I don't.'

'Yes, you do. You always have. You think Max is great because he does what he wants and always has. Max has always gone off on boys' holidays whenever he felt like it. He never, ever missed doing anything he fancied. He never even asked Sally if she minded. She was, I have to be honest, a bit of a doormat. But she loved him and she wanted him to be happy, so she never stopped him doing what he wanted. She was devoted to him, but it wasn't enough so he dumped her. And this man is Niall's role model.'

Niall glared at her. 'Bullshit. I can see perfectly well that Max can be selfish. I like Sally, too, and of course I feel sorry for her. But, no, I don't blame Max for wanting to be happy. He was miserable with Sally. They had nothing in common. To be honest, I think if she hadn't got pregnant when they were dating, he wouldn't have stayed with her. To be fair, he gave it fifteen years, which is more than a lot of blokes would have done.'

'He was hardly ever at home. He was either working, travelling with work or on holidays with his mates,' Alice said.

'He tried to make it work, Alice. That's all a guy can do. They were never suited. He's happy now.'

'Happy behaving like a teenager. It'll all come crashing down around his ears, Niall, just wait and see. And his kids aren't very happy, are they?' Alice turned to Maggie. 'Max has two teenagers, a fourteen-year-old son and a thirteen-year-old daughter and they're heartbroken.'

'How does that make you feel?' Maggie asked.

'Angry with Max for being a shit dad and putting himself first,' Alice replied.

'That's not fair, Alice,' Niall said. 'He's not a bad father. He sees the kids once a week, usually on Sundays, and sometimes, if they don't have sport, on Saturdays too.'

'Give him a medal. Father of the Year. He fecks off on his family and spends a few measly hours with them on a Sunday.'

'I'm hearing a lot of anger and fear here. Does Max's behaviour make you feel threatened, Alice?'

'Yes,' she admitted quietly. 'Very. Max just woke up one day and walked out the door. Niall could do that to me. If he decided to run off with one of Lizzie's hot friends, there's nothing I could do about it. Overnight your life can change completely and you can't control it and it's frightening, especially when there are innocent children involved whose hearts would be broken.'

Maggie turned to Niall. 'Can you identify what emotions Max's behaviour raises in you, Niall?'

Niall shifted in his seat. 'It's just . . . you know . . . I love my family and the kids and everything, but sometimes, if I'm being honest, sometimes I do think: Is this it? I feel there's more to me than just being a dad, you know? And I suppose maybe I'm just worried that I'm disappearing under the weight of responsibility – kids, mortgage, work, bills – and, well, it can feel suffocating at times.'

'This is a normal reaction,' Maggie said. 'Everyone reaches an age where they think: Is this it? They feel as if it was only yesterday when they were young and carefree and now they have responsibilities and duties that tie them down.'

'Yeah, I suppose that's it. I miss my old life sometimes.'

'Can you understand Alice's fear too?'

He nodded. 'I do, but it's crazy. I don't want to leave Alice. I booked this appointment because I want to fix our marriage, not leave it.'

'Does that reassure you, Alice?' Maggie said. 'Niall is here to get closer to you, not further away.'

'Yes, but lots of couples go to therapy with good intentions and end up realizing their marriage is doomed,' Alice said.

Maggie nodded. 'True, but equally lots of couples seek help and find that they reconnect with each other. It makes their relationship stronger. Okay, let's leave Max to one side for a moment. Can we discuss how you feel about each other? Alice, do you still find Niall attractive?'

Alice blushed. 'Yes.' It was true, she did. He'd aged better than she had. He hadn't put on much weight and his hair was only a little grey. She'd always fancied him. She loved his blue eyes and his smile. His two front teeth had a little gap between them and she'd always found that sexy.

'Niall, do you still find Alice attractive?'

Alice held her breath: he probably didn't any more.

'Yes, I always have.'

Alice exhaled.

'You braced yourself for his answer, Alice.' Maggie smiled kindly at her. 'How do you feel about Niall saying that?'

'Well, I'm glad he does. I suppose I feel relieved.'

'And you, Niall?'

'I'm relieved, too. I was beginning to think Alice had gone off me, to be honest. When someone pushes you away, you presume they don't fancy you.'

Alice felt bad. If Niall pushed her away, she'd feel awful, paranoid and rejected. She hadn't considered that the lack of sex might make him feel unwanted.

'I totally fancy you, Niall. I'm just tired,' she said.

'But when are you not going to be tired?' Niall asked.

'I don't know,' Alice admitted. Maybe she did need to call Lisa's personal trainer and get fit. But the thought of some toned gym bunny shouting at her to run faster and do more push-ups just made her feel weary and a bit sick. She'd rather eat carrots for a few weeks.

Niall sighed.

'It's not easy, Niall. The kids are exhausting.'

'You wanted the third kid, Alice. I said two was enough, but you pushed for the third.'

'Yes, I did. I wanted three kids, but I didn't bargain on having twins, did I?'

'So your youngest children are twins?' Maggie asked.

'Yes, we have a ten-year-old, an eight-year-old, and twins who have just turned six,' Alice explained. 'They're a handful.'

'That's a busy household,' Maggie said, nodding.

'We were just getting our lives back and having some fun again when Alice pushed for another child and then the twins arrived,' Niall said wearily.

'If you're being honest, do you resent Alice for pushing for that third child?'

'A bit, yeah. I love the twins and I wouldn't change it, but they are nuts and they never stop. I'm looking forward to when they calm down.'

'We made the choice to have another child together,' Alice said. Between Niall and her mother, it felt like she was being blamed for having a family. Niall had been every bit as much part of that decision as she had. 'I know they're a bit crazy, but in a good way. They can be so much fun and so sweet at times, too. I've felt swamped, but now that they're in school for a few hours, it's a little bit calmer.'

'You're still exhausted all the time, though,' Niall said.

Alice felt the old anger rising at the accusatory tone in his voice. 'That's because the older they get, the more demanding they are of my attention and my time. Homework and projects and sports and plays and music lessons and all of that stuff.'

'They don't need to do every activity going,' Niall pointed out. 'You're run ragged driving them everywhere.'

'All four of them enjoy doing their activities and they're easier to manage when they're busy. Besides, why do you care? I'm the one driving them around and organizing everything,' Alice snapped.

'I care because you're constantly wrecked,' Niall said. 'You've no energy left for me. You barely even speak to me, never mind have a glass of wine with me when I come in from work. You're usually already in your pyjamas or in bed.'

'Well, if you came home earlier and helped me put them

to bed, I might have more to offer. In fact, if you helped me at all, that would be wonderful. I'm a one-woman show, Niall, juggling absolutely everything. You can't wander in, having done nothing to help me, and expect to be met by a Stepford wife.'

'I'm trying to make senior partner, Alice. I have to work harder than Dana or Roger if I want to get the spot. I'm doing it for us.'

'Fine, but don't swan in at nine o'clock at night and moan about me being tired then.'

'I'm going to interrupt here,' Maggie said calmly. 'This is a sore spot for both of you, judging from the anger and hurt in your voices. So let's take a moment. We've identified a key problem, in that you both want to reconnect with each other, but your busy lives are draining you of time and energy. The solution is a commitment from each of you to make the effort to reach out. Niall, could you commit to coming home earlier maybe two nights a week?'

'I can try, but things come up and the managing partner, Denis, is a ball-breaker. He never goes home. If I leave a meeting to go home and put my kids to bed, he'll think I'm a lightweight. Cases we work on often have last-minute glitches or issues that need attention. I really can't say for definite that I'll be home early on certain nights. If I make senior partner, things will be easier – I'll be able to delegate more – but until then I'll have to work harder than ever. But I will try.'

'Okay, that's fair enough,' Maggie said. 'Alice, can you try to stay up and have a glass of wine and chat to Niall when he comes in maybe two nights a week?'

'I'll try,' Alice said.

'It's important in all relationships to carve out time for each other. You need to prioritize couple time, not just kids and work. So I think what would be helpful for you, and hopefully enjoyable, is a little homework based around regaining some intimacy.'

Alice's head shot up. She eyeballed Maggie. What the hell was she going to make her do?

Maggie smiled reassuringly at her. 'We'll take this slowly so that you don't feel overwhelmed. I'm going to ask you both to choose a night when the kids are asleep and you know you won't be interrupted. I just want you to lie down and massage each other with some nice scented oil. I don't want you to have sex. I don't want Alice to feel any pressure. This is not about sex. This is about physical touch. I just want you to be naked with each other and massage each other. Nothing else, just touch, which is so important in a relationship. Next week, you can tell me how it went and how it felt.'

'Okay, good,' Niall said.

Where the hell am I going to get massage oil? Alice thought. I doubt they have it in Tesco. Oh, God, she'd have to starve herself for the next few days so Niall wasn't massaging her flabby stomach and thighs.

As if reading her mind, Maggie handed her a small bottle of massage oil. 'Try to relax and enjoy it. There's no pressure for it to be perfect. Just touch each other and feel the warmth of your hands.'

Relax? thought Alice. She was already stressed out of her mind about it. Maybe Niall would forget. Maybe they'd never have to come back here. She really didn't want to have to come back and talk more about sex. It was so uncomfortable.

'Thank you so much, Maggie. That was great. See you next week,' Niall said, as he followed his wife out of the room.

Alice squeezed the little bottle so tightly she was amazed it didn't shatter.

15

Orla helped the children with their coats and made sure they all had their backpacks, their water bottles and lunchboxes inside.

'Thank you, Miss Orla,' Lulu said, when Orla handed her the unicorn bottle she had left behind on her desk.

'I wish I had a unicorn bottle,' Poppy said. 'Mine's just a stinky old purple one. Mummy said she's sick of buying pretty bottles because we lose them all the time.'

'My daddy buyed me this.'

'I wish my daddy was like yours. My daddy's always working or on his white couch, watching sport. I'm not allowed to sit on the white couch.'

'My daddy's couch is grey and we sit on it to watch princess movies. But my mummy's couch is cream and I'm never allowed to eat snacks on it.'

No surprise there, Orla thought. She imagined Sonja's furniture being all cream and minimalist and expensive. Poor Lulu was probably afraid to move.

'My mummy doesn't mind if we eat snacks on our TV couch cos it's dark blue and it's already been ruined by Jamie and Sarah spilling.'

'I wish I hadded sisters and brothers.'

Me too, Orla thought.

Poppy's eyes widened. 'Are you crazy, Lulu? I wish I was an only child, like you. You get all the Christmas presents to yourself and no one breaks your toys and eats your food and pushes you and pulls your hair.'

As if on cue, Ted ran up and pulled Poppy's ponytail. 'Come on, Mummy's waiting.'

'See?' Poppy said.

'I suppose so.' Lulu wasn't convinced. 'But you have people to play with.'

'Isn't your mummy having a baby?'

Lulu nodded.

'You'll have someone to play with soon.'

'I don't want that baby. Mummy is tired and grumpy and she says it's because the baby is getting bigger and bigger.'

'My mummy is always tired and she doesn't have a baby in her tummy. Last night she said a bad word to Sarah.'

'What?'

'She said Sarah was "a little bitch",' Poppy whispered.

'Oooh!' Lulu was shocked.

'Then she said she was sorry and hugged Sarah and cried.'

'Okay, girls, that's enough chat, time to go now.' Orla ushered them out of the door. Poor Alice, she thought. She was obviously strung-out. She looked like someone who was being pulled from all sides. The twins were great fun, but they were a handful. Alice was often a bit late dropping them at school and looked like she'd barely had time to get dressed. Orla never gave her a hard time. She could see that Alice had enough on her plate and she was always so apologetic and lovely, and often sent the twins in with homemade flapjacks for her.

Orla looked for Paul in the crowd of parents at the gate. She saw him waving at Lulu and beaming as she ran towards him. He picked her up and swung her around. He caught Orla's eye and smiled at her. She felt herself blushing. This was ridiculous. She turned and walked back into the class-room to hide her red face.

'Miss Orla, might I have a word?' a shrill voice called.

Oh, God, not Judith again. Orla looked at her watch. She had to be on time for her appointment. She'd have to deal with Judith quickly.

She turned to face her. 'How can I help, Judith?'

Judith closed the classroom door behind her and sat down. 'I wanted to talk to you about Miles.'

'Is everything all right?' Orla asked.

Judith pointed out of the window. 'As you can see, Miles is a total bookworm.'

Miles was sitting in the yard waiting for his mother with a book in his lap. He wasn't actually reading, though, he was watching some of the older kids playing.

'I can't get the books away from him. He's a voracious reader. I'd say he reads seven books a week. And his aptitude for maths is astonishing.'

Astonishing? Orla tried not to laugh. Miles was a very average student who was ticking along in the class. He was no maths prodigy.

'The thing is, Orla, he's not being challenged enough in school. I'm concerned that he's suffering from lack of stimulation.'

Orla chose her words carefully. 'Miles is a lovely boy, very polite, very considerate to his classmates, and he's doing well academically. I don't believe he's lacking stimulation. He is engaged during lessons, and while he's keeping up with the classwork, he isn't moving ahead of the others in any way.'

Judith bristled. 'The problem is, you haven't realized how clever he is and that's a worry for me.'

'As I said, Miles is doing well, but he is not top of the class or forging ahead of his classmates.'

'Who is top? Who is the cleverest?' Judith wanted to know.

'It doesn't matter. My point is that Miles is a good student who is challenged.'

Judith stood up. 'Miles is doing two-hundred-piece jigsaws at home. He's an exceptional child and I think it's unfortunate you can't see that. I'll have to speak to Mrs Long about this.'

Go ahead. Run to the headmistress – she'll be a lot blunter than I am, Orla thought. She'll tell you straight up that your kid is average and you're delusional.

'Absolutely. Feel free to speak to Mrs Long,' Orla said. 'Shall I see if she's available?' She stood up. 'We'll go to her office now, shall we?'

Judith looked taken aback. Orla had met mothers like her before and she knew exactly what she was thinking. She saw in Orla a young woman and assumed that meant she would yield under pressure. Others had made that mistake, thinking youth made her easy to manipulate. Orla might be young, but she was no pushover. The quicker Judith grasped that, the better.

'Well, no, I don't have time now. I have to go. I . . . Well, I came in to say I would like you to keep an eye on Miles and nurture his curious mind.'

Orla plastered a smile on her face. 'I can assure you that I nurture all of the children in my class every day.'

'Right, well, thank you for your time.'

'My pleasure. Have a lovely afternoon.' Orla held the door for the delusional mother and let it snap shut after her.

She rubbed her temples. Why couldn't all the parents be like Alice with the twins, or like Paul with Lulu? Loving, kind, affectionate but realistic . . . and, in Paul's case, so attractive.

Orla glanced at the classroom clock. It was later than she'd thought. Bloody Judith and her book-eating child. She grabbed her coat and rushed out of the school. She couldn't be late for this appointment.

*

Orla stood outside the pretty mews, hiding behind the hedge. Her appointment was for three thirty and it was three thirty-five. She had been standing there for fifteen minutes, paralysed. She wanted to go in, but she was terrified. How could she explain to this stranger that she was an embarrassing freak? What if this woman, Maggie Purcell, couldn't help her? What if this was her last chance at a normal life? It had to work. Orla couldn't live like this any more.

She took a deep breath and forced one leg in front of the other. Her hand shook as she rang the buzzer.

The door opened almost immediately.

'There you are,' the woman said. She looked very chic, but her smile was warm and welcoming. 'I was just about to pop my head out to see if you were on the way. Sometimes people find it hard to come in for the first session.'

Orla blushed. She'd been foiled. 'I did struggle to work up the courage,' she admitted.

'Well, I'm glad you managed it,' Maggie said, opening the door wide. 'Come on in.'

Orla followed her to a room and took a seat in a comfy armchair, sitting bolt upright, perched on the edge. Maggie sat opposite her. 'Your body language is speaking volumes, Orla,' she said, with a gentle smile. 'I'd say it took great courage for you to come to see me today. Did it?'

Orla nodded, relieved that Maggie understood how she was feeling. 'It's not something I've done before,' she said. 'I'm not sure I want to be here.'

'That's no problem,' Maggie said. 'It's hard to come into an unknown space with a stranger and talk about personal things. I totally get that you're feeling out of your comfort zone right now. But it's just you and me, and everything said in this room is completely confidential. I'm not going to judge you or demand anything from you. This is your space now, for you to talk about whatever you wish. I will listen and do what I can to help you. Is that okay?'

'That sounds really good,' Orla said. 'Thank you.' Her whole body was beginning to calm down. Maggie was so reassuring and kind that she felt better already. Maybe she'd actually be able to talk to her openly about her issue. Maybe she really would be able to help her.

Maggie smiled encouragingly. 'So, Orla, what would you like to address in this first session?'

Orla took a deep breath and dived in. 'I'm here because I have a problem. I heard you talking about it on TV and I thought maybe you could help me.'

'Can you tell me a little more?'

Orla's face was on fire. She looked down at the pale lilac carpet. 'I . . . The thing is, I . . . I find it difficult . . . well, impossible, actually, to . . . well, to have sex.'

Orla peeped up at Maggie from under her thick fringe. The older woman was completely unfazed.

'What do you feel is stopping you?' Maggie asked.

Orla cringed. 'I kind of clam up. Down there. I think I might have vaginis . . . vaginis . . .'

'Vaginismus.' Maggie helped her out. 'It's a lot more common than people think. I have quite a few clients with this condition. But because women are embarrassed to talk about it, it's a hidden problem, which is a pity because it's nothing to be ashamed about.'

'Really?' Orla looked directly at her for the first time. 'You have other women coming here who have it too?'

Maggie nodded. 'Yes. And it can be a very distressing condition. How has it been for you, Orla? Have you always had problems with vaginal penetration? For example, have you ever been able to use a tampon?'

Orla shook her head. 'Never. I first tried when I was about sixteen and it was a disaster.'

'Right. So you've been experiencing problems with penetration for a long time?'

Orla nodded. Maggie was talking about penetration and vaginismus so matter-of-factly that she began to loosen up – a little.

'I know women with vaginismus find smear tests very difficult. Have you ever had one?' Maggie asked.

Orla reddened. The memory of trying to have a smear made her want to weep. The humiliation of being naked from the waist down with her legs akimbo while the GP tried, in vain, to insert the speculum. Orla had shrieked and fled the clinic without even paying.

'Judging by your face, it didn't go so well.' Maggie smiled sympathetically.

'Disaster,' Orla muttered.

'Most women with vaginismus dread, or completely avoid, having smears.'

Orla exhaled. 'So it's not just me?'

'Not at all. Do you know much about the condition?' Maggie asked.

'Not really. I just thought I was a freak, and then I heard you talking about it.'

'If you take anything from this session today, Orla, I want you to remember this. You are *not* a freak. This is a physical condition, although it can have psychological roots. What's happening is that your body is rejecting penetration of any kind. It's an involuntary spasm of the muscles of the vagina that can make sex or smears or inserting tampons painful or even impossible. It doesn't mean you don't wish to experience penetration. It doesn't mean you have no libido. It doesn't mean you're any less a sexual being than any other woman. It is involuntary and it doesn't define you as a woman, okay?'

Orla nodded.

'Good. Now, we measure vaginismus in three categories, mild, moderate and severe. Where would you say yours is?'

Orla's eyes welled up. 'Severe.'

'Have you ever tried to have sex?'

'Yes, and failed spectacularly every time.'

'That's really tough,' Maggie said gently, handing Orla a tissue. 'But not at all uncommon.'

'It's so humiliating. You're lying there all steamed up and you want sex and he wants sex but when he tries to . . . I just clam up and I can't . . . I just can't let go. Am I frigid? Is that it?'

'No, you are not.' Maggie's voice was firm. 'You have a physical condition. You mustn't beat yourself up. This is not your fault.'

Orla wiped her eyes. 'Can you fix me?' she whispered.

'You're not broken, Orla,' Maggie said. 'But I know what you mean when you talk of being fixed. You'd like your body to respond as you want to, so that you can enjoy sex and have confidence in your relationships, right?'

Orla nodded. 'I hate being like this. I don't feel like I'm really a woman.'

'Regardless of what society would have you believe, being penetrated is not the definition of a woman. We're so much more than that. You're saying you'd like to be "fixed", but the answer we find may not be the one you were expecting. First off, the thing about patients with conditions like vaginismus is that there is no single, definitive answer. So I can't promise you a straight-up cure. However, I have helped some women to go on to have a normal sex life. With others, though, I've helped them to learn to work around their condition and not to feel broken by it, as you currently feel. So, right now, I can't tell you what your outcome will be, Orla, but I promise I'll do my very best to help you. Now, have you been to the doctor and been checked out so we can rule out any medical issues?'

'Yes. I've been told that I'm "normal" down there.' Orla laughed bitterly.

'You are normal, Orla,' Maggie reminded her. 'There are many women just like you and they're normal, too. For today, I think the best thing we can do is to explore how you feel about sex and intimacy in general, and what your childhood was like. Vaginismus can often stem from some incident that happened during a woman's past. So, can you take me back to your childhood and tell me what growing up was like for you?'

'How long have you got?' Orla said.

'Talk to me.'

Orla sighed and sat back in the comfortable chair. Maggie was so calming. Her heart rate was slowing and she wasn't frightened any more. She felt safe here.

'My mum died giving birth to me and my father has always blamed me for her death. He adored my mother and he feels that I stole the great love of his life. He lost his beloved wife and got a screaming baby instead.'

'I'm so sorry. It must have been really hard for you, growing up without a mother.'

'Oh, no. I did grow up with a mother – she was everywhere. There were photos of her in every room. I come from a small town in the west of Ireland and my mother is buried in the graveyard beside the church. My father made me visit her grave every Sunday after mass. He also had a special mass said for her on the first Friday of every month. On her birthday he bought a cake and we sang "Happy Birthday" to an empty chair. On Christmas Day he had presents for her that would never be opened. My mother was everywhere. I couldn't get away from her. I actually grew up hating my mother. I hated her for dying and I hated her for never being dead. She was ever-present. My father was the greatest widower that ever lived. He has been grieving relentlessly for twenty-four years. Joseph Kane, king of grief, champion of grievers. If there was an Olympics for grief, he would have won the gold medal for Ireland every year.'

Orla stopped to take a breath and looked at Maggie in astonishment. Had all of that just come out of her mouth? She had never told anyone her real feelings about her father, had never told anyone that his grief made her furious and had never admitted that she hated her mother for ruining her life. 'I'm sorry,' Orla said, 'I shouldn't have said that.'

Maggie shook her head. 'You absolutely should have said it, Orla, because it's quite clear that it's your truth. You're here to explore your true feelings and emotions. Being honest about how you feel is an essential part of therapy. I'm not at all surprised that you have complex feelings about your mother – and about your father. It must have been incredibly lonely to grow up in the shadow of a deified ghost. That's a heavy burden to carry.'

Orla's eyes filled with tears. 'It was, but I've never told anyone how I really feel about it all.'

'Well, that's a huge first step towards healing, Orla. I'm proud of you for being so honest. It gives us the best start possible to help you. But what about you? How was your relationship with your father growing up?'

Orla shrugged. 'My existence reminded him of what he'd lost, so he found it difficult to love me. He wasn't cruel or anything, just distant and awkward around me.'

'Can you remember a time when it didn't feel as if he was distant and awkward?'

Orla shook her head. Her father had never hugged her or kissed her like other dads did. He had patted her on the back when she won the class prize in English. He had squeezed her shoulder when she left home to move to Dublin. He had congratulated her when she qualified as a primary-school teacher, but fatherly affection – never.

'No. He was never tactile or talked to me like other dads talked to their kids.'

'Was there anyone else you felt close to growing up?'

'I had Shannon, my best friend. She had her own family problems, so we bonded over that. She would hug me and tell me she was proud of me, and I'd do the same for her.'

'Are you still friends?'

'Yes, but she lives in America now, so I hardly ever see her. I miss her.'

'Were there any relations around you growing up? Any aunts or uncles or grandparents?'

'My father's an only child. His mother died when he was six, and when he was twenty his father died and left him the farm. My mother's parents and brother moved to Canada twenty-eight years ago. They tried to get Dad to send me over to them, but he wouldn't. He said my mother wanted me to grow up on a farm, surrounded by nature. She wanted me to be raised in Ireland and have a magical childhood.' Orla began to sob again. 'Magical? God, Mum, if only you knew.'

Maggie handed her another tissue. 'So who did you go to, to ask about periods and sex and to buy a bra with?'

'Shannon's mum was really nice to me. Her dad was an alcoholic, but her mum was lovely. She had a lot to deal with, but she was kind. She took me and Shannon to get our first bras together and she showed me where to buy sanitary pads and what to do with them. She told my dad that I needed an allowance for women's things, which he was only too happy not to have to discuss, so I looked after all that myself. I just remember feeling lonely all the time.'

'How did you cope with the loneliness?'

'I read, I watched movies, I studied hard and I ran. I ran a lot. I joined a local athletics club. It helped me cope. Running was a safe place. It still is. My brain switches off when I run.'

'That's great. It's so important to have a physical outlet. So, talk to me about your first sexual experience, your first kiss.'

Orla tucked her hair behind her ears. 'I kissed boys as a teenager and fumbled about a bit, but in a small town everyone knows everything, so I didn't go very far with anyone. I met my first actual boyfriend when I moved to Dublin.' She paused, needing to gather herself to continue.

Maggie sat back and watched her in silence.

'His name was Mike, and he was gorgeous. He was on my teacher-training course. Tall, dark, handsome. He was from Cork and didn't know anyone I knew. He was a fresh start, a new beginning. I couldn't believe it when he told me he fancied me – me! We got together and kissed and went back to his place. I wanted to have sex with him, I was totally up for it, but I just froze and clammed up. He couldn't get inside me. I pretended I was just nervous. The second time we tried, I got really drunk. I thought it would help me relax. It was fine initially, I got excited and turned on when he touched me, but – but then he tried to put his finger into my vagina and I clammed up again. We tried a few more times to have sex, but I could never get my body to open up. He thought it was because I didn't fancy him physically, so he broke up with me.'

'How did you react to that?'

'I felt ashamed, humiliated, like a freak of nature, completely hopeless.'

'And how did you deal with all those emotions?'

'I ran a lot. Forrest Gump has nothing on me. I listened to a lot of angry rap music. I drank a bottle of wine every night just to get to sleep. I was a mess, but I moved on. I guess having a shitty childhood makes you quite resilient.'

'Have you tried to have sex since then?'

'Oh, yes, I've had three more excruciating incidents and now I've stopped trying. I can't put myself through it any more.'

'I'm so sorry you've had such a hard time, Orla. But I don't think it's surprising you've experienced this, given that your whole life has been overshadowed by your mother's death during childbirth and the fact that your father became stuck in his grief. Do you think that perhaps, because of all that, you associate sex and vaginas with negative rather than positive emotions?'

Orla hadn't thought about it like that. Maybe she did have a block because of her mother's death and her father's coldness. Was that what this was all about? Did she associate sex with grief or death on some subconscious level?

'Maybe,' she said uncertainly. 'I hadn't thought of it like that before.'

'What goes through your mind when a man tries to penetrate you?'

'Fear. I just panic. I don't know why because I'm fine with . . . you know . . . touching down there and I do get turned on and want him, but I'm not okay with . . . when . . . if . . .'

'If a finger or penis tries to penetrate you?' Maggie said.

'Yes.'

'Do you anticipate that it's going to hurt you?'

'Yes, and also I just feel scared, like something bad will happen. I can't explain it. I just seize up.'

Maggie nodded. 'The anticipation of pain can cause the

body to tighten the vaginal muscles automatically. With vaginismus, the mind and body develop a muscle-memory response against penetration of any kind – whether it's a tampon, a finger or a penis.'

'Oh, right. So even though I want it, my muscles sort of take over and clamp shut?'

'Exactly. It's not a conscious reaction. If it was, you could control it. This is coming from your subconscious, and of course our subconscious is where our inner child lives. And your inner child is traumatized and hurt and lonely, Orla, and might be afraid of letting people in because there's a fear there that it will all go horribly wrong. Your mother died in childbirth, and I think, on that deeper level, you're terrified of the same thing happening to you.'

'I can't believe I hadn't seen that before,' Orla said. 'When you say it, it kind of sounds obvious. Logical, I suppose. I just never thought of it that way.'

'Talking about things openly helps us to make sense of our issues and see them more clearly,' Maggie said, smiling at her. 'I'd like to hear a little more about your father. Have you ever tried to talk to him about your grief and pain around your mother's death?'

Orla sighed. 'On my thirteenth birthday – which was obviously also the thirteenth anniversary of my mother's death – Dad was going on and on and on about how much he missed her and how it wasn't the same without her and I snapped. I shouted, "I miss her too, Dad! I lost someone that day too! My mother!"'

'How did he react?' Maggie asked.

Orla laughed bitterly. 'Oh, the usual Dad stuff – how he'd loved her for years and his pain was acute. How I had never known her and how you can't really miss what you never had.'

'How did that make you feel?'

'Furious, but I knew then that there was no point in ever trying to talk to him about how I felt. He won't listen. He's so wrapped up in his obsessive grief that he isn't capable of ever seeing my side. It's all about him.'

'Perhaps we can look at ways you could talk to him now, as an adult, or maybe even write to him. Sometimes writing down how you feel can be a better way to get through to someone who finds it hard to listen.'

Orla shook her head. 'Honestly, there's no point. I want to forget him and fix myself.'

'I understand, but working through your feelings about your father is going to be an important part of healing.'

'Okay . . . but is there anything else I can do, something practical? I looked up vaginismus online and saw that there are dilators you can use to train your vagina. I've ordered some. They should arrive soon. Might they work, do you think?'

Maggie nodded. 'Sure, we can combine therapy with vaginal trainers that may help retrain the muscles. But only if you feel you want to. Only if you feel ready. There is no rush. We could wait until we've done a few more sessions.'

'I want to do everything I can. And I want to start now. Let's do both.'

'If you're sure, I want you to start off very gently with the smallest dilator, and if you don't like using it, stop. There is no pressure to do this. See how you get on over the next week with the smallest one. But, as I said, if you find you're getting worked up or stressed about it, stop. Opening up about your past, the way you have today, is a really big first step.'

'I'll try the dilators. I really want to fix this.' Orla reached over and took a long drink of water.

Maggie placed a card on the table in front of Orla. 'I'm

going to give you my mobile number. It might be an idea to call me before you try the dilators, or if you're struggling with them. I don't want you to push yourself too hard at this early stage.'

'Thank you.' Orla put the card carefully into her bag. She looked at Maggie's kind face. She hadn't planned on mentioning Paul, but Maggie was so sympathetic and Orla was desperate to confide in someone.

'The thing is . . . the reason I want to push myself now is that . . . You see, I'd cut myself off completely from sex. I go out with my flatmate, who is a sex maniac, and I kiss guys and then I go home alone. I don't let myself fancy people or allow myself to think that I'll ever have a relationship, but I've met this man and he's . . . I dunno . . . he's . . .' Orla ran her hands through her hair. 'It's going to sound so silly, but I felt a bolt of electricity when he shook my hand. His name is Paul. He's the dad of a kid in my class. He's separated and he's so lovely. I've never had such a strong physical reaction to someone. And he's not extremely handsome or anything. There's just something really attractive about him and he's a really nice person, too. Now whenever I see him, I feel all shaky, like a teenager. I don't even know if he notices me. Sometimes when he picks Lulu up he waves and smiles at me – which I know means nothing and I'm sure I sound like a ridiculous fifteen-year-old girl. I guess I'm kind of stunted when it comes to relationships because I've never had a proper one. When I see Paul, I get butterflies and I'm scared. I want him to ask me out, but if he does, he'll find out I'm abnormal and he'll run like all the others.'

'Now hold on there a minute, Orla,' Maggie said. 'We need to scratch words like *abnormal* and *freak* from your vocabulary because you're neither. You're a lovely, strong, resilient, brilliant young woman with your whole life ahead of you.

Feeling physically attracted to this man, Paul, is a good thing. What we're going to do together is talk through your fears and worries and look at the potential cause of the vaginismus from all angles.'

'Will I be able to have sex? Can you fix that?'

'As I said, some women can do so after therapy, some never find penetrative sex comfortable. But those women still have a great sex life. There are lots of ways to make love that don't involve a penis entering a vagina. We're schooled to think like that, but once you open your mind to wider possibilities, there's a whole world of intimacy for you to explore and enjoy.'

Orla was listening to Maggie, but she didn't want that. She wanted Maggie to make her a proper woman, who could have sex with a guy. She was going to use those bloody dilators and make herself normal. A normal woman that someone like Paul could fall for, not a frigid loser. She was going to force her body into being normal and that was all there was to it.

16

Alice scrubbed the floor around the toilet with bleach while Poppy howled from her bedroom next door.

'Mummy, I think I'm dying.'

No, you're not, you're just puking everywhere except into the sodding toilet. Alice just couldn't understand why Poppy couldn't vomit into the bowl. She vomited beside it, behind it, in front of it and all over it, but not actually into it.

'Mumm-*yyyyyyyyyy* . . .'

Alice rinsed the cloth in scalding water and went in to check on her dying swan.

Poppy was lying on top of her bed in her fifth set of pyjamas that day. They were her princess ones with a tutu attached to the bottoms. She lay with her arms and legs splayed. 'Can you die from vomiting?' she asked.

'No, pet.'

'What if you puke for weeks and weeks? I bet you'd die then.'

'Poppy, it's a vomiting bug that's going around. You'll be fine. It only lasts two days so you should start feeling better soon.'

'I won't be able to go to school for weeks. I'm very sick.'

Over my dead body, Alice thought. She'd had Ted puking all weekend and now Poppy. She'd had to cancel her appointment to get her hair coloured for the third time. She looked like a badger, her dark brown-grey roots showing the world her true colour. She was going to her friend Valerie's fortieth birthday lunch on Saturday and she had to get her hair done before then. She'd kind of hoped to get the vomiting bug from Ted earlier in the week so she could lose a few pounds. But now it was Wednesday, and if she caught it from Poppy, she'd be feeling awful for Saturday, so she was trying to look after her daughter without catching it.

'Mummy, the scarf around your face is kind of rude,' Poppy said.

'It's just so I don't catch the bug. Because if I do, who's going to look after you?'

'Daddy could.'

'Daddy is working very hard at the moment, so he couldn't.'

'I bet you Daddy wouldn't say bad words when I puke on the carpet.'

I bet you Daddy would say words that would make your head spin, Alice thought. As well as vomiting in the bathroom, Poppy had also managed it all over the carpet in the master bedroom and the duvet cover. Alice had spent hours scrubbing to get the smell out of the carpet.

'When I feel better, I want a ginormous chocolate chip muffin and a big doughnut with sprinkles all over it.'

'That would just make you vomit again.'

'Ted said you gave him a doughnut when he felt better.'

'Yes, I did, a plain one. You can have that too.'

'But I want one with sprinkles from the doughnut shop in town.'

'Let's get you better first.'

'I want to watch TV in your bed,' Poppy said.

'Okay, but only if you have the bucket beside you at *all* times. Do you understand?'

'You don't have to be so grumpy. I'm sick, you know.'

Poppy flounced into Alice and Niall's bedroom and snuggled under the fresh duvet cover. Alice handed her a bucket and the remote control. She kissed her head.

'It's not a real kiss cos you have the scarf on. A real mummy would kiss her little girl properly.'

Alice pulled down the scarf and gave Poppy a big wet kiss on her hot little cheek.

'Too much, Mummy. Just a normal kiss, please,' she squealed, but she was smiling.

Alice stroked her daughter's cheek and headed downstairs to boil the cloths she had used to clean the bathroom and put on yet another wash.

Two days later, Alice was walking into the hair salon with a take-out coffee in her hand, looking forward to three hours of reading magazines and getting honey highlights put into her dull hair, when her phone rang. It was the school. She didn't want to answer it. Calls from the school were never good news. They never rang to tell you what a fantastic child you had, or that your child had been kind to someone or had won a prize, only if there was trouble or sickness. Alice wanted desperately to ignore the call, but what if it was important?

She swiped and held the phone to her ear. 'Hi, Alice, Siobhan here from the school. Jamie has vomited and is feeling quite unwell. Looks like he has the bug that's going around. Can you pick him up?'

What Alice thought was, No, no, I cannot pick him up. If I pick him up, I'll miss my hair appointment. I don't want to look a state tomorrow in front of Valerie and all her glossy friends. It's Friday, and this is my last chance. But what she said was, 'Of course. I'm on my way.'

She rang Niall. No answer. She rang him again and again until he picked up.

'Hi, is it urgent? I can't really talk. I'm just heading into a meeting.'

'Yes, it is bloody urgent. I need you to pick up Jamie from school. He's got the bug.'

'I can't. I just told you, I'm about to walk into a meeting with my biggest client. Why aren't you picking him up? What are you doing?'

'I'm at the hairdresser's getting my colour done. Please, Niall, please just pick him up. I'll be home by one.'

'Alice, I can't cancel a meeting because you're getting your hair done. Just book another appointment.'

'I have,' she hissed. 'This is my fourth attempt to get my hair done.'

'So, cancel and make another. I'm in work, Alice. Sorry, but I've got to go.' Click. He hung up.

'Selfish bastard,' Alice shouted into the phone.

She tried her mother. 'Mum, I'm sorry to call you in work, but is there any chance you or Lisa could pick up Jamie and hold on to him for a couple of hours? He has the vomiting bug and I'm just about to get my hair coloured for a girls' lunch tomorrow.'

'Oh, Alice, I'm sorry, but I can't. Two of my staff called in sick because of the bug. Lisa and I are on our own here today. You can drop him into the pharmacy and we'll put him in the back and keep an eye on him, if that helps.'

'No, it'll take me too long to get him to you and the appointment will be gone.' Alice's voice shook. 'I asked Niall, but of course he's too bloody busy.'

'He can't help being busy in work, Alice.'

'I know, but I've had to cancel this appointment three times already because of the bug. Could he not do me this favour for once in his busy life?'

'Alice, blaming Niall is not going to help. We have some good hair products here. You could colour it yourself at home.'

I don't want to do it myself at home, Alice wanted to scream. I want to sit down in an actual salon and have it done for me. Besides, she knew she'd do a bad job, and she wanted to look nice and glossy, for the other women at the lunch to look at her hair and not her chubby stomach.

'It's fine, don't worry. I'll just put it up in a ponytail or something.'

'Alice,' her mother said, in her listen-to-me voice. 'I know you're upset, but don't take this out on Niall. It's not his fault.'

Alice sighed. 'I know. I'm just fed up.'

'It's hard when the kids are sick. Take a breath and put it into perspective. It's just a hair appointment. If you like, I can come around after work and help you dye it, but it won't be until well after nine. We're open late.'

'It's fine, Mum, don't worry.'

'You need to sort out some kind of back-up help, Alice. You can't seem to manage it all yourself.'

'Most of the time I can. They just all happen to be sick this week.' Alice was in no mood for a lecture on how she wasn't organized enough or coping efficiently with her four children.

Her mother and Lisa were similar in their *über*-organized personalities. Alice had always been more relaxed and less uptight about time management and routine. It drove them mad, and it drove her mad that they were so inflexible.

'Sorry I can't help. I have to go. We're crazy busy here. I hope Jamie feels better soon. Make sure you get liquids into him. Bye.'

Busy, busy, busy. Everyone was so busy. Alice turned around and walked back to the car.

She cried all the way to the school. She wiped her eyes and went in to get her son. Jamie was sitting in a chair, as pale as a ghost.

'Sorry, Mum,' he said, when he saw her.

Alice's heart melted. She put her arms around him and hugged him. 'Don't ever be sorry for being sick.'

'I know, but you've had to look after the twins all week and now me too. I promise I'll puke into the toilet bowl.'

'Oh, Jamie, love, please don't worry about anything but getting better. Come on, let's get you home and snuggle you up.'

Jamie put his hot, sticky hand into hers. 'Thanks, Mum. If you get the bug, I promise I'll look after you.'

'You're an angel, Jamie.'

Alice turned away so Jamie wouldn't see her tears. She felt guilty for even thinking about not picking him up. He was a sick child. Her sick child. It was her job to look after him. She felt guilty for being so selfish about her stupid hair. Jamie needed her.

Later, when he had fallen into a sweaty sleep in her bed, Alice tidied up around him. She put away the books she had been reading to him, put the TV remote on her bedside locker, and that was when she saw it. The massage oil.

Damnit. She'd forgotten about it, with all the vomiting and cleaning. Maybe Niall had too. She hid the bottle in her bedside drawer, underneath a pile of receipts and cards from the children. Out of sight, out of mind. The last thing in the world she wanted to do right now was massage Niall's hairy back.

That night, Alice woke up with the bug. She missed Valerie's birthday lunch. She tried not to turn green with envy as she studied the posts of everyone looking gorgeous and having a wonderful time. She needed a day out, a day when she got dressed up, left her family to go and drink prosecco with girlfriends, get giddy and go dancing. A day when she didn't feel like a fat, frumpy mother of four.

Although, if she was being totally honest, a tiny part of her was relieved. Her hair was a mess and the dress she had wanted to wear was too tight, even with industrial strength Spanx. She knew she would have felt fatter than everyone else and less interesting. The eight women Valerie had invited were all fellow journalists, girls she'd met in college or through work. Two were married without kids, two were single and the other four were married with kids, but they all worked. Alice would have felt a bit inadequate. What did she have to contribute to the conversation when they talked about juicy news stories, political shenanigans, healthcare scandals and work–life balance?

Her work–life balance was – scrub, shop, cook, help with homework, stuff her face with chocolate biscuits and repeat.

On Monday night, when Alice and Niall had finished chasing their now healthy kids around and into bed, Alice went into their bedroom and put on her pyjamas. It was nine thirty and she'd had enough of today and this poxy week. After a weekend in bed vomiting, when Niall had had to look after the kids and let her sleep, Alice felt much better. She was still tired from the bug, but almost back to normal. She was very much looking forward to watching an episode of *Poldark* in peace, ogling Aidan Turner striding about, his chest bare.

She was fast forwarding to the part where Aidan takes his top off when Niall came into the room.

'So.'

Alice frowned. 'So, what?'

'So, we're seeing Maggie soon and we need to do our homework, remember?'

Damn. Alice had thought he'd forgotten. Fat chance.

'Niall, I've had a crappy week and I'm wrecked. Can we just

pretend we did it? Or maybe we should cancel the appointment. We don't need her.'

Niall stood with his hands on his hips. 'No, Alice, we can't. The problem with us is that we keep putting things off. I'm wrecked, too, from looking after the kids all weekend. Maggie said we had to schedule time for us. Remember? It's just a massage. It'll do you good to have a nice massage.'

I don't want a massage! I just want to be left alone! Alice wanted to scream. But she pushed down her feelings and prepared to do something she didn't want to do to keep Niall happy.

'Come on, we need to work on this together.'

'Okay,' she said. It was just a massage, she told herself. She'd only have to take her top off and hopefully it'd be over quickly.

She fished the oil out of her drawer and turned around. Niall had whipped his clothes off and was naked on the bed beside her. That was quick. Alice reluctantly took her pyjama top off.

'And the bottoms.'

'Why?'

'Because it's a full-body massage.'

'That's not what she said.' Alice wasn't having this.

'Yes, she did.'

'No, it isn't. A back massage was what she meant.'

'No, she meant a full-body. It's supposed to be sensual.'

'It's not supposed to lead to sex. She said no sex,' Alice reminded him.

'I know that, but it's about touch.'

'So touch my back and I'll touch yours.'

'For goodness' sake, Alice.'

'What?'

'Just give me the oil.' Niall grabbed it from her.

Alice lay down on her stomach and tried to unclench her jaw as he poured oil all over her back. It began to drip down her sides onto the duvet. The duvet she had changed four times that week due to vomit stains.

'You put too much on – it's dripping. You're supposed to rub it into your hands first.'

'I'm new to this. Relax.' Niall began rubbing the oil all over her back, but some of it still dripped down. It was also going into her hair and her pants. Oil was really hard to get out of clothes and duvet covers and her hair looked bad enough without adding oil to it.

'Alice, your body is rigid, relax.' Niall rubbed his hands up and down her back and up her neck into her hair.

She tried, she really did. She tried closing her eyes and breathing deeply. She tried to enjoy the rubbing, but she just couldn't. Oil was getting onto her earrings now. She felt greasy and wet and the bloody duvet cover was ruined and her hair was full of greasy oil and she'd have to wash it now. She began to squirm.

'Chill out, Alice.'

'I can't. Stop.' Alice wriggled away from her husband's hands and stood up. 'I can't do this. The oil is going everywhere and all I can think about is that we'll have to change the bed before we go to sleep and the oil will probably stain the actual duvet as well and –'

'Jesus Christ, who cares? Who cares about the bloody duvet? Can you for once stop thinking about everything except us? Just focus on us.'

'I tried. I just can't relax. Look, get a big bath towel and put it under you – actually, get two because the oil is very greasy – and then I'll massage you. Wash your hands before you lie down, though, because they're covered with oil.'

Niall bit his lower lip. Inhaling deeply, he snapped, 'No,

thanks. Funnily enough, I'm just not in the mood now.' He grabbed his clothes and stormed out of the room.

Alice looked down at the oil-stained duvet cover and sighed. She pulled out a fresh one and began to change it.

17

Ann and Ken sat in stony silence in their respective chairs.

Maggie watched them closely. 'So, how has your week been? Did you get a chance to practise holding hands?'

Ann said nothing. She felt depleted. The party had been the last straw. She hadn't even made an effort today. She'd put on her oldest, comfiest jeans and a baggy jumper. What was the point in making an effort for a man who didn't even notice?

Ken, embarrassed by the silence, said, 'It felt a bit awkward and forced. Look, I don't mean to be rude, but I don't need some therapist to tell me to hold my wife's hand.'

Ann snapped out of her silence. 'Really? Don't you? So when have you held my hand then, or will you ever? Mmm? Tell me, because I'd really like to know.'

Ken stared at her. 'I'm just saying that this is not the answer,' he said, pointing at Maggie.

'What is, then?' Ann crossed her arms and glared at her husband.

'I don't know . . . Maybe we could go away for a night and talk.'

'Why can't we talk now?'

'Because I don't want to talk about personal things in front of a stranger,' he said.

Maggie stepped in. 'Ken, I understand that you feel uncomfortable, but perhaps you could talk about why holding hands with Ann felt awkward.'

He shrugged. 'It felt fake.'

'Why do you think holding hands with your wife felt fake?'

'Because we were doing it as homework, not naturally.'

'Do you ever hold hands naturally?' Maggie asked.

'Well, not recently, I guess, but we . . . I mean . . . we . . .'

'Never.' Ann wasn't letting Ken get away with anything today. She'd had enough.

'Not never,' Ken said.

'Never,' she snapped.

Ken said nothing.

'Okay. So we've established that at this time you're not physically interacting and touching each other has become awkward. Let's go back to when you were having sex. What was it like? Did you enjoy it? What did you like doing in bed?' Maggie asked.

Silence. Maggie sat back and let it settle around them. Silence was a very powerful tool in therapy.

Ann sat still while Ken twisted his hands together. Eventually he coughed and said, 'Well, I guess we had a normal . . . you know . . . uhm . . . sex life.'

'What did you like doing? For example, what was your favourite sexual position?'

'Well, now, I'm not sure about all of that. It's very personal stuff.'

'He preferred me to be on top,' Ann said.

Ken looked surprised, then nodded. 'Yeah, I guess I did.'

'Did you like being on top?' Maggie asked Ann.

Did she? Ann supposed she did. She'd preferred being under Ken, though. She'd liked feeling the weight of him on her. There was something comforting about it.

'I didn't mind, but I prefer to be on the bottom.'

'Really?' Ken was surprised.

'Yes.'

'You never said.'

166

'You never asked.'

Silence.

'Did you have regular orgasms when you had sex?' Maggie said.

'Jesus Christ,' Ken muttered.

Ann was feeling braver now. It was awkward and embarrassing discussing their sex life, but that was what they were there for, to mend their broken relationship.

'Sometimes. Maybe half the time.'

'Hold on a minute.' Ken's chest puffed out. 'More than that, Ann – come on now, be fair.'

'I'm being generous, Ken,' Ann said.

'What? You always seemed to be . . . to be . . . . well, to be satisfied.'

Ann shrugged. 'I faked it. All women do.'

Ken was affronted. 'Are you kidding me?'

'Nope.'

'So you're telling me that you only felt satisfied fifty per cent of the time?'

'Probably forty, to be honest.'

'Well, why the hell didn't you say anything? Why would you pretend?'

'Because I wanted you to feel good and I didn't really mind anyway. I'd just masturbate in the bath afterwards.'

'WHAT?' Ken almost fell off his chair. 'You did what?'

'I masturbated, Ken. These days, I watch porn and masturbate. It's the only action I get.'

Ken stared at his wife in shock.

'Women masturbate, Ken. They have needs and wants too,' Maggie said gently. 'Ann faking an orgasm doesn't mean you're a bad lover. It just means she wanted you to feel good.'

Ken was still staring at Ann. 'But when and . . . and . . .'

167

'In the bath and in bed. Sometimes I watch a little porn on my laptop and sometimes I just close my eyes and fantasize.' Ann wanted to shock Ken. She wanted to shake him out of his life coma. She wanted him to wake up and see her as a woman, a sexual being, not just the woman he lived with. She realized she was actually enjoying watching him squirm and being taken aback by her disclosures.

'Do you masturbate, Ken?' Maggie asked.

Ken took a deep breath and composed himself. 'All men do.'

'How often?'

'Not like I used to. I dunno, maybe once every few weeks or so.'

Maggie turned back to Ann. 'When you fantasize, what or who are you thinking of?'

'Oh, I'm kind of boring really. It's not dominatrix or anything kinky. It usually involves me and George Clooney in an office and he pushes me over the desk and takes me from behind.'

Ken stood up. 'Jesus, Ann,' he spluttered.

'What? I'm telling the truth, Ken. I haven't had sex in years – I have to get my kicks somehow.'

Maggie motioned for Ken to sit back down, which he did, reluctantly.

'How about you, Ken? Do you have fantasies?'

'I cannot have this conversation. Can we please leave, Ann?'

'No, we can't. I know this is hard, but you have to try.'

Ken folded his arms. 'I like straightforward sex. I'm not into anything weird.'

'But do you ever fantasize about oral sex, or threesomes or, like Ann, being intimate with someone you find very attractive?'

'Do you really want me to answer that?' Ken asked his wife. 'Honestly?'

'Yes.'

'Well, I guess I have occasionally thought about receiving oral sex from Jennifer.'

'Jennifer who?' Ann asked. 'Oh, I know, Jennifer Aniston – you always liked her in *Friends.*'

'Not her, no.'

'Jennifer Lopez?'

'No.'

'Jennifer Lawrence? She's a bit young, but I suppose it's okay in a fantasy.'

'No.'

Ann was getting irritated. 'Who, then?'

'Jennifer Hogan.'

Ann recoiled in her chair. Jennifer Hogan? The mother of their daughter Zoë's best friend?

'Jennifer Hogan, Kelly's mum?'

Ken nodded.

'You fantasize about our daughter's best friend's mother giving you a blowjob?'

'You wanted me to be honest, so now you have the truth. The answer is, sometimes, yes.'

'How long has this been going on?'

'I dunno. A while, I guess.'

'We've known her for about fifteen years. Have you been thinking about this all that time? Were you thinking it when she came to pick Kelly up? Did something happen between you? Did you have an affair with Jennifer Hogan, Ken?'

'No, I did not.'

'Did she give you a blowjob when my back was turned?' Ann's mind was whirring. 'Was she giving you oral sex when you dropped Zoë over for sleepovers?'

'I never did anything with her. You asked if I had a fantasy and I told you. You're the one who wanted to open up this conversation. You're the one who wanted to be honest and talk about our feelings. You're the one who dragged me here and forced me to talk about things no man should have to talk about in front of a stranger. So don't you start giving me a hard time.'

Ann was fuming. Jennifer Hogan was a low blow. Her fantasy had been about a man she'd never meet. Ken's was about a woman he'd met hundreds of times and had had plenty of opportunity to have oral and any other kind of sex with.

'I'd like to remind you both that we're in the realm of fantasy here,' Maggie said. 'Some people like fantasies to be fantastical – the idea of someone they'll never meet allows their imagination to run wild safely. That'd be your George Clooney dream, Ann. But for others, they get that same frisson from imagining someone real, someone they know, doing stuff they never will. It doesn't mean they ever intend to do anything in real life with that person.'

That was all well and good, Ann thought, but still – Jennifer Hogan, for the love of God!

'Do you still think about her that way?'

'Sometimes, I guess.'

'Do you think you enjoy this fantasy, Ken, because oral sex is something you particularly enjoy receiving?' Maggie said.

'What man doesn't?'

'And is that something you used to do to each other?' Maggie asked.

It was Ann's turn to squirm. She hated giving blowjobs. Always had. She'd done it a few times when they were first dating, but then she'd stopped. It had always made her gag and she'd felt as if she was going to choke. She hadn't known that Ken had been thinking about blowjobs for all these years – and with Jennifer bloody Hogan.

'Ann isn't keen on it.'

Ann felt she needed to defend herself. Ken was getting in some serious punches. 'I find it very uncomfortable. I think it's fair enough not to feel obliged to do something that makes you gag.'

'I never forced you to do anything,' Ken reminded her.

'I never said you did, but now you're all "Oh, I love blow-jobs and I want them from Jennifer."'

Ann grabbed her glass of water and drank deeply. To hell with Ken and his fantasies. Why couldn't he dream about celebrities he'd never meet instead of someone so bloody accessible?

'Ann, do you think oral sex is something you could revisit? There are techniques that you can learn to make the experience enjoyable and sensual for both of you.'

Ann didn't want to go to Blowjob School. She just wanted affection and sex, plain old sex, with her husband. More than that, she wanted him to hold her hand and kiss her and talk to her and laugh with her. She just wanted him to be like he used to be, when they were young. She didn't see why she had to learn how to give great oral sex. The therapy was supposed to fix Ken, not her. She wasn't the problem.

'How do you feel about giving oral sex?' Maggie asked Ken.

'I'm okay about it. We never really did it. Ann never seemed comfortable with it. She always seemed to prefer to have sex and not anything oral.'

Ann threw her hands in the air. 'I like sex, normal stick-it-in sex. What's wrong with that? Why am I suddenly the one who is abnormal? How did I suddenly become the problem here?'

Maggie held up the palms of her hands. 'We're just trying to explore your likes and dislikes and looking at ways to reignite your desires. Would you like to do something that would turn Ken on?'

'Does it have to be a blowjob?'

'No, but I wonder if your resistance stems from bad experience. Perhaps it's something you could explore and even grow to enjoy if you had the correct technique.'

Ann sighed. 'Fine. What technique?'

Maggie said she'd write down the name of some websites that had good demonstrations and guidelines for oral sex practices. 'Is there something Ken could do to turn you on?'

'Well, he can't turn into George Clooney, so I'd be happy with him just holding my hand, kissing me and hugging me. I'm not demanding much, just a little affection.' Ann's voice quivered. All she wanted was to be a couple again. She wanted Ken to love her again, look at her, hold her. Why was it so difficult? Why did she feel that now the onus was on her?

Maggie glanced at the clock. 'All right, our time is up. For next week, your homework is to hold hands and to hug. Ken, I want you to turn off the TV, look into Ann's eyes and talk to her. Ann, I want you to look at the websites I've written down. You don't need to do anything. This is just a gentle exploration.'

She stood up and shook their hands.

Ann and Ken walked out in silence. Ken tried to hold her hand as they walked towards the car, but Ann snatched it away. She was upset and felt pressurized into becoming the queen of oral sex or her husband would be down to Jennifer Hogan's house getting satisfied there.

18

Zoë hung up the phone and frowned.

'Is everything all right?' Orla asked.

Zoë rubbed her eye, smudging her freshly applied mascara. 'It's my mum. She just seems really down. I know she's missing John, but it's more than that. I think she's really had it with Dad. I don't blame her, really. I mean, Dad's great, but he's not exactly Mr Lively. He keeps banging on about being nearly seventy, like seventy's the end of the world. Look at Joe Biden, for goodness' sake – he's seventy-eight!'

'Maybe he's worried about retiring and not having anything to do.'

'I suppose so. Perhaps he's a bit depressed. But sitting around in that ugly chair isn't going to help him. Poor Mum – I'd kill him if he was my husband.'

'That's hard for her. She still seems young at heart.'

'Yeah, she is, and she wants to have a life. But whenever I've asked her to come away with me, she says she can't leave Dad on his own because he can't boil water. So she's kind of enabling it too. I bet you if she left him alone, he'd be fine. He's well able to do stuff. He just doesn't have to because she's always done everything for him.'

'I suppose they're used to things being a certain way,' Orla said. 'It's easy to get stuck in a rut. But the day she popped in looking for you, she was saying how she's always wanted to see South America. Do you think she'd take a trip there on her own or with you?'

Orla thought Ann should go away, whether to visit John in Australia or to Buenos Aires. She'd seemed so unsettled and lost the day she'd called in. Orla had sensed that Ann desperately needed to change her life because she was clearly very unhappy.

Zoë chewed her thumbnail. 'Yeah, she's always had a thing about Argentina. I dunno, though, if she does go away on her own, it might make her see that she doesn't want to be with Dad any more. They've never had a very loving relationship, my dad's not affectionate, but they used to get on well. They seem like strangers now. Whenever I call in, they're always in different rooms and they don't even sleep in the same bed any more. It's kind of sad. I want them to be happy, but they're not, especially Mum.'

What is 'happy'? Orla wondered. Is anyone really happy? Is happiness not being alone, or is it being alone but content? Is it staying with someone – even when you've grown apart – because you have a history together? Is it leaving and starting a new life? But what if the new life is worse than the old? What if the grass isn't greener? Orla had never known real happiness. She wondered if she ever would.

'Anyway, enough about my parents' marriage. Good luck for this morning. I hope the kids behave.' Zoë waved and headed off to work.

Orla had carefully thought out her outfit for today. She wanted to look pretty, but also professional. Today was the music morning for the parents and she was hoping Paul would be there. She decided to wear a blue dress that drew out her eyes. It was midi-length and figure-hugging without being too tight and had sleeves to the elbow, which gave it a professional feel. Today she was going to wear heels, which she normally didn't. Her feet would throb after a day standing in them, but she wanted to look her best. She put on high nude court shoes, then reapplied her lip gloss. She examined herself in the mirror. She looked as good as she could. If Paul didn't notice her or pay her attention today, he obviously had no interest in her.

The first parent to arrive was Judith, who was carrying a violin case. She'd insisted that Miles bring in his violin and play a piece for music morning, even though it was supposed to be all of the children singing a few songs. To keep her from causing a huge scene, Orla had agreed and told Miles he could accompany them on 'Do-Re-Mi'.

Judith had been cold to her since their conversation about Miles's academic prowess, so Orla had given in on the violin. Judith was full of smiles and chat now.

'Morning, we're very excited for today. Miles spent hours practising last night. He's note-perfect. I'll just put my coat on this seat in the front row so I can record him without any other parents' heads blocking me.'

While Judith commandeered the best seat in the class-room, Orla helped Miles get his violin out. She felt a tap on her shoulder. She stood up. 'Hello, Lulu – oh, don't you look pretty? Is that a new dress?'

'Yes, Mummy bought it for me.' Lulu swayed from side to side to show the dress swishing.

'I picked it up in London last week.' Sonja came up behind her little girl. 'They have such nice clothes shops for children, so much better than here.'

She was dressed up in a tight black pregnancy dress, cut low at the front to show off her considerable cleavage, sky-high heels and a beautiful long dark green cashmere coat. Her hair was perfectly blow-dried and her make-up flawless. Even late into her pregnancy she oozed sex appeal.

Sonja looked Orla up and down. 'You look nice. You should

make an effort more often. That dress highlights your figure. You're very toned – what do you do? Reformer Pilates?'

'No, I run.'

Sonja wrinkled her nose. 'I hate running. I think it ages you. Reformer Pilates is excellent for toning. When I get this baby out, I'm tying my fallopian tubes in a knot and getting my figure back ASAP.'

Orla didn't know what to say to that. She was wishing Sonja and her passive-aggressive remarks would sod off and she was really disappointed that Paul wasn't with Lulu.

The door opened and Alice came in with the twins. She'd made an effort to dress up although she had a jam stain down the front of her pink blouse. She was very pretty, Orla thought, and if she just made a bit more of an effort, she'd be super attractive. Her husband followed her, perfectly dressed, navy suit, crisp white, jam-free shirt, mobile phone glued to his ear.

'Ted, give me the sword now. You promised,' Alice said.

'No.' Ted sprinted away from her.

'I told you not to let him have it, Mummy. I said he wouldn't give it back.'

'Yes, thank you, Poppy, but it was the only way to persuade him to come and sing.'

Ted raced around the classroom, shouting and waving his sword.

'I'm so sorry, Orla. We'll get it from him before he takes someone's eye out.' Alice looked at her husband, who was busy on the phone. 'Niall! Get the sword from Ted,' she hissed. Niall held up his finger and continued to talk.

Orla stepped in. 'Ted,' she said firmly, 'I need you to put the sword down. You might hurt someone and we don't want that to happen, do we?'

Ted stopped. 'No.'

'Please give Mummy the sword and take your place.'

'I don't want to sing stupid songs.' Ted groaned.

Orla bent down. 'I need you, Ted. You have the strongest voice and you're the leader.'

'Am I?' Ted asked, wide-eyed.

'No, he isn't, I am,' Poppy stated.

'Ted is the leader of the boys,' Orla confirmed.

'Oh.' Poppy was appeased.

Ted handed Orla the sword.

'Now, go to your places.'

Alice smiled at her. 'God, I wish they listened to me the way they do to you.'

'To be fair, it's my job.'

'It's supposed to be my job, too.' Alice sighed. 'They can just be a handful at times. By the way, you look absolutely stunning. That colour really suits you.'

Her husband came over. 'Niall, nice to meet you. Sorcha, is it?'

'It's Orla,' Alice reminded him.

'Right, sorry. Orla.'

'Nice to meet you, Niall. The twins are a great addition to the class.'

Niall raised an eyebrow. 'Really? Their energy is quite something. Breakfast was like a zoo this morning. I need a coffee.'

'Today was a good day,' Alice said. 'Niall usually conveniently leaves for work early,' she explained to Orla, 'so he got a glimpse of what my mornings are like.'

'Are we starting soon?' Sonja called to Orla.

'Who's that?' Niall asked.

'Lulu's mum,' Alice said. 'Try to keep your eyes off her cleavage.'

'Hard to when it's on display like that.'

Orla could feel the tension bouncing between the couple. She decided to get things moving. She turned her back to them and clapped her hands. 'Children, everyone, into your places, please.'

The children all rushed to the front of the class and lined up. The parents sat down and pulled out phones and fancy cameras.

Orla was about to start the show when the door opened and Paul rushed in.

'Daddy!' Lulu left the class group and ran to hug him. 'I thoughted you were in Kerry.'

'I got up early and drove back to see you. I couldn't miss this.'

By the look of him, he had barely slept. It was a five-hour drive so he must have been up at four a.m. to make it. Orla came over to get Lulu.

'Sorry, I need Lulu in her place,' she said, avoiding eye contact.

'Wow! You look stunning,' Paul blurted out.

Orla froze. She looked up and saw his brown eyes watching her. 'I . . . uhm . . . thanks.'

'Sorry, that was probably inappropriate. I'm high on caffeine. I've been up since three thirty to get here on time.'

'It's fine, honestly.'

'I'll shut up and sit down now.' He shuffled away to his seat.

Orla felt ten feet tall as she walked Lulu back to the front of the classroom.

The children sang four songs. Orla watched as the parents gazed at their children adoringly. She also noticed that Sonja was texting during one song and that the twins' dad stepped out during the second song to take a call. Alice looked furious.

When Miles attempted to accompany the class on his violin to the finale of 'Do-Re-Mi', every parent winced at the awful sounds, except Judith, who beamed at him from behind her enormous camera. Orla reckoned she must be tone deaf.

The children bowed and the parents clapped enthusiastically. Then the children offered their parents juice and nut-free, gluten-free buns.

'I've got to go,' Niall said.

'But I want you to have a juice and a bun,' Poppy whined.

'Sorry, sweetie, but I have a meeting.'

'I don't care. This is Ted's and my big music day and you have to stay like all the other parents.'

'Just have a bun, Niall,' Alice urged him.

'Okay. Grab me a juice and a bun, then.'

Poppy wandered off to get her father some refreshments.

Out of the corner of her eye, Orla saw Lulu kissing her mother goodbye and going back to Paul, who was scoffing buns as his eyelids drooped. He caught her eye and walked over. Orla's stomach flipped. 'I'm sorry again about earlier. I hope you're not going to #MeToo me for my comment.'

Orla laughed. 'No, I promise not to.'

'Phew.' He popped the end of the bun into his mouth. 'I think I've eaten more of these than any other parent. I need the sugar.'

'Well, you had a very early start.'

'I had to make it. I knew how much it meant to Lulu.'

'You're a great dad,' Orla said.

'Thanks. And that's really nice to hear. No one ever gives you compliments for parenting. You're just supposed to do it. And, speaking of compliments, I meant what I said. You look really beautiful.'

Orla blushed.

'Sorry, I'll go before I say anything else inappropriate. Thanks for a lovely morning.'

'NO, DADDY!' Poppy yelled.

They both turned to see Niall trying to peel her off his leg.

'Poppy, let go,' he hissed.

'You said you were going to stay for a bun and you haven't eaten it.'

Niall took the bun from her hand and stuffed it into his mouth. 'There,' he said, spitting crumbs. 'Happy now?'

'No! Cos you spatted crumbs on my dress,' Poppy said.

Orla noticed Alice smile. Niall was a lot more uptight than his lovely wife, she thought.

'Poppy, I came to your show and saw you and Ted, and you were both fantastic. I'm very proud of you, but I have to go to work now.'

'Fine, but Ted wasn't fantastic. He didn't sing one word of "Do-Re-Mi".' Poppy flounced off as Niall hurried out of the door.

The parents began to leave. Paul waved at Orla from the door as he left. 'Thanks again, Orla. The kids are lucky to have you as their teacher.'

'Hear, hear,' Alice agreed. The other parents clapped and the kids whooped.

Orla felt her face go red, but inside she was dancing.

19

Alice tried to button her jeans. Damnit. Too tight. She thought back to the past few days. Since the disastrous attempt at massaging each other, she'd gone into overdrive on the sneaky cigarettes and biscuits. You'd think the fags would cancel out the need for the biscuits. Didn't all those stick-thin models smoke to suppress their appetite? Typical me, thought Alice, the one person who can still tuck away half a packet of chocolate digestives after a cigarette.

'*Muuuuuuum!*' Sarah shouted.

Alice ignored her and pulled out her 'fat' jeans. She put them on, with a loose-fitting shirt to hide her expanding muffin top.

Lisa kept texting to ask if Alice had rung her personal trainer to book a session: *You need to get fit – it'll help with the sex too*, she kept saying. Her mother was also on her case: *Contact Lisa's trainer. You need to lose a few pounds. If you feel better about yourself, you'll have more energy and life won't seem so overwhelming.*

Alice knew her sister and mother were right, yet she hadn't called the trainer. She'd meant to, but every time she picked up the phone she chickened out. She just couldn't face jumping around in leggings and swinging cow bells, or whatever they swung these days, over her shoulders. She just needed sleep and peace and quiet, and everything would be fine.

'Mum!' Sarah was standing at the door of Alice's bedroom, her arms crossed.

'What?'

'I've been calling you for, like, ten hours.'

'Or ten seconds.'

'Whatever. I need you to help me build an Eiffel Tower out of toothpicks.'

Bloody school projects, Alice fumed inwardly. Why the hell do teachers do this to busy parents? No one – well, no one in their right mind – wants to build a stupid replica of the Eiffel sodding Tower out of sodding toothpicks.

'And this time I want to turn up with something that doesn't look rubbish,' Sarah said, referring to the last project, which was supposed to have been a rocket. She had used up three full rolls of tinfoil trying to create it.

When Niall had strolled in from work, unaware of the numerous breakdowns, hissy fits and tantrums that had preceded this final version, he'd roared with laughter and asked his daughter why she was bringing a tinfoil penis to school.

Cue histrionics, and Alice had had to spend an hour talking to Sarah through her bedroom door, only persuading her to come out with a promise of Rice Krispie Mars Bar buns, which she then had to make.

But toothpicks? The Eiffel Tower? Come on, they'd be here until next year.

'Why don't you make it with lollipop sticks? It'll be easier,' Alice suggested.

'Because that's taking the easy road, Mum. I want this project to go well for once and I'd appreciate your help. All the other mums help their kids, and most of them have actual jobs and are way busier than you. Olivia's mum is helping her recreate the *Titanic*, with waves and icebergs and lifeboats and passengers and everything.'

Ouch. Sarah really knew how to stick the knife in. Feck Olivia and her *über*-creative (and competitive) architect mother. Why couldn't all mothers just agree to let their kids do the projects themselves? Then you wouldn't have kids turning up with replicas of the Sistine Chapel created by their engineer mother or sculptor father.

But, no, the tiger parents always got involved and then Alice was dragged in. Niall never helped: he was always at work, and if he did happen to be home, he'd make himself scarce, claiming he had to 'catch up on some important emails'.

Alice chose her words carefully, persuading Sarah that using lollipop sticks instead of toothpicks would save hours, if not days, of pain, frustration and meltdowns – and not just Sarah's.

'First of all, that was rude. I am busy, thank you very much. Second, I understand your wish to take the hard road, Sarah, but I'd be worried that the toothpicks wouldn't hold up. I think that as lollipop sticks are so much sturdier, they'd make for a better foundation. Then you wouldn't have to worry about the tower falling over or tilting during trans-port. Obviously it's entirely up to you, but I think you'd have more success with lollipop sticks.'

Sarah pursed her lips. 'I guess they would be less likely to break and I really want my project to win. We could make it higher, too. We could make it five feet tall instead of three feet, like I was going to. Yes, let's do that.'

Alice's heart sank at 'we' and 'let's'. She'd been hoping to persuade Sarah to do this project on her own. Fat chance. And five feet tall? Was she insane? Alice felt a headache coming on. She could see the days ahead – the kitchen filled with glue, lollipop sticks, and Sarah's wide range of intense emotions.

Alice wanted a cup of tea and a biscuit, but she would not give in to the temptation. She would have to force herself to book in with Lisa's trainer this week, no more excuses. She badly needed to feel better about herself.

As she was unpacking half-eaten sandwiches from the lunchboxes, her doorbell rang. It was her mother. She was immaculately dressed and made-up as always. 'I was on my way home from work and decided to pop in and give you some of these new skin products. They're fantastic.'

Alice's mother handed her a bag and walked past her into the kitchen. Damn! The place was a mess. Alice liked to have notice of when her mother was calling in. It gave her time to tidy up and look like she had some kind of control over her life. She rushed after her and scooped the strewn lunchboxes, copybooks and cups of cold coffee off the table.

Her mother brushed crumbs from a chair and sat down.

'Sorry, it's a bit chaotic, Sarah is doing a project and we got distracted. Cup of tea, Mum?'

'I'll just have hot water and lemon, thanks.'

Hot water and lemon? Why couldn't she just have a normal cup of builder's tea? Alice rummaged around in the fridge. She didn't have any lemons. 'Uhm, I seem to be out of lemons.'

'Hot water is fine.'

'Hi, Granny.' Sarah came into the kitchen holding an iPad. 'I'm building a replica Eiffel Tower out of toothpicks.'

'I thought we'd agreed on lollipop sticks,' Alice reminded her.

'I've changed my mind. Freya is doing it out of toothpicks. Her mother is helping her. She's an actual civil engineer who builds bridges and stuff and she said toothpicks are fine.'

Bloody Freya and her civil-engineer mother, Alice thought.

'Nonsense.' Alice's mother snorted. 'Your mother is far too busy to help you stick thousands of toothpicks together. Lollipop sticks are much more sensible. In fact, cardboard would be better, faster and more durable.'

Sarah turned to her grandmother. 'I want to win a prize,

Granny. My last project was a disaster. The other kids have parents who actually help them. Parents who have interesting and cool jobs.'

'Mind your manners, young lady. Your mother is worn out looking after you all. You should be helping her, not criticizing her. And projects are supposed to be done by the pupil, not the parent. These parents are ridiculous doing their child's project for them, which is cheating by the way.'

Go, Mum! Alice was delighted to have someone defending her.

For once Sarah was silenced. She turned on her heel and left the room. Alice handed her mother a cup of hot water.

BOOM!

They jumped as the football smashed against the French windows. Alice opened the door. 'Jamie! I've told you a million times! Do not kick the ball this way, only towards the back wall.'

'Sorry,' he shouted.

Alice turned back to her mother. 'Would you like a biscuit, Mum?'

'No, thanks. I'm going out to dinner soon. How are things with you?' her mother asked, as her eyes rested on the mountain of laundry sitting on a chair in the corner of the kitchen surrounded by discarded school bags and muddy shoes.

'Fine, thanks.'

'I'm a bit worried about you, Alice. You never seem to have time to do anything. Lisa said you still haven't called her trainer. I really think you need to get up and out and fitter. A healthy body equals a healthy mind. I think it's important for your marriage that you stay fit and healthy and look your best, too.'

'You're saying I need to lose weight so Niall won't leave me?'

Her mother sighed. 'No, Alice, I'm not saying that. Stop being so defensive. I'm just saying that in a marriage both parties need to make an effort. If Niall let himself go, you might not like it.'

'I haven't let myself go. Jesus, Mum, I've just put on a few pounds. It's no big deal.'

'I never said you had let yourself go. This isn't about weight, Alice, it's about self-esteem. I can see you don't feel good about yourself. I want you to be happy.'

'I am,' Alice lied.

'Are you?'

'I just wish everyone would leave me alone. Niall's always nagging me to go out more, and you're always at me to lose weight, and the kids are always wanting me to do stuff for them. I just need some peace.'

'Well, then, you shouldn't have had four children.'

'Yeah, you've said that before, Mum,' Alice said wearily. 'It's all my own fault and I should put up and shut up, I know.'

'Look, Alice, I was widowed at your age with two children to raise. You just have to get on with things. Feeling sorry for yourself is no good to anyone. You have to figure out a way to carve out some time for yourself and shake yourself up. You need to get on top of things here. Make a timetable for your day and stick to it. If you have a tidy house and feel in control of things, you'll feel so much better. It's all a bit chaotic here.'

Alice sighed. She didn't want a bloody timetable. She wanted to go to bed and sleep. 'I know it's a mess in here, but I lost a week when the kids were all vomiting, and I haven't quite caught up yet.'

'Why don't I send my cleaning lady to you? She can help you.'

'No, thanks. I'll sort it out this week.' Alice did not want a cleaning lady coming in and seeing how messy she was. She felt it was a sign of her failing at her only job if she had to hire someone to clean and iron.

She didn't understand why, but somehow there never seemed to be enough time to get things done. She knew her sneaky cups of tea in front of Netflix didn't help, but it was her only little treat. Daily life was so mundane and repetitive, and there were days when she didn't feel like cleaning the house. But Niall was working hard to pay for everything, and she couldn't justify asking him for a cleaner: it wasn't fair. She ought to be able to get it all done.

'I know the place is a mess, but I'll get on top of it. I will . . . I'll . . .' Alice's voice quivered as she fought back tears.

'Alice.' Her mother put a hand on her arm. 'I've been wondering if perhaps you might be a bit depressed. Maybe this way of life isn't for you, darling. Why don't you think about getting back to work? Lisa said she'd suggested you could help out at the pharmacy. We could find you something to do – we're always swamped. I think it would do you good to get out of the house and back into the real world, be an adult for a few hours a day, rather than always chasing your tail for the children.'

Alice shook her head. 'This makes me happy, Mum. I want to be a full-time mum. I chose this life. I want to pick the kids up from school and be there for them.'

'I know you do, but you don't seem very happy. Maybe it's time for a change.'

'But this is what I am. I'm a mum, that's my job.'

'A job should give you fulfilment,' her mother pointed out. 'And who said you have to be one thing, Alice? It's okay to want to be more, or different. In fact, I'd say it's a good thing to want to be more. Don't back yourself into a corner because of a decision you made ten years ago.'

Alice looked at the mess surrounding her. Was being a full-time mum what she'd thought it would be? Was she any good at it? Was she fulfilled?

'Look, Alice, I'm just worried about you. I keep thinking about how you said you're tired all the time. Maybe you should get your bloods done. You seem overwhelmed, and it could be perimenopause. I went through the menopause early. It's worth getting checked out.'

'I'm only forty-one.'

'It happens to women at different times.'

They heard a bloodcurdling roar. Alice sprinted into the TV room, her mother hot on her heels.

Ted was holding Poppy's precious American Girl doll by the hair in one hand. In the other he was wielding scissors.

'STOP HIM!' Poppy shrieked.

'Jesus Christ, Poppy, I thought someone was dead or mortally wounded.'

'You said another bad thing! You're always cursing, Mummy, and this *is* very serious.'

'Poppy, you gave us all a fright,' her granny said. 'You shouldn't scream like that unless it's an emergency.'

'Well, actually, Granny, it *is* an emergency.' Poppy was not backing down.

'What exactly is going on?' Alice asked.

'Poppy said I'm not her real brother. She said I'm adopted and my real parents are smelly hobos.'

'Poppy, why would you say that?'

'Cos he was annoying me. He kepted wanting to put Maisie into her football kit and I wanted to dress her up in her party dress and he wouldn't leave me alone and Maisie is *my* present from Santa, not Ted's. And then he said he was gonna chop her hair off. She has beautiful hair. If he cuts it off, she'll be ugly and I won't want to play with her any more.'

Alice decided to leave the It-doesn't-matter-what-someone-looks-like-it's-the-beauty-inside-that-counts conversation for later.

'Ted, you are not adopted. You were born three minutes after Poppy. You are one hundred per cent my boy. Poppy is being silly and mean. But you must not destroy her gift from Santa. You wouldn't like it if she cut up your football jersey, would you?'

Ted shook his head and lowered the scissors slightly. 'Do you swear I'm not adopted?'

'I swear. Look in the mirror, love. You're the image of your dad. Poppy is never going to say anything mean like that again, and she's very sorry, aren't you, Poppy?'

'Is he sorry for forcing Maisie to wear football clothes?'

'Poppy!'

Poppy pouted. 'Fine, sorry.'

Alice held out her hand. Ted gave her the scissors, then passed the doll back to Poppy, who held it to her chest dramatically whispering, 'You're safe now, Maisie. You're safe.'

Alice and her mother left the twins and made their way back to the kitchen.

'*Muuuuuuuuum!*' Sarah roared from upstairs. 'I need you to go to the shop and buy me toothpicks now.'

Her mother laid a hand on Alice's arm. 'I don't know how you do it, pet. You're amazing. It's a zoo in here. I've only been in the house half an hour and my head is throbbing. Work would be so much easier than being at home. Think about it, Alice.'

Alice shrugged. 'It's not easy, but I love them.'

Her mother kissed her cheek. 'I'm off. I need a large glass of wine. Don't forget to call Lisa's trainer.'

So do I, Alice thought. Wine and biscuits. The trainer could wait for another day.

Things had been awkward with Niall since the massage night, but they had managed to dance around each other, using the kids as a buffer. They talked about logistics, soccer pick-ups, ballet drops, hockey-match times . . . and while Alice watched a kids' movie with the children on Friday night, Niall worked on his laptop.

He hadn't come home early once that week, and Alice hadn't stayed up to chat to him. Nothing had changed. The therapy wasn't working. In fact, it was just making Alice worry more.

On Saturday evening, Niall strolled into the kitchen at seven, reeking of aftershave and wearing another new tight-fitting shirt. He announced that he was meeting Max for a few beers.

'Just Max?' Alice asked.

Niall shrugged. 'I think so. Lizzie might be coming, but I'm not sure.'

Alice frowned. 'What about Lizzie's friends? Will they be there?'

Niall picked up his wallet from the kitchen table. 'I don't know. Max just texted me to see if I wanted to meet for a beer and I said yes. I've had a hellish week, and I was up until two a.m. working last night. I need to get out of the house.'

What about me? Alice wanted to shout. Don't I need a night out? Mind you, Niall going out was great: she'd get the kids to bed early, put on her comfiest pyjamas, have some wine, a couple of sneaky cigarettes but no biscuits. She'd let herself watch one *Poldark* and then watch *Queer Eye*, which always cheered her up. Still, it stung that he hadn't even asked her if she'd like to come.

'Where are you going?'

'Some new cocktail bar in town. It's supposed to be really cool.'

So, her sexually frustrated husband was heading out to a trendy cocktail bar with Max and probably his hot girlfriend, plus her equally hot friends. Brilliant. Fan-fecking-tastic.

'Sounds great. Am I not invited?' she asked, trying not to sound bitter.

Niall looked surprised. 'You never want to go into town. You always want to stay local in case the babysitter calls, or so you can "not be out too late". You always complain when we meet people in town.'

'No, I don't.'

'Yes, Alice, you do.'

If she was being honest, he did have a point. She didn't like being too far from home. She had her reasons, though. She'd been called home by babysitters for vomiting, high temperatures, suspected concussions, a cut hand, a broken toe and once a missing child, when Ted thought it would be 'hilarious' to hide in the laundry basket for an hour.

When they went out, Niall turned his phone off or left it at home. Cool as a breeze. But Alice couldn't do that. She had to be responsible and contactable. 'If something happens, the babysitter will deal with it,' Niall always said. 'That's what we're paying her for.'

But that wasn't fair. An eighteen-year-old girl shouldn't have to deal with sick or injured children. But when they went out at night, Niall just walked out the door and shed his dad skin completely. When he was out, he didn't worry about the kids. Alice would love to be able to do that, but she couldn't.

'It'd still be nice if you asked,' she grumbled.

Niall ignored her comment and glanced at his watch. 'I'd better go.'

'God forbid you'd be a minute late for Max. Are you going to bother saying goodnight to your kids?'

Niall opened the TV-room door, and shouted, 'Night, kids.' None of them looked up from the TV. He headed to the front door and was about to leave when Alice asked him what time he'd be home.

Niall turned, looked directly at her and said, 'I have no idea, but I'd say it'll be late. Sure, you'll be asleep at ten anyway.'

As he closed the front door behind him, Alice raised her middle finger at his back.

'Hey, Niall, over here.'

Max beckoned him to a table. Niall strode over, grinning at his friend.

'Here, I have one lined up for you,' Max said, handing him a cold bottle of beer.

'Nice look.' He laughed at Max's T-shirt, which had a picture of a cockerel on it and said, 'I Don't Eat Cock I'm Vegan.'

He shrugged. 'Lizzie keeps buying them for me. She likes me to wear them.'

Niall thought his friend looked a total 'cock' in the T-shirt, but said nothing. He picked up his beer. 'Thanks,' he said, tipping it towards him. 'God, do I need this. What a week.'

'Get it down you. Lizzie and a few of her mates will join us in a while. Should be fun.'

Niall nodded at his friend's pint glass. 'So you're drinking tonight, then?'

'Ah, yeah, can't be teetotal all the time,' Max said. 'No hiking tomorrow – weather's set to be bad, thank Christ! So we'll just stay in the sack all morning instead.'

Niall shook his head and smiled. 'I hope you know how lucky you are. A kid-free morning of lounging and shagging! What I wouldn't give for that.'

'You sound fed up,' Max said, nodding at the barman for another round. 'Everything okay at home?'

Niall sank the last of his beer and grabbed the next by the neck. 'You don't need to hear me moaning on a night out,' he said lightly. 'Tell me more about the great sex you're having.'

'No, honestly, how are you doing?' Max said. 'You seem stressed.'

'It was just a long, hard week in work. The pressure of proving myself worthy to be senior partner is really tough. I'm one of three candidates for one senior partnership, and I really want it. You know yourself, four kids, big mortgage, and I'd like the kids to go to private senior schools if I can afford it.'

'I hear you,' Max said. 'Sally and Lizzie are sucking me dry. Sally keeps asking for more money for the kids, and Lizzie, well, she likes her weekends away and her designer clothes. That girl knows how to spend money! What's Alice like with spending?'

'She's great on that front. She doesn't blow money on designer gear or anything for herself, but she rarely says no to the kids when they want something. They do a ridiculous amount of expensive after-school activities, and then, of course, they want all of the paraphernalia that goes with them.'

'Whatever you do, don't let her get them into sailing,' Max said. 'Florence does it and it costs a fortune. Sally's playing the guilt card on me now, too, trying to get me to buy Florence a feckin' boat because she's so "traumatized" by my leaving.'

'Multiply that by four kids. The bills are endless.'

Max held up his glass. 'Well, here's to you making senior partner, mate. You certainly deserve it. You've worked your nuts off for this. I'd say Alice is so proud of you, yeah?'

Niall rolled his eyes. 'I don't think "proud" is a word Alice would use about me.'

'Ah, I was sure something was stressing you out,' Max said, nodding for more drinks. 'I know the signs, believe me. You look as unhappy as I did when I was with Sally and living that boring, suburban life.'

'I just . . . I mean, you'll understand this,' Niall said, pulling out his wallet and dropping a note on the bar. 'I don't want to sit in on a Saturday night, watch a kids' movie and go to bed at half ten. I want to go out, blow off some steam, have a laugh, be the other me for a while, not just "Dad", you know? But Alice is totally different. She loves staying in. I left her there tonight on the couch with the kids – we've spent all day with them, driving them from one activity after another – watching some animated film. She's changed. I miss her.'

'What do you mean?'

'I miss the old Alice, the fun Alice. She's narky all the time, tired and focused solely on the kids. I don't feature at all. She barely looks up when I walk in from work and, if she does, it's only to nag me about being late.'

'Jesus, that sounds grim,' Max said. 'We only have one life. We need to live it and enjoy it. Sounds like she's really changed. I must say, I thought she was in terrible form the night we went out for dinner. She was really snappy, especially to you.'

Niall sighed. 'I know. Do you remember when I first met her? She was so much fun, a total party girl.'

'Yeah, but she hasn't been like that for a while now, has she? Sally was the same. When they have kids they change and turn into old women.'

'I just wish she'd come out with me and let loose and have some fun. It would do her good.'

'Does she want to, though?' Max asked. 'From what

you've said, it sounds like she's happy to be at home and just caught up with the kids.'

Niall sighed. 'Yeah, I think she's happy not to go out. Happy not to be spending time with me anyway.'

Max slapped his back. 'It's not for me to tell you what to do with your life, mate, but I will just say that I haven't regretted my decision for a second. I know people think I'm a selfish bastard for leaving Sally, but that life was suffocating me. Things are brilliant now. You need to put yourself first sometimes. You deserve that, Niall. You're one of the good guys.'

The door swung open and a group of stunning girls made their way towards them.

'Lizzie!' Max shouted, jumping up to grab his girlfriend in a long kiss. Her friends swooped around Niall, giggling and introducing themselves. Niall lapped up the attention.

'Now this is living,' Max said, winking at him.

Niall switched his phone to silent and popped it into his pocket. He deserved a night off.

20

Orla locked the bathroom door. Even though Zoë was out, she didn't want her coming home suddenly and barging in on her.

She opened the packet she'd ordered online – she was far too embarrassed to go to her local pharmacy and ask for them. Five different dilators fell onto the bathroom floor. They went from the smallest at seven centimetres long and 1.5 wide to the biggest, at sixteen centimetres long and 3.5 wide. Orla felt her vagina tighten at the mere sight of them. She sighed. This was going to be a nightmare, but she was determined. She had to do this, or at least try.

Picking up the smallest and shortest dilator, she read the instructions.

This Vaginal Dilator Set has been clinically designed for women experiencing vaginal discomfort and penetration problems caused by vaginismus, dyspareunia (painful intercourse), gynaecological surgery, lichen sclerosus and trauma following childbirth. Dilator sets are used extensively within the healthcare system to help women experiencing any of these conditions, to eradicate painful internal discomfort and help keep the vaginal muscles supple and free from scarring.

It all sounded good. It all sounded relevant. The hard part was going to be inserting it without freaking out. According to the instructions, *The tapered design makes them very easy and, most importantly, comfortable to use.*

Orla wanted to laugh – *easy and comfortable to use*. The

person writing this leaflet had never experienced vaginismus. Nothing about it was ever easy or comfortable. The smallest dilator looked about the width of a tampon but was longer. Orla began to sweat.

She forced herself to read on.

In the comfort of your own home, using a water-based lubricant, you simply insert your chosen dilator inside your vagina at a pace that is comfortable for you. We recommend starting small and working up to larger dilators as you progress with your exercises.

Over time, this continuous penetrative action will help your vagina stay healthy and supple. Many women report that after using vaginal dilators discomfort is considerably reduced during follow-up examinations, sexual intercourse and further treatments.

Orla opened the lubricant jelly, plastered it over the smallest dilator, took a deep breath and inserted it. Her muscles contracted and rejected it.

She tried not to cry. If she couldn't even get the smallest, skinniest one in, what hope was there of her ever having sex?

She picked up her phone and dialled Maggie's number.

'Orla, are you okay?' Maggie asked straight away, when she answered.

Orla's voice shook. 'Not really. I'm trying the smallest dilator, but it won't go in.'

'Where are you?'

'In the bathroom.'

'Turn away from the dilators and focus on my voice. What is going through your head when you try to insert it?'

'Fear, frustration and anger.'

'Let's take a step back. How have the last few days been for you? Why did you choose tonight to do this?'

Orla closed her eyes. 'Because I saw Paul yesterday and he

told me I looked stunning and I think . . . I mean, I could be wrong . . . but I think maybe he finds me attractive and maybe fancies me a little bit. And I know, for sure, that I really like him.'

'How did you feel when he told you that you looked stunning?'

Orla beamed. 'Amazing, giddy, high.'

'Well, let's hold onto those emotions. When you try to insert the dilator, think about Paul. Think about his face, his voice and him saying those words to you. It should help your body relax. Whatever happens, don't worry. If it doesn't work tonight, you can try again later on. Don't put pressure on yourself.'

'But if I don't try, I'll never fix this.'

'I understand your urgency. You like Paul and you want to move forward. But if you are not successful in inserting the dilator tonight, it's not a failure. Do you want me to stay on the phone while you try again? I can talk you through it.'

'I think it would be even weirder to be talking to you while I'm trying to do this,' she said, and laughed. 'Thanks, but I'll try it again on my own. I'll let you know how it goes. Thanks for taking my call.'

'Remember, having vaginismus is not going to ruin your life. You can work around it. There are lots of ways to have a fulfilling sex life. Don't be despondent if this doesn't work tonight. Okay?'

'Okay. Actually, Maggie, do you think a glass of wine would help me relax?'

'Sure, I don't see any harm in that. But try to picture Paul's face and voice. And I'd also recommend that you get out of the bathroom and lie on your bed. You can keep the lighting low and relax more there.'

'Right, I'll do that.'

'Call me if you need to chat,' Maggie said, and Orla hung up.

She gathered up everything and went to her bedroom. There, she closed the curtains and turned on the lamp. Then she went to the kitchen, opened a bottle of wine, poured herself a large glass and drank deeply. She decided to bring the bottle into the bedroom with her. One glass might not be enough. This might require the whole bottle.

Orla drank a second glass for courage. She lay back, pictured Paul's face and tried to insert the dilator. Nothing.

She drank another glass. Focus, Orla, think about Paul, think about his smile, focus . . . She tried, but her body rejected the dilator again. She hadn't even got the smallest dilator the tiniest way up.

Why, oh, why was she such a freak? It was all very well for Maggie to say, 'Don't worry, you can work around this,' but Orla didn't want to work around it. She just wanted it to stop happening and for her body to be normal. She was twenty-four, and girls of her age were off having fun and sex all the time, and here she was, with a body that wouldn't let her do that. It felt like a cruel trick.

She curled up into a ball and sobbed into her pillow, crying for her lost future and the knowledge that she'd never have children or a husband or even a boyfriend. She was doomed to live alone for ever.

Her head was spinning from the wine. She thought she might throw up. She tried to concentrate on one spot on the ceiling to steady herself, but she wasn't used to drinking so much, so fast. Within minutes she was back in the bathroom, leaning over the toilet bowl, upending the wine and the sandwich she'd eaten earlier.

Orla rinsed her mouth and looked at her face in the mirror. How could she have thought for a second that someone like Paul, a man who had been married to a successful, sexy woman like Sonja, would ever look at a pathetic non-woman like her? Sex with Sonja would have been fantastic. She oozed hotness and confidence. Paul would have had incredible, full, normal, penetrative sex with her. Sonja was a real woman, a woman who knew how to satisfy a man. Paul would never go for someone like her. Orla was clueless when it came to relationships. She had no idea what it was like to be in a committed relationship, to love and be loved. She'd never experienced it. Now she never would.

Orla crawled back into bed and prayed for the relief of sleep. At least when she was asleep, she didn't feel the burning shame.

Orla was tidying the classroom when she heard a gentle knock on the door. She looked up. It was Paul, crumpled and gorgeous. Orla felt herself blush. She tried to busy herself putting books back on the shelf to give herself a minute to calm down.

'Sorry, I didn't mean to disturb you.' Paul walked towards her. 'Here, let me help.'

As he leant down to pick up some of the books still piled on the table, his arm brushed hers.

Orla felt a warm glow spread through her. This was ridiculous. She was like a teenage girl with her first crush. They tidied the books onto the shelf and then Paul turned to her. 'I wanted to pop in to thank you.'

'For what?' Orla peeped at him from under her thick fringe. Zoë had told her she looked French when she came back from the hairdresser with her hair cut in a short bob. Orla had been delighted. She'd secretly been hoping for that chic French look.

God, Paul was handsome.

His big brown eyes stared into hers. 'For what you've done with Lulu. She's like a different child. She's back to her sweet self. She's happy again.'

Orla brushed off his praise, but she was so pleased he'd noticed. She'd done a lot of work with Lulu, building up her confidence, making sure if she felt frustrated that she came up and talked to her, instead of arguing with her classmates.

'No, really.' Paul placed his hand on her arm. 'Both Sonja and I owe you a big thanks.'

Orla wanted him to leave his hand there for ever. She wanted to rest her weary head on his strong shoulder. She wanted to nuzzle into his neck and inhale the scent of him. She wanted to disappear inside this kind, handsome man. 'Honestly, it's really nothing. She's a wonderful child with lovely parents.'

'I'm not sure Sonja has ever been described as lovely before.' Paul laughed. 'But she loves Lulu in her own, unique way.'

There was a knock on the window. They turned. It was Lulu. She was beckoning her dad. Orla wanted to shout at her – *Go away! Come back later! Let me spend more time with your dad. Please.*

'I've been summoned.' Paul grinned. 'Uhm, so, anyway, Lulu and I just wanted to give you this as a small token. Lulu picked it out. I hope it's okay.'

He handed her a box with a scented candle inside. It had *Thank you for being awesome* on it.

'I know the message is a bit cheesy, but Lulu adores you and she insisted that this was the one. I hope the smell doesn't make you gag.' He laughed.

Orla opened the top of the box and held the candle to her nose. It smelt of vanilla, which wasn't a scent she particularly liked, but she didn't care. 'It's beautiful and I'm . . . well, I'm really touched.' Her eyes welled despite her best efforts.

Paul looked deeply into them, unafraid of or embarrassed by her response. 'Like I said, it's just a token. We really think you're a fantastic teacher and, well . . . person.' He stumbled slightly over his words.

'*Daaaaaaaad!*' Lulu roared, from outside the window.

'Right, time to go.'

Paul reached out his hand to shake Orla's, and she did something she hadn't planned to, something that was inappropriate for a teacher to do with a student's father. She kissed his cheek. 'Thank you, Paul.'

She knew it was probably the only time she'd feel his face so close to hers.

'You're more than welcome,' he whispered into her ear.

As he walked out to collect his impatient daughter, Orla touched the side of her face and closed her eyes.

21

Ann sat at the kitchen table and stared at the banana. She looked at her phone and scrolled down to the information she'd found: 'How to Give a Good Blowjob'.

She'd been mortified even writing the words into her search box, but she didn't want Ken going down to Jennifer Hogan for one, so she needed to try.

The idea that he was fantasizing about a woman they knew still shocked her. Jennifer Hogan, of all people. She wasn't particularly sexy. She looked good for her age, but she wasn't one of those women who wore low-cut tops and push-up bras. She didn't wear skinny jeans and high boots either. In fact, Ann thought she looked better for her age than Jennifer did. What was it that had made Ken fantasize about her? It must be her eyes, Ann thought. She had lovely hazel ones and a sexy voice. Jennifer smoked and her voice was kind of raspy. Maybe Ken thought that because her voice was sexy she'd be brilliant at blowjobs.

Ann's head throbbed. She rubbed her temples and sat up straight. Come on now. Let's get going.

She read through the instructions, relieved when she saw the bit about it not being necessary to have *an entire penis in your mouth* for the man to feel pleasure. That was a relief, at any rate. *For a man to enjoy oral sex, he does not need to be deep-throated.* Ann gagged at that. She was very glad to hear that men didn't need it because there was no way in hell she was deep-throating anything – neither a banana nor her husband's penis. If he wanted deep-throat action, he could go around to Jennifer with the deep voice, and possibly a deep throat too.

An enthusiastic blowjob can and should involve using your hands as much as your mouth. By using your hands, you'll stop yourself gagging, which is a lot more pleasant for everyone involved, especially you. No man should expect to be deep-throated, and if he does, don't give him a blowjob.

Yes! This woman was brilliant. Ann liked her style. But how did she use her hands to stop herself gagging? She needed advice on the mechanics of it all. She read on. Then she took a deep breath and peeled the banana. She held it at the bottom with both hands. She put her mouth over the tip of the banana, but she squeezed too hard with her hands. The banana broke in two, collapsing on the table with a gentle thud.

Dear God, if she squeezed too hard, she might do that to Ken. She had to get the pressure right. She reached for another banana and peeled it. She held it gently with one hand, focusing on the right level of pressure. She glanced down at her phone for the next bit: *Keeping your tongue flat . . . lick your way up like how you'd lick an ice-cream cone.*

What? What did keeping your tongue flat mean exactly? Did she have a flat tongue when she ate a Magnum? She tried to picture it. No, she usually bit into it, and that certainly wasn't going to work here.

Ann stuck her tongue out and did her best to keep it flat and wide. She started at the bottom of the banana and licked all the way up to the top. Then she put her mouth over the banana and tried to suck, but the banana got all mushy and the tip dissolved in her mouth, which made her gag.

Damn this! Ann flung the mushy banana into the bin.

What was she even doing? She was sixty-four: did she really need a degree in oral sex at this stage of her life?

Then again, therapy had been her idea and, despite his extreme reluctance, Ken had come to the sessions with her. Ann took a deep breath and peeled her third banana . . .

Milly threw back her second can of Coke Zero and groaned. 'I am never, ever, ever drinking again.'

Ann laughed. 'How many times have I heard you say that?'

Milly groaned again, theatrically. 'I know, but I really mean it this time.'

Ann had heard Milly swear off drink at least once a week for the past three months. The girl liked to party. Ann remembered being twenty, a wonderful carefree time. Your biggest worry was earning enough money to buy drinks. She envied Milly her youth, her don't-give-a-damn attitude and the confidence of young women. Zoë had it too, complete self-belief. The world was their oyster – they could do any-thing, be anything, go anywhere with anyone. There was such freedom in that. It almost made Ann breathless to think about it.

'Are you okay, Ann? You seem kinda down.'

'I'm fine, pet, just tired. I didn't sleep well.'

'Did Ken have you up all night?' Milly winked.

Ann tried not to let bitterness coat her words. 'Fat chance.'

'Maybe you need a fit young lover.'

'Where would I find one?'

'Online. I keep telling you. I could hook you up on Tinder. I swear you'd be getting action every day.'

Ann laughed. 'I don't think I'd have the energy for that.'

'But that's the whole point. You get to choose if you want it, when you want it and who with. Online, you can meet *waaaaaay* more guys than you can in normal life.'

Ann said nothing. The thing was, she didn't want other men. She just wanted Ken back. Her Ken, the one she'd fallen in love with. The one she'd had children with. The one who had stared into her eyes and told her he loved her over and over again. The one who had held her in his arms and comforted her when her parents died. The one who had brought her cups of tea in bed with hot buttered toast after her failed pregnancies. The one who had twirled her around when he got promoted. The one who had kissed her neck and made love to her like she was the most beautiful woman in the world.

But maybe this was ageing. Maybe this was what it was like for couples when you got old and stale. But she saw other older couples and they still had fun together and were affectionate and loving. Maybe she was the one who had changed most. Was she more needy now? She hadn't worried much about Ken's dwindling affection when the kids still lived with them and kept her busy. Was she obsessing about it now because she had more time on her hands, like Ken said? Was she asking him for the impossible? Could Ken give her what she wanted? Maybe the answer was no. Maybe she needed to go out and find it, on her own, and figure out what she actually wanted for her future. Talking to Maggie had made her start to think it wasn't all Ken's fault. Their relationship had changed because they had changed. Ken wanted less while she wanted more.

So, what did she do about it? If the Ken she wanted was gone, would she be better off alone and single? Would she be happier on her own?

'Ann!' Milly said. 'I'm serious. Maybe a night of passion with a random guy is what you need. Or you could do a threesome with Ken. Lots of women are into it. You hook up with a woman or a guy online and then you meet for a drink and, like, make sure each other isn't a freak and stuff. Then you bring them home or go to a hotel room and you all have sex, or two of you do and one watches or whatever.'

Ann tried to imagine Ken's face if she told him she'd organized a threesome. Mind you, if it was with Jennifer Hogan, he might be delighted. She could give him a decent blowjob while Ann watched and took notes. She'd read so much on it at this stage, she could give scores out of ten for technique.

'Or,' Milly continued, chewing a chocolate bar, 'you could be the threesome person. You could put up a fake profile online and you could be the person who's with the couple.'

Knowing my luck, Ann thought, I'd end up meeting someone I know, some couple I never knew were kinky, and it would be mortifying. I'd never be able to leave the house again.

'Or –'

'Thanks.' Ann cut across her. 'I do appreciate your suggestions and your concern. But I'm kind of old-fashioned when it comes to sex. I like it with one person and I want to be in love with that person.'

Milly crumpled up the chocolate wrapper and threw it towards the wastepaper basket, missing the target. 'I don't think that's old-fashioned, I think it's lovely. But,' she raised a finger, 'I have to be honest, the best sex I ever had was with a one-night stand in Paris. Hot, hot, hot.'

'Do you give blowjobs?' Ann blurted out.

Milly's jaw hit the floor. 'Whoa, Ann! Yeah, sure I do.'

'Do you like giving them?' She'd shocked the girl, so she might as well continue.

'Sometimes yes, sometimes no. It depends on the guy, the size of his willy and stuff.'

'Do you ever gag?' Ann had to ask.

'God, yeah. Lots. If the guy pushes forward when you're in the middle of one or if he has a really big penis or whatever. I even puked while giving one once.'

Ann gasped. 'Did you really?'

Milly grinned. 'Yeah. Now, to be fair, I'd had loads to drink and I'd smoked weed. I felt myself gagging, and before I pulled back properly, I'd vommed all over his stomach.'

The two women creased up, laughing.

'What did he say?' Ann wiped her eyes.

'Eff off, basically.' Milly giggled.

'Oh, Milly, you're such a tonic.' Ann hugged her.

A customer came in and Ann helped her find a warm coat, while Milly continued eating and drinking her way through her hangover.

'Thank you for your help,' the lady said. 'I'm going to visit my daughter in Iceland. It's cold there at the moment.'

'How lovely,' Ann said.

'I'm very nervous,' the woman added. 'My husband died last year and it's the first time I've travelled alone. I'm not a very good flyer. I get anxious, but my daughter said, "Mum, if you don't push yourself to do it, you'll be stuck at home for ever." So, I'm all booked.'

'Good for you.' Milly gave the woman two thumbs-ups.

'I think that's brave and wonderful,' Ann said. The woman was about her age. 'And I'm very sorry for your loss. I hope you have a really lovely time.'

'Thank you. I think I will. I'm nervous but excited too. We have to keep living, don't we?'

Ann looked into the woman's eyes. Without having to say anything, the two knew they didn't have the luxury of decades ahead of them and that life was for living, even if you had to push yourself to do things that frightened you.

Ann walked the woman to the shop door and wished her

luck. She thought of John in Australia. Maybe she should go and visit him. Maybe she should take the plunge.

'You see,' Milly said, hands on hips, 'you have to do stuff outside your normal. You, Ann, need to go to South America. You keep telling me you always wanted to go there. Go and dance the tango.' She clicked her hands in the air.

Ann smiled. One dance step at a time, she thought. The first step was learning how to give her husband of thirty-eight years mind-blowing oral sex. This wasn't what she had thought therapy was going to bring to her relationship, but it was shaking things up, and that was what she wanted, wasn't it?

22

Alice was wearing an oversized cardigan that she kept pulling tight around her and her arms were crossed. Niall was in a smart suit and kept looking down at his phone, scrolling through emails. Alice could sense Maggie sizing up their body language, which must be speaking volumes.

'How did you get on with your homework?'

Niall looked up from his phone and placed it face down on the arm of his chair. 'You mean the massages? Ha, total disaster. Alice was far too worried about the duvet cover getting splashed with oil to bother trying.'

'That is not what happened,' Alice said. 'It just was hard to relax because Niall poured half the bottle of oil all over me and it was dripping everywhere. The kids and I got the vomiting bug, so I'd spent the whole week changing sheets and I was exhausted.'

'You can never relax when it comes to sex or massages or anything. You're always uptight.'

'No, I amn't,' Alice snapped, in an uptight way. 'I'd just had a crappy week cleaning vomit and nursing the kids back to health, Niall.'

'It sounds like you had a rough time, Alice,' Maggie said.

'Yes, I did. Three of the kids had the bug. It was a nightmare and Niall just carried on working late and being no help at all.'

'I helped all weekend when you were sick.'

'Yes, but not before, when all the kids had it.'

'I'm sorry, Alice, but I was working on a huge case with a

deadline. I couldn't tell Denis – he's the managing partner' Niall explained to Maggie '– that I had to go home because my kids were sick. Denis never mentions his kids and never, ever leaves early. Anyway, it's your job to look after the kids and it's my job to work really hard and earn money. That's the arrangement we both agreed.'

Alice glared at him. 'I know I'm a full-time mum, but when the kids are sick it's bloody hard and I could have done with some help. I'm sure Denis would still promote you if you went home to help put your sick kids to bed.'

'You don't know him. He would totally see that as a weakness, that I was distracted and not focused or committed enough.'

Alice sighed.

'I think you're both feeling frustrated,' Maggie said. 'I'm hearing you feel unsupported, Alice.'

'Yes, I do.'

'Niall, how does that make you feel?'

'Fed up. It's always about the kids.' Niall sighed. 'Everything is always about the kids, never about me or my job.'

'We decided to have four kids and they need to be looked after, Niall. It's called parenthood. It's called responsibility.' Alice snuggled deeper into her cardigan. 'They are more important than either of us. These are the years when they need us most. We have to come second and we just have to suck it up. It'll get easier later, but for now we have to be committed to them. I just don't get why that's so difficult for you. It's just obvious. It's being parents, which is what we are.'

'Would you agree with that, Niall?' Maggie asked. 'I'd like to hear how you feel when you hear Alice saying that.'

Niall looked at Alice and sighed. 'If I'm being honest, sometimes I resent the kids a bit because I feel that they've taken Alice away. Motherhood's changed her and she's not my Alice any more. She's their mother. I realize that sounds a bit silly, and I love my kids, but I really miss Alice, my partner and best friend. I'm just feeling . . . I don't know . . . a bit suffocated by it all. Between the kids, the mortgage, work, arguing with Alice, Sarah becoming a right little madam . . . it's a lot and there's nothing to alleviate it. I sometimes miss the old days, when it was just me and Alice spending Saturdays in bed watching TV, hung-over, having lazy afternoon sex. I feel as if the kids have sucked us both dry. I love them, I really do, but there are times when I dread coming home.'

Maggie nodded. 'It's hard to admit those feelings when you're a parent. There can be pressure to be delighted with your kids all the time, can't there? But that's not realistic. I think every parent since the dawn of time has probably had days when they wanted to walk out of the front door and keep walking. Believe me, I know.' She smiled at them. 'So what you've said might have been hard to say, Niall, but it's perfectly normal, and it's okay to admit to it. I'll ask you to be similarly honest, Alice. What do you think about Niall saying he dreads coming home sometimes?'

'I feel hurt. I mean, it can be chaotic at home sometimes and the evenings are often the worst. The kids are tired and not at their best – nor am I, to be honest, but that's life. We wanted kids, and parenthood is a twenty-four/seven job. You never get a break, it's relentless, but they're our kids and they're amazing. I do understand that it can be overwhelming at times, I get that completely, but I'm always very aware that time is passing so fast. Before we know it, the kids will be eighteen and gone. This time is precious, and we'll never get it back.'

'But would you agree, Alice, that it's important to find a balance between being there for the children, enjoying them, having a good family life, and also putting time and effort into your marriage?'

'Yes,' Alice said quietly. 'If I have the energy.'

'That's just it,' Niall said. 'That's what I want, Maggie. I want to have an us life as well as a family life. I want to be a good dad, and I also want kid-free time with Alice. But she makes me feel like that's asking too much. I just can't accept that you have to sacrifice your relationship until your kids turn eighteen. Time is passing for us, too. We have to live our own lives as well and I don't think that's being selfish. I feel as if I'm being reduced to one thing – a dad – and I don't want that. Maybe that's wrong, but I just don't.'

'I don't think it's selfish to want to carve out time for your relationship. On that note, how has this week gone for you both as a couple? Have you had any physical contact or enjoyed any intimate moments?'

'I tried to initiate sex, but I got slapped away, as usual.'

Alice wasn't having this. 'Niall went out with Max and Lizzie and all her "fun" friends and stumbled in at four a.m. stinking of booze. Then at eight the next morning I get a penis shoved into my back and a leg thrown over me. Amazingly, I just didn't feel like having sex with him. He was still drunk.'

'You never want sex, Alice. When we do have it, it's like a chore you need to tick off your to-do list. Do you know,' Niall leant towards Maggie, 'that I once heard her mutter, "Just get on with it, for fuck's sake."'

'Yeah, I did. Sometimes, on nights when I'm really tired, I do just want you to stick it in and get on with it. I don't need, or want, long sex sessions. I don't care if I come or not. I don't want foreplay. I just want you to stop sniffing around me, like a dog in heat, and get on with it so I can go to sleep.'

Niall pointed at Alice. 'You see?' he said to Maggie. 'You see what I have to deal with?'

Maggie spoke calmly and quietly. 'Niall, I can clearly hear your anger and frustration and I know that it stems from hurt and rejection. For you sex is wonderful and bonding, and you aren't feeling that in return from Alice. While you, Alice, are feeling that sex is yet another demand on you, when you're overwhelmed as it is. It doesn't represent fun time off for you. Instead, it has become, as Niall points out, another thing you feel you have to do and that you're doing it for someone else, not for yourself, just like everything in your life. Would that be fair to say?'

Alice tried to explain: 'It's not that I'm trying to push Niall away or want to lose him or break us up or anything, it's just that . . . I don't feel sexy or want to have sex.'

'I think sometimes, as women, we forget that sex for men isn't just about a physical or biological need, it's also about connecting with your loved one. Men want to engage with their partners and feel close to them emotionally. I think that's what Niall misses too, the connection.'

Niall nodded.

Alice's eyes flashed. 'Well, as a woman, it's not fun to have a man following you around like a sex fiend, constantly sticking his erect penis into your back, looking for sex all the time when you don't bloody want it.'

'Niall, do you ever touch Alice when it doesn't lead to sex? Just a hug or a kiss, or cuddle her in bed?'

'Yeah, sure, absolutely.'

Alice was shocked. 'That's a blatant lie! You do not! If Niall so much as looks at me sideways in bed, he wants sex. I'm afraid to walk in front of him unless I'm fully clothed because he'll be sniffing around for sex. If he kisses me on the couch when we're watching TV, he'll be trying to take my top off within seconds. There is no such thing as cuddling, Niall. You're lying.'

Niall's face twisted with anger. 'Well, it's the only way I can get sex, Alice. Because you never seem to want it. So if I never initiated sex in our marriage, we'd actually never have it. Ever. And it's normal for married couples to have sex, Alice. Remember, we used to do it a lot and you used to actually enjoy it. You should be happy that I still want you.'

'HAPPY?' Alice roared. 'Oh, thank you, Niall. I'm so grateful that you still want to have sex with me. You're so kind. I'm so lucky.'

Niall looked uncomfortable. 'Okay, happy was the wrong word, but why don't you ever want to have sex with me or seem to enjoy it any more?'

'Because I'm exhausted all the time. So bloody tired. Everyone wants something from me. You. The kids. Your dad. My uncle. My mother with her constant lectures. Lisa and her well-meaning advice on how I need to get fit. Everyone has an opinion on what I should do and how I should do it. What about what I want?'

'Well . . . what is it that you actually want?' Niall asked. 'I get that you do a lot for everyone and I really appreciate how kind you are to my dad, but you seem angry and fed up all the time. Nothing I do is ever right. All you do is snap at me.' His voice rose as his frustration bubbled over.

Alice began to cry.

'Oh, Alice,' Niall said, looking pained, 'don't cry. I didn't mean to shout. I'm just looking for answers. I want to understand why you're so unhappy. Please don't be upset.'

'Sometimes we all need a good cry.' Maggie handed Alice a fresh tissue. 'The important thing now is for Alice to reach into those feelings, right into what's making her cry, and to say it out loud. I know this is hard for you, Alice. I think it means confronting thoughts and emotions that frighten you. I suspect this goes a lot deeper than just being upset because Niall raised his voice. Take your time, then face your fears and talk to us.'

Alice wiped her eyes and took deep, juddering breaths to stop the tears. Her head ached with it all. Just thinking about all of the things she had to do and all of the people she had to look after, who needed her, who depended on her, who swung out of her, morning, noon and night, made her feel completely overwhelmed. Some days when she woke up, she felt short of breath when she thought about the day ahead and all of the things she needed to get done. She didn't understand how some women did it all – worked, had kids, had parents who needed help, and still managed to look amazing, read Booker Prize-winning novels and go to the openings of plays. She felt like a total failure at life. Why, oh, why wasn't she more like her mother?

'Can you tell us what you're thinking, Alice?' Maggie asked.

Alice sighed deeply, then faced her husband. She needed to be honest, no matter how hard it was.

'I'm struggling with it all. I want to be there for everyone, but I can't seem to manage it. In the last ten years I've had three C-sections, two cases of serious mastitis and broken sleep every single night. My body has changed, and not for the better. Every time I try to join a gym or sign up for classes or even get my hair done, one of the kids gets sick or breaks a limb, or your dad needs dinners made or for me to drive him to and from hospital for his diabetes check-ups, or my uncle wants me to do a shop for him because his arthritis is bad . . . It never ends. I can't even stop long enough to think about what I want. I feel drained and empty. And when you start criticizing me and listing my faults, it's like you're putting me down and I feel bullied. From the very beginning you bullied me here to make me talk about sex, which I'm really uncomfortable doing, and I feel that I'm going to have to have sex all the time now and I just don't want to. I'm sorry, but I just don't. I want to go to bed, put the duvet over my head and sleep for days and days.'

Niall reached over and rubbed her arm. She didn't want him to rub her arm – what if he tried to have sex with her in the car on the way home? She pulled it back.

'So at the moment, Alice, sex is not how you want to be closer to your husband?' Maggie asked.

'I'm sorry, Niall, but at the moment, no, it's not. I'd like a hug, or a cuddle, but I don't want sex. It feels like another duty I have to perform, when I'm already performing all day long. I'm playing at being a mother, a wife, a daughter, a friend, and I just constantly feel I'm failing at all of them. I think part of my lack of desire for sex is because I'm not sexy any more. I feel really unattractive. I've put on weight and I hate being naked. In fact, I hate the idea of Niall seeing my blubbery stomach. So when Niall keeps pushing me for sex, I feel a lot of pressure and that makes me resent him. And then I feel bad about not having sex and I hate myself even more.'

'Okay. A number of things are coming up there in what you're saying, Alice, but for now I'd like to ask Niall how he feels when he hears that you have this sense of being bullied.'

'Well, awful, obviously. Alice, I don't want to bully you or make you do anything. I just want us to get back to the way it was. We used to have a laugh together. We used to go out and drink wine and come home and want to rip each other's clothes off. Now you always want to go home early to let the babysitter go and you don't want more than two or three drinks because you don't want to be hung-over when you have to be up with the kids. It's just always about them.

Never about us. I miss you and me hanging out together. This isn't just about sex at all, honestly. That's only a small part of it. You're my best friend and I feel as if I've lost you.'

'I don't drink a lot because I can't cope with the kids the next morning if I do. And if I stay out too late, I'll be tired and cranky with them and that's not fair.'

'But it's not all about them, Alice. That's what I keep trying to make you see. Parents are allowed to have lives, too, to be people in their own right. We're not ninety. We should be going out to cool bars and clubs and doing stuff we enjoy together.'

Oh, not this again. Alice was sick of Niall moaning about wanting to go to 'cool' places. 'I know we're not ninety, Niall, but we're not eighteen either,' she reminded him.

'Is this a strong feeling for you, Niall,' Maggie asked, 'that your lives are too narrow and you feel old before your time?'

He snorted. 'Yes! My friends are out having a blast.'

'Most of your friends are in exactly the same boat as us,' Alice said sharply. 'Your *friend* Max is out making a complete arse of himself with a bunch of youngsters. Your other friends are leading normal family lives.'

Niall's jaw set. 'We keep going around in circles,' he said. 'You know what, Alice? I had a blast with Max on Saturday night. I felt young again, and I liked not having to clock-watch. I liked being able to forget about responsibilities for a while. I'd had a really tough week in work and it was great to blow off some steam. What's wrong with that? I think you need to do that too. It would do you good to let your hair down and be fun Alice again.' Turning to Maggie, he added, 'Alice used to be the party queen. When we first went out, I could never get her home.'

'Yes, but I was twenty-five,' Alice said, throwing her hands into the air. 'I was young, carefree and had no kids. I loved my crazy nights. I had a ball, but I don't need that any more. I'd feel ridiculous prancing about a dance-floor with a bunch of twenty-year-olds. Unlike Max, I've grown up, Niall. Max is behaving like a selfish teenager. His relationship with his kids is in tatters. They're devastated by the separation and he spends all of his time with Lizzie and very little with them. He's crushed the hearts of his ex-wife and his two kids. So if he's your role model, we have serious problems.'

Niall bristled. 'I'm not saying he's my role model. I know he can be selfish, but he's also really happy. You know, I was looking at him on Saturday and the way Lizzie is with him, so affectionate and attentive and . . . Well, you can see they have fun together. That they *both* want to be with each other.'

He didn't add that Lizzie's friend had made a pass at him. It was late, they were all drunk and she'd kissed him on the lips. He'd been flattered and, if he was completely honest, tempted. But he'd pulled back. She was gorgeous, but she wasn't Alice.

'Did they have sex in the loo?' Alice asked.

'I dunno. Maybe. They're all over each other, but it's nice. I think he's lucky. I miss it, Alice. I miss you wanting to spend time with me, instead of always doing stuff with the kids.'

'Do you feel lonely, Niall?' Maggie asked.

Niall nodded. 'Yes, I do. Very.'

'For God's sake, Niall, the Lizzie-and-Max thing won't last. No couple is obsessed with each other for long. The novelty will wear off. He'll get dumped soon or she'll want a kid and he'll run a mile. He'll end up on his own or with some other random person he meets at the gym or lurking about in nightclubs. His life is sad and self-centred, and his kids will never forgive him for what he did.'

219

'Kids get over break-ups, Alice. They'll be fine.'

'Eventually – but their relationship with him is permanently damaged.'

Niall balled his hands into fists. 'You're not listening to me. Forget about Max. I just want us to be a couple again, have fun together, let loose a bit. I want us to be us.'

Alice sighed and looked out of the window. She was tired of Niall saying they were boring. They had a good life, four healthy kids, no major financial worries. People had real, serious problems out there. They should be counting their blessings, not picking holes in their life.

'You've both dug really deep during this session and I appreciate that,' Maggie said. 'Let's focus on the positives, on what you both want to achieve. Alice, what kind of relationship would you like to have with Niall?'

'I want Niall to engage with his family. He works late all the time and, yes, I get it, he wants to make senior partner, but I'm always on my own with the kids during the week. On weekends he does help with sports runs and all that, but he also goes into the office quite frequently or hides in his "den" watching sport. He's just never present. It's like he's physically there but he doesn't want to be with us. He says he wants more time for us as a couple, but it has to fit in with our family life. He can't demand one and not put into the other. It doesn't work like that.'

'Niall, how does hearing that point of view make you feel?'

'Okay,' he said slowly. 'There's truth in it. I do work hard and long hours, but it's because I want to provide for my family. And, yes, it's also because I like what I do and I'm ambitious. I admit that I find the kids a handful and do sometimes hide out in my den, as Alice calls it . . . But when I come home from work, I never find Alice waiting for me, like she used to, with a glass of wine, ready for a chat about our day. It's always the kids refusing to go to bed and fighting with each other, or if I get home later it's Alice cleaning up and feeling tired and I do understand that, because her days are long and hectic. Or sometimes when I get home the kids are asleep and she's in bed already and doesn't want to talk because she's wrecked. It's just very lonely.'

'Niall has mentioned the word "lonely" a couple of times, Alice. How does that make you feel?'

'Well, being a single parent is very lonely, too,' Alice said, shooting her husband a look. 'I might be at the centre of non-stop chaos, but I'm still lonely in there. I don't get adult conversation with colleagues or nice lunches and time to just . . . Jesus . . . just breathe and think, you know?' She ran a hand through her hair and took a deep breath. 'But I'm sorry Niall feels like that. I don't mean to ignore him. I'm glad to see him when he gets home, but I just don't have any energy left after I get the kids to bed. I'm utterly worn out. I'm find-ing it all a lot. I dunno, I used to be better at being a mum. Now, I find it . . . I find it . . .'

Alice began to cry again. She couldn't hold it in. 'I'm finding it really hard. I love them, I really do. I love every hair on their heads but I'm a bit sick of my boring, mundane days. I thought being a mum would be everything I'd dreamt it would be. Parts of it are, but some of it is just so dull. I wanted to be so good at it, but I don't think I am. The kids seem to be more demanding as they get older and harder to manage, and I feel like a total failure. I look around at all these women who seem to be doing it all so easily, and I'm just crap. Sarah said to me the other day, "What would you know? You don't even work," and I thought, Is that how she sees me? As someone who doesn't count? I gave up every-thing to be at home with the kids and maybe they don't care or notice. Maybe it's all for nothing.'

'That girl needs a good talking-to! How dare she speak to you like that?' Niall was horrified.

'Alice, I think you're getting to the heart of the problem now,' Maggie said, smiling at her. 'I know that took a lot for you to say. I think your whole identity for the past decade has hinged on being a mother – a full-time mother who prioritizes her children's welfare and happiness. You've put huge pressure on yourself to be this *über*-mother figure and I think the weight of that expectation is crushing you. Would that be a fair observation?'

Alice covered her face with her hands. 'Yes,' she sobbed. 'I was so sure I'd be a brilliant mum. But I'm not. Sometimes I actually want to scream at them all to sod off and leave me alone. I don't, but I want to. I'm just so disappointed with myself. This is what I wanted, the one thing I thought I'd be brilliant at. But I'm not. I'm rubbish.'

Niall handed her a tissue. 'Come on now, Alice, you're a great mum. You're there day in, day out, an absolute rock. The kids love having you around. It might seem like they take you for granted, but they light up when they're with you. You're brilliant with them and you have an incredible bond with all of them – even spiky Sarah. I envy you, in fact, because I know I'm not the best at being patient with them and they much prefer you.'

Alice shook her head. 'I was doing all right when they were smaller, but now I find it so much harder. That's why I'm tired and grumpy all the time. I can't even get my fat arse out for a walk. I just seem to go around in circles every day, achieving nothing. If I do have an hour free, instead of doing something constructive and worthwhile, I just want to flop on the couch. I'm such a loser.'

'You're incredibly harsh with yourself, Alice. Can you see that?' Maggie asked. 'The words you use about yourself you would never say to a friend who was struggling. So why do you aim them at yourself? Why are you so self-critical?'

'Because I'm a loser. I'm surrounded by can-do women. My mum and sister are really successful and the other mums in my kids' classes either work full-time and have brilliant nannies or are at the school gate in gym gear looking slinky and fit and together. I feel inadequate because I *am*. I'm failing at the one thing I always thought I'd be good at.'

'Oh, God, Alice! I hate hearing you say that. I had no idea you felt so bad about all this. You're not a failure, not by a long shot. You're a great mum, with the patience of three saints. You're devoted to the kids – they do every activity and sport going and you get stuck in with homework and nightmare school projects. You're absolutely brilliant. I don't know how you put up with the kids all day. After half an hour with them, I need a break. They're relentless.'

Alice shook her head. 'But they're amazing too. Like, the good times make all the bad worth it.' She sighed. 'I don't know why, but when they're in school I miss them, and when they get home, I want to run away from them.'

Maggie laughed. 'A lot of parents feel that way. You're definitely not alone, Alice. You're torn between loving them and wanting time for yourself. But I do think you're putting a lot of undue pressure on yourself to be a perfect mother.'

Alice nodded. 'I'd like to be. I mean, if I fail at this, who am I? What am I? A woman with no job or career who wanted to be a full-time mum and made a rotten job of it. That's the truth.'

'It is not,' Niall said, his voice full of concern. 'Why didn't you tell me you were thinking all this? I'd have told you how great you are at being a mother.'

'But I'm not, Niall, and I seem to be getting worse at it. And I'm a crummy wife too. I'm sorry. I really am. I'll try harder. I'll try to shake myself up and have more energy for everyone.'

'I think it's really important that you learn how to be honest about what you want, Alice,' Maggie said. 'It seems you often put everyone else first and don't speak up for yourself. Again, that's common, especially among mothers, but it's important to break the cycle. Living with all these conflicting emotions and negative self-worth is not good for you and is damaging to your mental well-being. So I'd like you to answer a simple question. You've been so brave about opening up today, and that has been a wonderful step forward. So, Alice, if you had twenty-four hours to yourself and could do anything you wanted, what would it be?'

Alice didn't even have to think about it: go to a five-star hotel with a spa – alone. Sleep, watch *Poldark*, sleep some more, have a proper massage, order everything on the room service menu, have a long bubble bath and then sleep some more. Could she say that? Probably not. She knew Niall would want her to say, 'Go away for a night with my husband,' or 'Go out partying with my husband,' but she'd give anything to go away alone. Just have that slice of time to think, to catch up with herself. She could leave the kids with him, turn her phone off, have no one asking her for anything, no one saying, '*Muuuuum*' . . . It would be utter bliss . . .

Maggie and Niall were waiting for her answer.

'I'd like a night away. Twenty-four hours of total peace and quiet.'

Niall perked up. 'Really? We can do that. I'd love to treat you, Alice. It'd do us both good to get away.'

Maggie looked intently at her and held her gaze. 'Alice, are you happy for Niall to go with you or would you rather go alone?'

Alone! Alice thought wearily. I want to be left alone. She

knew you weren't supposed to lie in therapy, but if she said what she really wanted, Niall would probably feel hurt, she'd feel bad, and she wouldn't be able to enjoy her break alone because of the guilt.

'With Niall,' she lied.

'Okay. Niall, will you organize that for Alice?' Maggie asked.

'Of course,' Niall answered confidently, as if he'd ever even organized a babysitter.

Alice tried to smile, but she felt sick. Oh, God, how had she got herself into this? Now she'd have to arrange babysitters and schedules and pre-cook meals and freeze them and have all the sports kits and uniforms washed and ready and . . . It would be a huge amount of work just to go away for one night. How could it be worth it?

Worse, she knew that as soon as they put their bags down in their room, Niall would want to have sex. And she'd have to pretend to be into it or he'd tell Maggie on her. Alice felt weary just thinking about it.

'I'll book the Old Grange. It's supposed to be really plush.' Niall sounded delighted.

Alice faked yet another smile. 'Great.'

'Try to take the time to talk to each other and reconnect. I look forward to hearing how you got on.' Maggie stood up and saw them out.

Niall put his arm around Alice and kissed her cheek as they walked towards the car. Maybe the night away would be good, she told herself. Maybe they'd have a nice time after all. She leant into his shoulder and hoped for the best.

23

Zoë came out of the bathroom wrinkling her nose. 'Oh, my God, did you light that candle again in there? It stinks.'

If Orla was being honest, she didn't love the scent either. When the candle was lit, it gave off a very strong vanilla smell and it was a bit cloying, but Zoë was not allowed to criticize it. No one was. The candle Paul had given her was, sadly and tragically, Orla's most treasured possession.

'I like it,' she said firmly, leaving no room for discussion.

'Okay, keep your hair on. Could you not leave it in your bedroom, though?'

Orla nodded. 'I can. I just brought it into the bathroom because I was having a bath.' And trying and failing to insert dilators into my vagina again, she thought glumly.

Zoë leant across to hand Orla the candle, but her hands were wet from washing them and it slipped through her fingers.

Orla watched as, in slow motion, the candle connected with the wooden floor and the pretty glass cup with *Thank you for being awesome* on it shattered into a thousand pieces.

'Shit, sorry.' Zoë crouched down to pick up the shards of glass.

'YOU FUCKING IDIOT!' Orla screamed. She hadn't intended to. But it flew out of her mouth. Raw red rage rose up inside her. She wanted to punch Zoë in the face.

Zoë jumped back and stared at her in shock. 'Jesus, Orla, calm down. It was an accident. It's only a candle. I'll get you another one.'

Orla concentrated on getting her voice under control. 'Just go away. Leave it. I'll clear it up.'

'Let me help you,' Zoë said.

'No,' Orla snapped. 'I'll do it. You've done enough damage already.'

'Suit yourself,' Zoë muttered, as she went into her bedroom and slammed the door.

Orla held the shards of glass in her hand. The candle, which had flown out of its glass cup and smacked against the wall, lay on its side on the floor. It had a chunk missing on one side. Orla put the shards into the bin and held the lopsided candle to her chest. She went to her bedroom and locked the door. She lay down on her bed and sobbed. It wasn't 'just a candle'. It was a gift. A precious gift from a man she had fallen in love with. Yes, she knew it was ridiculous to be in love with someone you hardly knew. Yes, she knew she was clueless about relationships and the whole thing was pointless and hopeless and it could never be, but she had fallen head over heels for Paul anyway, and this candle was probably the only thing she would ever have from him.

Orla sipped her take-out coffee, the one little luxury she allowed herself every morning on the way to school, and tried not to let herself spiral downwards about the broken candle and her failed attempts with the dilator. She had to shake herself out of this slump. She was taking the class to the zoo today and the kids would be hyper. She needed to get her energy levels up, but she had slept so badly the night before that she felt exhausted.

She did not feel ready to herd a class of twenty five- and six-year-olds around the zoo, with endless toilet breaks, snotty noses, screams, tears and probably one or two vomiters on the bus . . . She had a headache just thinking about it. Besides which, one of the three mothers who had volunteered to help with the trip was Judith. Orla was dreading having to spend the day being followed around and told about Miles's genius.

The two other volunteer mums were the twins' mum, Alice, who was lovely, and Una, Daisy's mum, who was quiet but seemed very nice. Orla was hoping they would both act as a buffer for her with Judith.

But when Orla got to school, Sharon in Reception told her that Una had called to say she wasn't feeling well and couldn't help out.

'But don't worry.' Sharon smiled. 'I've managed to get you a sub. One of the other parents was dropping their daughter in when they heard me on the phone and volunteered to help. They've been garda vetted, so it's all good.'

'You're a life-saver, Sharon, thanks. Who is it?' Orla asked, but Sharon's phone rang and she turned to answer it.

Orla finished her coffee and put her keep cup in the staffroom. She'd collect it later. She checked her backpack – tissues, wipes, plasters, toilet paper, antiseptic spray, sunscreen, raincoat, an inhaler, spare socks, pants and two pairs of tracksuit bottoms in case of any accidents. Orla had also printed out a list of animals the children had to find to keep them somewhat occupied. She was also going to remind the volunteer parents that the children were not allowed to enter the gift shop under any circumstances.

She went down to her classroom, and as she walked through the open door, Judith pounced on her. 'Morning, Orla,' she trilled. She was all decked out for the day in sensible walking boots, knee-length shorts and a rainproof jacket. 'I've printed out maps for all the children so that if they get lost they can find their way back to the front entrance, marked here.'

Orla stifled a giggle. These kids couldn't find their way out of a plastic bag, never mind a large zoo.

Undeterred, Judith continued, 'We need to make this as educational as possible, so that it's not just some waste of a day. I've compiled the top ten facts on forty of the animals in the zoo. I made sure to include mammals, birds and reptiles.'

Judith handed Orla a pile of sheets, dense with text. Orla knew that these sheets would end up on the floor of the bus or in the nearest bin.

'Thank you for this, Judith, but this outing is a fun day for the children and, yes, we will be talking about animals and teaching them some key facts, but all of this information in one go might be a little too much for them. I'll keep these here and we can look at them tomorrow, when we're talking about our day in the calm of the classroom. For today, I've organized a little animal hunt and some fun facts.'

Judith sniffed. 'They're not babies, Orla. They can handle serious facts and figures. You're young. You don't realize how much information children can actually absorb.'

Orla, normally so polite and careful with her words, was too tired and upset for this. She glared at Judith. 'I've been teaching for five years. I know exactly what material is appropriate for my class.'

'Morning,' a voice called out. 'Your last-minute substitute parent is here.'

Orla spun around. Paul was standing in the doorway holding his phone. 'Just had to rejig a meeting to tomorrow. But it's all sorted.' He grinned at her. 'I'm all yours.'

Orla tried to find words, but only managed to squeak, 'Thank you.'

She abruptly turned around and rushed over to her desk, where she pretended to busy herself while trying to get her hands to stop shaking.

229

Paul! Paul was going to be spending the day with her. The whole day. Oh, God, why hadn't she had some notice? Could she rush home and get changed? Could she nip to the bathroom and completely redo her make-up? It wasn't fair. She was wearing her 'spring school outing' clothes. Khaki trousers and trainers and a rain jacket over a shirt. Damnit. She knew she looked tired after a terrible night's sleep, too. Behind her, she could hear Judith ear-bashing Paul about Miles's brilliant mind.

As Orla was trying to gather herself, Sharon popped her head around the door to tell them that the bus had arrived.

Alice came tumbling into the classroom with the twins in tow. 'Sorry we're late.' Her hair was wet and she had mascara smudges under her eyes.

'No problem. Thanks for coming and helping out.' Orla smiled at her.

'That's what we stay-at-home mums do – school trips and school committees,' Alice muttered.

'Ted, you can go in Mummy's group. I want to go with Miss Orla,' Poppy said.

'Gee, thanks, Poppy.' Alice squeezed her daughter's nose affectionately.

'It's not that I don't love you, I just prefer Miss Orla on school trips.'

'I'll go with Mummy, but I want Nathan and Oliver in my group,' Ted said.

Orla calmed her breathing. Avoiding eye-contact with Paul, she called on the children to form a line and walked them onto the bus. She busied herself helping them to put their seatbelts on and then, when she had no more excuses, she slowly made her way to the front where Judith was sitting beside Paul and Alice.

'She's very young. I would have preferred a more mature,

experienced teacher. This is a key time in Miles's intellectual development. I'm having to do more with him at home to keep him from getting bored.' Judith's voice carried.

Orla felt herself blush. How dare that cow criticize her to Paul? Now he'd think Orla was rubbish at her job. And although Orla knew she was a disaster in many ways – self-confidence had always been an issue for her and self-doubt had crippled her for most of her life – the one thing she knew she was good at was teaching.

'I think Orla's fantastic,' Paul said. Orla froze, she was standing just behind them. 'She's been amazing with Lulu.'

Orla blushed again, with pleasure this time. Paul thought she was 'fantastic'. If only he knew how utterly incredible she thought he was.

'Hi.' Orla sat across the aisle from him.

'Have you checked all the seatbelts?' Judith asked.

'Yes. Everyone is safely strapped in.' Orla leant towards the bus driver. 'Thanks for waiting. We can go now.'

As the bus took off, the kids all cheered. Judith opened her mouth and talked at Paul, Alice and Orla for the entire journey. They heard about Miles's wide and varied diet, his love of seafood and sushi, his curious, insatiable mind. Judith raved about living in a house with no television, screens, iPods, iPads, iPhones . . .

'Hang on a minute,' Paul interrupted her. 'Are you telling me you don't have a mobile phone?'

'No. I have a phone, but I switch it off at six p.m. and Miles has never used it or played any of those awful video games. He likes to read and do jigsaws and play chess or practise his violin in the evenings.'

Alice gazed at her. 'Are you serious? Oh, my God, I'd lose my mind if the kids didn't have screens to distract them and keep them quiet.'

'Yes, well, your twins are very lively, I must say.' Judith sniffed. 'All that screen time could well be making them hyper.'

Paul looked at Orla and winked. 'Do you not worry about Miles getting bullied when he's older?' he asked Judith.

'What do you mean?'

'All kids are going to use technology. It's part of life. If your kid is the only one who's clueless, he'll get left out. When he's older and all the boys in his class are arranging to meet up, he'll be left behind.'

Judith patted Paul's arm. 'You don't need to worry about my son being left behind. He'll be streets ahead of all the other boys who spend their time staring at screens. Miles will be getting straight As while those poor boys will be addicted to gambling, watching pornography and whatnot.'

Paul threw back his head and laughed. 'Porn and gambling? Come on, Judith! Most kids use their phones to connect with their mates.'

Orla gazed at him. He had a lovely laugh – warm and infectious. His eyes crinkled with merriment and he looked even sexier.

Judith pursed her lips. 'Mark my words, Paul, children's brains and morals are being destroyed by mobile phones. Keep them away from your daughter. You'll thank me when she doesn't turn into a reprobate.'

Paul laughed even louder, much to Judith's annoyance. Then, turning to Orla, he mouthed, 'Save me from this lunatic.'

Orla grinned and distracted Judith by handing her a list of the children she was responsible for. Judith and Una were supposed to be paired together and Orla was supposed to be with Alice, but now she decided to switch the pairs.

'So you and Alice will take group A, and Paul and I will take group B,' Orla said.

Along with the list was a map of the zoo, with all the toilets marked with large Xs, some suggested routes and a copy of the list of animals the children had been asked to find.

'I think I'll add a few to this list. It's really very simple, more suitable to four-year-olds, I would have thought,' Judith muttered.

'Judith, this is the list that the children chose. I'd appreciate it if you stuck to it so that none of them feel they have outshone the others.' Orla was firm.

Judith muttered under her breath and Orla studiously ignored her.

'This looks great,' Paul said. 'Lulu's favourite animals are the red pandas. She'll be thrilled they're on the list.'

Orla smiled at him gratefully.

'I'll just be happy if we don't lose any of the kids.' Alice chuckled.

'We'll be keeping a close eye on them, I can assure you. No child will get lost on my watch,' Judith barked.

'I was kidding.' Alice rolled her eyes.

As they stood up to gather the children and dismount the bus, Paul whispered, 'Don't mind the old witch, she's certifiable.'

The feel of his warm breath close to her ear made Orla feel faint. This was ridiculous! She was like some soppy heroine in a chick-flick. She wanted him to kiss her ear and her neck and . . . Stop it, Orla! Pull yourself together.

The children split into their two groups. Orla gave Alice her mobile phone number. As Alice typed it in she said quietly, 'I promise only to call in an emergency. I won't interrupt your day with Paul.' She winked.

'What? I don't . . . Please do call . . . I'll be . . .'

Alice smiled. 'He's very taken with you – the chemistry

on that bus was electric. You're gorgeous! Of course he fancies you.'

'Do you . . . I mean . . .'

'Orla, he hasn't taken his eyes off you. Enjoy the lovely attention. I'll keep crazy Judith occupied. Maybe she can help me get my life in order. I need the help.'

'Thank you,' Orla said.

Alice turned to Judith and her group. 'Let's go, gang, and no climbing into the tiger arena.'

'Mummy.' Poppy ran to Alice.

'Yes, pet?'

'Is Ted going to be your favourite now cos I wented with Miss Orla?'

'He might be.'

'No, Mummy.' Poppy hugged her mother tightly.

'I'm joking, you silly goose.' Alice kissed Poppy's head.

'Promise?'

'Swear. I love you both the same.'

'But me a teensy bit more?' Poppy asked.

'No, Poppy, the same. Now, off you go. Have fun and behave.'

'I love you, Mummy, even though you're a bit shouty sometimes.'

Alice laughed as Poppy skipped over to Orla. Judith frog-marched her group up the hill in the direction of the tigers. Alice followed behind.

Orla could hear Judith's voice: 'Tigers are the largest cat species in the world, reaching up to three point three metres in length and weighing up to six hundred and seventy pounds . . .'

'So.' Paul smiled at her. 'Which way?'

Orla pointed in the opposite direction to Alice and Judith and they headed off.

'I wanna see the flamingos. I love flamingos. I love pink.' Poppy tugged on Orla's jacket.

'We're going this way, towards the dolphins, first. But before we do anything, we're all going to visit the toilets, which are just up here.'

Orla lined them up, then Paul took the boys into the Men's and she took the girls to the Ladies'. Orla used the precious minutes to apply some lipstick and mascara to her washed-out face.

'Why are you putting on lipstick?' Jessica asked her.

'I, uhm . . . Well, my lips are a bit dry, so I decided to put some on.'

'You putted a lot on. Your lips are all shiny now.'

'Good shiny or bad shiny?' Orla couldn't believe she was stooping so low as to ask a six-year-old how she looked. This was desperation at its finest.

'Good shiny. My daddy hates sticky lipstick. He says it's yucky.'

Well, let's hope Paul likes it. Orla rubbed her lips together to make it a little less obvious.

She heard a cry from a cubicle. Somehow Tara had missed the toilet bowl and peed all over her jeans.

Orla had to go in and change her into the spare clothes she had packed, then put Tara's wet jeans into a plastic bag in her backpack. They had been at the zoo for precisely fifteen minutes.

'Hey.' Paul waved to them. 'You were in there for ages. Everything okay?'

Orla's heart fluttered. 'Yes, sorry, a little accident.'

'Miss Orla was putting lipstick on,' Jessica piped up.

'It looks very nice.' Paul smiled.

'I felled down while we were waiting for you girls and cut my knee, but Paul putted a plaster on,' Liam said.

'Oh, you poor thing.' Orla gave him a hug.

'Thanks for giving me the plasters. They came in very handy,' Paul said.

'Someone always trips,' Orla said.

They started walking again. The kids ran ahead, so they were side by side.

'That Judith is heavy-going.' Paul grinned.

Orla had to be careful: it wasn't very professional to criticize other parents. 'She's a little old-fashioned, I guess.'

'Old-fashioned?' Paul cackled. 'She's like something from the nineteenth century. God love her poor son. He's going to be a social outcast.'

'He's a sweet boy. Hopefully she'll loosen up a bit as he gets older.' Orla tried to remain diplomatic.

'And pigs will fly. She's more uptight than my ex.' He shook his head.

'Dadd-*yyyyyyy*!' Lulu came over, interrupting them. 'We wanna see the monkeys.'

Paul stroked his daughter's cheek lovingly. Orla felt hers tingle as she watched.

They headed towards the chimpanzees with ten excited children surrounding them. This was how I wanted my life to be, Orla thought sadly, with a husband I adore, surrounded by children.

But he wasn't her husband and they were not her kids. They never would be. She pushed away the feelings of sorrow. She had to enjoy this moment. It might never happen again. This was a little gift in an otherwise really awful week, spent trying to make herself a normal woman, with a normal vagina, and failing miserably.

They reached the chimpanzees and watched the cheeky animals swing from the treetops and chase each other around. The kids were shrieking with delight. Orla and Paul stood behind them, joining in their laughter. Paul was standing close enough to Orla for her to feel the tip of his shoulder against hers. She had to suppress the urge to rest her head on it.

'What are they doing?' One of the children pointed to a couple of chimps to the left.

Orla and Paul turned to look. Oh, my God, the male was having energetic sex with the female. Orla's chest tightened, while beside her Paul let out a loud laugh.

'They're having a very good time by the look of it,' he whispered to her.

She moved away from him. She couldn't laugh and joke with him about sex. It was too painful.

She tried to think of something to say to the kids, but all she could think about was how much she wanted to have sex with Paul and how she never would. Thankfully, Paul jumped in. 'They're just having a cuddle.'

'But he's squashing her, Daddy,' Lulu cried out.

'No, he isn't, she's fine.' Paul coughed to disguise his laughter.

'He looks like he's dancing on top of her,' Karl said.

'They're dancing together, right, Orla?' Paul winked at her.

She knew she was supposed to laugh, but she couldn't be light-hearted about sex.

'Okay, children, let's move on. We've lots to see.' Orla had to get them all out of there before they asked any more awkward questions, or went home and told their parents that they had seen two chimpanzees hard at it.

She walked ahead, chatting to Luke and Karl. She always found it soothing to be with children. She felt her heart rate come down and her palms stopped sweating.

But soon Paul caught up with her. 'That was a bit tricky.'

'Yes, it was.' Orla tried to keep her voice light.

'I'm praying Judith's group saw that. A live mammal sex show. Oh, I'd give anything to see her face.' Paul roared with laughter.

Orla managed a chuckle.

'I was supposed to be in a boring governance meeting. This day has turned out to be very different.'

'Thanks for helping with the kids. Lulu is thrilled you're here.'

'I was glad to come. It's been nice hanging out with Lulu. She seems so happy, these days.'

Orla was on safe ground now. 'Yes, she really is. I'm sure her acting up was just a reaction to the baby.'

'Sonja handled it badly.' Paul's smile was gone now. 'She just blurted it out and presumed that Lulu would be ecstatic to have a sibling. She never thinks before she speaks or considers other people's feelings.'

'How do you feel about it all?' Orla asked.

'I'm fine. Sonja can do what she wants. All I care about is Lulu. She definitely felt sidelined but, to be fair, Sonja seems to have reassured her somewhat. I'm worried, though. I know when the baby arrives that things will change. Sonja's already telling me that she can't have Lulu for the first month or so while she's breastfeeding and up all night with the baby. Try explaining that to a six-year-old.'

Orla walked along, matching Paul's stride. She loved that he was over six feet tall. 'I think the most important thing with children is to make them feel secure. If you explain to her that Sonja will be up all night with the baby, babies cry a lot and Sonja doesn't want poor Lulu to be woken up all the time, maybe you can make it seem like Sonja is actually putting Lulu first. I mean, it's just a suggestion.'

Paul stopped walking and turned to her. 'It's a really good one. Thank you.'

Orla gazed into his beautiful eyes. It was as if he was looking inside her. She lowered hers.

'Why did you decide to go into teaching?' he asked.

'I've always loved kids, I love their innocence and I wanted to help the ones who were struggling. I loved school when I was a kid. It was my happy place.'

'Wow! I thought you were going to say because of the long holidays.' Paul seemed impressed.

She smiled. 'No. It feels a bit like a vocation. I hate the long holidays. I love being with the children.'

'These kids are so lucky to have you. It's rare to find someone who has a true passion for what they do.'

'What do you do?' Orla asked, although she knew already. She had looked him up online. Paul was a lawyer.

'I'm a lawyer, insolvency and restructuring mostly, but I do pro bono work with refugees to feed my black soul.'

A lawyer with a big heart. 'Do you enjoy what you do?'

'The day-to-day work? Not so much, but it pays the bills. I love the pro bono work. I'm hoping to do more of it this year. Although I think my work–life balance is completely arseways. Apart from Lulu, I hardly see anyone.'

'I guess Lulu takes up all your spare time,' Orla said.

'She sure does. What do you do in your spare time? Do you have a partner?' he asked.

'No.' Orla blushed.

'Well, I'm sure it's not from lack of offers,' he said. 'What do you do on the weekends? Do you go out much?'

If only he knew. I either stay in or go out with Zoë, pretend to go home with a guy, then spend hours alone in Starbucks. 'My flatmate is a bit of a party animal, so she drags me out a fair bit.'

'You don't sound very enthusiastic.'

'I guess I'm just a small-town girl who likes a quieter life.

I've never really enjoyed being in places jammed with people where it's so loud you can't talk.'

'An old soul. I like that,' Paul said. 'My mates keep trying to drag me out – "poor single Paul". I'm their charity case. But I hate nightclubs and, to be honest, I can never think of anything to say when I do meet someone. I'd rather stay in and watch a movie with a good curry.'

'I love movies.'

'What's your favourite?'

Orla bit the inside of her lip. Could she really tell him? Paul's eyes were so kind and interested. 'It's a bit cheesy and old, but it's *Clueless*.'

Paul stopped walking. 'Are you serious? I love that movie. "He's a disco-dancing, Oscar Wilde-reading, Streisand-ticket-holding friend of Dorothy" has got to be one of the best lines ever.'

Orla was speechless. She'd never met a guy who liked *Clueless*, or had ever even watched it. Not only did Paul love it, he could quote from it. 'I love that line,' she said.

Paul grinned. 'Sonja thought *Clueless* was "childish and boring". I should have called the wedding off then and there.'

Orla smiled at him, a proper look-into-his-eyes smile. Could this man be more perfect?

'You know what?' Paul said. 'This common love for *Clueless* is cause for a celebration. How about you come out for pizza with me and Lulu tonight? If you're free.'

Orla hesitated. What was the point in falling deeper for this man when she knew where it would end up? But she couldn't refuse him. She couldn't say no to those eyes.

'I'd love to,' were the words that came out of her mouth, and she was rewarded with the most beautiful smile.

24

Ken reached across the table in the restaurant and took Ann's hand. It still felt awkward and unnatural, she thought. His was sweaty, and she wanted to let go and wipe hers with her napkin but she knew she couldn't, so she smiled at him and tried to look pleased. At least he was trying.

She had booked dinner for them, and Ken had put on his good shirt and jacket for the occasion. The restaurant was small and intimate. It was homely and the food was Italian, served by Italian waiters who all seemed to be related to each other and the owners.

'How did you find this place?' Ken asked.

'I searched for romantic restaurants and this place had amazing reviews. They said it wasn't pretentious or over-priced. I liked the sound of it and I figured you would too.'

'I do.' Ken smiled at her.

Their food arrived and they pulled out of the hand-hold.

Ken ate quickly, shovelling his seafood pasta into his mouth at speed. Ann drank more than she ate. She was nervous and the wine calmed her jitters.

'You've a thirst on you tonight.' Ken went to pour her another glass but the bottle was empty. 'Should I order another? Or would a glass be better?' He was keen to go home, of course, Ann realized. He'd want to watch the Manchester United v. Arsenal match. If they left soon, he'd get most of the second half. If he ordered another bottle, they'd be there for at least another hour.

'A big glass for me,' Ann said. She needed more alcohol. She needed the courage it would give her.

'Right.' Ken ordered the wine and watched as Ann knocked it back.

Ken talked about work and they talked about Zoë and John, whether Zoë would ever settle down.

'Her flatmate, Orla, is a good influence on her,' Ann said. 'She seems sensible and grounded, although there's something sad about her. I can't put my finger on it, but she has a sadness around the eyes.'

'She seemed nice, a quiet country girl. I don't know about sad around the eyes. Only you would notice something like that.'

That's because I pay attention, Ken, Ann wanted to tell him. I look at people. I see them. I don't live with my head in the newspaper or TV screen. But she didn't say it, because she didn't want to ruin the nice evening. The wine was making her feel warm and mellow inside. She reached across for Ken's hand again. 'This is nice, isn't it? The two of us, out together, away from the house and TV, chatting . . .'

'Sure, yeah.' It had been nice for the first hour, but Ken wanted to go now. They'd chatted, they'd eaten, and now he wanted to go home and watch the match. To be honest, he'd have been just as happy to eat at home in the kitchen and watch the whole game in his comfy chair with a cold beer, but he was trying to make an effort. He didn't really get the big deal about eating out. He liked his wife's cooking. He liked eating at home. He didn't need to come to a restaurant and be fleeced for average food and overpriced wine.

'I think we should go away somewhere exotic, somewhere

adventurous,' Ann said, slurring her words slightly as the wine hit her. She was drinking like a sailor on leave, he thought. 'To celebrate your retirement.'

'Where?' Ken was wary.

Ann let go of his hand and waved hers. 'South America!'

'That's very far away. The flights would kill me! You know I hate flying.'

'Jesus, Ken, just take a sleeping pill,' Ann said. 'We can't stay stuck in Ireland for the rest of our lives because you don't like flying. I want to go away. I want to experience new things. I want to dance the tango in Argentina.'

'Off you go. I'm not stopping you. Maybe Zoë would go with you.'

'Zoë wants to dance the tango with a hot boy, not with her mother.'

'I dunno . . . One of your friends, then?'

'I want to tango with you, Ken. I want us to do it together – it'd be good for us.' Ann's eyes were glazed.

Ken knew his wife was tipsy now and he didn't want an argument. This tango thing was becoming an obsession. Why the hell did she need to travel halfway across the world to dance? They probably did lessons in the local church hall. Why did she suddenly want to change everything? He liked their life: it was pretty perfect. So they didn't have sex. He was sixty-eight – lots of people stopped having sex when they got older. They were just being their age. It was normal. It didn't bother him, but clearly it bothered his wife. Everything seemed to bother her these days. He was going to the awful therapy sessions for her, and that was enough, more than most men he knew would do for their wives. He was not going travelling across the world on some pie-in-the-sky whim to dance the tango. He was going to nip this Argentina nonsense in the bud. He was never going and she just needed to accept that. 'That's one dream that won't be coming true, I'm afraid.'

Ann sighed. Of course he'd say no. He said no to anything that involved going further than five kilometres from their home. She wanted to shout at him. She wanted to say, 'Try, Ken, try to work with me. Help me save our marriage. Help me save my sanity.' But she didn't want to fight. She wanted them to go home on good terms so she could carry out her plan.

'I just thought it would be nice for us to do something different.'

'You knew when you married me that I wasn't the adventurous-traveller type.' Ken was firm.

Yes, but back in the early days of their marriage he would at least go to Italy and France. She wished he'd get off that goddamn leather chair once in a while.

'What's wrong with trying something new? Come on, Ken. Say you'll at least think it over.'

'Ann, I will never go to Argentina, you know that.'

Ann sat back in her chair and tried not to get angry.

'Can I ask you something?' Ken looked at his wife.

'Of course.'

'Do you really think this therapy stuff is helping us? You don't seem happier.'

'We need Maggie to help us communicate with each other.'

'Why are you so unhappy, Ann?'

'I just think we've lost our way.'

'I don't feel lost. I feel fine. I like coming home from work and having dinner with you. I like watching sport on TV. I like having Zoë over for dinner on Sundays.'

'Aren't you bored?'

'No. I'm an old man who's happy to live a quiet life.'

'We're not old, Ken. We're just living like old people.'

'I'm nearly seventy.'

'Seventy is the new sixty.'

'That's just nonsense.'

'So, you see no problem with continuing to live the way we are now for the next ten or twenty years?'

'No, I don't.'

'Ken, we sleep in separate bedrooms, we have bland conversations, small-talk, really, and we never laugh together.'

'I don't need a big sex life. I don't need to laugh all the time. What married couples sit around cracking up all day?'

That Ken didn't see any problem in their marriage was terrifying to Ann. All she saw were holes and gaps where love, affection and humour used to be. Or was she delusional? Had all of those memories been based around the kids? Laughing on holidays or at dinner when one of the kids did or said something funny. Had she and Ken ever been the couple who went out to dinner, chatted non-stop, laughed until they cried and the owners begged them to leave as it was closing time? The realization hit her. No, they hadn't. So what was Ann missing? How could she miss something she'd never had? If Ken was still essentially the same, just older and grumpier, and their marriage hadn't changed, why was she so unhappy? Had the kids leaving home and Ken's upcoming retirement triggered a fear of being alone with him all day? Had it caused her to panic and reassess her life? Could she, in fact, be the source of the problem, not Ken? Maybe she needed to look to herself for the solution to her happiness and stop blaming Ken.

'I just don't see why you're suddenly so dissatisfied with our life. I don't think I've changed, but you seem to have all of a sudden. I don't understand it.'

'It's not sudden. I've been feeling lost for a while now. I can't

245

face spending the next decade doing the same things over and over again. It's killing me. I want us to shake things up a bit. Don't you?'

'I'm not sure what you mean by "shake things up". I'll be retired soon – maybe we could play golf together. Like I said before, I think you just need a hobby. If you're busy, you won't be picking holes in everything.'

'Aren't you worried about retiring? Aren't you worried about having no work to go to?'

Ken bristled. 'I'll have plenty to keep me busy. I plan to paint the shed and we need to clear out the attic. I might play some golf, read more, and there's always plenty of sport on TV, and . . . well . . . I'll find things to do.'

'I don't want to clear out the attic. I want adventure, Ken. New experiences. This is our last hurrah and I'd like to make the most of it.'

'Every day I hear about someone else my age getting cancer or having a stroke or a heart attack. I don't want to take risks. I want to have a nice quiet life.'

'You're sixty-eight, the same age as Liam Neeson, and he's starring in blockbuster action movies. For God's sake, Ken, live a little. Our good health is a blessing because it means we can go and do things. We can really live.'

'I *am* living. I'm living the same life I've always lived and enjoyed. You're the one who wants a different life, Ann. Not me, you. You're the one driving a wedge between us.'

Ann said nothing. She squeezed her hands together under the table. She needed to remain calm and collected. She wasn't giving up on her marriage without a fight. She was going to prove to Ken that shaking things up would be fun. Then he wouldn't be able to argue any more.

Ken asked for the bill and they got a taxi home. In the car Ann leant over and nuzzled his ear. She kissed his neck.

'Ann.' He pushed her away gently. 'Not here, come on now.'

She tried not to mind, but she did. The taxi ride seemed to take for ever. Ann was worried she'd chicken out. She was going to have to do it straight away or she'd lose her nerve.

When they stepped into the house, she slammed the door shut and pounced on him. It was now or never. She pulled his shirt out of his trousers and began to unbuckle his belt.

'What's going on?' he exclaimed.

'Sssh,' she said, kneeling down.

Ann undid the button of his trousers and pulled down the zip. She put her hand inside his boxer shorts and fumbled about, trying to find his penis. Eventually she pulled it out. It was limp.

'Jesus, Ann, steady on there.'

Ann put it into her mouth and began to suck. She tried to remember the instructions. She shouldn't have drunk so much wine. She'd needed it for courage but now her mind was foggy. What was she supposed to do – something about gripping the shaft and focusing on the head and licking. Squeezing was involved somewhere along the line, but she couldn't remember where she was supposed to squeeze.

Ann sucked and licked and squeezed. Ken's penis remained flaccid. Her knees began to ache. She should have waited until they were in the lounge. The wooden hall floor was very hard. Come on, Ken, she thought, I'm killing myself here, react.

Ken squirmed in front of her. 'Ann, now is probably not a great time. I think I drank too much wine and you kind of took me by surprise.'

Ann's knees were burning now, but she thought of Jennifer Hogan, sucked harder and squeezed tighter.

'Ouch!' Ken squealed. He pulled back abruptly, tucked

his manhood into his trousers and zipped up. Looking mortified, he said, 'Sorry, Ann. I guess I'm just tired. Uhm . . . thanks, though. I mean, thanks for . . . you know . . . the effort and all.' He scurried upstairs, leaving her sitting on the hall floor, covering her face with her hands.

25

Niall whistled as the hotel porter closed the bedroom door. 'I asked for a nice room, but this is more than I expected.'

The hotel he had booked was a castle that had been bought by an American billionaire who had completely refurbished it. It was very tastefully done. The bedroom was huge, its four-poster bedecked with a thick satin duck-egg blue cover. The carpet was soft and luxurious. On the table beside the couch, to the side of the bed, was a bottle of prosecco and chocolate-dipped strawberries.

'Nice touch.' Niall popped a strawberry into his mouth and threw himself onto the bed. 'This is the life,' he said, with a grin.

Alice checked her phone. She had left a long list of instructions for Danika. She had organized lifts for Sarah to get to and from hockey, for Jamie to get to and from football, for the twins to get to and from swimming, and for Poppy to get to her ballet. She had had to pull in favours from so many parents that her head was spinning. She'd have to find a babysitter who could drive: Danika kept saying she was going to take her driving test, but she still hadn't got round to it. Lisa and her mum had promised to pop in after work to make sure Danika was all right and had promised to call if there was a problem.

'Come on, Alice, turn your phone off.'

'I can't, with all four kids going in different directions all day. What if something happens, or someone forgets to pick them up?'

She glanced at the big bath and dreamt of lying in it, alone, surrounded by scented bubbles, listening to cheesy music and not having anyone interrupting her.

Stop it, Alice, she scolded herself. You love this man, and he's trying to get closer to you. He's been working incredibly hard and needs a break, too. You have to make an effort. While she still disliked all the intimacy talk, the sessions with Maggie had shown her that she did put the kids first and that it wasn't fair to Niall. She really did want to try harder.

'Let's have a glass of bubbles to relax us.' Niall got up from the bed and popped open the bottle.

Good idea. Alice needed some alcohol. She didn't have to get up early, and she wouldn't be interrupted by bed-wetting or bad dreams or thirsty kids or high temperatures or 'I want to sleep in your bed'. She could have a few guilt-free drinks.

Niall handed her a glass. 'Cheers.'

'Thanks for booking this gorgeous place.' She smiled at him.

As she was about to take her first sip, her phone rang.

'Don't answer it,' Niall said.

'It's Sarah.'

Niall looked frustrated, but she couldn't ignore her own daughter.

'Mum,' Sarah shouted.

'Yes, pet, are you okay?'

'No, I am not. We got beaten one–nil and the goal was my fault because I didn't tackle the striker and everyone was staring at me and I wanted to actually die! And then I had to sit in the car the whole way home with Karen, who you know I don't even get on with. Why did you get her mum to take me home? Why didn't you ask Penny's mum? I'm way more friendly with Penny.'

Last week Karen was your best friend, Alice wanted to remind her, but kept silent.

'And when I finally got home and told Danika, she said, "This is life, Sarah. Bad things happen." She didn't even care. She doesn't get how embarrassing it was for me. I am never, ever, ever playing hockey again and you can't make me, so don't even try.'

'I'm sorry about the match, love. I'm sure it wasn't your fault.'

'Oh, my actual God, did you not even hear what I said? I missed the tackle, Mum. It was one hundred million per cent my fault and I know I'm going to get dropped and be on the B team now with all the rubbish players.'

'Sarah, it was one bad moment. How did you play in the rest of the match?'

'Fine, but it doesn't matter. We lost because of me.'

'Why don't you ask Danika to make you a hot chocolate?'

'I don't want a hot chocolate. I'm not a baby, Mum. You've actually made me feel worse. Jamie wants to talk to you. Thanks for nothing.'

Alice closed her eyes and breathed deeply in and out. She had never known that a ten-year-old could drive you absolutely crazy. She took a sip of her drink as she heard Jamie's voice.

'Mum?'

'Hi, love, how was the match?'

'We won.'

Thank God. 'Great.'

'Yeah, it was. And Danny's dad brought us to McDonald's after and I had a quarter-pounder with fries.'

'That was nice of him.'

'Yeah, thanks for organizing it all, Mum. Are you having a good time?'

'Yes, thanks, love, we are.'

'Okay, see you tomorrow.'

'*Meeeeeeeeeeeeeee.*' Alice could hear Poppy screeching.

'Mummy?'

'Yes, Poppy.'

'When are you coming home?'

'Tomorrow.'

'What? No way. You have to come now. Danika is a pain. I hate her. I want you to come home now.'

'Poppy, Danika is very nice and you are to behave and be polite to her.'

'She put too much butter on my bagel and it's all slimy and yucky and I will not eat it and she saided that children are dying of hunger, and I saided I didn't care, I still wasn't eating it. And I will not, so there. I'm going to die now because you wented away and left me here by my own.'

'I'm going to die too,' Ted shouted down the phone. 'We want you back, Mummy. Now. Right now. Immediately.'

Alice smiled. It was nice to be wanted. It made her feel she mattered, that maybe she wasn't such a bad mother. Part of her was tempted to grab the car keys, drive home and hug them, comfort them and make them lightly buttered bagels. It was ridiculous, but she missed them already. She missed their sweet, and grumpy, little faces.

As if sensing her hesitation, Niall reached over and took the phone from her hand.

'Put me on speaker,' he ordered Poppy and Ted.

'Okay, grumpy Daddy.' Poppy sighed.

'Right, kids, can you all hear me?'

'Yes,' four voices answered.

'I have taken Mum away for one night for a little break. Mums and dads need time to themselves. You are to stop ringing and moaning about sports, food and whatever else you're giving out about. Mum is to be left alone. Do you understand? If there is an emergency, call your grandmother or Aunty Lisa. I do not want any more phone calls. This is our time. We will be back tomorrow to sort out any problems, but unless you're actually dying, do not call Mum again.'

'You're so mean, Daddy,' Poppy said.

'Have fun, Dad,' Jamie called.

'You're a stinker, Daddy,' Ted said.

'If I was actually dying, how would I be able to call you?' Sarah drawled.

'Goodbye.' Niall hung up and turned Alice's phone off.

'Stop!' she said, panicking. 'You can't turn it off – there might be an emergency.'

'Alice, it's one night.'

'I don't care. Put it on silent but don't turn it off. I cannot be completely out of touch. I'll only check it every now and then, I promise.'

Niall put the phone on the mantelpiece, away from Alice, and refilled her glass.

They sat side by side on the couch. Alice wondered if Niall wanted sex right away, or if they would wait until after dinner – or would he want it in the bath?

She was wearing her sexy black lace bra and knickers. The bra was digging into her sides and the knickers were riding up the crack of her bum. She kind of wanted to get the sex out of the way so she could take off the stupid lingerie and relax in her bathrobe. Maybe they could order lots of room service and watch a movie.

Alice had tried to stay off the biscuits in the days running up to this night away and she had done quite well. She had lost two pounds, which wasn't a lot, but at least it was something. She held her stomach in and tried to look sexy.

She knocked back her third glass of prosecco and, feeling

lightheaded, decided to be brave and initiate sex. The room was very bright, though. Alice needed darkness. She didn't want Niall seeing her stomach in the bright light of day. She got up and closed the curtains. Then she walked over, pulled Niall up and kissed him.

'Oh, yes,' he said, enthusiastically kissing her back.

Alice tried to keep her mind in the moment, but she kept thinking about what she'd order when this was over. Maybe she'd treat herself to a mid-afternoon warm brownie with ice-cream, or perhaps scones with cream and jam.

Focus, Alice. Niall was pulling her dress off and she tugged at the waist of his jeans.

He drew back to look at her. Thank God it was almost dark in the room.

'You are so sexy,' he muttered, as he kissed her hungrily.

Alice couldn't quite match his enthusiasm, but she tried. She made little 'ooh-aah' noises and nudged him towards the bed. She wanted to get on with it. But Niall was nuzzling and putting his hands all over her body. She just wanted to get him onto the bed, naked, and have sex.

He slowly pulled off her bra. She ripped his boxer shorts down in one swoop. 'Easy, Alice,' he breathed into her ear.

His hands slid down into her knickers. She whipped them off and pushed him back onto the bed.

But he kept pushing her back and exploring her body with his hands. For the love of Jesus, just stick it in, she tried not to shout.

He stroked her. She stroked him harder.

'Whoa, not so hard.' He pulled her hand back from his penis.

'Sorry, just got carried away,' she lied.

Back to slow petting again. Alice continued moaning and grunting in what she hoped was a sexy way. She couldn't relax enough to be turned on by his touch but she tried to make all the right sounds and movements. Eventually, she couldn't take any more stroking and faffing about.

'I'm ready, babe,' she faked.

They had sex.

Hallelujah!

Niall rolled off her and Alice wanted to punch the air. Job done. Now she could relax. Now she could let herself really enjoy the night away.

'Was that good for you?' he asked.

'Yeah, fab, brilliant.' Alice had no desire to discuss sex. Jesus, it was bad enough going to see Maggie – she didn't want to have a post-mortem every time they did it. It was done, the box was ticked. Night away in hotel, starve self into sexy undies, initiate sex with husband, have sex. Her work here was done.

She leant over and reached for the room-service menu. 'What'll we order?'

Niall was lying back with his eyes closed. 'What?'

'Food. Let's order something.'

'Not for me. I'm going to sleep now. You've worn me out.' He kissed her ear and lay back on the bed. 'This was great. I love this, just you and me,' he said sleepily. She rubbed his cheek affectionately. He closed his eyes and drifted off.

Alice picked up the phone and ordered the warm chocolate brownie with vanilla ice-cream and a large cappuccino. Time for the actual relaxation to begin.

Alice hummed as she put on her make-up. This was nice after all. It was good for them to be away together. She felt lighter than she had in ages.

'There's my sexy wife.' Niall slapped her bum as he came out of the shower. 'God, I feel so good after that nap.'

255

He seemed very energetic. Alice, on the other hand, had eaten a pile of sugar and watched Netflix. She hadn't slept and was now feeling the sugar crash. She was looking forward to a nice meal, a glass or two of wine and an early night of uninterrupted, blissful sleep.

They made their way down to the restaurant holding hands. Alice couldn't remember the last time they'd held hands. They used to all the time, even on the couch when they were watching TV, but they hadn't for ages, possibly years. It felt lovely, especially as she knew that she could touch him without worrying that he was going to want sex. They could be affectionate without that hanging over her, because it was done.

She kissed him. 'I'm really glad we came. Thanks for booking it.'

He beamed at her. 'Me, too. I love you, Alice.'

'I love you, too,' she said, and snuggled closer to him.

Dinner was lovely. Gorgeous food, wine, dessert, Irish coffees . . . they ate and drank everything.

As Niall signed the bill, Alice sat back and felt her stomach straining the waistband of her skirt. She felt full, and sleepy, and happy.

'Will we go up?' Niall asked.

'God, yes. I'm ready to call it a night.'

They walked back to their room, holding hands. As they approached the door, Niall pinched her bum and kissed the back of her neck.

Alice froze. Surely not. Surely to God he didn't think they were going to have sex now? They'd had it already. What was he doing? She ducked away from him and quickly opened the bedroom door. She was heading towards the bathroom when he pulled her back.

'Come here to me, you sexy thing.'

Seriously? Was he actually expecting more sex?

'I think my energy was used up earlier,' she said.

'I've got a surprise for you.' Niall rummaged around in his overnight bag and held something up.

Alice hated surprises, and she was pretty sure this was not going to change that.

Niall came close to her, holding something. It was hard to see in the dim light of the bedside lamps. What the hell was it?

'This came highly recommended by Max and Lizzie. Lizzie said all of her friends use them and love them. I thought we'd spice things up tonight.'

Sweet Mother of God, had he been talking to Max and Lizzie about their sex life? Had he actually betrayed her by telling that selfish bastard and the 'child' he was dating that they weren't having sex? Alice's face burnt with shame and hurt. How could he? How could he let her down like that?

'It's the Jessica Rabbit G-spot vibrator. Lizzie got it for me. She said it drives her wild.'

Oh, my God. Alice was having trouble breathing. Niall was sending Max's girlfriend out to buy sex toys for his boring, sexless wife.

'Let's give it a go. I think it'll be fun, especially for you.' He winked.

He was completely oblivious to her feelings. How could he be so clueless and thoughtless? How could he not know how hurtful this was? How could he not see how degrading it was for her that he was asking virtual strangers to buy sex toys to 'get his wife going'?

Niall turned on the vibrator, and as it whizzed and whirred between them, Alice burst into floods of tears.

26

There was a heavy, uncomfortable silence in the room as Ann and Ken sat across from each other, waiting for Maggie to start the session. Ann felt as if she might throw up, and Ken didn't look at either of them.

Maggie poured Ann a glass of water, which she accepted gratefully.

'I'm glad to see you both again,' Maggie said, 'but the atmosphere seems a little strained. Tell me, how are things?'

Neither spoke.

'How has your week been? Did you hold hands and hug as we discussed last week?'

Ken cleared his throat. 'Yes, we did.'

'That's good to hear. And how did that feel? Did you have a sense of reconnection?'

'It was okay . . . Yeah, it was nice.' Ken gave a side glance to his wife, who was saying nothing.

'I'd really like to hear what you're thinking, Ann,' Maggie said.

Ann put down her glass of water and stared at the floor. 'You might as well know that I tried to give Ken the oral sex he so desires. It was a total and utter disaster. I've never felt so humiliated in my life.'

'Why was it humiliating?' Maggie asked.

'He didn't respond, and he practically ran away from me – left me there on my knees, on my own.'

'Okay,' Maggie said, turning to Ken. 'Was it too much too

soon for you, Ken? How did you feel about Ann trying to pleasure you orally?'

Ken tugged nervously at his tie. 'It was, uh, nice of her. I suppose I was just taken by surprise and it all happened kind of fast and I . . . I couldn't really get into it as such.'

'So you didn't become aroused?'

Ken blushed. 'Uh, no.'

'Is this why you felt it was humiliating, Ann?'

Ann laughed bitterly. 'That's just the tip of the iceberg. I felt mortified, embarrassed, ashamed . . . and I wasted a whole bunch of bananas practising. I studied and researched my subject matter thoroughly. I thought I had the technique right, but I obviously didn't. I was clearly rubbish at it. Ken might as well trot on over to Jennifer Hogan and get her to give him one, because mine are useless.'

'It's not like that, Ann. It wasn't you at all. It was me. I appreciated the effort, I really did. It all just happened very suddenly and I'm sorry it didn't work out.'

'So perhaps it was a case of Ken being taken by surprise and then being unable to respond. It would have been unex-pected, given that you're moving from no intimacy to this. It was a big step for you to try, Ann, and I'm sure it wasn't easy to initiate it. Was there something Ann could have done differently to make you aroused, Ken?'

Ken squirmed. 'No, no, it was nothing to do with how she was doing it or anything. It was just very sudden. We'd barely closed the front door and I . . . Well, I was kind of blindsided.' He looked down at his hands. 'God, it's awkward talking about this stuff.'

'It's important that you communicate your desires to each other,' Maggie reminded him. 'It's good to be able to say what you do and don't want.'

259

Ken inhaled deeply. 'Well, she kind of pounced on me and ripped my trousers off. I think a bit of . . . well . . . a bit of preamble might have helped matters.'

Ann's face flushed with anger. 'I tried to kiss him in the taxi, but he pushed me away.'

'I can't be intimate in public, Ann. Come on now.'

'A kiss in the back of a taxi is not a sex show in public. You said you wanted a blowjob and I gave you one. What more do you want?'

'Let's take this back a step,' Maggie said. 'What I hear Ken saying is that he appreciated your efforts to pleasure him, but perhaps a slower build-up to it would have helped him to become aroused and enjoy it fully.'

'Yes, absolutely,' Ken agreed with Maggie.

Ann winced at the word 'aroused'. This whole process was becoming much more complicated than she'd thought it would be. She'd come to Maggie to encourage Ken to look up from the TV and notice her again, to connect with her and occasionally have sex with her, like a normal couple, and now she was looking up blowjobs on the internet and making a show of herself. Her head ached from too much wine, lack of sleep, crying and humiliation.

'Right, Ken, what do you want me to do? How am I supposed to "arouse you"? Go on, tell me. I thought a blowjob would do it, but clearly I was mistaken. How on earth do I get you to have sex with me?'

'I'm sorry, Ann, truly. I'm just saying that a bit of notice would probably have been helpful. I feel bad about how it ended. But I never asked you to do it. This whole therapy, talk-about-our-feelings thing, was your idea. This is all you. So don't go blaming me now.'

'I think what Ken's saying is that he's open to it, but he would have liked to know what you had in mind for him last night.'

Ann glared at Ken. 'So you want me to give you a heads-up? Spontaneity is out the window? Well, let's arrange for me to give you oral sex on Thursday night at eight. Does that suit you? Is that enough notice?'

'That's not what I meant. But let's be honest here, Ann, if I ripped your clothes off in the hallway, would you have liked it?'

'Yes! Yes, I would. I'd like you to rip my clothes off any-where, any time. I'm not fussy. I don't need a timetable.'

'I was caught off-guard. That's all.'

'How do you feel about having sex with Ann?' Maggie asked Ken directly.

His eyes avoided hers. 'Fine, I mean, okay. Last night felt odd and forced and it was as if Ann was pretending to be someone else.'

'That's the whole point!' Ann raised her voice. 'Being me is clearly not working because we never have sex. So I thought if I was more like Jennifer Hogan or something, you'd be turned on. That you'd actually want me. But, hey, I was obviously wrong and nothing I do is going to work. I give up.' Ann sat back and crossed her arms.

'Ann,' Maggie said gently, 'Ken understands that his re-action wasn't what you'd hoped for, but it's not a reflection on you as a woman or as a lover. You took a big and brave step last night and it demonstrates that you're really trying to reconnect with Ken and show him how much he means to you. I'm hearing that Ken appreciated the effort but would like to have taken things a little slower. Men and women often come at relationships and intimacy from different angles. Men often show their love by actions, providing for their families, being reliable . . . whereas women often show it in physical affection and comfort. It's important that you both recognize how the other shows their love.'

'That's all well and good,' Ann said fiercely, 'but I'm sick of making the effort to get him to talk to me, look at me, love me. I shouldn't need a translator to know what he feels about me.'

Ken rolled his eyes. 'I do look at you, all the time. What is wrong with you, Ann? Why is our life not enough for you any more? What do you want from me?'

'More than this,' Ann cried. 'More than dying inside. More than cooking and cleaning and watching TV. More than having to force you to go out for a simple dinner with friends, more than having to beg you to stay out past ten p.m. If you don't see that our marriage is in trouble, then I think . . . I really think we're doomed.'

As the words came out of her mouth, Ann realized she meant it. She hadn't planned on saying something so strong and definite. But she couldn't deny that the thought that she might be happier on her own had been hovering around the edges of her mind for some time. She wouldn't have to sit on the couch with her husband feet away from her, staring at the TV, ignoring her. She wouldn't have to make conversation with him over dinner. She wouldn't have to beg him to have sex with her. She wouldn't have to be the lively fun one when they went out, to cover up for his silences. She wouldn't have to persuade him to stay longer than an hour at a party. She wouldn't feel so utterly alone. She could eat what she wanted, when she wanted. No more steak and potatoes. She could eat salads or have wine and chocolate for dinner if she fancied it. She could walk around the house all day in her pyjamas. She could play music loudly, open a bottle of wine and finish it without Ken asking if she really needed another glass. She could throw out his horrible reclining chair and replace it with something tasteful that matched the style of the room. She could drown her meals in spices and eat hot food, instead of worrying about 'poor Ken's delicate stomach'. She could turn his bedroom into a little exercise room.

There was no getting away from it. Ken was right: she was the one who was pushing for change, so maybe it was time to act. Maybe it was time she stopped giving out about her marriage and blaming Ken and took charge of her own destiny. If Ann wanted to shake things up, she had to make that happen. Ken had said that he was happy with the way things were. She wasn't. She had asked him to move forward with her, but he didn't want to. It was suddenly all very clear-cut in her head. She could see what she wanted, and she could see what he wanted, and they were simply two totally different things. She had been fighting to change him, so he'd want the kind of retirement and life she wanted, but it wasn't going to work. She couldn't force him to be someone different. He was Ken, and he wasn't going to change with her or for her.

She felt a weight shift inside her. The answer was suddenly breathtakingly simple. It was time to stop moaning, stop pleading, stop arguing and *do* something. She had to stop talking about wanting to travel and just bloody well do it. If she was going to have a second spring, it had to be now, and she would have to do it alone. She felt a strange sense of lightness, as if she was floating above their heads, and had to focus hard to bring herself back to her seat. Maggie was speaking.

'Ken, would you agree with Ann's suggestion that your marriage is in danger of breaking up?'

'I don't know what to say,' Ken said. 'I'm lost. I'm trying to deal with my upcoming retirement and I thought Ann would be supportive of me at this time of change, but instead she's all about herself and what she wants and what she needs, and she's trying to change me and our marriage. It used to be good enough for her, but now it's not. I don't know what she needs to make her happy, so I don't know how to do it. So, yes, on that basis, I suppose we are at a crossroads.'

'You mentioned your retirement. Do you feel it's a factor in all this?'

Ken sighed. 'Maybe. I suppose it's making Ann feel anxious about the future. I can understand that because I've my own worries on that score. I've been at this company for thirty years. Financial controller. Now there's a young guy waiting impatiently for me to leave, snapping at my heels. He's practically moved into my office already. Work is all I know. In five weeks' time I'll wake up with nowhere to be. It's a bit daunting, I'll admit that. I guess I thought Ann and I could play golf together and . . . I dunno, grow older together in our house. I didn't know that she'd suddenly want to fly all over the world and change everything. I don't like change, I never have. When I was a kid we moved around a lot and I was in six different schools. I hated it. I like routine. I like familiarity. I like feeling secure. I've worked so hard to build this life, and it's a good one. It's a life I've shared with Ann. We've walked this road together and I always presumed we'd walk to the end together, but now . . . well, I don't know.'

'What about you, Ann? Do you feel Ken's retirement has been a catalyst in any way?'

Ann nodded. 'In a way, Ken's retirement is why we're here. I think the kids leaving home and now him leaving work have pushed me to re-evaluate things. I found myself thinking, What are we going to do when Ken retires? Are we going to sit around every day, waiting for old age and death? Is he going to spend every day in his big chair, watching sport on TV? I want us to have fun and not grow old before our time. I want us to live a full life while we're healthy and still can. There's already far more behind us than lies ahead, so this is the time to really grab life and do what we want to do, isn't it? I suppose I'm panicking a bit because I think that, if we don't change things, we'll just slip into old age and it will all be over before we know it.'

'I hear you,' Maggie said, 'but can you also appreciate that different things make different people happy? Ken has been very honest in saying he doesn't want change, that he likes familiarity.'

'Well, he's had it for over forty years. I don't think I'm being demanding by wanting to do something different.'

'But is the change for you or for Ken?'

Ann hesitated. 'I thought it was for both of us, but I'm not so sure any more.'

'It's not for me, Ann. I don't want change. Retiring is enough change for me. More than enough.'

Ann looked at her husband. 'I understand that – I know you so well after all these years – but I was asking you to change because I can't live like this any more.'

'Well, at least you're finally admitting it,' Ken said. 'This is all about you and what you want. You keep saying you're doing this for us, but you're not, Ann. You want this for you. I've provided a good life for you all these years, but apparently it's not enough now. Well, you know what, Ann? You're no picnic either. After you had John, you went off sex for a long while. I never pushed you. I gave you time and waited for you to be ready again. I never dragged you to therapy to show you up in front of a stranger. I respected you.'

'This isn't about sex, Ken. This is about everything. Our whole relationship is falling apart. Our lack of sex life is just one tiny part. I don't know who we are any more.'

'I haven't changed, Ann. You have.'

Ann gazed pleadingly at him. 'I think I have changed, Ken, but I don't think it's a bad thing. I want us to have a good old age together. I want us to be a real couple, a partnership again. But we don't communicate. We're like strangers. I have better conversations with Mrs Kelly in the newsagent's than with you. I want more now. I want more from my life.'

'Why do women always need to talk?' Ken asked Maggie. 'Why can't they ever just stop talking and be happy? Always talking, talking, talking and finding fault in things.'

Maggie shook her head. 'As I said earlier, women and men process emotions differently. Women often work things out by talking through their problems until they find an answer. Men process through action. It's a source of much conflict in long-term relationships. But I think it's fair to say that Ann suggested coming to see me because she loves you. By coming here, Ann is trying to tell you that she wants to save your marriage.'

'Yeah?' Ken snapped. 'Well, all I'm hearing is that Ann hates our marriage and is dissatisfied with everything. I love you, Ann, and I want to stay married, but this is all too much. I don't care if we never have sex again. I don't need it. I don't want to go on long plane trips to foreign places where it's too hot and the food is awful. I hate all this talking. It's codswallop. Our marriage is fine. I don't have problems. This is all you, Ann.'

'If you don't see that we have issues, we can't fix this,' Ann said quietly.

'I can't do this. I love you, Ann, I always have. But I cannot sit here and listen to all my flaws. I'm a decent man, and if that's not enough for you, I don't know what else to do. If you want to change your life, I can't stop you. I love you, but I can't change who I am for you. That's the honest truth.'

'Neither can I,' Ann said softly.

266

27

Orla beamed at Maggie, her face flushed as she described her pizza date with Paul and Lulu after the zoo.

'Oh, Maggie, it was so amazing, and it didn't feel like a date-date because Lulu was there, so there was no pressure. We laughed and talked non-stop. The conversation just flowed. Paul was so warm, and he really listens when I talk. He made me feel I was very special. And I didn't have to worry about him trying to kiss me or inviting me back for sex because Lulu was with us. I was able to just be myself. It was . . . it was perfect. I know this is going to sound really sad and soppy, but it was the best night of my life.'

Maggie smiled at her. 'It sounds great. Have you been in touch since?'

Orla grinned. 'Yes! He's been texting non-stop.'

She'd kept all of his texts. Her favourite was the one he'd sent her straight after the pizza night: *I had such a fun day. You are so incredible with Lulu, she adores you. I really loved spending time with you. Let's do it again soon?*

Orla had spent over an hour trying to come up with a suitable response. She'd wanted to say, 'I love you, you're the most amazing man and father . . .'

What she had written was, *Really enjoyed it too. Lulu is wonderful. Yes, let's do that.*

She had taken ten minutes deciding whether to add an exclamation mark after 'that', but decided it might seem a bit keen. But she was keen, very keen. Still, she didn't want to scare him off.

'Are you going to meet up again?' Maggie asked.

Orla nodded. 'He's invited me out for dinner tomorrow night, just the two of us.' Her smile faded. 'And I'm terrified.'

'What are you most afraid of?'

Orla sighed. 'The voice is back in my head telling me that someone like Paul isn't going to want to date me when he discovers I'm a frea–'

'Orla!' Maggie interrupted her. 'I thought we'd agreed you wouldn't use that word to describe yourself.'

'Okay, damaged then. I'm thinking of cancelling the date. I'm scared because I like him a lot. Like, really a lot.'

'You deserve love as much as anyone else. Don't let your fears stop you moving forward in life.'

'Do you think that maybe – I mean, now that I've found someone I really like, well, if I'm honest, I think I love him – I'll be cured?'

Maggie shook her head. 'It's not about being cured. It's about getting to the bottom of the issues around the condition. We need to continue to look at your childhood, your background and your negative associations with sex and childbirth. This isn't about Paul. This is about you.'

'Yes, but if I'm really in love, my body should respond, right?' Orla was desperate for Maggie to tell her that she'd be able to have sex with Paul.

Maggie paused. 'If you and Paul develop a close relationship, it will certainly help you emotionally and, hopefully, give you more confidence in yourself, but it won't necessarily change your body's reaction to penetration. It's early days in your therapy and in your new relationship. Let's take it one step at a time.'

'I want this to work – I need this to work,' Orla said, getting emotional. 'He's the perfect man.'

268

'How have you been getting on with the dilators?' Maggie asked.

Orla thought back to the night before, when she'd lain on her bed and tried so hard to force the smallest dilator inside her. She was bruised and sore today but trying to block it out. It would be different when it was Paul: dilators were so fake and clinical. 'Not very well. I don't think they're working for me. I feel tense even before I try to insert them.'

'Take a break. Put them away for a while and just try to enjoy getting to know Paul.'

'Oh, I am.' Orla smiled.

'Orla, what will you do if Paul asks you back to his place tomorrow?'

'I don't know.' Orla's voice shook with emotion.

'I think perhaps you should ask him if you can take things slowly. I'd advise not rushing into a physical relationship. Have fun together, hold hands, kiss, but keep it nice and slow, and in the meantime you and I will work together to get you to a stronger place physically and emotionally. How does that sound?'

Orla smiled. 'It sounds great. Thank you, Maggie. My instinct is to jump feet first into this relationship so I won't lose Paul, but you're right. I need to take it slowly. I don't want him to find out that I'm a frea– different.'

'That's more like it, well done.' Maggie smiled at her. 'And have fun on your date.'

Paul was pacing up and down outside the restaurant. He looked nervous, Orla thought. Not as nervous as she was – no one could be as anxious as she was. But, still, it was nice to think that he was nervous too.

He looked up, as if aware that he was being watched. He saw her and his whole face lit up. Wow! Orla had never had a guy look at her like that. He made her feel as if she was the most amazing person. She couldn't help laughing with pure joy as she crossed the road into his open arms. He kissed her cheek and hugged her.

'I'm so glad you said yes to dinner alone,' he said into her ear.

It was very strange. They didn't know each other well, yet it felt as if they'd known each other for ever. Orla was so comfortable with him. She hugged him back. 'I'm so glad you asked me,' she replied.

'You look smoking hot.' Paul took in her skinny black jeans, black lace shirt and high boots.

'Thanks.' Orla grinned. She had spent ages deciding what to wear and had gone for sexy. She had a good figure from all her running and she'd decided it was time to show it off to Paul. She wanted him to see her as Orla his hot date, not as Orla the teacher.

Paul took her hand and walked her into the restaurant. When they were sitting down, and had made their order, he told her she was beautiful.

Orla blushed. 'Would you go away out of that! I am not.'

'You are. Take the compliment.'

She laughed. 'Okay, thanks. So are you.'

'Beautiful?' He grinned.

'I think so, yes.'

'Well, I've never been called that before. Sonja used to tell me I dressed badly, had terrible haircuts, needed to tone up . . . and on and on. She was never happy with the way I looked.'

'She was wrong.'

'Thanks. She's just one of those people who will never be happy. Nothing is ever enough. Sometimes I almost feel sorry for her. We should never have got married. We panicked when she got pregnant and jumped into it.'

'I'm sorry.'

'I would be if it wasn't for Lulu. She is the one glorious thing to come out of a pretty shitty marriage.'

'Were you ever in love with her?' Orla asked.

Paul swirled the wine in his glass. 'I don't know. I think I was dazzled by her. She was so different from any other girls I'd gone out with. She was so driven and focused and self-assured and confident. I found her fascinating. She had always gone out with equally high achievers and I think she liked me because I wasn't trying to outdo or outshine her. And then Lulu came along and we got stuck. The marriage didn't last long. We knew before Lulu was even born that we wouldn't make it. Now she's with Oliver, who is another high-flying, super-successful hedge-fund manager. I guess her blip with me, middle-of-the-road steady but boring lawyer, made her run back to her own type.'

'She seems formidable.'

Paul laughed. 'That's a good word to describe her. I worry that Lulu will inherit her flaws – her selfish, self-centred, to-hell-with-everyone-else traits. I want her to be a kind and caring kid.'

'She won't be selfish, not with you as her dad. You're so kind, caring and fun with her.'

'Do you really think so?' Paul leant forward. 'I don't want to mess parenthood up. I feel bad enough that Lulu comes from divorced parents. I'm a clueless thirty-one-year-old man just making it up as I go along. I wish there was a hand-book or a degree you could do, but you just have to figure it out day by day, don't you?'

'I think you're doing a wonderful job. She adores you.'

Paul gazed at her. 'Thanks for saying that. Would you like kids?'

Orla froze. Yes, she wanted to say. Yes, I would. I want

kids with you. Lots of them. But I don't know if I can even have sex with you, so I think kids are out.

'I'm not sure,' she fudged the answer.

'You're young, you've plenty of time. You'd be an amazing mother, though. I see you with Lulu and the other kids and you're a natural.'

Orla drank deeply from her glass to push down the emotion rising in her throat. Thankfully, their food arrived so they were distracted.

'So, tell me about yourself. Where are you from?'

Orla was about to launch into her usual made-up, fantasy childhood. She usually told people she had a loving father whom she went home to see regularly. But Paul had been so honest about his marriage and his fears about raising Lulu that she decided to tell the truth for once. Well, not the whole truth, but some of it.

'I'm an only child. My mother died in childbirth and my father never got over it. He tried not to, but he blamed me for her death.'

Paul reached out and took her hand in his. 'Oh, my God, that's awful. What a tragic thing to happen. So you never knew your mother?'

'No, but my father talked about her all the time. He never got over her death. He made her out to be a saint. He had photos of her all over the house. She was ever present, but I have no idea what she was really like because my dad deified her.'

Paul's eyes were so full of compassion that Orla had to look away.

'I'm so sorry that happened to you. I'm even more in awe of you now. You're so lovely and you seem so together. How did you manage to come out of that childhood so . . . so . . . well, normal?'

272

If only you knew, Orla thought. 'I'm sure I do have scars, but I think getting away from my hometown and my dad, and the blame, and all the memories has really helped. I love living in a big city where no one knows your family or your past. I feel like I can breathe freely here.'

'Do you see your dad much?'

'Not really. I try to go home once every couple of months, but sometimes it slips to four- or five-month gaps. I know I should go home more often, but it's . . . it . . .'

'It dredges up all the memories?' Paul gently finished her sentence.

Orla nodded. He got it. He understood. 'Yes, exactly.'

'It's amazing you go home at all. Did your dad ever meet anyone else?'

'No, he never even considered it. He shut down that side of his life when my mother died. He built a wall around himself so high that no one could have got over it.'

'It's kind of tragic that he spent all of these years stuck in the past, never letting himself live again. It must have been so hard for you.'

Orla shrugged. 'It was all I knew. When you're a kid, your life is your normal. It's only when you grow up, meet other people and see other families interacting that you understand how dysfunctional your own is.'

'That's very true.'

'I've seen it with the children in my classes over the years. No family is perfect. Everyone is flawed in some way. Some are just more so than others.'

'That makes me feel a bit better about Lulu being from a broken home.'

'She'll be fine because she has two parents who love her. That's not really a broken home, believe me.'

'If I'm being honest, I was a bit down for a while after the

273

break-up. I put all of my energy into Lulu. She was the crutch that got me through the divorce. I barely went out for years. Lulu was all I needed.'

Orla felt emotional listening to him, thinking of how distant and cold her father had always been. And here was a man who talked about his daughter so lovingly. Lulu was a lucky little girl.

'I've only really felt like myself again in the last year. I hid away after my marriage failed. Eventually, a few months ago, my mates forced me to go on a blind date and it was a disaster.'

Orla was delighted to hear that. 'Have you dated since then?'

'A one-night stand that was drink-induced and so awkward the next day.' He rolled his eyes.

A one-night stand, probably drunken steamy sex. Orla's stomach dropped. Still, though, he'd said it was awkward, so maybe it was bad sex.

'After that I cried off women for a while, until I met you and wanted to go on a date.'

'I'm flattered.' Orla smiled.

'You should be. I'm very picky.'

'Except for the one-night stand.'

'I blame the shots of Jägermeister my best mate forced down my throat.' Paul looked sheepish. 'I met you sober and clear-headed.'

Orla laughed. 'So you're attracted to damaged country girls.'

'I'm attracted to one very gorgeous country girl. And you're not damaged, you're a survivor of a tragic childhood. That makes you even more attractive. You're obviously very strong and the fact that you chose to provide education, love and care to young kids is amazing. With all that you went through as a child, it's no wonder you're such a compassionate teacher.'

Orla looked down at her half-eaten meal. Did he really think that?

As if sensing her lack of confidence, Paul added, 'I mean every word. You have no idea how good you are with kids.'

'Thanks.'

'And pretty good with the dads too.' He winked at her.

Orla didn't want Paul to think she was a slapper who went out with any dad in the class who paid her attention. 'Just to be clear, I have never, ever gone out with a school dad before, and to be honest, I'm not sure I'm supposed to.'

Paul squeezed her hand. 'I won't tell if you don't.'

Orla laughed. 'My lips are sealed.'

'Very nice lips they are too.' Paul leant across the table and kissed them gently. Orla felt her mouth tingle as he pulled away.

'Shall I get the bill? Then maybe you'd consider coming back for a nightcap,' he asked, looking at her with eyes that had 'I want you' written all over them.

Damnit, what was she going to do? Lulu was staying with Sonja and she knew if she went back to Paul's house, he'd try to have sex with her. She didn't want him to find out. She remembered Maggie's words – take it slow. Her whole body yearned to be with him, but she knew what could happen. Orla felt beads of sweat rolling down her back as panic set in.

'Hey,' Paul said, taking her hand. 'You look hassled. Am I moving too fast? Sorry, I'm so out of touch with dating. But I wasn't inviting you back for sex – I mean, if it happened, that would be fine too, but I just wanted to keep chatting and for the night not to be over. I'm really rubbish at this. Tell me what to do.'

He was nervous too. Orla could have cried with relief.

'Thank you. I'd love to come back and chat. And, yes, if it's okay with you, I'd like to take it slowly.'

Paul's worried face broke into a smile. 'Oh, thank God, I thought I'd blown it. Would it be okay if I kissed you, though? I've been wanting to all night.'

Orla smiled. 'A kiss would be lovely.'

Paul took her face in his hands and kissed her. Orla closed her eyes and fell deeper for this tender, loving man.

28

Ann stared at the ceiling. How did she get here? Was this really marriage – to end up in a house living with a man she couldn't talk to and be content with that? To feel so lonely? Ann had never imagined that loneliness could feel so acute that it left you breathless. She could not live like this. She had to do something before it was too late.

I'm sixty-five, she thought sadly. Happy birthday to me. Sixty-five and the unhappiest I've ever been. This was even worse than the failed IVFs. At least IVF was based on hope and goals, whereas this feeling of daily dread felt devoid of any hope. She had a permanent pain in her chest and felt anxious all the time. She was terrified that her life was over before she'd got to experience all it had to offer.

Well, Ann, she thought, the only person who can change your life is you. But how? What was she going to do?

Her phone pinged. *Happy birthday Ann. Hope uv had a b'day shag & Ken is cooking u a fab brekkie & that he gave u loads of decent presents. See you next week. Love ya. Milly xxxxxx*

Tears dropped onto her phone screen. Ken had barely spoken to her since the last session with Maggie. All he had said was that he was never going back. If he wasn't willing to try, it was over. Ann knew it and she reckoned Ken did too.

Ann heard the doorbell ring and Ken answer it.

'Hi, where's Mum?' Zoë asked. 'Are you making her breakfast in bed? What did you buy her?'

Ann couldn't hear Ken's replies because he was speaking

in his low voice. She heard Zoë's footsteps on the stairs and quickly wiped her eyes.

The bedroom door burst open and Zoë rushed in, holding an enormous bunch of flowers. 'Happy birthday, Mum. These are from John and me. Love you.' Zoë handed her the flowers and kissed her.

'And this is from Orla.' Zoë threw a package onto the bed.

Ann's heart lifted at the sight of her daughter. She had done well when it came to her children. Zoë and John were wonderful. Her marriage hadn't been a total waste. John had sent her a beautiful message at midnight and said a gift was in the post. She missed him so much, but she was glad he was happy in Sydney.

Ann held Zoë's flowers. 'Thank you, love, they're gorgeous.' She tried not to let them, but the tears flowed.

'Aw, Mum, don't cry on your birthday.' Zoë sat on the bed and hugged her.

'Don't mind me. I'm just emotional and missing John.'

'God, me too, but he sounds so happy. I'm a bit jealous. All that sun and surf.'

'Don't even think about emigrating. I can't have both my kids on the other side of the world.'

'Nah, I'm not going anywhere. I'm having too much fun here. By the way, what's up with Dad? He seems particularly grumpy. What did he get you?'

'I don't know. I haven't seen him yet.'

Zoë rolled her eyes. 'I'll have a word with him. He should be showering you with gifts. You're an amazing wife and mother.'

Ann kissed her soft cheek. 'Thanks, Zoë.'

'You really are, Mum. You did everything for us. You always put us first. I think that's why I'll never have kids. I'm too selfish.'

Ann squeezed her hand. 'No, you're not. When you hold your child in your arms, you want to do everything in your power to make their life perfect. I loved being a mum. I honestly loved every minute. I miss it.'

'But isn't it nice to get your life back and have time for yourself again?'

No, Ann thought, it isn't. It's terrifying. The days and weeks and months lie in front of you – empty. All those hours to fill . . . and with what? What is your purpose? You're considered old by society. Take up golf or bridge to fill the hours? But she didn't want to play golf or bridge. She wanted to experience more and live more before it was too late.

'What are your plans? Please tell me Dad's taking you out for a nice lunch at least.'

Your father has barely uttered two words to me in four days. Our marriage is imploding. I somehow doubt we're going for a fancy lunch. 'I'm not sure, love, he hasn't said anything.'

Zoë rolled her eyes again. 'Honestly, Mum, he needs a good shake. I remember for your fiftieth he organized that surprise party. He's got lazy lately. He's so set in his ways. I'm going to talk to him.'

Zoë scrambled off the bed and went down to talk to her father.

This should be interesting, Ann thought. She went to the bedroom door, opened it a crack and listened.

'Dad, what are you doing for Mum's birthday? I hope you have plans. Are you taking her to a posh restaurant for lunch?'

'Well, she said she didn't want a fuss.'

'All women say that and they never mean it. You know Mum likes to be taken out. Seriously, Dad, step it up.'

'What do you mean?' Ken sounded annoyed.

'I mean, don't be complacent. Mum is amazing and the one day she deserves to be spoilt is her birthday, so spoil her. I think she's struggling a bit at the moment. She really misses John and she seems a bit lost. Do something nice for her. Here, I'll book a restaurant now and you can pretend it was your idea.'

'No, I'll do it.'

'Well, you'd better hurry up or they'll all be booked out. What did you get her anyway?'

'I got her that Dyson cordless she was talking about.'

'Oh, my actual God. You got her a Dyson?'

'Yes, she wants it. She's been talking about how good it is.'

'Jesus, Dad, no woman wants a vacuum cleaner for her birthday. Buy her a Dyson on a Monday, but do not buy her one for her sixty-fifth birthday.'

'I bought her something she wants. What do you suggest I buy her then?'

'Something romantic . . . flowers, perfume, silk nightie, weekend in Paris . . . something that says "I love you", not "I like the house to be clean."'

'If I got her perfume, it'd be the wrong brand, and she likes wearing pyjamas and you brought her flowers and I don't like flying. What's wrong with getting her something I'm sure she wants?'

'You're a disaster. You'd better book somewhere really fancy for lunch to balance out the Dyson. Seriously, Dad, you need to try to be more romantic.'

'Did your mother tell you to say that?'

'No, she didn't say anything. I'm telling you because someone needs to. If a guy gave me a vacuum cleaner for my birthday, I'd shove it up his arse and break up with him.'

'I give up. Nothing I do is right.'

'Oh, come on. Don't be a drama queen, just make an

effort. Book Chez Max and buy a bottle of champagne. She'll forgive you. Mum's not hard to please. She's so grateful for any little thing we do for her.'

While Ann appreciated Zoë's support she wondered if she was so easy to please. Was she *too* easy to please? Was she just a doormat? Maybe that was the problem. Maybe she should have spoken up years ago. Zoë would never accept a vacuum cleaner as a birthday gift. Yet Ken had always bought her practical gifts. He'd never been one for champagne and chocolates. He saw them as a waste of money. He'd rather buy her a good toaster than a bottle of Laurent-Perrier.

Ann had never complained. She'd just gone with it. She'd thought, That's how it is. That's how we are. We're a practical couple. But when she saw friends' husbands buying them romantic gifts of jewellery and perfume, she did envy them. She'd dropped hints to Ken over the years, but he couldn't understand why you would spend hundreds of euros on a bracelet when you could spend it on a good-quality barbecue that would last years.

Ann knew that if Ken had come in to her with breakfast in bed, flowers, perfume and a silk nightdress, she would have been thrilled. But he never had, and he never would. That was not who she had married.

Until recently, she hadn't minded that he wasn't romantic. After all, he had paid for her new kitchen. He had paid for their lovely home. Ken didn't do gestures, he did practicality. That was him. Why did it bother her so much now? Maybe she was more worried about his retirement than he was. She dreaded the thought of him being around all day. She dreaded that it would highlight their having nothing to say to each other, that they had little in common except the kids. Ken was right: maybe he hadn't changed all that much at all, but she had. Did she want to save her marriage or herself? Was all this really about Ann wanting to live a more exciting life? Was she being too hard on Ken? Was she trying to change him to suit her needs? Or had they just grown apart?

'I'm not sure your mother wants to go for a fancy lunch with me,' Ken admitted.

'Why not? Did you guys have a fight?'

'Well, kind of a disagreement, I think you'd call it.'

'About what? The Dyson?'

'No, I haven't given that to her yet.'

'What, then?'

'Just private stuff, between us.'

'Well, if you want my opinion, you need to start making more of an effort, Dad. It's just the two of you, and now John's gone to Australia, Mum probably feels lonely and a bit lost. You need to pay her more attention.'

'Hey, I'm very good to your mother. I provide her with everything she needs, a good home, a nice car – she used to be happy with that.'

'I know you're good to Mum, but it's not about sensible gifts, Dad, it's about love and kindness and romance,' Zoë explained.

Was she happy until recently? No, Ann thought. This had been creeping up on her for a long time. It had just happened so slowly that she could ignore it, sidestep it, until one day she had woken up and realized she was deeply unhappy. That her life had gone by without her making any impact on the world. That she had devoted her life to people who were busy living theirs. That her life was so small and insignificant, she might as well have been invisible. It was sobering and petrifying.

'Okay, Mr Grumpy, I can see you're in a mood so I'm going, but please be nice to Mum. I'll pop around after work to check up on what you did. She seems very down in the dumps, these days. You should make a big effort today to treat her and be extra nice to her. Go on, Dad, I know you love her, but you need to show her how much.'

The thing was, Ann didn't want to go out for a fancy lunch with Ken. He'd just fuss about the price of everything and having to get dressed up, and he'd take all the good out of it. Besides, they had nothing to say to each other. It was clear they had run out of steam. Their marriage, if Ann was being honest, was all but over.

Zoë left and there was silence. Ann closed the bedroom door quietly. As she got back into bed the gift from Orla fell onto the floor. Ann reached over and picked it up. She opened the beautifully wrapped gift. Inside was a book: *Tango Lessons* by Marilyn Grace Miller. Ann smiled. The card said, *I thought you might enjoy this. I hope you get to dance your tango one day. Love Orla xx*

It felt like a sign. It felt like a push towards change. Was Ann going to be one of those people who woke up at eighty full of regrets, wishing she had done all the things she'd dreamt of? Did she want to be sitting in an old folks' home, saying, 'I should have gone to Argentina and danced while I still could'? Could she blame Ken for not going? Or was it time to face up to the fact that it was she, Ann, who wanted this? It was she who wanted to change and shake things up. It was she who was dissatisfied, restless and unhappy. And she had now grasped that the only person who could change that, the only person who could make her happy, was herself. She had to stop blaming Ken and wishing he was different. If she wanted adventure, it was up to her to go and find it.

Maggie was right when she said that talking helped you figure out what you wanted. It was those sessions, when Ann had finally spoken her mind, that had led her to this understanding. She felt a deep sadness that it had also led her to the knowledge that her marriage wasn't what she wanted any more. But, deep in her soul, she knew this was the right decision for her despite the serious consequences. She knew now what she wanted, and what she didn't want. She knew Ken didn't want the same things. It was time to stop feeling sorry for herself and act.

Ann sat back on the bed and pulled out her laptop. She typed into the search bar 'Trips for single people to Buenos Aires'. It was time. Time to start a new life, where she did things that made her happy . . . and scared. But she would rather be nervous about an adventure than dead inside.

29

Alice handed Sarah her lunchbox.

'Mum, this is Poppy's,' Sarah said. 'If I went into school with a unicorn lunchbox, I'd be bullied.'

'I love my unicorn lunchbox,' Poppy shouted, grabbing it from her sister.

Alice rubbed her eyes and handed Sarah her plain red one.

'No way!' Ted said. 'I am not eating a cheese sandwich.' He pulled the sandwich apart and flung the cheese onto the kitchen counter. 'Mummy, you know I hate cheese. You gaved me cheese yesterday as well.'

'I hate bananas.' Poppy threw hers beside the cheese. 'I want crisps like Lulu has. Her daddy is really nice and gives her lunches that are not stinky.'

'What's wrong with you, Mum?' Sarah asked. 'You've been weird since you came back from the hotel with Dad. Are you sick?'

Am I sick? thought Alice. Yes, I guess I am. Sick of you all giving out about every sodding thing I put into your lunchboxes every bloody day. Sick of trying to get you to eat healthy food. Sick of being blamed for every tiny thing that goes wrong in your lives. But, most of all, I am sick of your father. Your selfish, sex-obsessed father. I want to shove that vibrator down his stupid throat.

'Mum, do you need me to get you medicine?' Jamie asked.

Alice looked at his concerned face. The other kids would suck her dry, but Jamie would look after her. She stroked his cheek. 'No, pet, I'm not sick, just tired. I slept badly.' She clapped her hands. 'Right, let's go. We're going to be late.'

'What about my sandwich?' Ted asked.

Alice slapped the two pieces of buttered bread together and shoved them back into his lunchbox. 'Butter sandwich today, Ted.' She grabbed her keys and headed for the front door. All she wanted to do was go back to bed and put the duvet over her head. But she had to keep going. These four little people needed her.

'You should ring Childline, Ted,' Sarah told her little brother. 'A butter sandwich is child abuse.'

Two hours later, Alice sat in Maggie's office with her husband, whom she currently hated. He was telling Maggie about the vibrator fiasco.

'I just thought it would be fun, but Alice got really upset.'

'Did you feel upset, Alice?' Maggie asked.

Alice nodded. 'Very.'

'And why do you think it upset you so much?'

'I suppose it might have something to do with the fact that he had discussed our sex life – which, according to Niall, is a disaster – with his friend and his girlfriend. That's pretty humiliating to me. Also, he hadn't discussed this little experiment with me beforehand, he pounced on me with it. And we had already had sex earlier that day. So it wasn't as if he was deprived of a shag. I'd done my bit.'

'Is that how you see sex? Doing your bit?' Maggie asked.

Alice shrugged. 'No. I just meant that we'd had sex, and I think once in a day is plenty. I don't need or want sex toys and I certainly don't want or need my bloody husband discussing me with a virtual stranger.'

'What's wrong with wanting to spice things up? It was just

286

a bit of fun. Max said it really turns Lizzie on. I was doing it for you.'

Alice thought her head was going to explode. 'For me? Bullshit. This is all about you, Niall. Everything is always about you. You wanting more sex, you wanting to go out to nightclubs because Max is, you wanting to use sex toys. You being jealous of your stupid bloody friend and his stupid girlfriend having sex all over the city. You want to be Max – no responsibilities, no kids to look after, except the odd weekend. I'm so sick of listening to how much fun Max is having. You're like some pathetic teenager who wants to be in the cool gang. Well, sod off, then. Go and join him in his vacuous, selfish life. I'm sure one of Lizzie's friends will accommodate you.'

'Yes, they would,' Niall snapped back.

Alice glared at him. 'You didn't? Did you?'

'No, but I could have.'

'How dare you even think about it?' Alice's whole body shook as she breathed, trying to calm herself. Niall stared straight ahead, not looking at her.

'That's a strong statement. What did you mean by it, Niall?' Maggie asked.

'I mean that one of Lizzie's friends was all over me. I'm not going to lie, I enjoyed the attention and I was tempted for a brief second, but I didn't do anything. I don't want to be with anyone but Alice.'

'Thanks so much. Am I supposed to be grateful that you let some young one maul you but you didn't act on it? Did you complain to her about your frigid wife, too? Did *she* give you any tips on sex toys? What should I expect next – handcuffs? Whips?'

'No, Alice.' Niall sighed. 'I actually told her that I loved my wife and she was wasting her time with me.'

'Do you feel reassured by that, Alice?' Maggie asked.

'Kind of, but I'm not exactly thrilled that he's out being flirted with and, besides, he still betrayed me by talking to Lizzie about needing to spice up our sex life with toys.'

'Why do you feel that was a betrayal? Perhaps Niall just wanted you to have more pleasure during sex.'

Alice slumped back in her chair. 'Because it made me feel so ashamed,' she said quietly. 'And humiliated and embarrassed. I know Niall and I have problems, but I've never discussed our sex life with anyone. I don't sit around gossiping with other women about sex. Our relationship is private. And yet there he was, talking about how rubbish I am in bed to Lizzie, someone he barely knows, and that makes me feel sick.'

Maggie took a deep breath. 'Niall, can you hear the hurt in Alice's voice? Do you understand how this looks from her point of view?'

'I never told her you were rubbish in bed! Come on, Alice, give me some credit. I did it for you. I did it to try to help you get more aroused,' he said.

'Okay, so your intentions were good,' Maggie said. 'But can you also see how, to Alice, it sounds like you went behind her back and talked about your private life with an outsider?'

'Yes, but I was doing it for her, for us. Lizzie said the vibrator was great for her and Max, and I thought it might be good for us too. I wanted to help Alice enjoy sex again. Shoot me for trying to reignite our sex life.'

Maggie looked at him, her head tilted to one side. 'Are you jealous of Max?' she asked.

'No, I'm not. I think he's behaving like an idiot. He's doing way too much coke, and a couple of weeks ago he told me he's going offside on Lizzie with one of her friends. I don't envy him his choices or his life. I don't think he was wrong to walk away from an unhappy marriage, but he's gone a bit nuts. He puts his own happiness before anyone else's, which is hard on his family.

'But at the same time, seeing him full of life and fun again showed me how dull we've got. I want to be with Alice, but I don't think we need to sacrifice everything for the kids. My parents loved my brother and me, but they didn't put us first. They put each other first. They left us with childminders and went off on weekends with friends and had nights away, and if they were a bit hung-over, they shoved us in front of the TV for the morning. It didn't do us any harm. But with Alice and me, it's always about the kids. All I'm asking is, can't we be a couple as well, instead of just parents all the time?'

Maggie looked at Alice. 'Niall has made an important point about how your life together is set up. How do you feel about what he just said? Do you think you put the children first too much?'

Alice paused. Did she? Probably, but they were young. They needed her and Niall. But, then, if she was being really honest, she probably did sometimes use them as an excuse not to go out or to avoid sex. She'd got lazy about making an effort with Niall. She'd got lazy about making an effort with herself. She'd stopped going to the gym and for walks. She wore the same clothes every day, jeans and a sweatshirt. Some days she didn't even bother putting on any make-up. Her hair was always pulled back in a ponytail. She kept saying she'd buy new clothes when she lost that stone, but she never did. She felt bad about herself – she didn't feel attractive or sexy. Lisa and her mother were always on at her to get a new haircut, some new clothes, and to wear make-up. 'You need to smarten yourself up,' her mother said regularly. Alice had largely dismissed it as nagging, but maybe her mother had a point.

'I suppose maybe I do,' she said. 'But I feel I have to. They need us.'

'So you feel that sense of responsibility as a parent to be there for your children, but do you also miss going out as a couple and having fun together?'

'I love all of us to snuggle up on Saturday night and watch a family movie. Niall thinks that's boring. I think it's special family time. It's something the kids will remember.'

'How would you feel about watching a family movie on Friday and going out with Niall on Saturday?' Maggie suggested.

'We could do that, but I . . . I just . . . Everything seems like a mountain to climb. I feel overwhelmed.' Alice began to cry.

Maggie handed her a tissue. 'So many mothers feel this way, Alice. You're not alone. There are multiple demands on today's mothers and it can be so hard to plot a path through that.'

'But it's my only job.'

'Does it feel like a job to you?' Maggie asked.

'Yes,' Alice admitted. She felt a rush of guilt, but she ploughed on: 'Yes, it does. And it's one where no one ever tells you you're doing well – in fact, you're told you're a rubbish mum daily and you never get a promotion or a bonus or a boozy Christmas lunch. I'm frustrated. I'm really upset that I'm not good at my job. My mum coped with all the pain and suffering life threw at her. She didn't sit around feeling sorry for herself, eating chocolate biscuits and smoking sneaky cigarettes out of the back door, she just got on with it. She was my role model, and although I wanted to be different, in that I wanted to stay at home with the kids, I thought I'd be better at it. I'm . . . I'm ashamed at how I seem to find it so hard. I'm disappointed in myself. I feel useless.' She gulped back tears. 'I'm a crap mum and I look like crap, too. I'm a real winner at life. Actually, I wouldn't blame Niall if he ran off with one of Lizzie's friends. I probably would if I was him.'

'You're being very hard on yourself, Alice,' Maggie said gently. 'You're giving so much to your children. Do you think perhaps you've lost yourself in there?'

Alice nodded. 'I keep saying I'll make an effort this week, then something happens – one of the kids gets sick or Niall's dad needs help or, well, there always seems to be some excuse I can use. So I don't go for a walk, I eat chocolate biscuits instead, and then I feel worse about myself. I feel flabby and ugly and . . . I don't know who I am any more.'

Niall put his hand out and rubbed her back. 'You're still you, Alice, lovely, gorgeous you. I don't care what you wear. You're still sexy and stunning to me. I hate hearing you being so negative about yourself and calling yourself ugly. I have no intention of running off with some young thing because I only want you, Alice.'

'Can you accept what Niall is saying, Alice?' Maggie asked.

'I suppose so. I'm just not sure why he's still in love with me. I don't even know who I am any more. I don't see myself as sexy or attractive or fun or funny or good company. I'm just a boring blob. When I see women like Lizzie, I feel so insecure. She's fun and bubbly and sexy – all the things I used to be, but amn't any more. I want to want sex again. I want to find my way back to the fun, enthusiastic, energetic Alice, I just don't know where to start. I'm not sure I can find her.'

'That's very honest of you, Alice,' Maggie said. 'It's not easy to admit that you don't see yourself as a sexual being at the moment, but that's not because you're not a sexual being, it's because you're worn out. Once you make the changes that address those hurdles, I think you'll find your spark again. I'm looking at two people here who love each other and who want to work towards finding each other again.'

'But I'm not working towards it,' Alice said tearfully. 'I'm tired and boring and getting chunkier by the day and I think . . . Niall's going to leave me . . .' a sob escaped from her '. . . and run off with some pert-bummed, bouncy vegan gym bunny who has a cupboard full of sex toys and will do tequila shots until five a.m.'

Niall laughed and grabbed her hand. 'Don't be mad. I only want you, Alice. But you never seem to want to hang out with me. I miss you.'

'I miss you too. I do know I need to shake myself up. I just find it hard to motivate myself when I feel like I'm doing a bad job all the time.' She looked at Maggie. 'My mother thinks I might be perimenopausal. I'm booked in to see the GP next week. To be honest, though, I think it's just years of interrupted sleep and feeling like a failure that's causing it.'

'It's no harm to get checked out by your GP,' Maggie said. 'But I do think stress is a big factor here, Alice. There's a conflict within you that you have to resolve. But I also think you might try to focus on your physical wellbeing, because it will help give you the mental clarity to figure out what you need. And it will help with your negative feelings about your-self. The physical affects the mental and vice versa.'

Alice nodded wearily. 'I know you're right.'

'Why don't you start slowly?' Maggie said. 'Would you con-sider getting a babysitter on Sunday mornings for two hours? Go for a walk together and grab a coffee after. There'll be no pressure to dress up or have sex. You can just talk to each other, get some exercise and fresh air, and reconnect.'

'Unless Niall shoves me into a hedge for sex and produces furry handcuffs.' Alice gave a watery laugh.

Niall laughed. 'I promise not to.'

Alice smiled through her tears.

'And, Alice, will you try to plan forty minutes every

morning for a walk? Leave the laundry, leave the unmade beds, and invest some time in yourself. Niall, will you encourage Alice to take time for herself?'

'I will, absolutely. I'll set an alarm on my phone and call her to make sure she's out walking.'

And I'll have to throw out the secret stash of biscuits and cigarettes, Alice thought. And stop watching endless reruns of *Poldark*, fantasizing about Aidan Turner ripping my clothes off. I need to think about Niall doing the undressing.

It wasn't going to be the same, but she had to try. She knew she had to do something or she'd never find herself again. She'd be buried alive under laundry, school lunches and ungrateful children. Something had to change.

30

Orla was sitting on one of the two counter stools, drinking wine, while Paul stood on the other side, chopping mushrooms.

She drank deeply to push away the negative thoughts of her failed attempt to insert the dilator again that morning. She had to focus on the *now*. Maggie had told her it was important that she lived in the moment and tried not to let that negative voice take over her thoughts.

The *now* was perfect: Paul cooking her dinner, music playing in the background, easy conversation and those big brown eyes smiling across at her. Lulu was with Sonja, so they were alone. She had Paul's full attention and it felt like the sun was shining on just her. Having spent her whole life being ignored and living in the shadows, Orla was cherishing every second.

'So, Miss Orla,' Paul grinned, 'how do you like your steaks cooked?'

'Medium rare, please.'

'Thank God you didn't say well done. I may have had to break up with you if you had.'

'I would never ruin a good steak by cremating it.' Orla smiled back.

Paul leant across and kissed her. 'Much as I adore my daughter, it's very nice to have you here in the house all to myself.'

Orla felt her stomach drop. They'd been on five dates and he had dropped her home after each one and kissed her on her doorstep, but nothing more. Lovely, long, lingering, passionate kisses. He had respected her request to take things slowly. But Orla knew that Paul would be hoping to have sex tonight. They were here, alone, about to have a candle-lit dinner: it was time for the next stage.

Maybe I'll be okay, she thought. Maybe the dilators are too clinical. With Paul she felt such desire that her body would surely let him in. She yearned to be naked with him, to rub her hands all over his body. But what if . . .

'Hey, where have you gone? You've got that faraway look in your eye again.'

'Sorry, I was just thinking how perfect tonight is,' she said.

'Yeah, it is. Actually, there's something I wanted to ask you.'

'What?' Orla tensed.

Paul transferred the chopped mushrooms into the frying pan. 'Would you consider coming on holidays with me and Lulu this summer? I've booked a campsite in France for a week. Don't worry, we won't be sleeping in a tent, they have nice cabins. But if you were free, I'd love you to come.'

I want to, I really, really want to, but we'd be sharing a bed, and . . . Stop it, Orla. She brought Maggie's voice to mind. Just say yes. Live in the moment.

'I'd love to.'

'Phew, you had me worried there – long pause!' Paul said. 'I thought maybe I'd frightened you off by moving too quick.'

'You could never frighten me off,' Orla said.

'Good, because I want you with me as much as possible.'

He came around and took her in his arms. They kissed and she felt his hands in her hair. Her body leant towards his, desire pulsing through her.

BANG! BANG! BANG!

'Jesus, who's that?' Paul pulled back.

He went to open the front door. Orla followed him out to the hall, watching from a distance to see who it was.

Sonja stood on the doorstep, looking, for once, a little dishevelled.

So she is human, Orla thought. But what was she doing here?

'What's going on?' Paul asked.

'My waters just broke. Oliver's driving me to hospital. You'll have to take Lulu.'

Lulu appeared from the car, carrying her bag.

'Is this a bit early? Are you all right?' Paul asked, as Lulu walked by him into the house.

'Only two weeks, nothing to worry about. She's a big baby, so they said it might happen. I'll let you know when the baby's born. Can you –'

'Orla!' Lulu spotted her teacher and ran to hug her.

Sonja looked to the left and saw Orla hugging Lulu. 'Seriously, Paul? Lulu's teacher? Could you be more of a cliché?'

Orla told Lulu to go upstairs and unpack her bag. She stood back, out of sight and listened.

'That's rich coming from someone who slept with her work colleague while married to me.'

'Of all the women in Dublin, you have to shag our daughter's teacher?'

'Her name is Orla and we're not shagging. We're going out with each other.'

Go, Paul, Orla cheered silently.

'So, what happens when you break up? How is that going to affect Lulu? Have you thought about that?'

'We're not going to break up.'

Sonja snorted. 'How long has this been going on? A couple of weeks? You never think things through, Paul. You're always driven by your emotions. It's ridiculous.'

'We've been together more than a couple of weeks and I really like her, Sonja. She's very special.'

Very special! Orla hugged herself.

'I give it another month and she'll be off. What age is she? Twenty-two? She's not going to want to be lumbered with you and Lulu. This is really stupid of you, Paul.'

'She's twenty-four and she adores Lulu.'

'Do me a favour. When this little fling implodes, keep your hands off Lulu's teacher next year. Find someone who isn't educating our daughter to sleep with.'

'Do *me* a favour and keep your snide remarks and your put-downs for Oliver. The wonderful thing about being divorced from you is that I don't have to listen to your crap any more. Good luck with the baby.' Paul slammed the door shut.

Orla went back to sit at the counter so he wouldn't know she'd listened to the whole conversation.

He came in, looking furious. 'How did I ever marry that bitch?'

'Have a drink.' Orla poured him a glass of wine.

He knocked it back. 'Sorry, she just winds me up.'

'So I see.' Orla rubbed his arm. 'Hey, she's gone now. Take a breath.'

Paul laid his head on her shoulder and nuzzled into her neck. 'I'm so glad you're here. I love you, Orla.'

Orla froze. What? Did he just say he loved her?

'I know it's very early in our relationship, but I love you,' he said again.

Orla stayed in the moment, the beautiful, precious moment. 'I love you too,' she whispered. It was true: she did, completely and utterly.

Paul pulled his head back and held her close, kissing her all over her face. 'Where have you been all my life?'

'In Ballystone, miserable, waiting for mine to begin.' Orla laughed.

'Well, I'm very glad you came up to the big city.'

They were kissing when they heard 'Daddy?'

They turned to Lulu. She was crying. Paul crouched down. 'Hey, sweetheart, what's wrong?'

'I don't want Mummy to have another baby,' she cried. 'I know it's mean and she'll be my sister, but I don't want a stinky sister. I want it to be the same. Just me.'

'Well, you'll have a sister, but only in Mummy's house. Here, in our house, it'll still be just you, the Queen Bee.' Paul hugged her.

'Promise you'll never have another baby?'

Paul looked at Orla over Lulu's shoulder. 'Well, I . . . It . . .'

'He promises,' Orla said. 'It'll only ever be you.'

Whether she ended up being able to have sex with Paul or not, Orla didn't need to have a child. Paul and Lulu were enough for her. She'd never believed she'd have her own children anyway. The thought of childbirth terrified her – look at what had happened to her mother. It wasn't something she'd thought would happen so it wasn't a sacrifice. She loved Lulu and she adored Paul. She didn't need anything else.

'Orla?' Paul frowned.

'I mean it, Paul. Lulu is enough.' Orla turned to Lulu. 'Hey, guess what I brought for dessert? Chocolate cake. Would you like some?'

Lulu nodded. Orla held out her hand and the little girl clutched it. Orla sat her up at the counter and cut her a big slice of the cake.

Orla chatted to Lulu about everything and nothing, distracting her from the worry of her new sibling's arrival.

Orla and Paul ate their steaks on their laps in front of the TV, watching Lulu's favourite film, *Inside Out*.

'Sorry about this,' he whispered. 'Not the romantic evening I'd had in mind.'

'It's perfect,' Orla whispered back.

Towards the end of the film, Lulu fell asleep.

Paul lifted her and brought her up to bed. Orla tidied up and stacked the dishwasher.

She felt arms around her.

'I didn't think it was possible to love you more, but I do now,' Paul said. 'You were amazing with Lulu tonight.'

Orla turned and kissed him.

'But we need to talk about the kid thing. I can't ask you to give up having children for Lulu. It's not fair.'

Orla stroked his cheek. 'It's not a sacrifice for me. I meant it. You and Lulu are all I need or want.'

'Are you sure?' Paul looked deep into her eyes.

'One hundred per cent.'

'God, I love you, Orla Kane.'

He kissed her passionately and Orla leant in and let herself go. Within minutes they were naked on the couch, Paul was exploring her body with his hands and she was responding. This is it, she thought, this is finally it. She wanted him inside her, her body craved it. She opened her legs as he straddled her. Moaning with pleasure, he . . .

No! Please, God, no.

'I can't seem to . . .'

Orla closed her eyes and tried to force herself to open up. Paul tried to enter her again. The pain was excruciating. Orla knew it was hopeless.

'Sorry, was I too hasty?'

'No, it's me.' Orla's voice shook.

Paul stroked her cheek. 'We'll just try again, I'll go slower.'

'You don't understand. I can't do this.' She began to cry.

'Did I do something wrong?'

'No, it's not you. I . . . I have to go.'

'Hey, Orla, wait.'

'I'm sorry. I'm so sorry.' Orla threw on her dress, grabbed her bag and fled the house before Paul could stop her.

She ran to her car and drove off. Two streets away she pulled over, rested her head on the steering wheel and howled. Once a freak, always a freak. Why had she ever thought she could be normal and have a happy life? It was over. Her last chance at happiness was gone. She loved Paul and wanted him so much, but her stupid body couldn't even let him in. She should never have let herself think it was possible. She was never going to be in a relationship. This was it, her life, alone.

Orla sobbed as the last remaining flutters of hope died inside her. It was over. Orla Kane had been born doomed. Nothing and no one would ever change that.

31

Ann stood outside the shop, locked and bolted the front door. She checked the shutters were secure, then handed the keys to Milly. 'Over to you now,' she said.

Milly threw her arms around Ann's neck. 'I'm gonna miss you so much. I never thought I could be such good buddies with an old person. When I first got the job and saw you, I thought it was going to be a nightmare, that you'd be all bossy and narky and stuff. But you rock, Ann. You really do. You're so nice and you never judge me when I tell you my mad stories. I hope you have a brilliant time because you deserve it.'

Ann kissed Milly's cheek. 'Milly, it was you who planted the idea in my head. You made me realize that life isn't over, and that even us oldies,' she winked, 'can have adventures and fun.'

'Did I really? Well, I'm glad. I hope Ken doesn't come into the shop and blame me, though.'

Ann laughed. 'He won't. He knows this is my decision. I'm doing this for me. But thank you for nudging me along. You're a wonderful girl, Milly. Don't ever forget that. And, remember, only be with a boy who deserves you and treats you well.'

Milly nodded. 'Thanks. You always make me feel like I deserve the best. I want you to go and have a passionate affair with some hot guy and live in a beach hut and sell jewellery made of sea shells, but I also want you to come back.'

Ann smiled at her young friend. She'd booked for three

months. She planned to come back, but who knew? For once, Ann was going to please herself. She was going to Buenos Aires to dance the tango. Part of her was terrified, but she was embracing it. She hadn't felt this alive in years. She'd spent all of her time researching and planning the holiday. She'd rented an apartment near the beach in what was described as a 'safe area'. She'd booked tango lessons online in a dance studio near her apartment. She didn't know a single person in Argentina, but she had signed up for Spanish lessons in a language school and was hoping to meet people through the classes.

'I'm gonna go now before I start blubbing. I love you, Ann, you're the best. *Hasta la vista*, baby.' Milly waved as she walked off, her lower lip wobbling like a little girl's.

'Bye, Milly, keep in touch.'

Ann watched Milly slouch off down the road. She'd miss her a lot.

Ken stood at the bedroom door and watched Ann pack. 'You're not actually going ahead with this?'

With her back to him as she folded her orange summer dress into the large suitcase, Ann replied, 'Yes, Ken, I am.'

'But this is ridiculous. I get it, you're angry with me. I need to make more of an effort. I need to take you out more and talk to you more. I'll do it. I know I've got a bit set in my ways. I'll try harder, Ann. Come on now, stop this nonsense.'

Ann turned to face her husband. 'It's not nonsense, Ken. I'm going to clear my head and have time to think. I'm going because I want to and, frankly, if I don't, I think I'll have a nervous breakdown.'

Ken spluttered, 'That's a bit dramatic. You're just having an empty-nest wobble. There's no need to go to the other side of the world to work it out.'

Ann turned back to her packing and tried to inhale and exhale slowly to remain calm. She packed her two new swim-suits, chosen by Zoë, who was full of encouragement and was planning to come and visit in the last month. John had been less enthusiastic. He was worried for her safety. She'd tried to reassure him that she would be careful, but he was like his father, a natural-born worrier. He'd made her promise to FaceTime him every day.

Ken cleared his throat. 'Ann, you can't go. It's danger-ous. People get killed in these places all the time, especially female tourists. You'll be a sitting duck for thieves and God knows what else.'

Ann didn't answer.

'Did you hear me, Ann? You cannot go to this crazy place. What if you get into trouble? Who's going to help you? I won't be there to protect you. What will you do?'

'I'll figure it out, Ken. I'm a fairly intelligent woman with good sense. I'll be fine.'

'But you're not, Ann. You're very casual with your bag – you're always leaving it open. You'll get pickpocketed. What if they steal your passport?'

'I'll get another one.'

'Jesus Christ, Ann, will you stop this nonsense! You can-not go gallivanting off to the other side of the world.'

Ann placed her cream sandals in the suitcase. She longed for the sound of waves and to feel the sun on her face.

She turned slowly to face her husband. 'Ken, I'm going. Tomorrow morning, I will leave for Argentina. I'll keep in touch and check in with you. But apart from that, I'm going to be on my own, to dance and feel alive again. If I get into trouble, that's on me.'

'I don't know what the hell is wrong with you, Ann. Why are you running off on some cockamamie trip to Argentina to learn how to dance? Go to tango lessons here, for God's sake. It's ridiculous.'

Ann shook her head. He didn't get it. It wasn't about dance lessons, it was about living. It was about not dying inside. It was about not giving up on life and adventure. It was about having sacrificed so much of your life for others and now wanting to do something for yourself.

The sessions with Maggie had shown her that Ken wasn't the problem. She was. Ken was the same solid, kind, protective, strong man she had married. Yes, he had got lazy and took her a bit for granted, but that wasn't a sin, and she was partly to blame because she had never complained.

But the children leaving home had shifted something in Ann. Her purpose was gone. Her *raison d'être*. She had realized she was going to be old soon. This was her window of opportunity to do the things she'd always wanted to do but had used the children as an excuse not to. No more hiding behind them. No more dreaming. It was now or never, and Ann knew that 'never' wasn't an option. She refused to die regretting things not done and adventures not lived. She was scared of getting old, she was scared of life slipping her by, so she was going to grab it with both hands while she could. Yes, it probably was crazy to go to South America alone, but so what? Crazy felt really good.

'This is bullshit.' Ken stormed off down the stairs and she heard the front door slam. Ann finished packing. She closed her eyes, picturing a sandy beach and a blue sky.

Ann was sitting in Zoë's apartment sipping a cup of tea and chatting to her daughter.

'Promise to FaceTime every day so I know you haven't been kidnapped by drug lords or gone off with some zillionaire on his yacht and abandoned your family for ever,' Zoë said, grinning at her.

'I promise.'

Zoë squeezed her mother's hand. 'I'm glad you're going, Mum. You look so excited and buzzed. It's great to see.'

'Thanks, love.'

'Has Dad come around at all?'

'No. He thinks it's foolhardy.'

Zoë shrugged. 'You're not going to change him now, Mum. It's too late. Just go and have fun, but remember to come back to us. I'll try to shake him up while you're away.'

Ann laughed. 'Good luck with that. Is Orla here? I have a book for her.'

Zoë lowered her voice. 'Yeah, she is, but she's in her room. I don't know what happened. She was seeing some guy, but I think he must have broken up with her because she's been in her room crying for two days.'

'Oh, no, poor pet.'

'I've tried talking to her, but she won't even open her door. She only comes out when I go to work.'

Ann stood up. 'Let me try.'

She knocked gently on Orla's door.

'I'm fine, Zoë. I just need to be alone.'

'Orla, love, it's Ann, Zoë's mum. I have a little something for you. I'm heading away to Buenos Aires tomorrow and I wanted to say goodbye and give this to you. Could you open up for a minute?'

Silence, then Ann heard the key in the lock. Orla's blotchy red face peered out from behind the door.

'Oh, pet, you poor, poor thing. You need a hug,' Ann said.

Orla dissolved into tears and let her in. Ann held the girl in her arms and closed the door behind her. She made cooing sounds and rubbed Orla's back until the sobbing subsided. 'What has you so upset?'

Orla blew her nose with a tissue and added it to the mountain of soggy ones in the wastebasket in her room. 'I . . . I broke up with a guy I really liked.'

'Oh dear. What happened?'

Orla hesitated. 'It's a long, complicated story, but the bottom line is that we can't be together and it hurts so bad because I love him.'

'Does he know that?'

Orla nodded.

'Does he love you?'

Orla nodded again.

'Well, then, maybe you can work it out? Communication is so important in a relationship. Have you tried talking to him?'

Orla shook her head. 'I can't really explain it, but it's never going to work, and I just have to accept it and shut that idea off. Sometimes love isn't enough.'

That was true. Look at her and Ken. She loved Ken and he loved her, but she was going away alone.

'Well, maybe a change of scenery would do you good. Your book gave me the impetus to book my trip to Buenos Aires. So I'm returning the favour.' Ann handed her a book on the Inca Trail. 'I've popped in the name of the travel agency I used. They specialize in South American holidays for single people. Perhaps if you got away and had time to reflect, you'd see a way to work things out with this man, or at the very least a way to get past the heartbreak.'

Orla threw her arms around Ann's neck. 'Thank you. This is so thoughtful.'

'Not at all. Look, Orla, life is short. Don't spend it crying in a dark room. I've done that and it does you no good. Lick your wounds and make a plan. You need something to look forward to in life, something to work towards. I don't know you well, but I sense you've had a hard time and known sadness. You need to look after yourself. A trip like this will help mend your broken heart. Since I booked my trip, I've felt alive again. I'm frightened, but in a good way.'

Orla looked at the book. 'Maybe I'll do it. I've got nothing to lose and nothing keeping me here any more.'

'Well, if you go to Peru, come to Buenos Aires and visit me. Maybe we can dance the tango together.' Ann smiled at her.

'I'd like that very much. Thank you.'

'I'd better go and say goodbye to Zoë. I wish you all the luck in the world. I hope you take the leap, do the Inca Trail and fulfil your dream.'

They hugged and Ann left to say a final goodbye to her daughter.

Ann was drinking a glass of wine in the kitchen when she heard the front door. She glanced at the clock. It was half past ten. She heard Ken climb the stairs. He obviously wasn't going to talk to her. Maybe it was for the best. She'd slip away in the morning and let him cool down. They'd said all they had to say for now. A bit of distance would do them good.

She was in bed when she heard a knock on the door. She really didn't want another argument with Ken, so she said nothing.

He knocked again, louder this time. 'Ann, can I come in?'

Ann sighed. 'Sure.'

The door opened. Her bedroom was in darkness, but the light in the hall was on. Framed in her bedroom door was Ken, in tight boxer shorts, wearing a mask. She peered at him. Oh, dear God, it was a George Clooney mask.

Ann was so surprised and caught unawares that she burst out laughing. Ken strode into the room and climbed on top of her.

'I know George is your fantasy, so tonight that's going to come true.'

He kissed her and she could taste whiskey on his breath. He tugged at her pyjamas and she helped pull them off. Closing her eyes, she let herself go. Ken was pretty drunk, so the sex was short-lived, but it was nice. It was lovely to be physically close to him again.

They lay side by side, holding hands.

'Where did you get the mask?' she asked.

'I went to a printer with a photo of George Clooney and they printed it out on thick paper for me. Then I just cut out the face and stuck a piece of elastic through it.'

'I'm very impressed. It was ingenious.'

Ken squeezed her hand. 'See, I can be spontaneous and fun.'

She squeezed back. 'It was lovely.'

'I had to drink half a bottle of whiskey to get the courage to do it. I was nervous as hell, Ann. It's been a long time, I wasn't sure if . . . well, if I could still . . . you know . . . but, hey, there's life in the old dog yet.' He laughed and punched the air.

It was the first time she'd heard Ken laugh in ages, the real, happy, whoopy kind of laughter. It reminded her of how he used to laugh at things. She'd forgotten the sound.

He rolled onto his side to face her. 'Was that okay for you? I know it was a bit quick. But I'll get longer with practice. I'm just rusty.'

She smiled at him. 'It was great, Ken. Like old times.'

'Yeah, it was.' He beamed at her. 'We're good now, aren't we? Maybe I'll move back in here to the bedroom with you.

And if you want a little break, we could go to the South of France. It's a short flight – I could manage that. I'll be retired in three weeks so we can do more together. You can cancel your flights and see if you can get some of your money back on the apartment.'

Ann's heart sank. One intimate moment in years was not going to fix their marriage. Ken thought it was all tickety-boo now that he had had sex with her. She didn't want to hurt him, but she had to stop him thinking that she wasn't going to Argentina.

'Ken, I'm still going.'

His eyes narrowed. 'What do you mean? Don't be ridiculous, we're all sorted now.'

'Tonight was a lovely surprise, but our marriage is not fixed. I need to go away and fix myself, and you need time to think about things too. We need to figure out what we want in life and from our relationship. One night isn't going to miraculously solve all our problems. Talking to Maggie has made me see that I have unresolved issues and I need to go and sort out my head. I'm afraid of growing old before my time. I don't know who I am any more. I need to see the world and get out of my comfort zone. If I don't, I'll always regret it. I'm not leaving you, Ken, I'm trying to find myself.'

Ken sat bolt upright. 'Why do you have to go? Why do you need to find yourself? You're still you. I'm doing everything I can. I went to therapy with you and I'm trying to be more attentive and closer to you physically. What more can I do? I'm lost here, Ann.'

'I'm not trying to hurt you. I'm really not. I was trying to fix our marriage with therapy, but I realized that I need to sort myself out first. I need to force myself out of this half-life I'm living. I'm a mother and a wife, but who am I? Who is Ann?'

'Why can't we work it out together? How can we fix our marriage if you're on a different continent?'

'I need to go, Ken. I have to get some space. I need to fix myself.'

Ken stood up. 'If you go, this marriage is over.'

'I'm going.'

Ann watched her husband storm out of the room. The George Clooney mask fluttered to the floor.

32

Orla was broken. She was barely able to speak. Every word was an effort.

They sat in silence, Maggie waiting patiently until Orla could tell her what had happened. She had described the wonderful dates, the candle-lit dinner, the 'I love you', and then she had started to cry with a grief that was heartbreaking to witness. Still Maggie waited.

Orla blew her nose and took a long, deep breath.

'I've stopped taking his calls,' she said, her voice dead. 'There's no point. I've called in sick to work this past week. I can't face seeing Lulu, or seeing Paul when he picks her up. It's too painful.'

'Has he tried to contact you?'

'A hundred times a day. He keeps ringing, keeps texting, keeps leaving messages that he loves me and he's sorry and he doesn't understand what happened and will I please talk to him. It's killing me.'

'It sounds like he's almost suffering as much as you,' Maggie said.

Orla looked at her sharply. 'Don't say that. I can't bear to think of him feeling bad.'

'That's because you're crazy about him,' Maggie said. 'Orla, everything you've told me points to you and Paul being a good match. You're being offered a true chance at happiness. The only thing holding you back is a physical condition that you can work around. Lots of women with vaginismus have wonderful relationships because they're honest with their partners and they figure out how to work with it. You have to let go of the mindset that sex has to be penetrative. You can be physically together and intimate in lots of wonderful ways if you just open your mind to those possibilities.'

Orla shook her head firmly. 'No, I won't do that to him. He deserves to be with a normal woman. He's a great guy.'

'And you're a wonderful young woman,' Maggie said. 'Orla, you deserve to be happy. You've said you opened up to Paul more than any other man before. You've told him about your difficult childhood and you said he was very understanding. So, doesn't it follow that if you opened up to Paul about your vaginismus, he would also be understanding and supportive?'

Orla's eyes flashed. 'He might stay with me for a bit, out of pity, but he'd end up dumping me. Come on, Maggie, what man wants to be with a woman he can't have sex with? His ex-wife is stunning and super-confident. I'd say their sex life was amazing.'

'They split up, and he seems to dislike her,' Maggie said bluntly. 'Even if the sex was good, it didn't keep them together. You said he told you he loves you, which gives you every chance of working through this together. I'd be happy to help you as a couple.'

There was no way Orla was going to drag Paul to couples' therapy because she had a messed-up body. There was no way she was going to ruin his life by telling him and have him stay with her out of pity. She knew exactly what would happen. They'd limp along with this huge black cloud hanging over them. Every time they were close physically, it would be the elephant in the room – *She's not a normal woman, I can't have sex with her, ever, for the rest of my life.* It would be hell to know she could never give him what he wanted. Hell to watch him pretend he didn't mind. Hell to know that their relationship was doomed. She loved him too much to put him through all that.

'Look, Maggie, I know you're trying to help, but the bottom line is, men love sex. They think about it all the time, they crave it, they need it. I'm not going to rob Paul of a normal sex life. And I don't want him to have to go through another painful break-up, so it's best that I end it now, before we get even closer.'

'Breaking up with him without explaining why is going to hurt him. Why not give him the chance to make his own decision?'

'Because he's so nice, he'd try to stay with me, and then when he finally did leave me, it would kill me. There's a child involved, too. I wouldn't just be hurting him, I'd be hurting Lulu, and I love her.' Orla wiped away a tear. 'I know what it's like to be hurt as a child. I couldn't do that to Lulu. She doesn't need another break-up in her life. If I cut them out of my life now, it won't be so bad for them. If I wait any longer, get closer to Lulu and spend more time with her, it will be much worse. I'm going away, Maggie. It's all booked. I'm leaving for a while, long enough for him to move on.'

Orla knew that she would never get over breaking up with Paul. The thought of living without him and Lulu was unbearable. She felt as if she couldn't breathe a lot of the time. When she woke up now, she wished she was dead.

She knew she couldn't stay in Dublin: the fear of bumping into Paul or Lulu was too great. She'd thought a lot about what Ann had said to her a few days ago in her bedroom. Ann was like a different person from the one she'd had coffee with in the kitchen a few weeks earlier. Ann, now, was full of life and possibility. Her upcoming adventure had given her back her zest for life.

Orla had decided that she'd go to Peru, far, far away from Dublin and everything here. In Peru she could be someone else, Orla from Ireland – no baggage, no history, no drama. She could disappear for a while and try to heal. Maybe she'd eventually piece her heart back together, maybe not. Hiking the Inca Trail to Machu Picchu would be a blessed distraction from her pain.

Maggie sat forward and gazed intently at her. 'Let's look at this from a different angle,' she said. 'If Paul came to you and told you he had a physical problem he was embarrassed about, like erectile dysfunction, would you stop seeing him? If he told you he had a heart condition that meant your sex life would be limited, would you leave him?'

Orla sighed. 'That's silly. Of course not.'

'No, of course not, because he's so much more than just sex to you. Love is about the whole person, the core of who they are, yet you're saying his love is contingent on being able to penetrate you. You're not allowing for his love to be as deep and wide as yours. Why is that? Is it because you believe you don't deserve his love?'

Orla's head had a dull ache now, from all the crying. 'You're twisting my words,' she said. 'You can't deny that men want to have a full and brilliant sex life. They do.'

'And what do you want, Orla?' Maggie said, fixing her with a stare. 'In all this, you keep talking about Paul's desires, Paul's needs. What are yours? Don't you deserve love and physical closeness? People have all kinds of physical and psychological challenges and they organize their sex lives in myriad ways in response to that. We only hear the "normal" stories. But you'd be amazed how few people actually have straightforward lives, sexual or otherwise. In my experience, people lie to present as "normal", society's idea of normal, and then they do their own thing behind closed doors. Vaginismus could even be seen as a blessing. It encourages creativity and experimentation between couples and precludes laziness and a predictable sex routine. If you change the lens, Orla, you could see and embrace the alternatives it throws up for you.'

'I can't,' Orla whispered. 'I just can't, Maggie.'

'I know the dilators haven't worked so far and that you couldn't have penetrative sex with Paul when you wanted to, but that doesn't mean you never will. You're only twenty-four. There are decades of love-making ahead of you. I think we're making progress and that you might eventually be able to have penetrative sex or, at the very least, accept your condition and have a wonderful intimate life. I'm asking you, Orla, how you would feel about staying in Ireland and continuing therapy? I think it's worth it because you love this man. You're saying this is what you want – so help me to help you grab it with both hands.'

Orla looked at Maggie, her eyes brimming with tears. 'There's no point. I'll never fix this – no one can. If I can't even have sex with the man I adore, it'll never happen. I was born a freak, the freak who murdered her mother. I've been a freak my whole life. Yes, Maggie, I am a freak. That is the word that best describes me. No amount of therapy is going to change that. It's just who I am.'

'Orla, you are one of the bravest young women I've ever met. What you have had to endure and survive is astonishing. You're much stronger than you think. Choosing to be honest with Paul will take courage, but isn't it worth taking a chance on love? Isn't it worth giving yourself a chance at a happy ending? You've spent a lifetime putting up protective barriers to help you survive. But you also had the strength to get away from your past, to move away from your father's long shadow and into the sun. Follow that strength, Orla. Let your barriers down. Don't let vaginismus define you.'

'You're very kind, Maggie, and you've helped me a lot. But I'm not going to let my problems ruin Paul and Lulu's lives. Nothing you can say will change my mind. Maybe when I'm far away from all this, I'll start therapy again. I have your number. But for now, I just need to disappear.'

Orla stood up and shook Maggie's hand. Maggie tried to persuade her to stay longer, to talk more, to book another appointment, to keep in touch . . . But Orla just kept shaking her head. No. No. No.

'Thank you for trying, Maggie. You've done your best. But no one can fix me. I realize that now. Goodbye.'

As she walked towards her car, Orla's phone pinged. It was the confirmation of her itinerary from the travel agent Ann had recommended. Her flight for Peru left on Sunday morning at 7.45 a.m.

She looked up at the grey sky and let the light rain fall on her face. She felt numb. She'd go to Peru and leave her past behind and, who knew, if she liked it, she could stay and carve out a little life for herself over there. She could teach English to kids and live in anonymity for ever. She could visit Ann and dance the tango in Buenos Aires. She'd become known to the local Peruvians as the strange single Irish woman who taught their kids English.

The raindrops splashed onto her cheeks, but she felt nothing.

33

Poppy and Ted blocked the front door. 'We want to come too.'

'Guys, move. Mum and I are going for a walk. We'll be back soon.' Niall picked Poppy up and placed her down behind him. She screamed and thumped him on the back with her little fists as he tried to peel Ted from the front door.

'Why can't we come too, Mummy?' Ted asked.

'Because Dad and I want to have some time to exercise and chat,' Alice explained. 'Danika is here and we'll be back before you know it.'

'I know it,' Poppy shouted, from behind Niall's legs.

'Poppy, you're being annoying now.' Niall tried to untangle his legs from her not insignificant grasp.

'Mum, you said you'd bring me to get new trainers today,' Sarah said, from the stairs.

'I will. Later,' Alice said.

'You always say the shops are a nightmare on Sunday afternoons and it's better to go in the morning,' Sarah reminded her.

'Yes, I do, but it'll be fine this once.'

'How can it be fine this once?' Sarah was not letting go. 'How can it suddenly be fine this Sunday and not any other Sunday?'

'Jesus, Sarah, will you leave your mother alone! We're going for a walk, not abandoning you.'

'I wasn't talking to you, Dad. I was talking to Mum.'

'I don't like your tone. You've got a bit cheeky lately.'

'How would you know? You're never here. You're always in work.'

'Sarah, I'm your father and —'

'A father spends time with his kids. You hardly ever do.' She crossed her arms and eyeballed him.

'So who was it who drove you to hockey yesterday, watched your match, then drove you and your three friends home?' Niall snapped.

'You didn't watch my match. You spent the whole time on your phone. At least when Mum brings me, she actually watches.'

'I had a few work emails to deal with. How do you think your lifestyle is paid for, Sarah? By me working my arse off, that's how.'

'The other mums and dads were watching.'

'Well, maybe they aren't as busy as I am.'

'You're always busy, Daddy,' Ted said. '"Not now, Ted, I'm busy." That's what you *aaaaaa*lways say.'

'Yeah, you do!' Poppy shouted. 'All the time. Busy-busy-busy.'

Alice stayed silent. This was good for Niall. He needed to hear how his disconnection was affecting the kids. He was constantly distracted by work and it wasn't fair on them.

'You used to do way more stuff with us, but now it's all about work,' Sarah said. 'Mrs Jenkins says it's very important in life to have a good work–life balance. Yours is rubbish.'

'Well, maybe Mrs Jenkins should shove her —'

'Niall.' Alice stopped him insulting Sarah's beloved teacher. She rested her hand on her husband's shoulder to calm him down. 'Sarah, you're being rude now. Dad works very hard to provide us with a lovely life. I said I'd bring you to get trainers today and I will. But you need to behave yourself or there'll be no shopping and no trainers. Now, Dad and I are going for a walk and I want you all to be good for Danika.'

'I hate Danika and I don't understand what she says. Her accent is all va-va-va,' Ted shouted.

'Ted!' Alice hissed, hoping that Danika, who was locking her bike in the front garden, hadn't heard him. 'Danika is lovely and her English is excellent and a lot better than your Polish, which is non-existent.'

'*Muuuuuum*,' Jamie shouted, from the TV room. 'Can I go over to Kenny's house?'

'Yes, but not right now. I'll drop you over later.'

'When?'

'At twelve.'

'But that's ages away.' Jamie's head appeared around the door. 'He wants me to come over now and I really want to go, Mum.'

Alice wavered. Was it worth it? She did need to get Sarah new trainers and Jamie deserved a bit of fun after falling and smacking his head against the goal posts yesterday, resulting in a black eye this morning.

'I want a play date with my friends,' Poppy shouted.

'Me too,' Ted joined in.

Alice looked at Niall. 'Maybe –'

'No, Alice,' he said firmly. Turning to the kids he said, 'You're all being really selfish. Mum does everything for you all week and all weekend. This is one little thing she wants to do for herself, just a simple walk, and you're all trying to stop her. That's not fair. Stop thinking about what you want and think about Mum for once.'

'Sorry, Mum, go for your walk. I'll tell Kenny I'll see him later.'

'Fine, but if the queues in the shops are long later, don't moan,' Sarah said.

'Okay, but if I ask Danika for Weetabix and she gives me a Nutella sandwich, it's not my fault, it's her bad English,' Ted said.

'Ted, you are not to eat –' Alice never got to finish her sentence.

Niall grabbed her hand and pulled her out of the door. 'Leave them. If they eat Nutella sandwiches, so be it. We'll never get out of the house if we keep negotiating. Jesus, they're a nightmare.'

'This is why I sometimes envy you, cocooned in your office, drinking swishy coffees from the Nespresso machine and having coherent conversations with adults. Meanwhile, I'm here being answered back to, ignored or screamed at.'

'I see your point.' Niall grinned at her. 'Maybe you should think about going back to work.'

'Maybe. It would have to be part-time, because I do still want to pick them up from school. The twins are only six. I'm not sure.'

'Could you do part-time in the pharmacy? Your mother would understand that you want to be there for pick-up time.'

'Maybe. Lisa's looking at options for me, but I'm embarrassed.'

'Why?'

'I feel like it's a pity job. I don't want Mum and Lisa seeing me as a charity case because I'm failing at my life. I want to feel useful. But what can I bring to the table? I'm kind of useless and qualified for nothing.'

Niall turned to her. 'Hey, stop that. You're amazing and smart and a quick learner. You could help them with their orders or stock-take or deal with customers, or meet the medical sales reps. There's loads you could help with.'

Maybe he was right. Maybe she could actually be useful.

Lisa and her mum were always saying how busy they were. 'I'll see what Lisa comes up with,' she said.

'Alice, you'd be an asset to them, and I think it'd make you feel better about yourself, to be out and interacting with adults.'

'God, yes. I do miss adult conversation.'

They walked in silence at first, each lost in their thoughts. But as the rhythm of their steps quietened their minds, they began to chat. Idle chat, nothing serious, nothing heavy, just chit-chat. Easy, Alice thought. Easy chat. She hadn't felt relaxed in Niall's company for ages. She always felt tense or resentful around him. Worried that he wanted sex, angry that he wanted to be out partying, furious that he was shoving a vibrator in her face, jealous of his time in work . . . But now, walking along, with no concerns about being hopped on for sex, or asked to go out to a nightclub, or having a child swinging out of her, she was able to relax and be herself. It was lovely to be out in the fresh air, with no kids moaning about the walk, wanting ice-cream, treats, drinks or lying down on the road and refusing to walk another step.

It felt like freedom to Alice. She should do it more. She really could carve out forty minutes every day, as Maggie had suggested. She would. She needed this. She felt lighter, happier.

After an hour's walk, they went to get a take-out coffee and sat on a bench looking out at the sea.

'This is nice, isn't it?' Niall said.

'Bliss.'

'We should do this every week.'

'I'd like that,' she said.

Niall reached over and took her hand. She didn't flinch because she knew it was just a hand-hold and nothing else.

His hand felt warm and familiar. Like putting on a

favourite old jumper. They drank their coffees in companionable silence.

On the way home, Niall said, 'Do the kids really feel I'm never around?'

Alice wasn't going to sugar-coat it. 'Yes, they do. They miss you.'

'But I do stuff with them on the weekends.'

'You don't really, Niall. You drive them to sports but, as Sarah pointed out, you don't watch them or really engage with them. It's like you're present physically but not emotionally. They feel it. They need their dad.'

'I suppose I am on my phone a lot. It's just that work is so full-on and I really want to make senior partner. Denis is going to announce the new partner soon.'

'I understand that, and I really hope you get it, but you'll have to leave work in the office at the weekends, or just allow yourself a specific time slot to check your phone. The kids are growing up fast, Niall. Don't miss out on their lives or you'll regret it.'

They walked on in silence.

'I've forgotten how to be around them. I seem to have lost my patience,' Niall admitted.

'They're not easy. They can be a right handful, but they're our kids and they're brilliant.'

'I know. I guess I've just pulled back and focused on work. The sessions with Maggie have made me see that I sometimes work late so I don't have to deal with bedtime. I just find I come in wrecked after a long day and can't handle them running around, refusing to go to bed, shouting, spilling toothpaste everywhere, climbing all over me, coming up and down the stairs ten, twenty times . . . It drives me nuts.'

'It drives me mad, too. But when they eventually lie down and you read them a story or kiss them goodnight and they hug you and tell you they love you – that's magic. It makes all the hard work worth it.'

'I guess I've forgotten the good stuff.'

'Sarah is ten, Niall. We have about three more years of her wanting to spend any time with us.'

Niall ran his hands through his hair. 'When you put it like that, it makes me feel a bit sick. I'd hate her to think I wasn't there for her. I've got some catching up to do. I'll take her to get her trainers today.'

'Really?'

'Yes, I want to.'

'Be warned, she's a nightmare to go shopping with. She'll try on every single pair of trainers in the whole shopping centre before deciding which ones she wants.'

'I'll consider it a baptism of fire.' Niall grinned.

Alice giggled. 'Be careful you don't get third-degree burns.'

They walked on, and as they rounded the road home, Niall told Alice he had a surprise for her. The last surprise had been a vibrator, so she was immediately on high alert. She stopped walking. 'What is it?'

'You're going to love it.'

'Really?' Please, God, let it be something normal.

He grinned. 'Yes. It's not a sex toy, I promise.'

'Thank God, so what is it, then?'

'I've booked us a family trip to France for the May bank holiday next week. It'll mean taking the kids out of school for a few days, but I don't see that as a problem. It's a family-friendly hotel beside the sea. They have a kids' club in the morning from nine to twelve, so we'll get some chill-out time for us.'

Alice wanted to laugh. Did Niall actually think that any of their children would go to a kids' club? He really was clueless.

'So?' he asked. 'Are you pleased?'

A holiday in France did sound nice. Personally, Alice was still holding out for the surprise weekend in a spa hotel alone. But Niall was trying, and she had to give him credit: it was a good idea. 'It sounds lovely. I'm not sure the kids will go to the kids' club, though.'

Niall smiled. 'Don't you worry about that. I'll make sure they do.'

Good luck with that, Alice thought. 'Great! When do we leave?'

'Next Friday.' He put his arm around her. 'I think it'll be good for us all. Change of scenery, sun, sand and relaxation.'

Sun, sand and sex, Alice thought. She had five days to lose a stone so she'd look presentable in a swimsuit. Would Niall want lots of sex? The holiday suddenly seemed like a lot of work. Be thin, be up for lots of sex, be with the kids all day with no break for school . . . Alice went from thinking it was a good idea to absolutely dreading it.

34

Zoë surveyed the mess of clothes all over Orla's bedroom and handed her a cup of freshly made tea.

'Thanks.' Orla took the tea gratefully. 'How's your mum getting on?'

'I spoke to her at four this morning – neither of us could sleep. She sounded excited. I want her to go and have an adventure, but I'll miss her badly.'

'I'm sure you will. She's lovely. You're lucky to have a mum like her.'

'Yeah, she's great, and she deserves a break. She was thrilled when I told her you were heading to Peru. She really wants you to visit her, if you can. I'll text you her mobile.'

Orla smiled. 'Thanks. I'd love to see her if I make it to Argentina.'

'Sorry I'm missing your last weekend in Ireland. I feel as if everyone's leaving me. John in Australia, Mum in Argentina and you about to head off to Peru. I feel very boring.'

'You'll have a blast at your friend's wedding. And you're the least boring person I know.'

Zoë played with the zip on her jacket. 'I'm a bit worried about Dad. He's going to be lost without Mum. He has no idea how much he relies on her. I'll have to keep an eye on him. By the way, he loved your chocolate fudge cake. It was the only time he'd smiled since Mum said she was leaving. He says a big thank-you.'

'It was just a small gesture to cheer him up. Has he come around to your mum going, or is he still cross about it?'

'He's acting furious, but underneath I know he's just really worried she might not come back, or she'll come back and decide their marriage is over. I'm going to have a proper talk with him next week. He'll lose Mum if he doesn't get out of that bloody chair and start living. I'm glad Mum is doing this trip for herself. I think she's been a bit depressed, to be honest. But now it's as if a light has switched on inside her. She's so happy and excited.'

'Maybe it'll be good for both of them. Your dad will realize how much he misses her, she'll have the adventure she wants and then come back.'

Zoë chewed her lower lip. 'I dunno. She might like it over there and never come back. God, relationships are so complicated. I'm never getting married.'

Tell me about it, Orla thought grimly.

Zoë's phone pinged. 'My lift is here.' She put out her arms and hugged Orla. 'I'll miss you. I know we're not best mates and I behave like a horny teenager and you behave like an actual grown-up, but you've been a great roomie. I'm sorry things didn't work out with that guy you were dating. Good luck in Peru, have fun with hot South American guys and forget all about him.'

Fat chance, Orla thought. She'd never forget Paul. He was The One. But for weirdos like her, there could never be The One.

'Bye, Zoë, it's been fun living with you. I hope it all works out for your mum and dad.'

Zoë shrugged. '*Que será, será.*'

Orla breathed a sigh of relief when she heard the front door shut. She was so lucky that Zoë was out of town this weekend. She was finding it a struggle to talk. She was constantly on the verge of tears and her nerves were raw. She found Zoë's energy and constant chat hard to take. She needed silence.

She needed to spend the weekend focusing on packing and organizing to go away. And then, on Sunday morning, she was going to the airport and would leave all of this heartache behind.

Orla hadn't told the school she was leaving the country. She didn't want them to make a fuss: she didn't want leaving parties and gifts, and she didn't want Paul to find out through Lulu. So she just told the headmistress that she was sick. She'd email her from Peru and apologize. She hated being so unprofessional. She hated leaving her class, but there were only four weeks left of the summer term and Harriet, the trainee teacher, would manage fine. Still, Orla felt sick not to be able to say goodbye to the kids in her class, but she was terrified of seeing Lulu and Paul. It would hurt too much. She'd send the class a long email and gifts from Peru, too. She hoped that would take the sting out of her leaving.

The minutes felt like hours. Orla just wanted to be on the plane and far away from here. Her phone buzzed. Paul again. He'd rung and texted and emailed non-stop. He'd even turned up on her doorstep. Orla had asked Zoë to tell him she had moved out and she had no idea where Orla was.

Orla had felt bad about it, but she couldn't see him, it was too painful. She knew he was confused and upset, probably angry too. It was better just to disappear.

Orla picked up the phone to make the one call she had to make before leaving.

'Orla?'

'Hi, Dad.'

'Is something wrong?' He sounded suspicious. Orla only rang him on birthdays or anniversaries, never out of the blue. He was clearly thrown.

'No, Dad.'

'Are you in trouble?'

'No, Dad.'

'Did you meet a fella? Are you getting hitched?'

'No, Dad.'

'You're not pregnant, are you?'

'No, Dad.'

'What, then?'

Orla kept her voice calm. 'I just wanted to let you know that I'm going away for a bit.'

'Where?'

'Peru.'

'Peru?'

'Yes.'

'Like, away over there in South America?'

'Yes.'

'Why in God's name are you going there?'

'To travel. I need to get away for a bit.'

'What's wrong with you?'

Where do you want me to start? Orla thought. 'Nothing, I'm fine. I just need a change of scenery.'

'Why don't you come home for a bit?'

No, thanks. That would push me right over the edge. 'I want to go somewhere different, and I've always wanted to hike the Inca Trail.'

'You never mentioned it before. How long will you be gone?'

'I'm not sure – a couple of months, maybe longer. I'll see how it goes.' She decided now was not the time to tell him that she wasn't sure if she was ever coming back.

'It seems sudden. Are you sure nothing is wrong?'

Orla wanted to shout, *Yes, everything is wrong. Since the day I was born, it's all been wrong. Why couldn't you love me? Why did you make me feel like I'd ruined your life? I was a baby, Dad, an innocent child. And now I'm a completely messed-up adult.* 'I . . . I kind of got my heart broken,' she admitted.

'What? How long were you with this boy?'

'Not long, but . . . well, it was kind of serious.'

'That's not a broken heart, Orla, that's a small bump in the road. You'll bounce back in no time. A broken heart is what I have. A broken heart is when your wife of eight years dies. Running away will do you no good.'

Fuck you, my heart is broken, she wanted to scream. But, as usual, it was back to Joseph Kane and his pain. It was *always* about him.

Orla balled her hands into fists. 'Well, I'm very upset, Dad, and I'm going to Peru.'

'Tell me you haven't given up a good job for this.'

Orla decided to lie. It was just easier. 'No, I've taken a leave of absence.'

'Good. You can't be going around giving up a good pensionable job.'

'I know, Dad, but life isn't just about work.'

'Don't I know it. I hope you're lucky enough to meet someone half as wonderful as your mother one day.'

Orla took a deep breath. Maggie had told her it was important to try to be more honest and open with her father. Easier said than done, though. 'I did, Dad. I did meet someone really wonderful, but I can't be with him because I'm so messed up.'

'What do you mean?'

Orla knew she had to tread carefully or she might break the thin tie she had to her father. 'I missed having a mother. I missed having a mother's love and care in my life.'

'Did I not provide well for you? Were you not well looked after?' Joseph was defensive.

329

'Yes, Dad, I know you did your best, but I still missed having a mum. It left a hole.'

'Don't I know all about that? Haven't I a hole in my life as big as a crater?'

Orla tried to stay calm. 'Yes, and so do I, Dad. I didn't just lose a mother, I also was the cause of her loss. That's a lot . . . it's a lot to deal with.'

'We all have our crosses to bear, Orla. We just have to get on with it. Your mother dying was the worst thing that ever happened to me, but I had a baby to look after, so I just had to get up and get on. That's life, I'm afraid. It can be fierce cruel. Running away will do you no good. You have to face things. But if you feel you need a little holiday, I suppose it won't do you any harm.'

Orla said nothing. There was nothing left to say. Her father would never see past his own pain. It was part of who he was now. It defined him as a person.

'Right. Well, good luck, then.'

'Thanks, Dad.'

'Will you still call?'

'Of course.'

'Don't forget your mother's birthday's coming up.'

'I won't, Dad. I never do.'

'Beautiful she was.'

'Yes.'

'The pain never goes away.'

'I'd better go, Dad. I have to finish packing.' Say something nice, please, Dad. For once in your self-centred, self-pitying life, say something nice.

'Mind yourself, Orla. I hope your trip cheers you up.'

'Thanks, me too.'

'Call if you need anything.'

'Okay.'

'Right, well, bye, then.'

'Goodbye, Dad.'

He hung up.

Orla sighed. He was incapable of seeing her pain. He was never going to change. She had to accept that.

35

Ann lay awake with a pit in her stomach. It was a combination of dread, excitement, fear and happiness. How could you feel all these emotions at the same time?

She was about to go on the adventure of a lifetime, but would it be an amazing experience that would fill her with joy and energy, or would she get mugged, raped and murdered? You know what? she thought. I'd rather feel afraid than numb.

It was her first long-haul flight. In sixty-five years of living, Ann had never been on a flight longer than three and a half hours. The south of Spain was as far as she had got Ken to go. Milly, who had travelled extensively for such a young girl, had given her lots of advice.

She'd said it was really important to be comfortable on long-haul flights and that you had to bring your own snacks because the food was 'manky'. She told her to wear loose trousers and a loose shirt that was made of soft material. She told Ann that if she had a cashmere cardigan, or one of those 'pashmina things grannies wear', to bring that, because the temperature on the plane went from hot to cold. Also, she recommended bringing sliders because you couldn't go to the toilet in your socks: 'People pee everywhere and it's gross.' She told Ann to download movies and boxsets on her iPad, too.

Ann got up, dressed and put her final bits and pieces into her backpack. Milly had found a really good one, with padded straps, in one of the donation bags in the shop and bought it for Ann. She'd paid seven euros for it and Ann had been very touched.

Ann pulled her large suitcase to the edge of the stairs and, as quietly as she could, bounced it down. She went into the kitchen and made herself a last cup of coffee. She had had the kitchen done up ten years ago. She'd been so happy and proud of it. Now it felt like a prison. It was the place she'd spent hours, days and weeks preparing meals she didn't want to eat, cleaning, tidying, staring into space, wondering where she had disappeared to. Now, she was about to leave it all behind. Ann wondered if she'd ever be able to come back. This kitchen, this house, this life felt like a noose around her neck. It was slowly sucking the life out of her. Please, God, may I find myself in Argentina, she prayed silently.

She rinsed her cup, dried it and tidied it away. She wiped down the surface for the last time. Then, she pulled out a list of practical instructions for Ken and laid it in the middle of the countertop. Basic recipes, cleaning tips, products to buy, where to find things, and the number for a dry-cleaner who would pick up his shirts, wash and iron them. On top of the instructions, she left a note.

Dear Ken, this is not about you, it's about me. I love you and I always have, but I gave up my life to be a mother and a wife. I'm lost and I need to figure out who I am and what I want from the rest of my life. Stay safe and well. Ann xx

Her phone buzzed: the taxi was outside. Ann took a deep breath and walked out of the kitchen door.

She bumped straight into Ken. He was standing in a T-shirt and pyjama bottoms, looking dishevelled.

He handed her a piece of paper. 'I looked up some of the things women travelling alone have to look out for.'

1. Don't use your phone in public – it can get snatched.
2. Duck into a café or shop if you need to check something.
3. Only carry the essentials – leave your passport, cash, and jewellery in your room.
4. Wear your bag across your body when you use public transport.
5. Don't flash money or expensive jewellery.
6. Always be aware of your surroundings and act like you know exactly where you're going.
7. Seek tourist police if you need help.

'Thank you, Ken.'

They stood in awkward silence. Ann leant in and kissed her husband's cheek, rough with stubble. 'Goodbye, Ken.'

He grabbed her arm. 'Don't go, please, Ann – don't leave me. We can work this out. This trip is madness.'

Ann gently pulled her arm away. She put her hand to his cheek. 'I need to go away and live a little. Try to find my spark, figure out how I want to live my life. I can't go on like this. It's eating me up.'

'But I love you, Ann.'

'I love you too, Ken.'

'Then don't go.'

She opened the front door and stepped out, dragging her suitcase. 'I'm sorry, but I have to.'

'Please, Ann.'

Ann turned to him for the final time. 'Goodbye, Ken, look after yourself.'

She walked towards the waiting taxi man, who lifted her

case into the boot of his car. Ann climbed into the back and waved one last time at her husband.

Then she turned to face forward.

'Here I go . . .'

36

Orla was rummaging in her coat pocket for her keys. She was standing outside her apartment holding the shopping bag in her other hand – it contained a microwave dinner and a bottle of wine for her last supper in Ireland. She was fishing about for the keys when she felt a hand on her shoulder. She jumped and dropped the shopping bag. The wine bottle smashed on the footpath. 'What the hell?'

'Orla.'

It was Paul. No, no, no. Orla turned and began to run in the opposite direction, but Paul was too quick for her. He grabbed the back of her coat and spun her around. 'Orla, what's going on? What did I do wrong? Talk to me. Please. I'm going out of my mind here.'

Orla looked down to avoid his eyes. She couldn't look at his eyes. 'Nothing. It's not you, Paul. It's me. I have to go.'

'What do you mean it's you? Orla, I'm begging you, talk to me.'

She peeped up. Oh, God, his eyes. They were so full of confusion and pain. She had done this to him. She shook her head. 'I can't explain. Please, Paul, just know it's me. It's all me. I'm a freak. You don't want to be with me. I'm going away tomorrow, to Peru. It's over.'

Paul's face registered shock. 'What? Peru? Jesus Christ, Orla, what the hell is going on? Why are you running away? What did I do? Why can't you talk to me? I thought we had something special. I really like you and I thought you felt the same. I don't understand.'

Orla looked over his shoulder. 'I promise you that this is for the best. I'll ruin your life. I'm a mess. Please believe me, Paul, I'm doing this for you and Lulu. You need to think of her.'

'Lulu's crazy about you. What do you mean a mess? Talk to me. We can work it out.'

Orla made herself be cold. She had to push him away. 'We can't. We can never, ever work this out. Go, Paul, please, just go. I have nothing to say to you. It's over.'

'Who are you? I thought I knew you. I guess I was wrong.'

'Yes, you were.' Orla turned around and began to walk away. She made it to the end of the road and around the corner before she collapsed into a heap and sobbed her heart out. The pain was unbearable. She bawled into her hands, broken-hearted at hurting the man she loved.

Someone picked her up. Paul pulled her into his arms and held her in a vice-like grip.

'I'm not that easy to push away. Whatever this is, we're bloody well going to work it out. I'm not losing you. Do you understand?'

Orla couldn't speak. She cried and cried into Paul's shoulder until she felt faint. Holding her up, he walked her back to her apartment and laid her on the couch. He took off her shoes and brought out her duvet, which he tucked around her.

He found a bottle of whiskey under the sink and made her coffee laced with whiskey. Neither of them spoke.

Orla sipped, feeling the alcohol hit her stomach and warm her body. Paul sat in the chair opposite.

'Talk to me. I'm a good listener.'

'I don't know how to explain it. I'm a freak of nature,' Orla said.

'What does that mean?'

'Look, you were married to a fabulous, sexy, successful woman. That's what you're used to.'

Paul laughed. 'Sonja was a nightmare. I told you, we should never have got married. You're my type, not Sonja. I love that you're caring and kind and thoughtful. Sonja was selfish and cold.'

'But she was sexy.'

Paul looked confused. 'No, she wasn't. Cold and selfish is not sexy.'

'But she was a real woman,' Orla whispered, as tears ran down her face.

'You're much more of a woman to me.'

'But I'm not, Paul. I'm broken. I'm not normal.'

Paul rubbed his eyes. 'Orla, I don't know what you mean. You're beautiful and gorgeous and wonderful. Is this about the other night, when we tried to have sex? Did I hurt you? We can take it slower next time, whatever you need.'

Orla had to tell him. There was no other way. It was time to tell him and make him see that she was abnormal. 'It is about the other night when we tried to have sex, but you didn't hurt me, I just . . . I can't . . . I can't have . . . I can't do . . . sex.'

Paul's hands dropped to his lap. 'What do you mean?'

'I have vaginismus.'

Paul looked blankly at her.

'It's a condition where your muscles seize up and you can't be penetrated.'

'Oh, God, okay. Right, that explains it. I've never heard of the condition. Well, that's . . . well, it's awful for you. Is it painful?'

Orla nodded. 'It can be, yes.'

'I'm sorry. Can you help it at all with drugs or . . . or something?'

'Some people can cure it with therapy, but not me apparently.' Orla sighed. 'I've been seeing a therapist, and when I met you, I thought that maybe with the right person . . . I love you and I want to have sex with you more than anything, but I couldn't and I can't.'

'Maybe you need a different therapist.'

'Maggie, the therapist I went to, was great, but even she couldn't help me. I've tried so hard to "train" my vagina with dilators. I can't even get the smallest one in. The pain is horrendous. I'm a total disaster, Paul. This isn't going to get better. Don't you see? That's why you have to go. You don't want to be with a woman you can't be intimate with. You need to be with a normal woman, who you can have a normal sex life with.'

Paul was quiet. She could see he was trying to process this bomb. He'd say nice things, then leave and she'd never hear from him again.

'Please, Paul, just leave now. I understand. I want you to go and meet someone you can be happy with. I'm going to Peru tomorrow. You'll never see me again. It's okay, what we had was lovely but you can move on now.'

Paul stood and began to pace up and down the small living room. 'Hold on, give me a minute here. I'm digesting. So you can probably never have sex, but you can do . . . I mean, we can have a sex life that . . . that just doesn't include actual sex. We can do lots of other things. I mean, you're okay with other things, right?'

'Yes.'

'Is touching down there okay?' he asked gently.

'Yes.'

'So you can . . . you can get excited, but just not have actual sex?'

'Yes, I can orgasm, just no penetration.' Orla was amazed

339

at how easily she was able to use words like 'penetration' and 'orgasm' now – Maggie had done some good work on her.

'Okay, then, we'll work around it. We'll have fun with all the other stuff. I mean, when you come to think of it, foreplay is often the best part.'

Orla loved him for trying, but she couldn't get her hopes up. Men needed sex. 'Paul, I love that you're trying, but you'll miss sex. You'll want it. You're a gorgeous man who is used to having sex. It won't work.'

'First of all, do you think I'm gorgeous?'

She blushed and nodded.

'Second, I didn't have sex for almost three years after breaking up with Sonja. The last time I had sex was that awful one-night stand I told you about. It was the worst sex I've ever had. And as for "sexy Sonja", for the last year of our marriage we didn't have sex at all. I slept on the couch. So I'm not someone who is used to regular sex or gagging for it. Besides, I think we can have lots of fun without it.' He winked at her.

Hope was creeping into Orla's heart. She was terrified: hope could be so cruel. 'Paul, you can't make this decision here and now. You need to sleep on it and think about it and really consider what you're giving up.'

Paul came over and knelt beside her. 'I'm not giving you up. I've never been so happy with a woman. When you ghosted me, I almost had a nervous breakdown. I want to be with you, Orla, in whatever way I can.'

Orla closed her eyes as tears rolled down her face. 'Don't let me get my hopes up, Paul, please. It's too painful if you change your mind. I'd rather you let me go now. Please don't make promises you can't keep.'

Paul kissed her eyelids. 'I'm crazy about you. In a few months you've lodged yourself in my heart. We'll work around this. I want you to have hope. I want you to be happy and have the life you deserve. I promise I'll never hurt you. Trust me, Orla, please, trust me.'

Orla stood on the edge of a cliff. Could she jump? Would she fall to a painful death or would she, could she, be happy? Was it wise to allow hope back into her heart? Could this amazing man put up with her messed-up body long-term? Wouldn't he leave her eventually? Would that break her?

Maggie kept telling her she deserved love, but did she? She'd never really had it. She didn't know what it looked like, but this felt right. This man, staring into her eyes, pleading with her to trust him. This was love. This was what she had always wanted. Was she going to sabotage it because of her past? Was she never going to allow joy and love into her life because of her condition? Didn't people always say love conquers all? Could it conquer a relationship that didn't involve sex? Did Paul love her enough? She knew she loved him enough to accept anything. If he lost a leg tomorrow, she'd love him. If he went blind, she'd love him. So, if he felt the same way, then . . . then it was enough. Maggie's words echoed in her mind. It was time to be brave.

Orla opened her eyes and looked into Paul's. They were full of love and kindness. Orla took a very deep breath and jumped.

37

Alice wrestled Poppy into a pair of shorts. Poppy's legs kicked wildly, smacking Alice in the face.

'Ow, Poppy, stop it.'

'I will not go,' Poppy roared.

'Me too.' Ted supported his sister. 'We're not going to some stinky kids' club.'

'It's only a couple of hours. You'll meet lots of lovely children from all over the world and make new friends.'

'I don't want new friends,' Poppy said. 'I have loads already.'

Sarah stormed into the bedroom, followed by a frazzled Niall. Raising her index finger, she said, 'Just to be clear, Mum, I'm not going to some dorky kids' club with a bunch of strangers to play stupid tennis, which I don't even like. There's nothing you can say or do that will make me go.'

'I'll go to the football camp,' Jamie said. 'I'm fine with that.'

Alice sometimes secretly wished that they'd had only one child – Jamie. Imagine how easy life would be with just him.

Niall clapped Jamie on the back. 'Thank you, Jamie. Now look here, Sarah, you are going to the tennis club and that's the end of it. This is our holiday, too. Mum and I need a break.'

Sarah glared at him, hands on hips. 'Well, then, why did you have four kids, Dad? You decided to have us, so you have to suck it up.'

'Don't speak to me like that. You're behaving like a spoilt brat. Do you know how many kids would love to be in this beautiful resort, going to play tennis?'

'How many?' Sarah asked.

'A lot,' Niall snapped.

'Come on, guys, let's give Mum and Dad a break,' Jamie said.

'Shut up, you lickarse.'

'Sarah saided a bad word.' Poppy squealed with delight.

'I wanna go to football with Jamie,' Ted moaned.

'It's for eight- to twelve-year-olds,' Niall said.

'Tell them I'm eight.'

'You look about three, squirt,' Sarah told him.

'Sarah's mean, Mummy. She should go on the bold step,' Ted said.

Alice knew this wasn't going to work. She'd told Niall the kids wouldn't go into any club. They were just wasting their time and energy.

'Niall, let's just –'

'NO!' He held up his hands. 'I'll sort this out.' Turning to the kids, he roared, 'Get your runners on NOW or you will not look at one screen for this whole week. I have them all locked in the safe in our bedroom. Move it.'

Reluctantly, they put on their shoes.

'Daddy, you're mean,' Poppy grumbled.

'Yeah, go back to work, Daddy. We want Mummy to be the boss of us,' Ted agreed.

'Out,' Niall ordered.

Alice watched them shuffle out of the door. They'd be back in fifteen minutes. He'd never get them to stay.

Fifteen minutes later, Niall returned, grinning and childless.

Alice was amazed. 'How?'

343

'I was going to lie and say it was my brilliant persuasive powers, but I stooped very low, Alice. I bribed them. Five euros for every day they go.'

'Wow! And they went for it?'

Niall looked a bit sheepish. 'Well, Sarah negotiated ten for herself, and they get their iPads or iPods for a couple of hours every day.'

'Define a couple of hours.'

'As much as they want when they're in the apartment.' He winced.

'Niall, I'm trying to reduce their screen time!'

'I know, but they broke me. Sarah did the negotiating – she'll go far in life. But to hell with it, it'll give us a break.'

He was right, but Alice was the one who'd have to argue with them when they got home about less daily screen time. Oh, well, she had to try to forget about that now.

Niall reached for her and pulled her into a hug. Alice froze. Was he going to want sex now? Was that why he'd paid the kids to go to their activities? Oh, God, would he want sex every day?

Niall stood back and smiled at her. 'How about a walk and a coffee?'

Alice almost cried with relief. 'I'd love that.'

They walked along the beach barefoot. The sun warmed their faces and the waves tickled their toes. Alice felt the knot in her stomach begin to untie. The kids were safe and occupied; Niall wasn't trying to rip her clothes off; she didn't have to do anything or be anywhere. She inhaled and exhaled the warm air.

They sat in a beach bar and drank strong coffee, side by side. Niall put his arm around her and Alice leant into his shoulder.

'This reminds me of old times,' he said, 'when we didn't

344

have babies and kids to look after. Remember that great holiday we had in Ibiza?'

Alice nodded. It had been their last holiday before she'd got pregnant with Sarah. They'd partied till sunrise and slept all day on the beach.

'I have to say, Alice, I love our kids but, God, they can be hard work. I don't know how you do it every day. As soon as one is happy, the others kick off.'

Alice smiled. 'Welcome to my world.'

'I think I'd be on a bottle of gin a day.'

'I've thought about it.' She laughed. 'But I opted for biscuits instead.' She prodded her smaller, but still protruding stomach.

'You're gorgeous.' He kissed her lightly on the lips. Alice snuggled into his shoulder.

This – this – was what she'd missed. Being close without always having the shadow of sex hanging over her. She loved being close to Niall.

He glanced at his watch. 'No! How could three hours have already gone by? I feel like I've only just left them. We have to pick them up now.'

Alice chortled. It was how she felt about school. She had to pick the twins up at half past one every day and it always came round so fast. 'It was three hours of bliss. Thanks for bringing them to the club. Keep it up. No matter what you have to pay them.'

'With Sarah's negotiating skills, I'll be broke within the week.'

They laughed and wandered off, holding hands, to pick the kids up. It felt so natural and unforced. They reached instinctively for each other.

Sarah didn't see them approach. She was chatting to a group of girls her age and giggling.

Niall and Alice stopped and watched their grouchy almost-eleven-year-old having a good time.

'Our daughter is smiling,' Niall whispered.

'And laughing. She's actually making happy sounds.'

'It's a miracle.' Niall shook his head.

Sarah turned and saw them. A scowl immediately replaced the smile. She stomped out of the door to the tennis court.

'So, how was it?' Alice asked.

'Crap.'

'Really?' Niall said. 'You looked like you were having fun with those girls.'

Sarah's eyes flashed. 'I'm a good actress.'

'Not that good,' Alice said. 'Admit it, Sarah, you had fun.'

'No, I did not. Was it as horrendous as I thought? No. Was it good? No.'

'Are those girls going to the beach later?' Alice asked, praying the answer was yes. If Sarah made friends, everyone's life would be easier.

Sarah flicked her hair over her shoulder. 'Yeah, they said they were.'

Alice pinched Niall's arm and they beamed at each other across Sarah's head.

Jamie had had a good time at football camp and made lots of friends. The twins came out and said they'd had the best time ever 'cos the teacher was super-nice and not grumpy like you, Mummy and Daddy'.

Alice squeezed her husband's hand. 'I think we might actually have a nice family holiday,' she whispered.

'Me too.' They beamed at each other.

Later that night, when all the kids were conked out in bed, exhausted from all the fresh air, swimming and sport, Alice and Niall sat on the balcony of their apartment, sipping wine, looking out at the moon reflected on the water. The air was still warm and the sound of waves was like soothing background music.

'Cheers.' Niall clinked Alice's glass. 'Good first day.'

'Great first day,' Alice said.

'You're looking brown already.'

Alice looked down at her arms: they already had some colour. Alice had always got a great tan. She loved the summer because with a tan she looked better, less chubby and healthier. Niall never really went brown, just pink, then white again.

Niall began to rub Alice's arm. Uh-oh. She was tired, she wanted to sit together and chat, not have sex.

'I got some news today,' he said.

'Oh, my God, did you make senior partner?'

'Yes, I did,' he said, beaming.

'Congratulations!' Alice hugged him.

'Thanks.'

'I'm genuinely thrilled for you. But is this going to mean even longer hours?'

'No. You get to delegate a lot more as senior partner. Proving yourself is the really hard graft. Once you reach the top, it gets a little easier. I promise I'll be more present with the kids. I know I need to put more effort in. I promise to put my phone away at the weekends and to come home as early as I can. The sessions with Maggie have opened my eyes and made me see I need to do more. I really want to be a better dad and husband.'

Alice squeezed his hand. 'As much as I hated going to therapy, it has been good. I've realized something, too. I kind of feel bad saying this, but I think being a full-time mum isn't enough for me.' She looked at Niall, half afraid of what he would say.

347

'Why would you feel bad about that?' he said. 'It's great you know you need more.'

'Really?' Alice said. 'Thanks. I just . . . It feels like I'm saying I don't love the kids enough or something. I think that's what's been stressing me out so much. I kind of knew it, but I was afraid of saying it. I just feel guilty. Then Maggie talked about a conflict inside me, remember, and I thought about that and realized what it was. I do want to be more than a mum. But I told everyone I wanted to stay at home and be a full-time, full-on mum, so now I look like a total fraud because it isn't what I thought it would be, and I'm not the mother I thought I would be. I've failed. It's been really hard to admit that to myself. But the truth is that I'd like to have something just for me, earn a bit of money, get out of the house, achieve something separate from family life. I think it'll help me find myself again.'

'You're not a failure, Alice. Wanting something for yourself is completely normal and I fully support you,' Niall said. 'And if you need extra help at home, we can look at getting someone in. I'd say Danika might be on for more responsibility, if we discuss proper payment terms with her. What do you think?'

'That'd be great,' Alice said, surprised at how easy this was. 'And, Niall, I do realize that I've become a grumpy old cow and not a barrel of laughs to live with. I promise to be less of a nag and to stay awake past nine thirty.'

They laughed and clinked glasses again.

'It's a deal,' Niall said.

He leant over and kissed her. She pulled back slightly.

'Don't worry, I'm not going to hop on you. I'm too tired. All that swimming and sandcastle building has worn me out. Being a full-time parent is exhausting. I understand why you go to bed so early. I'm going to crash out.' He stroked her cheek. 'Night, Alice. I love you,' he said softly.

'I love you too.'

Alice sat on the balcony and finished her wine. She was relieved he hadn't wanted sex, but she was also worried. She wanted to want sex with her husband. She used to want it. She used to really enjoy it. When would that come back? Was it a case of practice making perfect? Should she initiate it? How could she get her sex drive back?

Alice tiptoed into the bedroom and lay down beside her husband. She was asleep within seconds.

The week flew by. The kids made friends, went to camp, spent their bribes on sweets and ice-creams. Alice got browner by the minute. She felt her whole being relax. Every day she went for a long walk with Niall and they held hands and hugged. They talked of everything and nothing. He didn't pressure her to have sex. He stood patiently in the sea for hours, flipping Poppy, Ted and Jamie over his shoulder. He built elaborate sandcastles with them and let them bury him in the sand.

'Dad's actually being like a real dad,' Sarah said, as she lay beside her mother on their beach towels.

'What do you mean?'

'Well, usually he comes in from work late and spends about five minutes with us. On the weekends, he's always on his phone or watching rugby or football matches. But now he's doing dad stuff.'

She was right, Alice thought. Niall had spent more quality time with the kids in the last six days than he had in months. 'This holiday has been good for all of us,' she said.

'Definitely for you, Mum. You look about ten years younger. Having a tan really makes you look better and way prettier. You looked really white and kind of old before.'

Alice tried to focus on the complimentary part and ignore

the rest. 'You know, Sarah, it's what someone is like on the inside that really matters. Beauty comes from within.'

Sarah rolled her eyes. 'Mum, stop with the olden-days sayings. It's like this. If you're an ugly pig, no one is going to spend the time trying to find out what you're like inside.'

Alice shook her head. 'Sarah, I want the nice, sweet side of you to show itself more. It's been hiding a lot lately. Say nice things to people.'

'I just told you that you look pretty and I'm happy that you and Dad are getting on well. I was scared – I thought you were going to break up.' Sarah looked away from Alice, but she could see her daughter's lower lip wobbling.

'Hey.' She placed a hand on Sarah's shoulder. 'Dad and I love each other very much. We'll never split up.'

'Look at Max and Sally. They did.'

'I know, sweetie, but they had a lot of problems they couldn't fix and Max is . . . well, he's a lot more selfish than Dad.'

'So you and Dad are really fine?'

'Yes, pet, I swear we are.'

Sarah wiped a tear from under her sunglasses. 'Good, because I don't want to have to move between two houses every second week. It'd be a drag.'

Alice hugged her daughter and kissed her head. 'You have nothing to worry about.'

'Except being more beautiful on the inside,' Sarah reminded her.

'I love you just the way you are, you gorgeous, grumpy, wonderful, clever girl.'

'Get off me now, Mum. My friends might see us.'

Sarah stood up and went down to the sea to join her friends, who were messing about on a blow-up doughnut. Alice watched her, her heart bursting with pride.

Later that day, Alice told Niall she had booked a babysitter for the evening.

'Really?' He was shocked.

'Yes, it's Paola from the kids' club. It's our last day and we deserve the night out. I have a plan. Dress casually.'

'Okay.' Niall smiled. 'This is all very intriguing.'

At eight o'clock, Alice and Niall left the apartment and Niall followed his wife down to the beach.

Alice took his hand and led him to a private corner where she had laid out beach towels and a picnic. Cheese, bread, olives, cold meats, and a bottle of wine.

'I love it.' Niall's eyes sparkled.

They sat side by side, eating and drinking as the sun set over the horizon.

'Damnit, I forgot dessert,' Alice said. 'I'll be back in a second. Don't move.'

'Alice, I don't need dessert. Come back,' Niall called after her.

He was pouring them both another glass of wine when he saw her. Alice was naked.

'Whoa.'

'Fancy a skinny dip and some dessert?' She grinned.

Niall yanked his clothes off and they ran towards the sea, holding hands and laughing like teenagers.

In the sea, Alice wrapped herself around her husband, and for the first time in a long time, she wanted him. She felt her body sing again. She wanted him inside her. She wanted to feel their bodies unite as one. She wanted to feel the physical closeness that sex brings.

She wanted to be with Niall, together, for ever.

38

Paul's hand was sweaty as he shook Maggie's. Orla rubbed her tired eyes and sank into a chair.

'This is Paul. As I told you on the phone, I wanted him to come to meet you so we could talk honestly about my issues.'

Maggie smiled at him. 'Very nice to meet you, Paul. I'm delighted you're here to support Orla.'

Paul cleared his throat and wiped his sweaty palms on his jeans. 'I want to do whatever I can. I love her and I want us to be together.'

Tears ran down Orla's cheeks. Maggie handed her a tissue and gently patted her arm. 'I can see it's been a difficult and emotional few days. How are you feeling, Orla?'

'Happy and terrified.' Orla sniffed.

'That's perfectly understandable. This is a huge step forward for you. But being honest is vital to a healthy relationship. I'm really proud of you.'

Maggie turned to Paul. 'As I'm sure you understand, opening up to you has been a huge leap of faith for Orla. How do you feel about the fact that she has vaginismus?'

Paul shifted in his chair. 'I'm fine about it. I mean, I didn't know anything about it, but I've been reading up on it to try to understand it better. I want to do everything I can to help Orla and reassure her that it doesn't matter.'

Maggie nodded. 'You understanding the condition will be a big help to her. But it's also important for you to recognize that while she may one day be able to have sexual intercourse, she also may not. Vaginismus can be a condition that women have for life and vaginal penetration may never be possible.'

'I understand.'

'I told him to go and find a normal woman, but he won't,' Orla said. 'I wanted us all to meet because . . . I think we shouldn't go ahead with this, Maggie. Paul has Lulu and she can't be subjected to another break-up. And even though I know Paul feels strongly about me and I'm mad about him, I think we'll break up when he realizes what he's actually taken on and given up.'

'Would you agree with what Orla is saying, Paul?'

Paul took Orla's hand in his. 'No. It really upsets me that she feels that way. Orla is the most normal woman I've ever met. You should meet my ex-wife.' He grinned.

Maggie laughed. 'I think Orla is a very special young woman, too. Now, as I explained to Orla, having vaginismus does not prevent you having an active physical relationship. Couples can have a very healthy and happy sex life without vaginal penetration.'

Paul winked at Orla. 'We've already had quite a lot of fun this week.'

Orla blushed.

Maggie smiled. 'That's good to hear.'

Orla's face turned serious. 'It's true, we have had great non-sex sex. But I want Paul to be sure. I don't want him to give up having a real sex life without thinking it through properly.'

Maggie turned to Paul. 'As I'm sure you understand, it can be heartbreaking for a woman to be given a diagnosis of vaginismus. But sexual intercourse isn't everything. In fact, sometimes couples find that it can make a relationship deeper and more meaningful because they have to focus more on trust, understanding, compassion and kindness. The sex can often be better because they have to work on other areas apart from penetration.'

'That's what I keep telling Orla. I don't see this as a negative. We can work it out. I want to be with her, no matter what. To me, it's not a big deal and we can be just as close physically without, as you say, actual penetration.'

Orla winced when he said 'penetration'. It sounded so clinical. 'You say it doesn't bother you now, Paul, but what about in a year's time when you aren't so mad about me and you want proper sex, or another child?'

'Is that something that's on the cards for you, Paul, a sibling for your daughter?'

'I don't want another child. Lulu is enough for me. And I want to be with Orla a lot more than I want to have sex with her. She's amazing and, as you said, we can still have a really good sex life.'

'Do you believe Paul when he says you're enough, Orla?'

Orla gulped. 'It's obviously lovely to hear, but I'm worried he'll regret it. I just want him to be absolutely sure. This is a big sacrifice.'

'Paul?'

Paul took Orla's hand. 'It's not a sacrifice. I told you, I've barely had sex in years. I've had more fun sexually with you in the last week than I ever have. I was very lonely before I met you. After my divorce and a few awful dates, I thought I'd never find someone special. I thought it'd just be me and Lulu. In fact, I'd accepted it as my life. But then you came along and changed all of that. I love you for who you are, not what you can do physically. I've been in a bad relationship and I can assure you that this one is good, really good, and I'm not letting you go.'

'Does that make you feel less afraid, Orla?'

Orla wiped her eyes with a tissue. 'Yes and no. I just never thought I'd be happy. All of my life, I've felt abnormal. First for "killing" my mother and then for not being able to have sex or even use a tampon. I felt I didn't deserve to be happy. That I was destined to be alone. That by my mother dying in childbirth I was cursed never to have children of my own. Some people are born blind or deaf, and this is my burden. I'd felt alone my whole life, until I met Paul. I'm scared. I'm scared to admit how I really feel because I don't know if I have the strength to come back from this if it doesn't work out.'

'But isn't blocking love out what your father's done?' Maggie said gently. 'Didn't he wrap himself up in his misery and never let go or allow himself to live again? He refused to have hope ever again. Is that how you want to live your life?'

Orla froze. 'I'm not like him,' she said, staring at Maggie. 'I'm not.'

'You keep putting up obstacles and reasons not to move forwards, reasons to stay safe and not to take a leap of faith. Paul is here, willing to give this relationship every chance possible. You need to do the same. You grew up surrounded by negative thoughts and beliefs about yourself. You have to fight to push them aside and allow yourself to move towards joy and possibility and love.'

Orla's head was spinning. She'd never seen herself in this light before. Was she doing what her father had done? Was she refusing to move forward and allow love in? Jesus, the very idea of it made her blood run cold. Did she want to turn into him, live a life like his? A lonely, bitter man who wore his pain like a badge of honour? NO! 'I don't want to be like him. I want love, I really do,' Orla cried.

'Well, then, you need to let it in,' Maggie said. 'I hear you when you say how difficult it is for you to trust and let down your guard. But I also see Paul, who is here today by your side. Paul has told you that he knows everything and that he loves you and wants to build a life with you.'

'It just seems too good to be true.' Orla got upset. 'When you grow up thinking you're unworthy of love, it's hard to believe it when it happens.'

Paul put his arms around her and rocked her. 'You deserve it more than anyone I've ever met. Let me love you, please, Orla. Listen to Maggie, let me in. I swear I'll never hurt you. All I want to do is take away your pain and make you believe how incredible you are.'

Orla looked up at him. 'You can't promise that, Paul.'

Paul took her face in his hands. 'I want to make up for all the pain and loneliness you've suffered. I want to fill your life with love and laughter. I want to wake up beside you every day. I want you to be Lulu's step-mum. I want to kiss you and hold you and do lots of other things that I won't mention here with you. I think you're the most incredible woman in the world.'

'Do you really promise not to let me down or leave me?' Orla searched his face for the truth.

'I promise.'

'Are you one hundred per cent sure you can accept me as I am?'

'One hundred and fifty.'

'Swear?'

'Swear.'

Maggie smiled. 'Promising never to let each other down is a lovely sentiment, but none of us knows what the future holds, so you can't give each other cast-iron guarantees. That's why all relationships require a leap of faith. All you can do is have faith in each other, be honest with each other and take it from there. Orla, can you take a leap of faith and allow yourself to trust in Paul's love for you?'

Slowly, Orla began to nod. Yes, she could. She had to. She would not end up like her father. She would not close her heart. She would not push love away. She had to try. She had to give herself a chance at happiness.

'Is that a yes I see?' Paul reached over for her.

Orla buried her face in his neck. 'I love you so much I feel as if I can't breathe,' she whispered.

'Me too,' he replied.

Maggie beamed at them. 'I'm delighted for you both. I'd like to suggest you keep coming to see me, as a couple, and, Orla, I'd like to see you one-on-one as well. We still have work to do, but what you have done today, Orla, is a huge accomplishment and I'm very proud of you.'

Orla reached across and threw her arms around Maggie. 'Thank you, thank you for making me feel like I'm worthy of love and happiness.'

Maggie laughed. 'It's been an absolute joy to watch you blossom.'

Paul held out his hand and the young couple stepped out into the spring day as pink cherry blossoms, from the tree in Maggie's garden, fell around them like confetti.

39

Maggie poured two glasses of water and smiled. 'I have to say I'm surprised by your visit,' she said, 'but it's very good to see you again. How have you been?'

Ken picked up a glass and took a sip of water. 'Why are you surprised?' he asked.

'Well, I know the sessions were Ann's idea, and I know you often felt uncomfortable, so I'm pleasantly surprised that you would come to talk to me again now. What's on your mind?'

'Ann,' Ken said. 'She went to Argentina to dance the tango. I managed to push her to the other side of the world.' He laughed sadly.

'Oh, I see. How are you feeling?'

'Not good. She's been gone two months and no sign of a return yet.'

'How are you finding being on your own?' Maggie asked. 'I take it you're now retired?'

'Yes, I finished up a little over a month ago.' He sighed. 'The house is so quiet. I mean, I'm free to watch sport, do my own thing, but it's not the same without Ann there.'

'You were a long time sharing that house,' Maggie said. 'It has to be a huge transition for you, especially alongside retiring. Are you and Ann in touch?'

'In the beginning, she texted me regularly, about her dance classes and going to the beach and meeting new people through her Spanish-language class, just her day-to-day news. She always sounded very happy. I never had much to say back, though. Work was busy until it ended. Zoë still calls round on Sundays. I saw our friends Peter and Cathy one night for dinner and, to be honest, it was a strain. I didn't realize how much I rely on Ann to keep the conversation going. She's the lively, chatty one who makes these dinners fun.

'And now lately, I'm hearing from Ann less. She seems to be having a really good time. She has lots of new friends and . . . I dunno, I can't stop thinking, What is she doing? Who is she with? Will she ever come back to me? I think she's slipping away from me.'

'How does that make you feel?'

'Terrified. I'm lost, Maggie,' Ken admitted. 'I don't know what to do. I keep forgetting things and misplacing every-thing, my glasses, car keys, socks. I can't seem to concentrate on TV or reading books any more either.'

'Do you think that's because you miss her?'

'Yes. I never realized how much Ann does for me and how much . . . how much I need her. I'd never really appreciated how little I did outside of work. My life felt full because Ann was always there, bustling around in the kitchen, organiz-ing dinners with friends or Sunday dinners with the kids, or booking movie tickets or just chatting about the char-ity shop. It was just normal stuff, but it filled my days. Ann injected colour into our lives. She's the one people like and warm to, not me. I never knew that it was having her by my side that made me feel confident, more interesting and more likeable. Without her there, I feel like everything is grey and washed out. She's the light in my life.'

'Have you told her you miss her, Ken?'

'Not really. I don't want to annoy her.'

'Why do you think it would annoy her?'

Ken shrugged. 'Because she's having a ball and she doesn't

want her boring old husband ruining her buzz. She doesn't need me moaning in her ear. That's what she ran away from. It's funny, I always thought my job was who I was, that it defined me. But now I know it isn't. My relationship with Ann is what defines me. Being a husband is my most important role and I wish I'd been better at it. I need Ann. I need my Annie. She's the one who makes everything good and nice and homely. She *is* my home. Without Ann the house is just so empty, no life or light.'

Maggie nodded. 'Ken, have you thought about telling her this? Telling her how you're feeling.'

Ken shook his head. 'I'm scared – scared she'll tell me it's over. At least this way, I can still cling to a little bit of hope that she'll come back.'

'You've had a lot of upheaval in the last few months. It's not easy to deal with all of that. But these realizations are really helpful.'

'I took her for granted. I see that now. Ann has always been there, so I just assumed she always would be. Now it's all changed, and I hate change. It makes me feel anxious. Ann's gone and my job's gone and John's gone, and Zoë's busy with her own life. What am I going to do with mine? I thought we'd grow old together. I was happy to have a quiet life, but I never imagined it was going to be this quiet. I always presumed Ann would be by my side, making plans and organizing things for us to do with all the extra time we'd have together. But she's not there. It's just me, and I don't want to do anything without her. You know, we had those awful talks with you about sex. Just godawful.'

Maggie smiled. 'I remember well, Ken.'

'I hated it. I thought we were fine, separate rooms, peck on the cheek, we're old anyway. But I'm not too proud to admit it, Maggie, I'd give anything to walk into Ann's bedroom and find her there, lie down beside her and take her in my arms. Just to feel the warmth of her skin again and have her look at me and smile. I'd give anything. And when she was there, I didn't do it.'

Maggie handed him a tissue.

He dabbed at his eyes. 'Sorry, this is very unlike me. It's just, I see it now, far too bloody late, of course, but I see it. I got lazy. I lost her because of that. And now I'm lost without her.'

Maggie smiled and took a deep breath. 'Ken, I think this has been a real breakthrough for you. I know this is so hard for you and that you're grieving for what you feel you've lost, but you're understanding so much about your relationship. You've really opened yourself up.'

Ken sighed. 'Zoë thinks I need antidepressants. She said they'll shake me out of my slump.'

'What do you think? Is that something you'd like to consider?'

'Not really. What I need is Ann. If I have her by my side, I can get through anything. She's my rock. But I think I've lost her.' Ken dabbed at his eyes again. 'You know, we'd never been apart for more than two nights before this.'

'Ken,' Maggie said gently, 'maybe you should think about telling Ann how much you miss her, about what you're feeling now. She did say she wanted you to communicate more, and this could be a good opportunity to do that.'

'What if she rejects me?'

'If you don't tell her how you feel, she'll never know. And you'll never know. Sometimes in life you have to take risks.'

Ken took off his glasses and wiped them with the edge of his shirt. 'Zoë said I need to go over there, throw her over my shoulder and bring her home.'

Maggie laughed. 'Have you thought about going to visit her? It would certainly be a big gesture.'

'I hate flying. Ann knows that, and she knows I don't like hot countries either.'

'Exactly. So she'd know what it meant if you went over there to tell her how much you want her to come home.'

Ken looked at her. 'What if she doesn't want to come back?' he whispered.

'How much do you think she's worth fighting for? How far are you willing to go to show her how much she means to you?' Maggie asked.

How far was he willing to go? His life since she'd left was hell. He hated being without her. He needed her, he wanted her, he loved her. He had to do something. Zoë and Maggie were right: he had to get off his arse and show Ann what she meant to him. If it meant a godawful journey to Argentina, then he'd just have to brace himself and go. Was she worth it? He didn't have to think twice about that.

'I'll do it. I'll go.' Ken stood up. He felt a fire in his belly that he hadn't felt in a very long time. Adrenalin coursed through his veins. 'Maggie, I'm going to leave, because if I don't book this flight now, I may chicken out and I'm not going to let myself lose Ann. Thank you, thank you for helping me to see straight.'

'I really hope it works out, Ken. Just be honest and tell her how you feel.'

'I will. I'll tell her everything.'

'And, Ken, will you come back and tell me what happened?'

He smiled. 'I owe you that much, Maggie.'

Ken raced home in his car. He knew he had to act now, before doubt set in and the little negative voice in his head told him not to be silly and impulsive. He had to act before fear took over.

He parked the car in the driveway and went inside. He

closed the front door. Silence. He stood in the hall, listening to the tick-tock of the clock on the hall table.

Ann had said she couldn't live like this, and now he knew what she meant. He couldn't do this either. The quiet, empty house, the endless days that stretched before him, gripped him with panic. For so long, he'd thought she was crazy, with all that finding-myself nonsense. But being alone these past weeks had made him see that Ann was right, there was more life behind them than ahead. He had to make the most of what was left. What other option did he have? Die slowly in his chair watching TV? Ken realized he *did* want more from life. Unfortunately it had taken his wife leaving him to make him see that.

He opened his laptop and clicked on a flight comparison website. His fingers paused on the keyboard. Would he be welcome? Would Ann want to see him? Had she already moved on? Would she tell him to go home and leave her to her new life?

Ken took a deep breath and typed in 'Dublin to Buenos Aires'. If he didn't try, he'd never find out.

Acknowledgements

Every book is a collaboration and I have many people to thank:

A huge thank-you goes to Rachel Pierce, my editor, whose insight and guidance help make every book better and for being a brilliant person to work with.

Patricia Deevy, for the brainstorming sessions, the encouragement and her unwavering support.

Michael McLoughlin, Cliona Lewis, Carrie Anderson, Brian Walker and all the team at Penguin Sandycove for their continued support and help.

To all in the Penguin UK office, especially Tom Weldon, Joanna Prior and the sales, marketing and creative teams.

To my agent, Marianne Gunn O'Connor, for being a rock in stormy waters and for always believing in me.

To Hazel Orme, for her wonderful copy-editing, her beady eyes and her warm and wonderful feedback.

A big warm thank-you to Jenny Carty for talking me through the role of a therapist and showing me the skills to draw people out, skills that she has in abundance.

To my fellow writers, thanks for your support during this strange and unsettling year. It has meant more than ever to have a walk, socially distanced coffee and a Zoom call.

To my mum, sister, brother and extended family. Thanks for cheering me on always and for the family Sunday Zoom quiz nights.

To all of my friends: in a strange way, Covid has brought

us even closer. Thanks for keeping me sane and for always making me laugh.

To Hugo, Geordy and Amy, the brightest-shining lights in this difficult year.

To Troy, for being the best person to be stuck in a house with during Covid.

This book is dedicated to Lily Capot, who died very suddenly this year, too young, too soon. Her big warm beautiful smile is missed by all who knew and loved her.

And to all those who lost loved ones during Covid, I hope you get to say a proper goodbye and to celebrate their lives when lockdown is over.

Stay safe and stay well.